THE CAMBRIDGE MURDERS

THE CAMBRIDGE MURDERS

by

DILWYN REES

LONDON
VICTOR GOLLANCZ LTD
1948

NOTE

Every character in this book is entirely fictitious and no reference whatever is intended to any living person.

First Published October 1945
Second Impression (first cheap edition) January 1948

To the Master and Fellows—and more particularly the Dean—of my own College, the College of St. John the Evangelist

PRINTED IN GREAT BRITAIN BY RICHARD CLAY AND COMPANY, LTD., BUNGAY, SUFFOLK.

CONTENTS

BOOK ONE

Death in the Screens

BOOK TWO

Murder at High Table

BOOK THREE

Superintendent Robertson-Macdonald Investigates

BOOK FOUR

Sir Richard Cherrington Investigates

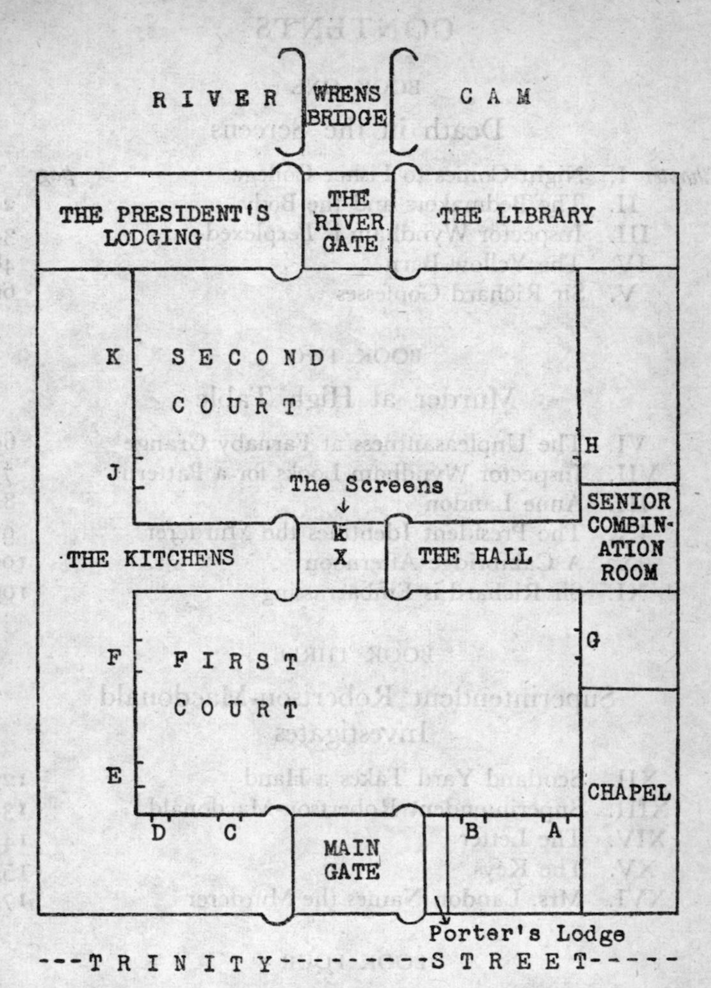

PLAN OF FISHER COLLEGE

A to K are the letters of the staircases.
X marks the place where the body was found.

BOOK I

DEATH IN THE SCREENS

CHAPTER ONE

NIGHT COMES TO FISHER COLLEGE

To those who were educated in the older and more beautiful of the two ancient Universities there is no need to explain that Fisher College lies between Trinity and St. John's, and stretches from Trinity Street down to the Cam, but to those who were not so fortunate we should explain that Fisher College—the abbreviation "Fisher" is never used—comprises two excellent sixteenth-century brick courts, both tremendously praised by Ruskin. The First or Old Court—it was completed in 1580—fronts on Trinity Street, and is entered through a tall brick gateway from the street, while the Second or New Court—so called though it was finished only some fifteen years after the First—lies between Old Court and the river. A wide brick bridge, a later addition falsely attributed to Wren, crosses the Cam from the River Gate of New Court and gives on to those immemorially lovely lawns and gardens called the Backs or Backsides of the Colleges, and through the Backs on to the elm-shaded quiet of Queen's Road.

Fisher College had fortunately escaped the zeal of restorer, renovator, and improver so often met on College Councils, and it stands to-day, or rather stood in 1939, when our story begins, much as it was when finished in 1595, save for the "Wren" bridge and a new block put across the river after the last war to house a few baths and some garages for the Fellows. It was a College of great architectural and æsthetic charms, although it had many disadvantages from the point of view of creature comforts. It had a tradition of Spartan learning, and the undergraduates and junior Fellows of 1939 upheld this tradition, shivering in their draughty rooms, and walking in their pyjamas and dressing-gowns through the Courts in the early mornings to get their baths, the while raw, sharp winds blew around them from off the dank Fens and the grey-cold North Sea.

Such an undergraduate, and one who might one day turn into a junior Fellow, was Giles Farnaby, who on this evening of Monday, March 10th, 1939, was in his rooms on G Staircase, packing his trunk, for it was the last evening of the Lent Term, and with the greater part of his fellow undergraduates he would be going down the next morning. Giles lived in a large converted farmhouse at Whistley near Twyford, which his father, an old member of Fisher College, had bought and made habitable and attractive while avoiding the consciously picturesque.

Here, and again for the sake of the less fortunate, we should explain very briefly the staircase system which lies at the basis of all College life in these ancient Universities. Those who understand this system can rush ahead and get to the bedmakers and the body all the quicker. To those others we should say that apart from the Kitchens, Dining-Hall, Library, Chapel, and the Junior and Senior Combination Rooms, where the undergraduates and dons combine socially, the whole of Fisher College was split up into open staircases leading from the courts and giving on to six sets of rooms or flats. These sets varied in size: each undergraduate has one large room for working in and eating in and drinking in—this is his "keeping room", for one "keeps" rather than "lives" or "stays" in Cambridge—and a small bedroom and an even smaller "gyp-room" for the "gyp" or servant. The dons had several keeping rooms in their sets, which are usually twice the size of the undergraduate sets. The President of Fisher College, as befits such a wise and learned man as Dr. Quibell, and such an important figure as the Head of the College, had a set of rooms four times the size of an undergraduate set, and this delightful set of rooms overlooking the river Cam was called the President's Lodging. Each set of rooms, whether it be that of undergraduate or Fellow or of Dr. Quibell himself, had two doors giving on to the staircase. The outer of these two doors is the "oak", and is usually left open: when shut it is "sported", and cannot be opened from the outside without a key. A sported oak means the owner is away or asleep or does not wish to be disturbed.

Each staircase is serviced by a man-servant or "gyp" and a woman servant or bedmaker. G Staircase had an excellent and dignified old gyp called Kilmartin, who was also College Butler, and presided over the mysteries and rituals of dinner in the Hall. Kilmartin and his wife looked after the five men who kept on G Staircase: two undergraduates called Simpkin and Debenham on the ground floor; Sir Richard Cherrington, the Vice-President of the College and Professor of Prehistory in the University, occupied the whole of the first floor, while the top floor housed Giles Farnaby and Dr. Landon, the College Dean. Sir Richard was a bachelor, and lived in College throughout the year, and his rooms were filled with the bachelor luxuries and comforts he substituted for the pleasures and hardships of married life. The Dean, Dr. Landon, did not normally keep in College: he was a married man, and had a small house out on the Madingley Road. He slept in College two or three nights a week, as was the custom of all officers of the College, and his small undergraduate set of rooms did him very well. It is hardly necessary to remind our readers that the Deans of Colleges most often are responsible not only for the services in the College Chapels, but also for the exercise of disciplinary authority in the College. Dr. Landon combined these executive functions, as do all dons worth anything, with a lectureship in Theology and with extensive theological researches, which brought him into violent controversy with the more rationalist and materialist dons. Among these was Dr. Traherne, another Fellow of Fisher College and Reader in Comparative Anthropology in the University. The disputes of Landon and Traherne often rang up and down the Fisher College High Table when the dons were at dinner. Dr. Landon was a stern, unsympathetic disciplinarian as well as an uncompromising scholar, and if the truth be told, no one in Fisher College liked him very much. Some feared him, some hated him—you could not be neutral in your reactions to this firm, cold, self-possessed, tight-lipped scholar. He remained in Fisher College despite his unsympathetic discipline and his hatred of music in the Chapel Services and his violent personal and academic rages, because with it all he was a scholar and a personality and, as Dr. Quibell wrote in his charming book of Cambridge memoirs called *The Backs are Green*, "A few interesting people, even a few mad people—provided they are scholars—make a College more worth while than a shoal of dull, sane, mediocre placeholders".

Giles Farnaby got on well with Dr. Landon as a next-door neighbour, which shows that the Dean was not really the inhuman, unsympathetic creature which he unfortunately became in his dealings with the normal undergraduate. Occasionally late at night Farnaby and the Dean would drink some tea or some beer together, the while Landon explained what a pagan young man Farnaby was and how, without a belief in the value and social sanctions of Christianity as a minimum faith, he was bound to lead an immoral life, and Farnaby accused the Dean of being a misguided divine as steeped in superstitions as the Trobriand Islander or the West African Negro, the only difference being that the Christian superstition had the approval of the English State in which they were living. In short, they often conversed and argued on all subjects late into the night, which is, after all, whatever the formal educationists say, one of the main purposes of the older Universities, or for that matter a University anywhere in the world.

II

Giles Farnaby had finished his packing, and, with the assistance of the gyp Kilmartin, had manhandled his trunk out on to the narrow landing that separated his rooms from those of Dr. Landon. He was drinking some beer in his rooms with another undergraduate who had looked in to see him, when there was a light knock at his door.

"Come in," said Giles, and the door opened slightly, and a head with a shock of steel-grey hair, and a long, lined face with a pair of black horn-rimmed pince-nez on the end of a thick black ribbon, put itself round the door.

"Busy?" queried the head, looking over the top of its spectacles.

"Hello, Uncle Dick," said Giles, getting up. "Do come in. No, we're not busy. Just gossiping and finishing up my beer. Let me pour you out a glass."

The door opened farther, and the whole body followed the head into the room. It was a tall body, dressed in a rough tweed jacket over a faded yellow cardigan waistcoat and grey flannel trousers. All these were partly hidden in a Doctor's silk gown.

"Ah, good!" said the body, and advanced into the room.

"Do you know John Parrott, by the way?" said Giles. "I'm so sorry." He turned to Parrott, who had just got up. "This is my uncle, Sir Richard Cherrington."

"How do you do, sir," said Parrott politely.

"How do you do," said Sir Richard.

"I thought you made it your business to know everyone in the College," chaffed Farnaby.

"I used to, you know," said Cherrington, "I used to, and as a matter of fact I still remember everyone's faces." He turned to Parrott. "I've seen your face about College quite a bit and in one or two other places." He paused. "It's my job, in a kind of way. I'm an archæologist, you know. It puts a premium on visual memory. As one gets older one's mind is just full of images of pots and paintings and details of decorations and tomb-plans and so forth. I still think I never forget a face. Had yours for a very long time in the compartment labelled 'unidentified faces'. Now I can put it in the other compartment in my head." He smiled. "Well, here's luck," and he drank off the beer his nephew had brought him.

Cherrington turned to his nephew. "Nice drop of beer," he said. "Well, Giles, I only looked in a moment to wish you a good journey tomorrow. Give my best wishes to your father and mother, and I shall be calling for you with the car in ten days' time. Giles and I are going on a short motor trip in Brittany," he explained to Parrott. "I want a change myself, and have one or two archæological sites I want to refresh my memory with. It's a chance to give Giles an outing and prevent him getting back next term quite stale and unable to work for the Tripos."

From outside in the court came the muffled tolling of a bell.

"Ah, First Hall bell," said Sir Richard. "I must be away." He got up to go. "I hope, Parrott, you won't think I'm very rude if I ask you one question."

"Oh, but certainly, sir," said Parrott.

"It's your jacket," said Cherrington. "I'm rather a connoisseur of tweeds myself. As a matter of fact the archæologist is supposed to go about in loose-fitting tweeds as he paces the countryside looking for barrows and ditches and so forth. I've just never seen a coat of the exact pattern and texture of yours. It's most attractive. You're not offended, I hope?" he added hastily.

"Why, of course not, sir," said Parrott. "I'm glad you like it. It is unusual, I suppose, being a Welsh tweed."

"A Welsh tweed?"

"Yes," went on Parrott. "There's a mill making small lengths of this and one or two other patterns in West Cardiganshire. I bought a length while I was on a geological field-class, and Rattenburys of Silver Street made it up into a coat for me."

"I see," said Sir Richard, turning to go. "Well, come and see me next term and tell me the address of this mill. Meanwhile, have a good vacation."

Farnaby saw him out on the landing. "Blast your old trunk!" said Sir Richard. "It's cluttering up the whole landing. I wish I could get proper lighting put on these staircases. Good night, Giles."

When the door of Farnaby's room had closed, Sir Richard paused a moment. "Parrott," he said to himself. "Parrott. Now where have I seen him recently?" He sighed. "Ah well, I must really be getting old. And yet sixty is not old." He crossed the landing and knocked gently at the Dean's door.

"Come in," said a voice.

The room Sir Richard entered was a large one. A fire was burning brightly in the grate. All the windows were closed and the curtains drawn. The walls were lined with books. Two leather armchairs stood on either side of the fireplace, and in the middle of the room was a large desk, at which sat a short, bald-headed man in clerical collar. It was the room of a married don whose real life was here and not in his home, and Dr. Landon looked that part.

He glanced up as Sir Richard came in.

"Oh, it's you, Dick," he said, peering towards the door. "Come in. I very stupidly left my long spectacles at home, but Anne is bringing them in after dinner. I shall need them tomorrow, or I shan't be able to conduct the final prayers of term."

He got up. "Why, it's nearly time for Hall," he said. "Let's have a glass of sherry before we go down. There's time."

"I'd be delighted," said the other.

The Dean opened a cupboard at the side of the fireplace and took out a decanter of sherry and two glasses. He poured out a glass and gave it to Sir Richard.

"Not to be compared with your own, I am afraid, Richard," said the Dean. "But tolerably good to drink."

"Your good health," said Sir Richard, tasting the wine. "Ah," he added, passing his tongue over his lips. "I find it good. Pleasantly dry and appetising."

The other put down his glass untasted, and was leaning against the fireplace. At the moment he looked almost ten years older than the forty-one years he really was. His grey hair was thinning, his face was drawn and tired, and his whole figure seemed to droop in a dejected way. Sir Richard noted this, but put it down to the fact that Landon had had a very busy and tiring term, and little change of any kind for many years.

"Drink up your sherry, Bill," he said. "It'll do you good. You look tired, man. Don't let the end of term get you down. It's a time for rejoicing, to my mind, not dejection."

The other looked up and picked up his glass. "Yes, I expect I do seem tired and dejected," he said slowly. "But it isn't due to end of term. No." He paused. "The truth is," he went on, "I've had a very great shock to-day—a very great shock indeed—and I don't know what to do. I asked you round to my room before dinner so that I could tell you and you could give me some advice. I don't want anyone else among the Fellows to know, and quite frankly I don't value the advice of any of the others—no, not from our revered President, Dr. Quibell, down to our new Prize Fellow."

"I'm honoured," said Sir Richard. "But come now, what is it? You're probably exaggerating it's gravity. One doesn't see things in the right perspective after eight weeks of teaching and tutoring to the tune of eleven hours a day."

"Make no mistake, Richard, I'm not exaggerating this," said the Dean. "Judge for yourself. I had a visit from Evan Fothergill while I was having tea in my rooms to-day."

At the mention of Fothergill's name, Cherrington had put down his glass of sherry and lit a cigarette.

"Yes," he said, blowing out a cloud of smoke and narrowing his eyes. "Yes, go on."

"You know how I opposed Fothergill's election two years ago when he was put up. I didn't like him as an undergraduate. I thought he was a man of loose morals, and I was right. Last year he took away that girl June Westmacott, the Tutor's niece, from John Parrott. God knows I think Parrott a poor type, and I've been proved right recently, but Fothergill wasn't honest then. He was just trifling with the Westmacott girl's affections. Now, though still technically engaged to her, he has the impudence to come and tell me that he is in love with my wife—with my wife Anne." He passed his hand over his forehead.

Sir Richard lived in College, and very little escaped him. He had heard rumours in the past three or four months of a growing attachment between Evan Fothergill, one of the younger Fellows of Fisher College, and a very brilliant mathematician, and Anne Landon, the Dean's very lovely wife, whom he had married about five years ago, when she was then about twenty-four or twenty-five, the elder sister of an undergraduate of the College. He remembered these things, but all he said was:

"Fothergill had the courage to come and tell you this?"

"He did," said the Dean; "and, what's more, he wants me to divorce Anne so that he can marry her. Of course I thought it was nonsense, and rang up Anne; but that's where I had my great shock. She says it is true, and that though she doesn't want to hurt me—hurt me, mark you!—if I don't agree she will just go away and live with Fothergill. She's coming round to-night to my rooms and we're going to discuss the situation. But it's quite intolerable. I mean my life as Dean of this College is finished, finished," he said, stamping his foot. "If I am involved in a divorce case, or if it became known that my wife had set up house with another Fellow, it wouldn't be so good for the College as a whole either! What would our Dr. Quibell say if that happened?"

"It need not happen," said Sir Richard quietly.

"No, I know it need not happen," replied the Dean, crossing to his desk and snapping open a drawer. "Look at this," he said. In his hand was a small revolver. "I've kept this in my desk ever since those outrageous happenings a few years ago in Lancaster College. I determined no one would catch me unarmed. Now, I may solve a difficult tangle in a simple way."

Sir Richard had not spent a life-time of service in the University for nothing. He was an excellent judge of character. He pretended to be unmoved by the show of the revolver and asked quietly:

"Who are you going to shoot—yourself, or your wife, or Fothergill, or the whole lot of you? And do you think it would do the College and your Church a lot of good?"

"I know, Richard; I'm distraught," said the other, dropping the revolver back into the drawer and closing it. "But what can I do?"

Sir Richard had been thinking quickly. "If I were you," he said—"and you have no need to take my advice—I should tell Anne when she comes to-night that the affair with Fothergill is a temporary infatuation and that you have no intention to assist it in any way. I would say to her that divorce and separation are out of the question, completely out of the question. And then I should go to the President to-night and tell him you are on the verge of a breakdown and must have a sabbatical year. You've never had one, and are entitled to it two times over. Fix your affairs: go away as soon as possible and as far away as possible. Don't come back for six months at least. I promise you you will not only be a happier man yourself, but that Anne will be glad to welcome you back."

"You really think so," said the other.

"I'm sure of it," said Sir Richard; "and now let's go down to the Combination Room, or we shall be late for Hall."

Landon knocked out his pipe, placed it in his pocket, and put on his black gown.

"You're a splendid fellow, Richard," he said. "You've put new life into me. I will take your advice. I'll go to Palestine and Syria. I've always wanted to go there. I suppose this is a good time of year for visiting the Near East, is it?"

They passed out of his room and clattered down the stairs.

III

The Combination Room of Fisher College is a small but beautiful room, its interior decoration dating from the time of its construction with the rest of the First or Old Court in the sixteenth century. It is panelled with linenfold, roofed with a delightfully designed plaster ceiling, and had two wide bow windows looking out on to the lane between Fisher College and St. John's. These windows flank a large, open, stonework fireplace. None of the original furniture remained, but the Fellows of a later generation had sensibly furnished it with a fine set of chairs which Mr. Chippendale had made for them, and had covered the polished floor with good Persian rugs of a deep, warm colour. It seemed a small room whenever the Fellows gave a party, but on an average night, when only the Fellows were dining in, it was almost cosy, with the curtains drawn, the candles burning in the sconces—for each generation of Fellows had wisely voted against putting electric light in the room—and a large wood fire burning in the open fireplace.

Thus it was when Sir Richard and the Dean came in. Sir Richard, despite his easily given advice, was perturbed by the unpleasant news he had just heard. Dr. Landon, however, seemed to have shaken off his gloom, as one will on seizing violently on a new course of action when all action seemed futile.

They were the last to arrive, and the small group of Fellows in their black gowns stood waiting round the fire, some drinking sherry, others scanning the London evening papers, which had just been delivered. Dr. Quibell, the short, white-haired, bespectacled President of the College, was standing with his back to the fireplace, his head thrust forward and peering myopically at Roger Westmacott, the Tutor. He broke off what he was saying to the Tutor as Cherrington and Landon came in.

"Good evening, gentlemen," he said. "You're nearly late."

"Good evening, Mr. President," said Sir Richard. "Are we the last?"

"Yes, you are," replied the President. "We're a small company to-night." He looked at the little hornbook which had been given him earlier by Kilmartin, who, as we have said, not only acted as Gyp for G Staircase but was also Senior Butler to the College. "Just the seven of us. No visitors to-night. Nevertheless," he went on, "however small, we remain, I hope, as any collection of Fisher College dons should always be, distinguished and scholarly." He bowed to the company.

The door leading into the Hall opened, and Kilmartin appeared, carrying in his hand a long ebony stick with a silver top. He caught Dr. Quibell's eye and struck the polished floor three times with his stick.

"Mr. President, Sir," he announced in a clear, impersonal voice, "dinner is served."

The President looked at Sir Richard. "Mr. Vice," he said, "shall we go in to dinner?" And they all filed into the Hall in the order of their seniority, and stood behind their chairs at High Table. The undergraduates and graduates who had been waiting for them stood up at their approach. After they had all found their places, Kilmartin, who had preceded the President into the Hall, struck a gong, and immediately Giles Farnaby, who had been waiting for this moment, gabbled a Latin grace as quickly as he could. When it was over, and amid a shuffling of chairs and benches, everyone sat down: the second Hall bell was rung in the Chapel Tower. Dinner was served.

Dr. Quibell sat at the head of the table. Sir Richard, as Vice-President, sat on his right, and the Dean on his left. Next to Sir Richard was Roger Westmacott, the Tutor, and beyond him young Dr. Wedgwood, the College Organist and Director of Musical Studies. Next to the Dean was Dr. Mervyn Traherne, the Reader in Comparative Anthropology in the University, and a fierce debating adversary of the Dean's. Traherne fortunately separated the Dean from Evan Fothergill, who sat opposite Dr. Wedgwood. It was, as the President said, a small and distinguished gathering. Everyone, including the Dean, seemed cheerful except Evan Fothergill, who sat moodily looking across the table at Wedgwood, meanwhile fumbling at the bread and toast which thoughtful waiters brought to him.

"Ah," said the President. "Let us see what Gough Clarke has arranged for us to-night."

This was his usual opening to his dinner talk. Gough Clarke was the young Librarian and Steward of the College, and as he arranged the College dinners and food and wine cellar, he perhaps more directly influenced the College than anyone else.

"Let me see," went on the President, scanning the menu and holding it as though it might contain some frightful tidings. "A Soup, Filet de Sole Varsowie, Game Pie, Crême Brûlée, and Cheese Souflée." He put the menu down. "Not too bad. A trifle pedestrian, perhaps, but it will do very well. Gough Clarke doesn't do us too badly, not too badly. At least there are no experiments, like his predecessor, eh, Richard?"

Sir Richard had been the previous Steward of the College.

"Mr. President, Sir," he said drily, "I was attempting to educate the College—both the High Table and the mass of the College," he added, waving his hand towards the body of the Hall. "You know our oath of allegiance to maintain the College as a place of education, learning, religion and research. I believe we should include food and drink among our subjects of education."

"Ah, yes. Drink, now," went on the President. "There I agree with you. Let me see, it being the last night of term, let us have some wine with our dinner. Mr. Vice, Mr. Dean, will you join me in some claret? It would go uncommonly well with your game pie."

"Delighted, sir," said the Dean.

"I'd be charmed," said Sir Richard.

"Good," said the President, turning to Kilmartin, who was standing behind him. "Have we any claret chambré this evening?" he asked.

"We have, sir," said Kilmartin. "I have taken the precaution of having up a bottle of the Château Mouton Rothschild 23 and the Pontet Canet 24."

"Excellent man," said the President. "Let's make it the Pontet Canet, gentlemen, shall we?" He turned to Kilmartin. "The Pontet Canet it is," he said. "Uncork it, let it breathe, and do not serve it before the pie." He looked round the Hall, and then turned to Sir Richard. "I could not see who read grace this evening," he said. "Did you notice; or you, Mr. Dean?"

"Yes, I did," said the Dean. "It was young Farnaby, my next-door neighbour, and Sir Richard's nephew here."

"Ah, yes, Farnaby. I am getting worse and worse about faces. Quite impossible. Do you know, that nice new assistant from the Library came to see me the other day and I thought he was a pupil. I got him to sit down and asked him to produce his essay. He was most embarrassed. Such a pity when the absent-minded don becomes a reality in oneself, eh, Sir Richard?"

Sir Richard was toying with his fish. "Better that, sir," he said, looking up, "than that you should cultivate absent-mindedness in your old age, as do others who shall remain nameless."

"Quite so, quite so," said the President, cackling merrily to himself in a high-pitched voice. He peered round the Hall again not seeing or recognising anybody. "So that was Farnaby, was it? Nice boy. Read the grace a trifle fast, but quite clearly." He paused. "I remember his father well when he was an undergraduate here. Surely it was here that he met his future wife, your sister, Sir Richard, was it not?"

"It was, sir," said Sir Richard. "Their engagement was announced at a May Ball."

"I remember perfectly," said the President, having some vague recollection of the occasion. The young things were always getting engaged during May Balls. "I remember it well," he went on, adding, "I was tutor at the time," to give his statement conviction.

"I am taking young Farnaby with me on a ten-day motoring holiday in Brittany this vacation, sir," said Sir Richard. "He's been working very hard and needs a short break, and I'm particularly anxious to see some archæological remains in Finistère."

"Ah, yes," said the President. "You archæologists are like the geologists—always ready-made scientific excuses to take you off on jaunts anywhere and everywhere." He paused. "Ah, here comes the claret." Kilmartin poured him out a quarter glass. He savoured it carefully. "Yes," he said. "Admirably to my liking."

The claret was poured out and the game pie taken round.

"My sight is going, as you know, Mr. Dean," said the President, "but it seems to me there are very few of our young men in Hall to-night."

"Very few, sir," said the Dean. "It being the last night of term."

"So," said the President, "and I suppose they are all out at parties. Last night before the vacation. More work for you, Mr. Dean, I fear me."

"Perhaps so," agreed the Dean.

"And where," went on Dr. Quibell, turning suddenly on Roger Westmacott, the Tutor—"where, Mr. Tutor, do the young men of to-day go for a great party? You, who so recently have been Proctor, should know all the haunts."

Roger Westmacott was rather taken aback at this surprising request. "Well, sir," he said. "There's the University Arms and Arts Theatre Restaurant and the Lion and——"

"No, no," said the President, lifting up his second glass of claret. "These places are too respectable. Too respectable by half. I want somewhere really low," he said, surprisingly, and beamed on the Tutor and Sir Richard. "When I was a young man," he went on, "there was a splendid place out on the Newmarket Road, half-way between here and Newmarket. What was it called, now? Yes, the Yellow Barn—that's right."

Sir Richard and Roger Westmacott exchanged glances. The Yellow Barn was nowadays little more than a well-conducted night club and road house.

"Full of life," went on the President. "Full of life and gaiety. Dancing. Charming women." He paused, his spoon ready to break a dish of crême brûlée that had been placed in front of him. "Do you know, I'd like to go there again. Let's make up a party, shall we? That would be fun."

Westmacott began explaining why it would never do for the President of Fisher College to be seen in such a place. Sir Richard was thinking of nothing in particular when suddenly something clicked inside his head.

"Of course," he said to himself. "I knew I never really forgot a face. So that's where I've seen young John Parrott. At the Yellow Barn. On the two occasions Sir Richard had been there in the last six months he had noticed Parrott, and on both occasions he was with the girl from the tobacconist's in Bridge Street."

The Dean had lost interest in the President's ramblings about the Yellow Barn, and turned to Dr. Traherne on his left. Landon and Traherne were violent in their high-table disputations on religion and magic and superstition. Landon was a devout Anglican and some considerable theologian: Traherne had a much better mind, but held with equal force rational and evolutionary doctrines. He was Reader in Comparative Anthropology in the University, and perhaps knew more about primitive religions than Landon did about the Anglican Church.

He had written several books that had been universally praised in the scientific world but looked on askance by Cambridge theologians such as Landon.

"Been busy lately, Traherne?" said Landon. That was at least a safe way of beginning a conversation. But it proved not so.

"Very busy indeed," replied Traherne, turning to him and smiling. "I've just been reviewing the new edition of your *Introduction to Comparative Religion.*"

"Oh, you have?" said Landon rather warily. "Found anything good to say about it?" he queried.

"Not a single good word," said Traherne roundly. "No, I am afraid I could not give you a single good mark. Your facts on the major religions are, of course, all right. You give a good account of the rise of Christianity and Mohammedanism and Hinduism and Buddhism and so forth—oh yes, that part is all right, but you miss two vital points which compel me to deny you the status of a serious student of religions."

"What are they?" asked Landon. The certain feeling that he was going away for a while made him for once quite tolerant of Traherne.

"They are very simple and very essential points," said Traherne. "In the first place, you give no definition of what religion is, and therefore only consider the major established religions, paying no attention whatsoever to the religions of what you call the primitive peoples and I would call the Preliterate peoples."

"I know, I know," said Landon. "We've been into all this before, and you know my view that religion cannot coexist with superstition and magic, and cannot be said to begin before the written word was available."

"Ha," said Traherne contemptuously. "What a shallow view! Anyway, I'm giving you all I can on this point: I'm enjoying myself."

"And the second point?" queried Landon, helping himself to some cheese soufflé that was just being brought round.

"It's almost as bad," went on Traherne. "You have twelve chapters in your book describing twelve religions. All of them have gods and so forth, but in one chapter only do you spell that god with a capital G. Why is that, please?"

"My dear Traherne. Surely that's obvious. I am a Christian."

"I know that, but shouldn't you say somewhere in your book: 'Of these twelve religions, only one has any particle of truth in it. The others are snares, delusions, the work of the devil'?"

"My dear Traherne, come," began Landon.

"But you must believe something like that," went on Traherne rapidly. "Why don't you Christian apologists come out into the open and say this? 'Most of the millions of religionists in the world are wrong: I, who am a Christian, am right, and this is why.' Do me the favour of writing such a book."

Landon turned to him smiling. "I most certainly will do," he said.

"I'll do it in the next six months. I'm going away on a long holiday almost immediately, and I'll do it then."

During all this discussion Evan Fothergill had sat looking moodily ahead and eating his food sparingly. Nothing in his life had surprised him more than the way in which Landon had taken the news of his wife's projected elopement with himself. At first he had been incredulous, then, having telephoned his wife, he had grown furiously bad-tempered and sent Evan out of the room. And now here he was in Hall apparently unmoved and gossiping about religion and theology with old Traherne. Suddenly Fothergill heard the references to Landon's forthcoming long holiday. This was too much for him. He had been through curious emotional crises this year. A young Welshman, he had come up poor and a scholar, and only in the last two or three years since his Fellowship and Lectureship in Mathematics had he had time or money to think of women. He had genuinely fallen head over heels in love with June Westmacott, the Tutor's niece, and as genuinely fallen out of love with her when he first got to know Anne Landon properly. His hot, tempestuous, Celtic nature had made him rush into a wild affair with Anne, and she, recovering slowly from five years' dull married life with the Dean, had responded very readily. At the Dean's remark of a holiday, he wondered if Landon could have got round Anne and she had promised to go away with him. Surely it was incredible that she would do that to him. But he must know. He could not wait until the end of the meal. He got up hurriedly and bowed to the President. "Excuse me, sir," he said, "I feel ill," and went out of the Hall as quickly as possible, making for the nearest telephone.

"I'll bring my review round to you to-night, when I've finished it," said Traherne, paying no attention to the interruption. "You can tell me what you think of it."

"Delighted," said Landon, smiling, but what really delighted him was Fothergill's obvious discomfiture on hearing that he was going away for a long holiday. "I'll break that young man," he thought, "I'll break him gradually into little bits," and he smiled again.

"What the hell's the matter with Fothergill?" said Dr. Wedgwood to Roger Westmacott, the Tutor.

"I don't know," said Westmacott. "I've no clear idea, but I think it's to do with my niece, June. She's in a sad state these days. Can't work. Has fits of crying. I think Fothergill and she have fallen out, and I'm expecting the engagement to be broken off any day."

"You are?" said Wedgwood. "Well, well, you surprise me."

"My dear Oliver," said Westmacott. "You live a really cloistered existence, hardly out of the Chapel any day longer than it takes you to lecture and eat. You don't know what goes on in this College." He dropped his voice. "I happen to know that Fothergill and Mrs. Landon are carrying on a very serious affair."

"Really, you surprise me," said the organist.

"Yes," went on the other. "Matters are coming to a head, I believe. It may be we shall have to recommend Fothergill for a Professorship in the Provinces somewhere, or perhaps in America. We got rid of Stephenson that way."

"I've got a better solution," said Wedgwood, his voice going hard. "Get rid of Landon."

"What do you mean?" asked Westmacott, caught by the sudden seriousness of Wedgwood's voice.

Wedgwood said firmly, "Landon is the canker in this College. He has been trying to control my services in the Chapel ever since I came back here from Wells. He declares, if you please, that the music—my music—and the choir—my choir—are merely adjuncts to the religious service. The man's mad. For two pins I'd throttle him myself."

"Oliver, please, hush!" said Westmacott. "He'll hear you."

"I don't very much care if he does," said Wedgwood, now thoroughly roused. "I've put up the service list for next term. If he alters it at all, I warn you, either he goes or I go. This College has for long had a reputation of providing the best music in either of the older Universities. That's why I gave up my job at Wells to come back here. It's one of the best musical jobs in England. And that paltry cleric is not stopping me."

He paused, and Westmacott looked across the table apprehensively, lest anyone else had heard this surprising outburst. He hoped there would be no more, and was saved by the end of the dinner.

The President rose to his feet, and so did all the others. The undergraduates had left a while ago, eating their smaller meal in a much quicker time and having made away to the nearest pubs and cinemas as fast as they could.

Kilmartin handed the President a hornbook with the Closing Grace on it, and Dr. Quibell read it slowly and in a good, firm voice. But he was not looking at the board: he knew the Grace after forty-five years, better than he knew most other things. He was thinking, "What a good College this is, and how lucky I have been while President! No major trouble of any kind." He looked round the table. "What a good company!" he thought—"all so contented, and all, in their ways, so scholarly and learned. Sir Richard and Traherne both scholars of European reputation. Wedgwood one of the greatest organists in England. The Dean and Tutor both excellent in their jobs, and yet finding time for research. What praiseworthy diligence!" And Fothergill—yes, he hoped he wasn't ill—"a brilliant young man, one of our forthcoming mathematicians. What a fortunate, contented High Table!" You must not forget, gentle reader, that Dr. Quibell was very short-sighted.

Grace was over, and they were walking out into the Combination Room. "An excellent dinner, gentlemen," said Dr. Quibell. It was his stock remark as they walked into the Combination Room. A table had been set near the fire and chairs for seven. On the table was a decanter of port, another of madeira, a box of cigars, a dish of walnuts, a dish of apples and a large silver snuff horn.

"Shall we take some wine and desert, gentlemen?" said the President.

They sat down to table. Outside in the cold, dark night undergraduates were scurrying through the streets and escaping into the lighted doorways of public-houses and hotels and cafés. Elsewhere last feverish packings were taking place. In the Combination Room all the candles were burning in their sconces, the fire was blazing merrily and the silver on the dessert table reflected back this warmth.

Dr. Quibell now had the Dean on his right. He poured him out a glass of port, then poured out one for himself and passed it to Oliver Wedgwood, who was now on his left. He picked up his glass and savoured the port slowly. They do not toast the King at Fisher College since the days when the Combination Room was sharply divided as to whom the real King was.

"Ah," said the President, "Excellent, excellent. Nothing could possibly be better."

IV

The College, even on last nights of term, usually went to sleep soon after twelve o'clock, and until six o'clock, when the main gates were opened again and the next day begun, it usually slept fairly quietly, except for one or two stray revellers returning from a party, or a studious undergraduate returning from a late-night discussion on moral philosophy or dialectical materialism or Shaw or sex over tea or ovaltine in another graduate's room, or even a don returning from another's room after a talk or a game of chess and glass of whisky.

To-night, as twelve o'clock struck on the College clock, to be followed by the same hour struck on at least fifty other clocks in Cambridge—a process which took over five minutes and made the exact computation of the hour conveniently difficult—the Head Porter came out of his lodge with Mr. Sam Gostlin. Old Gostlin was not a regular porter: he had been one some five years before, but after two years of College portering had given it up for night watchman at the gasworks. "Less faces to watch," he had said when asked over a pint of beer at the Bishop's Arms why he had made this change, so degrading to the hierarchy of College porters. "I got tied up sometimes remembering all the faces of the undergrads. And fifty new ones every October. It was too much hard work." But the gasworks job had not proved too interesting, and in the end he had left it, and was now out of work. Hearing this, the Head Porter, Mr. Baynes, had called him in when another of the porters had fallen sick, and Gostlin was enjoying his temporary return to Fisher College.

He carried the heavy front gate keys out, top hat on his head and his large torch in his hand. The Head Porter was going off duty, and Rodgers, the Deputy Head Porter, was already asleep in the Porter's Lodge, and would not normally be awakened until just before six o'clock the next morning. The last undergraduates were hurrying through the gate just before it closed, some tottering away rather uncertainly to their rooms.

"Now remember, Sam," said the Head Porter. "Give 'em a few extra minutes to-night, it being last night of term, but clamp to the gate at five-past at the latest. Even the Catholic church clock has struck midnight by then. And don't forget to do the rounds at two and four. You'll not wake up Rodgers unless there is an emergency."

"All right, Mr. Baynes. I'll not forget," said Sam.

"There'll be several late ones tonight, I expect. Note them down. The Dean won't do much, as it's the last night. He never keeps his list through to next term."

"All right, Mr. Baynes," said Gostlin, rather shortly. He had been given all these instructions before.

"There'll be a good few climbing in, I'll be bound," said Baynes. "Note their names down, and I'll go through the list in the morning. We've no need to report them to the Dean on the last night of term, but I like to know myself just what's going on." He made for the gate, but as he got to it an undergraduate tottered through very shakily waving his black square mortar-board in one hand.

"Goo' night. 'Night," he said to the world in general.

"Why, that's Mr. Farnaby of G Staircase," said Baynes, as the undergraduate tottered away into the darkness of the court. "Don't often see him in liquor. Studious type, he is. Now, his father, when he was up, was always in his cups. But, then, he was a real gentleman," he added. He paused, half out through the gate. "And by the way, Sam," he added, "Farnaby's is one of the trunks we didn't get down tonight. Must be done first thing in the morning, remember. Railway cart will come at eight."

"Yes, yes, Mr. Baynes, I will."

At last Baynes was gone and the front gate firmly locked.

"Old fuss-pot!" muttered Gostlin to himself. "One might think I'd never spent a night duty in Fisher College, from the way he talked."

The area behind the gate was full of trunks waiting to be collected and sent off to the station. He flashed his torch on them and went in to the Porter's Lodge. He seated himself in a comfortable armchair by the telephone switchboard, and in front of a window, from which he could see the whole of First Court. Rodgers' snores came loudly through from the next room.

Sam took out his pipe and lit it slowly. He was going to watch very carefully tonight. This was a real chance. For months now his daughter Diana, who worked as an assistant in Fleury and Driberg's, the tobacconist's, had been having an affair with one of the Fisher undergrads called Parrott. Mrs. Gostlin approved of it, but, then, she was silly and weak. Had some sort of an idea the undergrad meant well, and that Diana would better herself by marrying him. "Marriage!" Sam Gostlin snorted. "That's not what he wants. He's trying to ruin my girl, and I won't have it." He had been very firm about Diana meeting Parrott, but you couldn't watch the girl all the time. In the end he had expressly forbidden her to meet the boy at all. She had refused. So he had determined to take action himself. Tonight as he came to work just after ten o'clock he had seen his daughter slip into the Cam Tea Shoppe in Bridge Street. He had waited in the dark shadows by the river for a while, and then had seen Parrott come down the street and go in to the café.

That had made up his mind. He knew Parrott had been gated until the end of term—that is to say, could not be out of College after eight o'clock in the evening. "That means he must have climbed out of College." He was not yet back in his rooms in First Court, so he was bound to be going to climb back into College. "He's reckoning without me," Gostlin said to himself. "I'll catch him, and I'll give him a thorough thrashing he'll never forget. What's more, I'll report the whole story to the Dean tomorrow morning, Mr. Baynes or no Mr. Baynes. Might get him sent down for good. That would fix the whole thing. The bastard!" he muttered to himself. "Monkeying around with my girl. I'll fix him."

And with these benevolent thoughts he dozed off in his chair.

V

Giles Farnaby woke up in the middle of the night to find himself fully clothed, lying on his bed. His shoes were still on and he still had on his black gown. He switched on the light and blinked several times.

"Ah," he said, shielding his eyes with his hand. "What frightfully bright illuminations!" He sat up and groaned. "My goodness me," he said. "I must have been very tight last night."

He stood up very uncertainly and swayed backwards and forwards.

"Must get undressed," he said. "Filthy state, being in bed with your clothes on."

He took off his shoes and then undressed. When he had put on his pyjamas with some difficulty, he carried his shoes out into his keeping room, so as to put them outside the door. He could not find the light-switch and stumbled about, barking his shins against chairs and tables.

"Oh, dear me," he said wearily. "Not a good show, I am afraid. Not a good show."

He opened his outer door and put his shoes down on the landing by his trunk.

"Tut, tut," he thought to himself. "My trunk not gone yet. The Porter's Lodge are slipping up." He paused for a moment, looking across the landing blearily at the Dean's doorway. "That's funny," he said. "Could have sworn the Dean's oak was sported when I came up just after twelve. I was glad because it meant I wouldn't have to go in and see him. But maybe I was too tiddly to see straight." He went back into his room, closed his door and tottered away to bed.

As Giles Farnaby's footsteps died away and the sound of him banging his bedroom door was heard, the Dean's inner front door was opened slowly and stealthily. A figure came out in a dark overcoat and a soft hat pulled down over his eyes. He closed the inner door and then the outer door or oak carefully and quietly—not, as is the daytime custom, by banging the oak to, but softly with a key. He put the key in his pocket and crept down the stairs as quietly as possible. Only a stair-board here and there creaked and made audible his progress. Once at the bottom he turned up his coat collar and crept away through the Court into the night, keeping within the heavy shadow of the walls.

CHAPTER TWO

THE BEDMAKERS AND THE BODY

NEXT MORNING at five minutes to six the customary crowd of bedmakers and gyps were surging around the front gate of the College waiting for Sam Gostlin to open the gate and let them loose on their respective staircases, where from six until half-past seven they would make it impossible for the inhabitants of the College to sleep by banging about in their keeping rooms, cleaning out the fireplaces, laying and lighting new fires. Then at seven-thirty, or in some cases even earlier, they would batter on all the bedroom doors and say cheerfully, "Seven-thirty, sir," as if you had not been made painfully aware of their presence for the previous hour or more.

To-day the last late bedmakers had arrived and the College clocks began the round of striking six o'clock. Usually this was a signal for the front gate to be opened immediately, but to-day there was no rattle of keychain: the front gate of Fisher College remained immovably, imperturbably shut.

"Oh, come on, dearies; hurry up," said one bedmaker in a shrill voice, banging on the gate.

"Yes, come along," said another. "We've lots to do this morning."

"I think they are all asleep," said Kilmartin, who with his wife was waiting patiently in the crowd. "Here, let's ring the bell and see what's doing."

They rang the bell, and after a considerable wait steps were heard within, a key was fitted into the lock and the small wicket in the main front gate was opened.

The bedmakers and gyps all surged in, looking a little surprised at the sight of Rodgers in pyjamas and raincoat. His hair was tousled, and he seemed as surprised to see them as they to see him.

"Well, Charlie," said one bedmaker cheerfully, "have we disturbed your beauty sleep? There, there, what a pity! But some people 'as to work, you know."

"Where's Sam Gostlin?" said Kilmartin, as the others dispersed to their jobs, some making for the First Court staircases, others making straight ahead for the Screens leading to the Second Court. They were soon lost in the darkness of the Court.

"Don't rightly know," said Rodgers. "He's not here. Should have called me just before six, but he didn't; and the main keys are missing. Used the duplicate lot to let you in."

"Perhaps he's gone to——" began Kilmartin, but he was never allowed to finish his sentence. It was cut short by a piercing shriek from the direction of the Screens. "Hi, what's going on here?" asked Kilmartin, and both he and Rodgers ran across the Court to the Screens.

Here a strange sight met their eyes. The bedmakers and gyps on their way from First Court to Second Court through the panelled passage-way known as the Screens had been halted by a sight fortunately unfamiliar in Cambridge colleges. Mrs. Harris had shrieked and fainted, all the others were shocked and frightened. For lying across the stone passage-way of the Screens was the body of Sam Gostlin, the porter. His top hat was some feet away from him, and his electric torch lay against the wall a good distance off.

Rodgers swore beneath his breath and bent down over the body. He had been taking first-aid classes through the winter, and wanted to show how useful they had been. But one quick examination satisfied him that there was nothing he could do for Sam Gostlin. Neither was there anything anybody else could do.

"He's dead," he said in a whisper to Kilmartin—"been dead some time, I should say."

"Good God!" said Kilmartin. "What a thing to happen in College, and on the last day of term!"

Rodgers immediately took charge. "Now, Kilmartin," he said. "Please go and telephone the police. Mrs. Kilmartin, please go and get Sir Richard Cherrington at once. We won't disturb the President yet awhile. And all the rest of you, go on with your jobs as if nothing had happened. And don't gossip about it all to your gentlemen. Though that's a lot of use me telling them that," he added to Kilmartin. "It'll be all round College in five minutes."

"That's true," said Kilmartin, as he made off to telephone.

Mrs. Harris had come to from her faint and was being assisted away to her staircase.

"Horrible!" she kept saying; "horrible! What a turn it gave me! First thing in the morning, too. Horrible!"

Sir Richard usually got up quickly in the morning, but he leapt out of bed on hearing Mrs. Kilmartin's news, and with only a few seconds' delay to put on a dressing-gown and some slippers, picking up his spectacles and a torch, rushed down the Screens. Here he found Rodgers standing guard over the body, and also Evan Fothergill, who had just arrived.

"What's the matter, Rodgers?" said Sir Richard.

"It's Gostlin, sir," came the reply. "Dead. Been dead some time, I should think. Didn't wake me up at six. I was awoken by the bedmakers ringing the bell. Got up and let them in, and when they got to the Screens this is what they found. Mrs. Harris first saw him, and she fainted."

"Ah, ha." Sir Richard bent down over the body. Gostlin was lying spreadeagled on his chest. In the middle of his back was a small neat hole with dried blood around it. He frowned. "He's been shot," he exclaimed.

"Yes, sir," said Rodgers. "I've sent for the police."

"Good man," answered Sir Richard. "Better go and telephone the Head Porter, Mr. Baynes. Get him down here as soon as possible. Mr. Fothergill, please go and tell the Tutor, Mr. Westmacott. I'll guard the body here until you send a relief, then I'll tell the President myself. See that he doesn't hear this news by gossip from the servants."

As soon as they had gone, Sir Richard flashed his torch carefully all over the body. Without moving it he could not see whether Sam Gostlin had been shot from front or back, but as far as he knew anything about shot-holes the little hole in his back looked like an exit hole. Without moving him, too, Sir Richard had no idea whether or not there would be a weapon underneath him. "May be suicide," he said, trying to persuade himself. "But it's a damned odd and dramatic way of committing suicide. And a damned inconvenient one," he added, thinking of inquests and what Dr. Quibell would say, and indeed what he himself was going to say to Dr. Quibell in a short while.

"I mustn't touch the body until the police come," he said to himself, "must I?" But he couldn't resist lifting up the left arm to look at Gostlin's watch. "May be broken and tell us the time of the—er—accident," he argued to himself. "These things usually happen in stories." But the watch was no help. It was not broken, and recorded the time correctly at twenty-five past six.

Sir Richard flashed his torch round the Screens. There was nothing to see except the top hat and the torch. The torch had been dented and the glass broken by its fall. It was one like his own: the College probably had a stock of them. He looked at it nonchalantly and then compared it with his own. Suddenly his attention was riveted on the broken torch, for the light-switch was in exactly the same position as was his. The torch had been on when it was thrown down and broken.

He whistled softly to himself. "Well," he conjectured quietly. "Even if dramatic College porters do commit suicide in the Screens of their own Colleges, they surely do not do it the while they hold lighted electric torches in their hands. This is going to be a little more complicated than I thought."

He straightened his back and half closed his eyes. "A man is coming through the Screens and sees Gostlin," he said to himself. "He doesn't want to be seen, and he has a gun. He immediately shoots Gostlin, who is shining his torch on him and has recognised him. Gostlin falls forward to the ground, dead. His hat rolls away from him to the left and his torch falls out of his right hand and pitches where it now is. Yes," he said, "that will do very nicely: that means the man, if he existed, was coming from the First Court and trying to pass through into the Second. But who? The whole idea is fantastic."

Sir Richard heard a car draw up at the front gate. "The police, I suppose," he murmured as he bent over the body again, flashing his torch over it carefully. And then he saw on the far or Second Court side of the body, caught under Gostlin's coat, a button with a piece of material fastened to it. He looked at it with great interest. "I wonder does it come off the coat of my mystery man with a gun?" he thought. Somehow the material looked familiar: he could not think how, but before he could do any more about it a party of people had loomed out of the lightening darkness of First Court.

It was the police. "Ah, well," thought Sir Richard. "That's the end of my career in detection." He introduced himself. "I'm Sir Richard Cherrington," he said, "Vice-President of this College."

"Good morning, sir," said the first of the new arrivals, a tall, pleasantly spoken man in plain clothes. "I'm Inspector Wyndham of the Cambridge C.I.D. I think we've met before, sir, haven't we?"

"Have we?" asked Sir Richard. "I don't usually forget a face."

"Yes, sir," went on the other. "Do you remember the case of the stolen books some two or three years ago?"

"Of course, of course I do," said Sir Richard. "How stupid of me! Well, this is rather a different business. Rather more serious, I'm afraid."

"Ah yes, sir," agreed the other. "Well, we must get down to it."

The doctor who had come with him was already examining the body.

"I'll leave you now," said Sir Richard. "I must go and inform the President, Dr. Quibell. One thing you must decide. Most of the undergraduates would normally be going down in the next few hours. I assume that will no longer be possible?"

"I'm afraid not," replied Wyndham apologetically. "If you would be so good as to summon all members of the College who were in the College last night to the Hall, we will interview them there."

"I'll have that done for nine o'clock," said Sir Richard, "if that suits you?"

"Very well indeed," replied Wyndham.

"And may I suggest you breakfast with me when you are through with your—er—examination," said Sir Richard. "My rooms are on G Staircase—Set no. 3 on the first floor. I am sure you will need some sustenance before interviewing people at nine o'clock."

"Most kind of you, Sir Richard," said the other. "I shall be delighted."

II

It was nearly eight o'clock before Sir Richard got back to his rooms after interviewing the President and making arrangements for all the undergraduates to cancel their goings down that morning and attend a meeting in the Hall at nine o'clock. Dr. Quibell had received the news of the murder of a College Porter on the steps of the Screens first with frank disbelief, then with horror, and finally with a complete nervous collapse.

"Such a thing has never happened before in the annals of the College," he kept repeating and then, "What will the other Heads of Colleges say?"

To Sir Richard's assurances that such a strange occurrence reflected no discredit on Fisher College and its direction he paid no attention, but declared that he had had a premonition of evil the previous night, which was nonsense. He had merely eaten and drunk too much for an old man and been afflicted with nightmares and indigestion. He declared it quite impossible that he should attend the general meeting summoned for nine o'clock.

"Quite impossible," he had said. "Quite impossible that I should be mixed up in anything so undignified. My dear Sir Richard, you, I know, will be able to deal with the whole matter much better than I. You are so much a man of the world."

"And the police?" Sir Richard had asked.

"The police?" Dr. Quibell had queried.

"Why, certainly," Sir Richard said firmly. "The police will want to interview you, sir."

Dr. Quibell was horrified. "The police interview me?" he had said. "What nonsense! I can tell them nothing. I did not commit the murder. I shall tell them there has been no murder—merely an unfortunate accident—and perhaps I may persuade them to move the venue of this accident from the courts of Fisher College to some convenient lane or alley-way of the town. It would really be much more suitable there."

And with this strange and unreasonable pronouncement, Sir Richard had had to leave the learned President.

He had been in his rooms only a few minutes when there was a knock at the door, and in answer to his greeting Detective-Inspector Wyndham came in.

"Ah, good!" said Sir Richard. "I'm just about to sit down to breakfast myself." They sat down at table and were served by a rather shaken Kilmartin. When Kilmartin was out of the room Sir Richard said, "You were through with your examination very quickly. I always thought these things took hours."

"Oh no," said Wyndham. "I've left my assistants measuring and photographing and making plans. There really was very little for me to see. The whole incident of death was very straightforward."

"Really?" queried Sir Richard.

"Oh, yes," said the other, "remarkably simple. He was shot at point-blank range through the heart. Died at once, of course. We're looking for the bullet now. Probably lodged in the woodwork of the passage-way somewhere."

"There's no chance of suicide, I suppose?" asked Sir Richard.

"Not the slightest," said the other. "To start with, there's no weapon."

"Quite so," agreed Sir Richard. "But if we are going to be logical we should say this may have been removed—during the night or when the body was discovered this morning."

Inspector Wyndham waved his hand. "Yes, yes, I agree, suicide is logically possible, but really, why should a College porter commit suicide in such a dramatic way, to begin with?"

Sir Richard smiled. "Some more breakfast, Inspector?" he asked, lifting the top off a large silver serving-dish that Kilmartin had just brought in. "These are a speciality of the College. Crustades à l'Eveque. They are pieces of fried bread cut in the shape of an hour-glass, filled with minced chicken surmounted by a poached egg, and the whole hidden in white sauce. Do let me help you."

"Very nice of you indeed," said Wyndham. "And may I trouble you for some more coffee?"

"Certainly," said Sir Richard. "By the way," he went on, "I have told all the undergraduates to cancel their arrangements to go down, and have asked them to be in the Hall at nine o'clock."

"Good," said the Inspector. "I should be glad if you will say a few words to them first, unless the President will be there."

"No, no," said Sir Richard hastily. "The President is rather shattered by the news and excuses himself. He hopes to see you later," he added, not quite truthfully.

"Quite so. Well, after your introduction I want to say a few words to them. You know, usual thing. Any little things they noticed that had the slightest bearing on the crime. I shall ask those who have anything to tell me to come and see me somewhere."

"Very sensible indeed," said Sir Richard. "I have thought you would want some kind of office in the College while you were dealing with this case, and have arranged for Dr. Sanderson's room to be at your disposal. He's away at present—lecturing in the States—and you will find his rooms most convenient. They are on A Staircase, First Court, and have a telephone. The porters are opening them up for you now and lighting a fire."

"That's most kind of you, Sir Richard," said Wyndham. "You are certainly doing all you can to help me."

"I am anxious that this mystery attached to the College should be resolved as soon as possible," said Sir Richard, bowing.

"Perhaps you could help me even more," went on the other.

"In any way you like," responded Sir Richard.

"Well, sir, tell me what you know of this porter, Sam Gostlin, and of any reason you know why he should be murdered."

Sir Richard sat back in his chair and took out his pipe.

"Do smoke, Inspector, when you have finished," he said as he filled his pipe. He paused. "I am afraid you have asked for rather a lot," he said. "But I'll tell you what I know. The Gostlins are a large Cambridge family, and we employ a number of them in various capacities here in Fisher College. They have always been associated with Fisher College. Sam, this wretched man who has been murdered, was a porter here some five years ago. You can check all this up in the College records, but I should say he was porter for two or three years, from about 1932 to 1934 or 1935. Then he left and went off to other jobs. Rather a restless type. This term we were short of porters, and Baynes—that's the Head Porter—gave Gostlin a temporary job as Under Porter. He's been back with us about three or four weeks."

"Good, sir; this is very helpful," said Wyndham.

"I'm afraid I don't know any more," went on Cherrington. "I should have said that no one has a reason to murder Gostlin, or if so, it should be easy to find out. If you don't find such a reason it confirms my theory that this is a cover murder."

"A cover murder, sir?" queried the Inspector.

"Yes, a cover murder. Look at the way the body was lying, and I expect you noted that the torch was on. To my way of thinking Gostlin was walking through the Screens and saw someone at the other end. He shone his torch on this person, who shot him dead."

"Yes, sir, but why?"

"Because," continued Sir Richard—"because, my dear Inspector, he did not want to be recognised."

"Quite so, Sir Richard," agreed the other. "But if we all shot the people who saw us when we didn't wish to be recognised, there would be a great epidemic of crime."

"All of us are not prepared to do so," retorted Sir Richard sharply. "But this man was so prepared. Prepared physically, in that he had a gun, and prepared psychologically, in that he had already performed some other crime."

The Detective-Inspector smiled. "My dear Sir Richard," he said. "This is all supposition, of course."

"Of course it is, but that's what I do all my life. I find some pottery or some metalwork in some strange place and I have to explain how they come to be there. Here we have a man murdered. I say if there is no reason in his private life why he should be killed—blackmail, theft, etc. —that he was murdered by someone fresh from another crime, perhaps murdered with a gun still smoking from a previous murder."

If he had been seeking for an effect, the result could not have been more satisfactory. The detective spun round in his chair.

"What can you mean?" he asked.

"I mean nothing," said Sir Richard. "But I say there is no sense in this murder unless it be a cover murder, and therefore my advice to you is briefly, look for more corpses."

"Rest assured we will, Sir Richard," replied Wyndham, recovering a little. "We shall look everywhere. Even, with your permission, all round your rooms."

It was Sir Richard's turn to look surprised.

"You don't suspect me?" he said.

"I suspect everyone," said Wyndham, "who had means, motive and opportunity to do this murder. You certainly had the opportunity, Sir Richard," he added suavely.

"Good gracious me!" said Sir Richard, "I suppose I did."

"That is just the trouble," went on Wyndham. "The trouble in this case is that certainly all the residents in the College last night had the opportunity, which, as far as I can make out, goes for sixty undergraduates and five or six Fellows."

"H'm, your task is not easy," began Cherrington. He paused.

"Any clues? Or shouldn't I ask that?" he said.

"Just one, sir," said Wyndham. "This."

He took out of his pocket a small package wrapped in tissue paper, and unwrapped it. He held it in his hand and showed it to Sir Richard. It was the button with the piece of material fastened to it that Sir Richard had seen near the corpse.

"Ever seen this before, sir?" asked Wyndham.

"Why, no, certainly not," said Sir Richard, and could have kicked himself immediately afterwards. But it was too late.

"It's nothing," said the other. "But as I came across First Court this morning to the scene of the crime I saw you bending over the body, and thought maybe you had noticed this."

"No, no," said Sir Richard. It was too late to go back now. "I'm afraid I noticed nothing."

"Now, that's interesting," said Wyndham to himself. "That's most interesting. The old boy is lying. I'm sure he saw it. Damn it, he's an archæologist and trained in exact observation. Couldn't possibly have missed it. Now, why is he lying? Because he knows whose coat it comes from? That's possible. Or because he put it there? My God, that's an idea! Whew! this is going to be a complicated case." But all he said was: "A pity. I'd hoped you might tell us whose coat it came off. That coat will lead us straight to the murderer, in my opinion."

Further discussion was cut short by a loud knock at the door and the entrance of a large, blustering person in green Norfolk jacket and knickerbockers, a green felt hat on his head and a bushy, curling, white moustache.

"Ah, ha," he said, advancing into the room. "Good morning, good morning. Bad business this. Very bad business. Just going shooting out on the Breckland. Had to put it off to another day. Bad business."

Sir Richard and Inspector Wyndham got up from the breakfast table.

"I think you know each other, don't you?" the latter began. "Sir Richard Cherrington, the Vice-President of the College, sir, and Colonel Cunningham Hardy, the Chief Constable."

"How do you do," said Sir Richard.

"How d'ye do," said the Colonel. "Never met you before, I think. No. But know you by name. Very well. My son was up at St. John's. Went to your lectures. Said they were very interesting. Ready to believe him. Most interesting subject, archæology," he went on, blowing out his moustaches. "Yes. Archæology, anthropology, ethnology, prehistory," he listed. "All most interesting. No money in them, though. Don't get you anywhere. Bad business. What?"

There seemed no immediate necessity of answering this question, so Sir Richard offered the Colonel some breakfast.

"No, no, no," he said. "Most kind of you, I'm sure, but much too late. Always breakfast at seven. Habit I got into when serving with the Indian Army. Never given it up. In any case," he went on, surveying the breakfast table with disfavour, "I always eat very sparingly. One's breakfast should consist of a little porridge and some fruit. Always eat the skin of the apple. Roughage. The system wants roughage. Keep healthy. Too many fats and faldilals being eaten all day long now by everybody. Don't expect you have any of your own teeth in your head, Sir Richard, what? Too much soft food. Not good."

Sir Richard chuckled. In more favourable circumstances he would have enjoyed this old Colonel and added him to his large collection of delightful creatures, but to-day the moment seemed unsuitable.

"I'm sure you have a lot to discuss with Inspector Wyndham," he said tactfully. "So I'll leave you together. We'll meet again in twenty minutes and go into the Hall." He withdrew into his inner room.

Colonel Cunningham Hardy turned on the Inspector. "Glad you are on this job, Wyndham. Need an educated man to deal with these Colleges. Funny places. Very funny places. Now tell me the facts."

"Well, sir," began Wyndham. "I got here at six-thirty this morning. Found the body in the Screens—the passage-way between First and Second Court, with Sir Richard bending over it."

"Why?" asked the Colonel.

"He was on guard, sir," went on Wyndham. "The body was apparently discovered at six-ten or thereabouts by the bedmakers and gyps as they were going to work on the various staircases. The murdered man is a College porter, by name Gostlin. He was on duty last night, and should have let the bedmakers in at six o'clock. When no one opened the gate they rang the bell, and another porter, by name Rodgers, let them in. Said he hadn't seen Gostlin since he went to bed at midnight."

"Yes, I see," said the Colonel.

"Doctor puts the time of death between three and five hours previously."

"Let me see," pondered the Colonel. "That's between one-thirty and three-thirty."

"Yes, sir. The only other indication we have is that while porters could wander about the College as much as they liked during the night, they had to make compulsory tours at two and at four. It's possible that Gostlin was murdered while making his two o'clock tour."

"Yes. Any clues?"

"One, sir," and Wyndham again exhibited the button and piece of cloth.

"H'm," said the Colonel. "Bit of a tweed jacket. Harris, I should say. Rather nice pattern. That should be easy to trace. Get on to old Jack Rattenbury in Silver Street. He'll know how to track down this cloth. Anything else?" he queried.

"Well, sir," said Wyndham, lowering his voice, "there is one rather strange thing. I told you Sir Richard Cherrington was bending over the body when I arrived. He was flashing a torch, and I'm sure he saw this clue. But when I showed it to him he said he had never seen it before.

The Colonel snorted. "Very odd. Very odd indeed. But what do you suggest?"

"Either that he knows who it belonged to and wishes to shield that person, or——" began the Inspector.

"That's not very convincing, Wyndham."

"No, sir?"

"If he wanted to shield someone, he could have done it better by taking the clue away."

"Quite so, sir; but that would really have made him an accessory after the fact."

"H'm, yes, there's something in that."

"It's either that, sir, or else——" the Inspector paused. "Or else he put it there to implicate someone else and confuse the issue."

"Pooh! Come, come," said the Colonel brusquely. "Too much theorising too early in the morning. The time for theorising is over the port at night. Take me to the scene of the crime."

Sir Richard was having a few unpleasant minutes in the other room.

They could not have been more unpleasant if he had overheard the conversation that was going on in his outer room between Colonel Cunningham Hardy and Detective-Inspector Wyndham. For not only was he kicking himself for having so stupidly concealed the fact that he had seen the button and piece of cloth before, but he had suddenly remembered where he had seen that particular grey-green shade of tweed previously. There could be no doubt that it was the Welsh tweed which John Parrott had had made into a coat for himself and which he had commented on in Giles Farnaby's rooms last night.

CHAPTER THREE

INSPECTOR WYNDHAM IS PERPLEXED

AT FIVE minutes to nine the Hall of Fisher College was filled with a heterogeneous mixture of undergraduates, porters, bedmakers and gyps—for at the last moment Inspector Wyndham had asked for the College staff to be included as well. There was much chattering and speculation as to the purpose of the meeting. Some of the undergraduates had not heard of the murder; others had heard of it, but in a very garbled and improbable way. The bedmakers had all heard of it, and were speculating furiously.

"I heard it was Dr. Quibell who did the murder," said one of them. "Who'd have thought that old man would have murdered anyone, leave alone poor Sam Gostlin?"

"I've heard there are several other murders as well," another declared.

"Yes," chorused a third. "Someone told me Sam Gostlin's daughter, that worked in Fleury and Driberg's, 'as been murdered as well."

"Nonsense," said Mrs. Kilmartin firmly. "It's all lies and rubbish. It's only Sam Gostlin is dead."

"Horrible! horrible!" repeated Mrs. Harris, who had fainted earlier on. "What a turn it gave me! All blood and murder and things it was. Horrible! First thing in the morning too, and last morning of term."

Their speculations were cut short by the entrance of Sir Richard Cherrington, together with Detective-Inspector Wyndham and Colonel Cunningham Hardy. Cherrington was definitely ill at ease. In the first place, he did not like the task of addressing the College on such a distasteful subject. And, secondly, he could not help feeling that Wyndham knew he had been lying about the button, and that probably the Chief Constable knew this by now, too. He stood on the dais in front of the high table nervously twiddling his spectacles on the end of their black ribbon. After a moment or two Mr. Baynes, the Head Porter, who had been checking the entry of the undergraduates and graduates and servants at the door, came and told him everyone was present.

He cleared his throat, put his spectacles on his nose and began.

"Gentlemen," he said, "you have all been called together for a reason fortunately very rare in the history of this or any other College in the University. Last night Sam Gostlin, who was acting as temporary porter here, met his death in circumstances which demand full investigation by the police if the good name of this College and of yourselves is to be protected. The President is indisposed, but has asked me to instruct you that you must afford to the police investigating this case all the assistance you can. It is particularly unfortunate that this should have happened on the last morning of term, and I have readily agreed to the police suggestion that your going down should be postponed by one day at least, to permit of police examination. Detective-Inspector Wyndham is in charge of the case, and wants to say a few words to you. I repeat you must give him all the assistance you can."

"Thank you, Sir Richard," said Wyndham, and turned to the assembly. "I'm sure you will give me all the assistance you can. You will realise that in detective stories the first thing the police do is to interrogate everyone who might have a bearing on the case, or who might have heard or seen something during the time the crime was committed. To do that in this case, I would have to interrogate all of you in this Hall, as a beginning, as well as all the dons and many others besides. This is very difficult, and with the permission of the Chief Constable here I do not propose to do it. Therefore I ask this of all of you: if you have any information that concerns Gostlin, or his movements, or his life, let me have it. It does not matter how trivial it is. The College have kindly placed at my disposal Dr. Sanderson's room on A Staircase in the First Court. I, or my assistant, Sergeant Mossop, will be there most of the next few days, and want you to tell us anything you think may help us. This is a difficult case, but we can solve it with your assistance. Now I want all the porters and other College servants to leave, but I have a few more words to say to the undergrads."

During the noisy exit of the bedmakers and servants and porters, a police constable brought a note to Wyndham. He read it with evident delight, and smiled grimly at his audience. What it had said was:

> "Sir, a tweed coat of the material in question is being worn by an undergraduate called Parrott. He came into the Hall wearing it. It has a button missing,"

and it was signed "J. Mossop, Sgt."

"Good old Mossop!" thought Wyndham, and then he thought, "Hell, what does this imply? Does the boy not know he lost the button? It is a plant, then? I must get the truth out of this Cherrington merchant," he thought grimly. "That's the first thing. That, and question this Parrott boy."

He addressed the assembly again. "I've asked you all to stay behind because, apart from Rodgers, the Porter, and a few Fellows, you represent those who were here, or those who had a right to be here, in this College from midnight last night until six o'clock this morning. You will come and tell me anything that bears on the strange and brutal affair of last night. From the front gate register I know the last official entrants to the College a few minutes after twelve. I'm not a University man myself, but I've lived many years in Cambridge town, and I know that, especially on the last night of term, many of you will have come into College and left College after twelve by, shall I say, less recognised means than the front gate. I want all those who did to come and see me and tell me exactly what they saw in the Screens as they came by. Only by such co-operation can we hope to confirm the exact time of this crime. I want, then, from you two things: first, anything you know about this poor man Gostlin, and secondly, anything you know about the events of last night. I need hardly add," he said, looking round the Hall fiercely, "that those of you who knowingly conceal information likely to lead to the capture of the criminal are in danger of being treated summarily as accessories before or after the fact."

He paused.

"I want you all also to agree to remain in College for the whole of to-day, so that I can get hold of anyone I want. There will be police guards at all gates. Do not give them the necessity of enforcing your temporary imprisonment within the College walls. All of you may go to your homes to-morrow, except those whom it may be necessary to detain for further questioning.

"One final thing. The important clue we have in this case has made it necessary that while you are all here your rooms should be searched. You will appreciate that in the interests of justice this has had to be, and I want you all to remain here until the examination is complete. Thank you."

In the buzz of conversation that greeted the speeches of Sir Richard and Inspector Wyndham, the latter busied himself mopping his forehead.

"Hot work, speaking in public," he said. "'Fraid I'm not used to it."

"It was a jolly good speech," said Sir Richard tolerantly. "By the way, you are also searching the rooms of the Fellows?"

"No, sir. But I shall ask their permission to do that soon. How many Fellows were in the College last night?"

They were now walking away from the Hall towards the rooms in First Court allotted to the Inspector.

"Only four of us normally live in," replied Sir Richard. "There's the President—Dr. Quibell—and myself, and Mr. Westmacott the Tutor, and Dr. Fothergill, a young Mathematics don. We are a small College, you know—only eleven Fellows, and three of them are away at present. Dr. Sanderson is lecturing in the States, Mr. Whiblaye is in the Grenville Nursing Home, and Sir Archibald Jeffries, our Bursar, is away on estate business. That leaves only four: Dr. Wedgwood, the organist, who lives in Grange Road; Dr. Traherne, a Lecturer in Anthropology, who lives in the Hills Road; Mr. Gough Clarke, our Librarian and Steward, who lives with his mother in Madingley Road—you probably know Lady Gough Clarke—and then, finally, Dr. Landon, the Dean, who lives next door to them in Madingley Road." He stopped. "Wait a minute. That's an odd thing. I thought the Dean was in College last night, but apparently not. I haven't seen him about to-day."—"Goodness me," thought Sir Richard: "in the hurly-burly of this morning I'd completely forgotten Bill Landon's troubles."

"Thank you, Sir Richard," said Wyndham courteously. "I wonder if you could be so good as to let me have all that information on a sheet of paper?"

"I will indeed," said Sir Richard, only too glad to be of some assistance after his previous mistake. "I'll go off and do it now." And he went off.

"Well, Wyndham," the Colonel had said. "You've got this thing in hand. Don't want me hanging around. I'll leave you in peace now. I'll look in this evening to see how everything is going." He glanced at his watch. "Think I may get out to my shooting party, after all. Have some lunch with 'em, anyway. Got my bearer to pack some damn' good pigeon pie in the hamper. What!" And he, too, had taken himself off.

Inspector Wyndham stood with his back to the newly-lit fire in Dr. Sanderson's rooms and thought over what had happened since the phone call woke him at six-fifteen that morning. "There are five things to do," he said to himself. "First, get what dope I can out of these undergrads. Hope to God they can fix the time nearer than between 1.30 and 3.30. Second, I must interview Rodgers and get what I can out of him. Third, I must interview all the Fellows, particularly the four who were here last night, and especially our friend Sir Richard, with the expensive taste in breakfast dishes. Fourth, I must get on to Gostlin's family and see what angle I can get that way. And fifthly, lastly, but really first," he said, "Mr. Parrott must explain how a bit of his coat comes to be associated with a corpse." He rubbed his hands. "If we can fix this without bothering the Yard, it won't be so bad for me," he thought.

There was a knock at the door, and in came a short, thick-set, red-faced Sergeant.

"Good job you did with the coat, Mossop," said the Inspector. "Careful bit of observation. I appreciated it."

"Thank you, sir," said the Sergeant. "Now I've got two of the undergrads outside that has something interesting to tell about last night. They won't tell me. Insist on seeing you, sir."

"Splendid!" said Wyndham. "Splendid show! And I suppose one of them is called Parrott."

"No, sir."

"*No?*"

"No, sir," went on the Sergeant. "Parrott is sitting still in the Hall; looking a bit pale, but not moving in this direction."

"H'm. Strange," mused the Inspector. "What are these boys called?"

"One's Poynter. The other's Willerby, sir."

"Well, let's have Poynter first. Hope they have something interesting to tell us."

Poynter was a tall, fair-haired youth with a slight lisp.

"Good mowning, sir," he began. "'Fwaid I haven't much excitin' infowmation fo' you, but you asked if any of us had been about after midnight."

"That's right," said the Inspector; "and you were, were you?"

"Yes, yes," agreed Poynter. "Bit of a jolly pawty last night. Chap's wooms in Second Couwt. I live in First Couwt. Next staiwcase to this. Was coming back vewy dwunk, I'm fwaid. 'Bout half-past one. Can't be cewtain of the time, d'ye know, but between half-past one and two o'clock. No bodies."

"I beg your pardon," said the Inspector.

"No bodies," repeated the other. "I mean, I saw no bodies anywhere. And you know I would have," he added fatuously, "'cos I came wight thwough the jolly old Scweens. No cowpses. No shootin'. Nothing like that at all."

Wyndham saw he was likely to get nothing out of Poynter except some confirmation of the Doctor's times. "Thank you," he said. "That's very helpful. But you know nothing else that has any bearing on the case?"

"'Fwaid not," said the other languidly. "'Fwaid not. Hardly knew the cowpse. Knew his pwetty daughter by sight, but not the cowpse."

"His daughter?" queried Inspector Wyndham, pricking up his ears. "His daughter worked in College?"

"No. Not in College. With Fleuwy and Dwibewg, the pipe and tobacco people, you know."

"Oh yes, yes," said Wyndham, making a mental note of this statement. "Well, that'll be all, thank you."

"Not at all," said the other foolishly. "Only too glad to help. Like to give more infowmation, but 'fwaid wather dwunk at the time," and he ambled out.

"I wonder," said the Inspector to himself. "Damn me, I wonder. What is it the French say? *Cherchez la femme.* So old Gostlin had a pretty daughter? Wonder if he was blackmailing someone over her. Perhaps Sir Richard. You can never be sure with these old men."

The Inspector's musings were cut short by the appearance of the second undergraduate—a medium-sized, sandy-haired, pimply boy with spectacles.

"Willerby?" he queried.

"Yes, sir."

"Come in and sit down."

"Thank you."

"Now, Willerby, what have you got of interest to tell me about last night?"

Willerby hesitated a moment and then said, "Well, sir, I think, from what you told us this morning in the Hall and what the bedmakers are gossiping, I must have been a witness to the murder last night."

"What?" said Inspector Wyndham, staring at Willerby with the keenest of attention. "You saw the murder take place?"

"Well, sir, not quite saw it." Willerby hesitated. "May I tell my story?"

"Please do. I am all attention."

"It was this way. I was out rather late at a party last night. End of term and so forth. It went on later than I had expected, and it was nearly two o'clock when I climbed out of St. John's—I should have said the party was there—and I heard it strike two as I got over into Fisher College. I came in over the Library and dropped down into Second Court. I made my way towards the Screens to get into First Court—my rooms are on C staircase—but just as I got to the Screens I heard footsteps, and stepped back in the shadow of the Hall. There was no reason why I should have done this, as I was in the College, and had every right to walk about inside in the middle of the night. I suppose subconsciously I thought I was still engaged in the wicked act of climbing into College after twelve."

"Yes, man. Tell me what you saw," said Wyndham impatiently.

"I saw Gostlin come through the Screens. He had a torch in his hand, and he walked through the Court and went towards the River Gate. Suppose he was doing his usual nightly testing of the gates."

The Inspector rubbed his hands together. This was something. Gostlin was alive until two o'clock. That narrowed the time down to between 2 and 3.30, if the doctor was right. But Willerby had said he knew more.

"Well, what next?" questioned Wyndham.

"I crept through the Screens quietly and crossed First Court to my rooms and to bed."

"Yes," said Wyndham impatiently. "Is that all?"

"Well, sir, it isn't quite all," said the other slowly. "I want to be very careful in the impression I give you in my next statement. As I went up the stairs to my room I heard a noise."

"You did?" interrupted Wyndham. "What sort of a noise? A shot?"

"No, it was not a shot. It was more a dull thud, accompanied by a metallic noise. I thought nothing of it at the time. I wasn't drunk, but I was by no means normally alert, I'm afraid. It was late at night, and I'd been to a good party. But I'm wondering now if I didn't actually hear the murder taking place. It was a fairly quiet night, though dark:

the windows of the staircase were open on to the Court, and indeed faced right across the Screens. It is possible."

"It is indeed." Inspector Wyndham was very much on the alert. "And this would have been about what time? Can you fix it exactly?"

"Well, not exactly. I mean I didn't look at my watch at the time, and in any case my watch is with Mountsays, being mended. It was striking two as I got over the roof of the Library and began to come down the drain-pipe on the Second Court side. I should say the noise I heard—shall we call it that?—was about a quarter-past two."

"Thank you very much, Mr. Willerby," said the detective; "you've helped us a great deal. Sergeant Mossop will take down your statement in the outer room, and perhaps you will be so good as to sign it."

"I will, certainly."

"And if you recollect any other detail of last night, I know you will let us know. For instance, you saw no one else in the College last night except Gostlin?"

"No, sir," came the unhesitating reply. "No one except Gostlin. But it was dark, remember."

"Yes, quite. Well, that will be all, thank you."

The Detective-Inspector ushered Willerby to the outer room, where Sergeant Mossop was setting up a kind of temporary office.

"Sergeant, Mr. Willerby has an interesting statement to make. Will you take it down and get it witnessed? No one else wants to see me, I suppose?" he said, looking meaningly at Mossop.

"Well, sir," began Mossop. "There's none of the young gentlemen to see you, if that's what you mean. But there's a young lady here that Mr. Baynes, the Head Porter, thinks you should see."

Mossop tactfully piloted the Inspector back into the inner room and closed the door.

"What's the mystery, Moss?" asked Wyndham.

"The girl's Gostlin's daughter."

"Really?"

"Yes. She's quite a pretty one. Had a peep at her meself. Works in the tobacconist's in Bridge Street—Fleury and What-not, you know, sir."

"Yes, I know, Fleury and Driberg. So she wants to see me?"

"No," said the other excitedly. "No. That's the rub. She's asking to see our friend Parrott."

"Parrott?" queried the Inspector. "Are you sure?"

"Yes, she's asking for Parrott, but Mr. Baynes, the Porter, said as how no one could see no one to-day, and thought you would like to see her. She didn't seem keen on seeing you, so he kept her on purpose like."

"Good man Baynes! Well, Mossop, wheel in the lady. And afterwards I want to see Rodgers, the Under-Porter who was on duty last night with Gostlin."

"Ah, here's something at last," thought the Inspector to himself. "Now we are getting somewhere. Murder committed perhaps at 2.15 this morning. Button off this boy Parrott's tweed coat found near the body. Murdered man's daughter seeks interview with Parrott. Parrott does not come forward to explain how he lost his button. Strikes me this Parrott merchant has to do a lot of explaining. This case is going to be too simple, just too simple."

"This is Miss Gostlin, sir," said Mossop as he ushered in a small, neatly dressed girl with a mass of flaxen, curly hair.

"Good morning, Miss Gostlin," said Wyndham, getting up. "Have a seat by the fire. This must have been a very sad shock to you."

"Indeed it is, sir," said the girl. "When Mr. Baynes came round and told my mum and me this morning, we could hardly believe it."

Inspector Wyndham studied her carefully. Yes, there was no doubt she was very pretty—very pretty indeed, and unsophisticated. She'd been crying, and even now she was dabbing her eyes occasionally with a small pocket handkerchief.

"Yes, very sad indeed," said Wyndham. "You have my sympathies."

"Thank you, sir," said the girl, and looked up at him.

As she did so Wyndham caught the look in her eyes, and had a great shock. This girl was not grief-stricken: she was frightened. The look in her eyes was a tearful and frightened apprehension. "Now, I wonder why?" thought Wyndham.

"I know you will help me in the questions I am forced to ask you, Miss Gostlin," began Wyndham. "You will want as much as I do to get our hands on the murderer of your father."

"Yes, of course," said the girl, and began to sob again.

"What brought you to College this morning, Miss Gostlin?" asked Wyndham suddenly, and the tears began to stop. She eyed him warily.

"I came to see an undergrad called John Parrott," she said.

"Will you tell me why?" asked Wyndham.

"I will, of course," she said. "We had been friendly for three months. We was going to get married as soon as he took his degree. After my mum, he's the only real friend I have. So I naturally came to see him."

"Yes, yes, quite," said the Inspector out loud, but he thought: "Ho! the plot thickens. By God, it does! Now I wonder."

"Miss Gostlin," he said. "Did your father approve of your friendship and projected marriage with Mr. Parrott?"

She looked at him unwaveringly. "Yes," was all she said.

"I beg your pardon?"

"I said yes," she said. "Yes, he did approve."

"Oh, ho, my lady," said Wyndham to himself. "Did he, my goodness? You're lying. And why? Of course, to shield Parrott and to hide a motive. It's not much of a motive, though, is it?"

"Could you tell me your movements last night, Miss Gostlin? Purely routine enquiry, you know."

"Yes, I can," she said. "I worked in the shop until seven o'clock, then went home and had some supper, and then came back and met John—that's Mr. Parrott."

"You met him last night?"

"Yes. We used to meet in the Cam Tea Shoppe. It's down by the river in Bridge Street. I got there about ten o'clock last night, and John came just after half-past."

"And what then?"

"We had some coffee and biscuits, and then walked about a bit on the common."

"Midsummer Common?"

"Yes. We must have walked about for an hour or so. Then John took me home."

"What time would that be?"

"Can't say."

"You've no idea?" queried the Inspector.

"No, none at all," she went on. "We was thinking of other things. It was John's last night."

"Yes," said the Inspector encouragingly. "But didn't you hear a clock strike, or notice the time when you went in?"

"'Fraid not," said the girl. "I let meself in with my own latch-key. Mother'd gone to bed. I was soon asleep, and was making the breakfast this morning when Mr. Baynes brought us the news."

Inspector Wyndham was not to be put off so easily. "You'd have got home, then, some time between half-past eleven and half-past one?"

"Goodness, I don't know," the girl answered. "I expect it wasn't very late really, as John has to be in by twelve."

"When does your mother go to bed?"

"It varies. Why don't you ask her?" she added cheekily.

"All in good time, Miss Gostlin," said Wyndham, ruffled. "Everything will come out in good time." He paused. "Well, that's about all I want to ask you at the moment. I am afraid you can't see Mr. Parrott to-day, but probably to-morrow. I must ask you to repeat your statement to Sergeant Mossop or one of his assistants next door. Thank you for your assistance."

"Not at all."

As she went out the Inspector noticed her tears were dry and she seemed less frightened. It was as if she had been afraid of the interview with him and it hadn't turned out as badly as she expected. Perhaps he had missed something. And yet he was sure she was lying about two things: her father's approval of her seeing Parrott, and the time. "Now, why lie on these points?" he mused, and made a few notes in his book.

"Mossop," he said to the Sergeant, who had just come in, "take down

Miss Gostlin's statement very fully. Concentrate on her opinion of her father's statements with regard to her affair with Parrott."

"She was having an affair with Parrott, sir?" said Mossop, his eyes gleaming.

"Yes, my old Moss, she was. Put that in your pipe and smoke it. Old Uncle Sex appearing again, you see."

"Yes, sir."

"And another thing, Moss. Get a clear statement from her of what she did last night and try to fix what time she left Parrott."

"They were together last night?"

"Yes. It appears they were prancing about on Midsummer Common until round about midnight. Get her statement and bring it me. I want to check it up against what she told me. Then get her out of College, but meanwhile send someone—old Cobb will do—up to wherever the Gostlins live. Interview the mother and find out what time the daughter got back last night. Interview the neighbours. Somebody, perhaps, saw Parrott escort her home. If he was about and awake after one-thirty last night, and his button lying near the corpse, or 'cowpse', as that affected young man Poynter called it, he's got a lot of explaining to do."

"I'll get Cobb on to that, sir. It's just the job he'll love. And I've got Rodgers outside. Will you see him?"

"Fair enough, my old Moss. Wheel him in."

Rodgers had been so busy since his rude awakening earlier that morning that he had not yet had time to shave.

"Was just going to have a shave," he said, "when I got your message. Dunno as I can help you much."

"I think you can. I've got your facts the first time. You went off to sleep about half-past eleven last night. Gostlin should have awakened you at five-thirty, but you were actually awoken by the ringing of the front gate bell just after six. You were talking to Mr.—er—Kilmartin"—here the Inspector consulted his notes—"at the front gate when you heard a shriek from the Screens, and on running to the spot you found the bedmakers round the dead body of Gostlin."

"That's right, sir. You've got it all right."

"And you heard absolutely nothing during the night?"

"Absolutely nothing. I sleep very heavily. Gostlin used to tell me I snored very loudly."

"You knew Gostlin well?" queried Wyndham.

"Better than most of the other porters, and I liked him when he was here before. Four or five years ago. I tried to persuade him not to leave, but he wouldn't listen to me. Then I saw him occasionally when he was at the Gasworks and when he was out of work. We used to have a drink together in the Bishop's Arms round the corner."

"Now I'm going to ask you a question you will probably think very silly. Was his life at any time threatened by anybody, do you think?"

Rodgers smiled. "Oh, no, sir. I'm sure that is very unlikely. Gostlin was just an ordinary chap, like any of us porters."

"Nothing peculiar in his life. Blackmail? Thefts? Racing? Gambling? Anything that can give me a line on somebody?"

"Not that I know of, sir. Gostlin was just an ordinary chap," he repeated.

"Yes, I know," persisted Wyndham. "But was there no knowledge he might have got hold of that would make him worth getting out of the way?"

"I don't rightly know, sir," replied Rodgers. "But it doesn't seem very likely. This is only a College, like, and the dons haven't many secrets they'd commit murder to hide, or, if they have, I've got 'em all sized up wrong."

Wyndham smiled. Then he tried a last line. "You haven't heard old Gostlin being very vindictive about anybody lately, have you?"

Rodgers didn't make an immediate reply. "It is so difficult to say," he began.

"Remember, Rodgers," said Wyndham, "that it is your duty to put me in possession of all facts likely to bring the murderer to book. If we fail to do this, other College porters may be murdered."

"Oh yes, I see that," said Rodgers hastily. "And anyway you're bound to hear it sooner or later. Gostlin had for days now been uttering threats against one of the undergrads. Against Mr. Parrott."

"The hell he had!" said Wyndham, startled in spite of himself.

"Yes," went on the other, rather uncomfortably. "You see, Parrott was seeing a lot of Gostlin's daughter that works in the tobacconists in Bridge Street. Gostlin didn't like this. Had forbidden the girl to see Parrott; but she went on seeing him nevertheless. Gostlin was sure Parrott would get her into trouble, like, and leave her in the lurch. So he was watching Parrott, and was going to report to the Dean anything Parrott did wrong, so as to get him sent down. Parrott was already in the Dean's bad books, and had been gated."

"Gated?" queried the Inspector.

"Yes. He was found climbing into College. Caught by Gostlin three weeks ago. Dean gated him for the rest of term. Confined to College after eight o'clock each evening."

"Ah," said the Inspector. He began to see more light.

"Yes," went on the other. "But he broke the rules. Gostlin caught him climbing in two nights ago, and was expecting to catch him again last night."

"I wonder if he did," said the Inspector, half to himself. He began to see the crime taking shape. Parrott climbing into College just after two. Being caught by Gostlin. Opportunity, yes. But motive?

"If he was reported to the Dean, what would the penalty be?" he asked Rodgers.

"He'd get sent down for good and all. You see, he'd failed his examination this time again, so Pettet, the Tutor's gyp, told me."

"An end to his University career?"

"Oh yes."

"But was it sufficient motive?" thought the Inspector. "Surely not. And yet, what with that and disapproval of his association with the girl. After all, we are only dealing with undergraduates. Adolescents. They may get things out of proportion as compared to grown men."

"I think I'd better have a word with young Parrott," he said.

Rodgers got up. "I hope I haven't got him into any trouble, sir," began Rodgers.

"No, certainly not. You've been very helpful. I should have got all this information sooner or later. Thank you for making it sooner," said the Inspector.

The Inspector showed Rodgers out and instructed Mossop to get hold of Parrott and bring him for interview straight away. "Send in the constable when Parrott comes," he said to Sergeant Mossop. "I want a shorthand account of our conversation."

"Certainly, sir," said Mossop. "And here is Miss Gostlin's statement. All signed, sealed and delivered, so to speak."

Inspector Wyndham glanced through the written statement while waiting for Parrott to be brought to him. There were no discrepancies from the verbal account she had given him. The girl insisted that her father approved of her association with Parrott: that was lie number one, of course. Rodgers had proved that. She insisted that she could not fix the time Parrott delivered her back to her home, which was apparently 110 Milton Road. "Is that lie number two? I wonder," he said to himself.

The door opened and Sergeant Mossop brought in John Parrott. We have already met Parrott in this story, but to-day he was a very different Parrott from the one who had drunk some beer with Giles Farnaby the night before. Here he was, very nervous, seemingly afraid, and pulling at a cigarette all the time.

Inspector Wyndham introduced himself, the while looking carefully at Parrott. He took in the nervousness and the look of frightened apprehension in the man's eyes. "It's the same look as I saw in the girl Gostlin's eyes," he thought. "And yet, is it the look of a murderer?" Inspector Wyndham was a fair man, and he was bound to confess to himself that it was not. "And yet, you know," he said to himself, "it all points that way." He began his examination.

"Mr. Parrott," he said. "I expect you are wondering why I asked you to come here. I cannot examine all the undergraduates, but I am questioning all those who had any connection, however remote, with the murdered man. I understand you were friendly, if I may use that hackneyed phrase, with the murdered man's daughter?"

Was there a perceptible slackening in the tension of Parrott? Inspector Wyndham thought there was. Parrott had been surprised at the opening of the discussion. And then Wyndham noticed Parrott's jacket. Yes, it was of the same material as the fragment found near the corpse, and the bottom button was missing. What seemed so odd was that Parrott appeared unaware of the significance of all this.

"Yes," said Parrott. "I've been friendly with Diana Gostlin since January. I intend to marry her when I've taken my degree."

"Ah ha. Quite," said the Inspector. "Did her parents approve?"

"Her mother did, but her father was not very enthusiastic," was the reply.

"He never forbade you to see her?"

"That was hardly in his power," said the other, flushing.

"He never forbade Miss Gostlin to see you?"

"No, no." The answer came pat, but it was a little unconvincing.

"You saw a great deal of Miss Gostlin?"

"I did. What has that to do with the situation?"

"I mean did you see her much in the evenings?"

"I did, rather."

"Although you were gated?" It was a shrewd blow of the Inspector's.

"That is surely a College, and not a police matter?"

"Perhaps." A pause. "Did you see her last night?"

"I did."

"Could you give me the details?"

"By all means. I met her just after ten-thirty in the Cam Tea Shoppe, and walked home with her via Midsummer Common."

"What time was all this?"

"I got back into College just before midnight."

"Ah," thought the Inspector, "now we're getting somewhere."

"Did anyone see you come in?" he asked.

"Yes."

"Whom?"

"Sam Gostlin. I came in through the front gate a few minutes to twelve."

"Very clever," thought the Inspector—"very clever indeed. Build up your alibi by means of a dead man. Very difficult to break, or, for that matter, to prove."

"What did you do then?"

"I went straight to bed, and was woken up this morning by my bed-maker at about six-thirty saying that Sam Gostlin was murdered."

"Were you wearing that coat yesterday?"

Parrott looked puzzled. "Why, yes," he said. "But what has that got to do with it?"

Then Inspector Wyndham exploded his charge. "Just this. If you went to bed at midnight, can you offer any explanation how the missing button of your jacket was found close to the corpse this morning."

At first Parrot was incredulous. "That's just not true," he said, and then he looked at his jacket, and at the button and piece of tweed the Inspector was holding in his hand. Slowly the colour began to drain out of his face.

"You found that by the—er—body," he said weakly.

"We did," said the Inspector, "and we naturally thought you might be able to explain to us how it happened to be there."

"I can't," said the now very frightened Parrott. "Unless someone deliberately put it there to involve me."

Wyndham waved his hands in the air. "Listen, Parrott," he said. "I have already interviewed Miss Gostlin."

"You have?" said Parrott, brightening. "How is she? All right?"

"Yes, she is all right. You both declare that Gostlin did not object to your being seen together. From other sources I learn that he was violently opposed to this."

Parrott lowered his eyes.

"I put it to you," went on the Inspector, "that you were much later coming into College than you say you were."

Somehow the mention of Diana Gostlin seemed to have cheered up Parrott immensely. He half smiled. "Now you sound like prosecuting counsel rather than the police," he said. It was a shrewd remark, and pulled up Wyndham in time. "No, Inspector," went on Parrott, rapidly recovering his poise. "You may think I had cause to murder Gostlin: true, he didn't like me seeing his daughter—we misled you there—and I know he had it in his power to give information about me to the Dean which could have caused me to be sent down. But I don't think these motives for murder. In any case, the Dean had already sent me down. I went to see him at ten o'clock, and he drew a line across my University career. That removes one of my motives, doesn't it? And then, Inspector, you know I haven't a gun."

Inspector Wyndham smiled. "You're quite right," he said. "But you will appreciate that it is our job to suspect everyone. And despite what you say I am not satisfied with your explanation of how your button got near the murdered man. I must ask you, therefore, to stay on in College until I get a satisfactory explanation, or you provide one yourself."

"I see," said Parrott. "I'm still definitely on the list of suspects, am I?"

Inspector Wyndham waved his hand noncommitally.

"I know you will co-operate with us," he said as he showed him out.

Sergeant Mossop came in. "Any luck, sir?" he said.

"Well, so so," said the Inspector. "The girl Gostlin and Parrott don't give quite the same story about what they did last night, but it tallies generally. Nevertheless, I don't believe the story. This ruddy button has got to be laughed off somehow. We must shake them up over the time. Cobb's got going on the Milton Road angle, has he?"

"He has, sir; and sir——"

"Yes?" said the Inspector.

"When we was searching the undergrads' rooms this morning to find the tweed coat, Mitchell found a note in one of the rooms. He kept it 'cos it seemed to have some bearing on the case. Here it is."

He handed to the Inspector a half-sheet of scribbling paper on which was written:—

"SIR,

The Dean has sacked him, and is reporting the matter to the Police to-morrow. Please to do what you can to-night.

(*Signed*) A. KILMARTIN."

"Good heavens!" exclaimed the Inspector. "This is astonishing. Why—Kilmartin, that's the servant on Sir Richard Cherrington's staircase, isn't it?"

"Yes, sir."

"And where was this found?"

"In a Mr. Farnaby's room on the same staircase."

Inspector Wyndham passed his hands through his hair. "Perhaps this case is not so straightforward as I thought," he said. "Let's go and have some lunch."

CHAPTER FOUR

THE YELLOW BARN

SIR RICHARD ate a solitary but excellent lunch in the Combination Room. It was not his custom to drink port at lunch, but the events of the morning had been so unusual and the Stilton with which he was finishing his lunch was so good that on this cold March day he permitted himself the indulgence of a glass of port. As he sipped the wine he began to think over again the curious circumstances of the morning. He would like to have discussed them with the Dean, but he was apparently at home to-day. I suppose, thought Sir Richard, that all this sudden College scandal will overshadow his own troubles and keep him busy a while.

He had had a talk with young Willerby just before lunch, and he had told him much the same story as he had told the police. Together with the police doctor's evidence which Wyndham had told him, it did seem as though the murder might well have taken place soon after two o'clock, perhaps at two-fifteen, as Willerby suggested. That fitted in with Sir Richard's theory of Gostlin having been murdered while on his two-o'clock rounds.

"The problem is not first of all, By whom; it is Why?" argued Sir Richard to himself. "Surely it must be because if he had lived he would be able to testify to the presence of someone in the College who oughtn't to be there, or someone walking through the Screens at two in the morning who would have no proper reason for doing so. Now," argued Sir Richard, "if that person was prepared to murder Gostlin to prevent that testimony being given, he must already have committed some other very serious crime, and as he had a gun ready with him, probably this earlier crime was a murder. *Ergo*, look for more bodies."

Sir Richard got up and stood with his back to the Combination Room fire. He dangled his spectacles aimlessly from their black ribbon. "Yes," he thought to himself, "that's the inescapable conclusion, as I told that rather stupid Inspector this morning. Look for more corpses. Who is missing? All the undergraduates appear to be here. What of the Fellows?" The Dean, Wedgwood, Traherne—he hadn't seen any of them to-day. Should he ring up and ask if they were alive? The whole idea was preposterous. "And yet, unless we find the original crime, we shall get nowhere," he argued.

"The only thing about the second crime to help us is this button. I wonder, did it come off Parrott's coat, and if so what is the explanation? I was a fool to tell the police I had not seen it. I shall explain myself to them later. Well," he thought, "at any rate we can solve the button mystery. I'll go and see this man Parrott."

He walked across to the College directory. Parrott? Yes, E Staircase. In First Court. He walked out, past the Screens and up the staircase. Parrott's room was on the top floor. He was standing with his back to the fireplace, the remains of a meagre lunch of bread and cheese on the table. He looked very worried. He was not, Sir Richard noted, wearing the same coat as last night.

"Good morning, sir," said Parrott. "This is a pleasure, and a surprise."

"We didn't expect to meet again so soon, did we?" asked Sir Richard. "Mind if I sit down?"

"Please do, sir."

"Good," said Sir Richard. "I've come to ask you one question which you needn't answer if you do not wish to. After all, I'm not the police."

"I'll answer it if I can."

"Right. Last night, when I saw you, you were wearing a very attractive tweed jacket. I commented on it at the time and you said it was a Welsh tweed."

"That's right, sir." John Parrott felt he knew what was coming, and steeled himself.

"I was one of the first on the scene of the crime this morning," went on Cherrington. "While looking round before the police came, I saw a piece of that cloth with a button attached to it. It looked as if it had been torn from a jacket. Was that jacket yours?"

"Yes, sir, it was."
"It was?"
"Yes, I'm afraid it was."
"Then how the devil did it get there?"
"That's what I don't know, sir. It must have been planted there by somebody else. Leastways, that is what I suggested to the police."
"The police?"
"Yes, sir. The Inspector questioned me about it this morning. He suggested I lost it there while murdering Gostlin, but that's nonsense."
"Why is it nonsense?" asked Sir Richard sharply.
"Why, sir, when I came into College last night just before twelve Gostlin was alive and at the front gate. I went straight to bed, and slept until the morning."
"You didn't get up in the middle of the night and shoot him?"
"Why, no, sir," protested the other. "I haven't got a gun."
"You haven't got a gun now, I've no doubt; but did you have one last night? Do you belong to the Cambridge University O.T.C.?"
"Yes, sir."
"Plenty of revolvers there, you know."
"But, sir, if I shot a man, I don't see why I should leave a piece of my coat behind."
"H'm," said Sir Richard. "Nor, quite frankly, do I. It's a mystery."
He got up to go, and his attention was attracted by a portrait of a girl on the desk.
"Sister or fiancée?" asked Sir Richard sharply.
"Fiancée, sir."
"Nice-looking girl. Seen her somewhere before. Of course," he said. It was coming back to him now. Odd little pieces of information were fitting into a pattern. "It's the girl who serves me with tobacco and snuff in Fleury and Driberg's."
As if it reminded him, he took out his silver snuff-case and elaborately began to take some.
"Some snuff, Parrott?" he asked.
"Don't take it, sir."
"Should," said Sir Richard sharply. "Clears the head. I remember, too," he went on. "I've seen you with her in the Yellow Barn."
"Oh, did you, sir?" said Parrott. "When was that?" he added.
"Oh, some time ago. What does it matter?"
"I wonder, sir, if you could get a message to her? I know it's absurd of me to ask you this, but the police will not allow me out of College."
"I will if it's important," said Sir Richard kindly.
"Thank you, sir. Tell her I'm all right and not to worry, and that I will come and see her as soon as I can."
"I will do if you think it necessary," said Sir Richard. "Where can I get hold of her?"

"In the shop, sir, or at her home, 110 Milton Road."

"110 Milton Road," said Sir Richard, noting it in his diary. "What's her name?"

"Oh, I thought you knew, sir," said Parrott, much surprised. "It's Diana Gostlin. She's Sam Gostlin's daughter."

"Goodness me!" said Sir Richard, and he was really surprised. "I had no idea—no idea at all. I will most certainly take your message. And now I must be going off. Any funny business with the police and don't forget to let the Tutor and myself know. We're *in loco parentis* here, you know, and that's not an empty phrase."

Sir Richard walked back across First Court and Second Court, let himself out on the Backs with his Fellow's key and then into the Fellows' garden. "Very strange business," he thought to himself as he paced up and down the lawns. "I wonder if it is a cover murder, after all, what with this button and the girl? It all seems to tie up with Parrott. No, no," he said, "Parrott can't be a murderer. That's quite absurd. And yet, how did the button get there?"

Sir Richard took out his pipe. "Let's treat this thing as though it were an archæological discovery," he mused. "The murder is committed at 2.15. At 6.15, when I arrive, it is associated with a piece of cloth and button torn out of Parrott's coat. Now what are the possibilities? First, that it was there before the murder was committed and by ill chance the dead body slumped on top of it. By God, that's not impossible," he thought. "Second, that somehow during the murder it got snatched off the murderer's jacket. That is to say, Parrott did the murder. Not impossible, but not very likely. What is the third possibility? That it got there between 2.15, when the murderer went away, and 6.15, when I arrived. There is a fourth possibility, of course: that the murderer dropped it there at the time of the murder deliberately to involve Parrott and throw the scent off himself."

He considered the four possibilities. "I plump for the third," he said. "It arrived subsequent to the body, and its association with it is fortuitous." His training as an archæologist made him think like this. "Very likely, but how did it get there? Chance? Impossible. Design? Likely. But then we get back to the malevolent intention of someone involving Parrott or distracting attention from himself."

Suddenly he spun round sharply in his tracks. "Well, I'm damned," he muttered. "Fancy, after all these years, ruling out chance. It could well have been dropped by chance. Suppose young Parrott had walked through the College after the murder had been committed. He might have gone through the Screens, noticed the dead body, and bent down to see who it was. As he did so the button might have dropped off, and he, Parrott, would be unaware of this."

"All theory; all theory, my boy," he said to himself. "And yet very attractive. There are two snags. The first: why, if he saw the body, did he not go and inform the Porter's Lodge at once? No answer to that. Yes, there is. Yes, there is. What if he was afraid of being associated with the crime? Why? Maybe he'd got the Gostlin girl into trouble and Gostlin was blackmailing him. Perhaps that would account for his apparent concern now for the girl and asking me to take a message to her," said Sir Richard. "It's possible."

"Then the second snag. Buttons don't fall off coats at the sight of corpses. Unless they are loose. Was this loose yesterday? Ask his bedmaker. Or, by God, if they have suddenly been loosened. How? Ah," said Sir Richard, "I've got it at last. He climbed into College late last night, tore his coat a little as he came in. Came through the Screens, bent down over the body—the button came off—and he went on, all unknowing."

"Yes," he pondered, "that is possible. But, if so, why lie about it? And, if so, where was he until after half-past two last night. It is still March, and very cold. Good God!" thought Sir Richard, "I wonder." He stood stock-still, took out his snuff-case and reflectively inhaled some snuff from the elegantly poised back of his left hand.

"Good God!" he said again. "Is that why he asked me nonchalantly when I had seen him at the Yellow Barn? There's something in all this, and I'm going to find out. I'll get the car and drive out to Stanton Quy and find out."

As he drove along the Newmarket Road, the enthusiasm engendered by his self-argument in the Fellows' garden began to wane. "It is all rather hypothetical, isn't it?" he thought to himself, "and I'm probably very foolish to be driving out to the Yellow Barn on the offchance of Parrott and this girl Gostlin having been there last night. Never mind," he argued, "it's a fresh cold afternoon, the Fens on the one side and the hills on the other as I drive along, and in any case I haven't seen Babs Chilcott for a good while." And then, as he topped the slight rise out of Cambridge before Quy, he said to himself, "Now let's be honest. This murder has provided me with a problem as intriguing as any archæological one I have had for a long time. I've got a very great deal to do, and it's worth trying one's hand at solving it. Let's regard the police as rival archæologists. They will proceed by their routine methods: minute examination of everything, detailed checking of every point. I shall interview all the connected parties and let them gossip to me." And having at last become honest with himself, he drove in through the gateway of the Yellow Barn and up the drive to the main entrance.

The Yellow Barn had originally been a farmhouse standing on a slight crest of the dry land looking down over the Cambridgeshire fens between Quy and Stanton Quy. Just before the last war it had been bought by an enterprising business manager called Chilcott, who had turned it into a sort of luxury inn where the wealthy from Cambridge and Newmarket could drive out and drink when their own pubs and hotels palled on them. After the war Chilcott had developed it, and when he died in 1925 his daughter Margaret—"Babs" to everyone who knew her really well—had developed it further along the lines the dancing 'twenties wanted it, and then later, being a clever woman, changed it again in the 'thirties to meet the more exotic and less noisy tastes of those years. It now stood, a very large establishment, on the hillcrest edge of the Fens. The barn itself had been joined to the farmhouse, and both had been incorporated in further buildings which Babs had got a sensible unknown young architect in Cambridge to do. "This place when you've finished with it," she had told him, "has got to look as if it had always been there, and not as though it was a great road house stuck on the Cambridge–Newmarket Road." He had done a good job, and the place looked, as it was, in the best of taste. That taste was Babs Chilcott's, and so the place provided for those who wanted good food, good drink, dancing and a good cabaret, and those who wanted to stay the night without their room-mates being questioned. The more prudishly minded in University circles called it a high-class brothel: those who thought the word "brothel" rather begged the question of the frontier of pleasure and vice called it "that rather pleasant place out on the Newmarket Road". Certainly it flourished, and was often booked up for days ahead with the party-minded of Cambridge and Huntingdon and Ely and Newmarket and Royston.

Sir Richard put his car in the park and walked in through the main entrance to the Hall.

"Is Miss Chilcott in?" he asked.

"I'll see, sir," said a flunkey. "What name shall I say?"

Sir Richard took out a visiting-card from his notecase. On one side was printed, "Professor Sir Richard Cherrington, F.R.S., F.B.A., D.Sc., M.A.," and in one corner "Fisher College, Cambridge," and in the other, "Athenæum, United University." He turned it over and wrote on the other, "Babs, can I see you for a few moments, please?" and signed it "Ricky".

In a few minutes the flunkey was back saying Miss Chilcott would see the Professor. "Yes, certainly, sir. Come this way, please, Sir Richard. Miss Chilcott is in her private room."

Babs Chilcott was resting on a chaise-longue as Sir Richard came in. Some newspapers and magazines were on her lap, and a long cigarette-holder in her hand.

"Ricky," she said, half getting up, "you ought to come oftener."

"I will do," he said, taking her outstretched hand and squeezing it firmly between his.

"You always say that," she said. "Sit down. What will you drink?"

"Nothing, thank you," he said, drawing up a chair and sitting down beside her. "This is the one hour of the day when no drink of any kind is possible. I mean the latest post-luncheon tipplings are over by three o'clock, and no civilised person will drink tea before four o'clock."

"There you make a mistake, Ricky. You're too dogmatic, as always. It's a failing all you dons develop at your high tables." She lifted up a telephone at her elbow and dialled a single-figure number.

"John?" she said into the telephone, "bring up a King's Evil to my room. It is for a very special visitor."

"What in heaven's name is a King's Evil?" asked Sir Richard. "You know I really don't need anything."

"Its the only thing for a cold March afternoon," she insisted. "Now tell me why you have come to the Yellow Barn at this odd time of the afternoon. Were you just passing and thought you'd look in to see how I was ageing?"

"No," he said, smiling. "And in any case," he went on, bowing courteously, "you don't age. You just get more beautiful. Mind you, I don't know whether that is because you and your maid are getting more and more expert."

"Ricky!"

"No. On the whole I think it is that your charms are maturing. You get less coquettish every year, and more what I like."

"Really?" she began.

"Enough of this," he said firmly. "I want to ask you if you know an undergraduate of my College called John Parrott."

"I do."

"Good," he said. "Do you know his girl?"

"The one that serves in Fleury and Driberg's?"

"Yes."

"Yes, I do. That's his present girl. He used to come here with June Westmacott a lot."

"Oh, did he?" said the Professor. "You know everything, don't you?"

"No, no. I just keep my eyes on all the folks who come here. By the way, here's your drink."

"Thank you," said Sir Richard, taking a half-pint silver tankard from the waiter. He peered inside rather suspiciously. "What in heaven's name have you given me?" he asked.

"Try it and see."

"Well, here's health," and he took a firm draught of it. "Oh," said Cherrington, setting the tankard down. "Excellent—most excellent, and most potent. What is it? Some kind of specially spiced beer you have invented?"

"It's a secret of the house, but I'll tell you this much. It's some No. 1 Ale slightly mulled with some spice and a light lacing of spirits. Very good for the cold Fen winds. Guaranteed to keep away the Fen ague and the King's Evil and other horrid plagues."

"Gracious powers! I believe that it will," said Sir Richard. "But you are keeping me from the real purpose of my visit. What I want to know is this: were there any members of my College here last night?"

"Why do you want to know?"

"I'm trying to help somebody. I'll put the question another way. I'm guessing that an undergraduate called Parrott—John Parrott—was here last night with the girl from the tobacconist's in Bridge Street. Am I right?"

Babs Chilcott lit another cigarette. "This isn't getting them into trouble, is it?" she asked.

"It's helping them. They were here?"

"Yes, they were."

"Excellent!" said Sir Richard. "Now, when did they leave?"

"When the dancing ended, at about a quarter to three. They arrived round about eleven o'clock, and drove away after the dance in one of the house taxis."

"You can guarantee that these two were here from midnight until three o'clock."

"Well, I and my staff can," replied Miss Chilcott. "I was checking up the car runs this morning. The house car took them first to an address in the Milton Road and then dropped Parrott at the corner of Bridge Street and Trinity Street."

"Just as I thought," said Cherrington. "Just as I thought."

"What is the mystery, Ricky?"

"You'll see it in the papers this evening, Babs, so I might as well tell you now. It's just that last night, or early this morning, the girl's father, who is a temporary porter with us, was murdered in the Screens between First and Second Court."

She stared at him for a moment. "Is this true?" she asked.

"Afraid so," he replied. "And if the Yellow Barn can provide a water-tight alibi for Parrott and the Gostlin girl during those important hours of the night, well"—he paused and slipped into his suave lecturing style—"it will be doing a service to the University, and to Fisher College in particular, over and above its normal service of good food, good drink," he lifted up his tankard and finished the brew—"a good dance band and floor, and—er—shall I say good company?" He got up. "Now I must go."

"My dear Ricky. A murder has surely made the University dovecotes flutter, eh? What does Dr. Quibell say? I used to remember him coming here a lot when I was a little girl and my father was running the place."

"Dr. Quibell is prostrate with distress, my dear," replied Sir Richard. "I must go off and comfort him."

"Well, come again soon, Ricky, and come oftener. And if we can give you any more aid about alibis, we will." She walked down with him to the entrance. "Oh, there's Piggott," she said, pointing to a man polishing a car. "That's the driver that took them home last night."

They walked over to the car. "Good afternoon, ma'm," said the man Piggott, touching his forelock respectfully.

"Good afternoon, Piggott. I was just checking on your late run last night. This gentleman here was interested in the time."

"Well, ma'm," said Piggott, "I left here just after three, and drove straight to the first address—110 Milton Road it was—and then back down Bridge Street. I dropped the gentleman at the lights and drove straight back here. Horn stuck down just outside the aerodrome on the way back, but I got that fixed in a few minutes. I was back here about ten to four. I know I was in my room and in bed by a quarter past."

"Thank you, Piggott. Just what we wanted."

"Thank you indeed," said Sir Richard. "Now I must drive off."

"You won't stay and have tea, Ricky?" she asked.

"No, Babs," he said as he got into his car. "Next time. Many thanks, and don't forget to call on me when you are in Cambridge."

He drove off down the drive and out on to the road, turning right back towards Cambridge. He did not normally drive fast, but this afternoon he raced his old Bentley along so that the people said as he passed: "One of those wild undergraduates, I suppose," and little thought it was a respectable member of the Athenæum and a Fellow of many learned societies.

"I don't know whether it was that spiced beer, or whether it is the fun of the chase and having found one little hypothesis proved," he said to himself, "but I feel pleased. Here goes," he said out loud to nobody, and raced down the road past the aerodrome and the cemetery and over the railway bridge. He slackened speed as he came more into the centre of the town: "After all," he reflected, "I am a Justice of the Peace, and this is no way to drive a fast car in the gathering twilight of a March evening."

"What next," he asked himself, and then, without hesitation, swung the car round at the Jesus Lane roundabout and drove off down the Milton Road. "I'll see the girl," he said. "110 was the number, wasn't it?"

110 Milton Road was a small, semi-detached house: as he drew up he noticed all the blinds were down. He knocked quietly at the door, and after a short interval it was opened by a young girl aged about eighteen or nineteen. It was Diana Gostlin, and he recognised the girl who served him in Fleury and Driberg's when old Mr. Driberg was busy. She was also the girl of the portrait in Parrott's room. She looked pale and tired.

"Good afternoon," he said.

"G'afternoon, sir," she replied.

"My name is Cherrington," he began—"Sir Richard Cherrington. You've served me many times in Fleury and Driberg's."

"Yes, sir," she agreed. "I remember."

"I want to say first how horrified I am at the tragic death of your father. I want you to convey my sympathies to your mother."

"Won't you come in, sir?" she said.

"Thank you," said Sir Richard, and was ushered into a little room on the right of the passage. It was a typical unused, over-furnitured lower-middle-class front room. He looked around with the professional interest of the archæologist for the type objects of a culture. No, there was no aspidistra in the window, but there was a hideous cross-legged bamboo table on top of which was a bead mat and a bowl of bulbs. The mantel-shelf was draped with a plush material from which depended at intervals hideous plush balls. The mantel-piece itself was crowded with family pictures, hideous vases, and an extraordinary fan-shaped object of pieces of slate, picked up, no doubt, during some holiday in North Wales.

He sat down on the edge of one of the leather chairs.

"You probably know that I am Vice-President of Fisher College, and as such have the welfare of all the undergraduates at heart," he began rather pompously. He did not say that he had not known John Parrott until yesterday.

"Yes, sir," she said.

"Now, your young man, John Parrott, has been questioned by the police, as have all the undergraduates of the College," he went on hastily.

"So have I," she broke in.

"So have you? And what did you tell them?"

"I said I was out with John last night, but that we parted before mid-night because he had to get back into College."

"Ah!" said Sir Richard. He took off his spectacles, polished them carefully with a blue silk handkerchief, put them on again, looked at her and said slowly, "Why didn't you tell them the truth?"

"The truth?" she queried.

"You see, I know the truth," said Sir Richard. "I know that you spent the evening at the Yellow Barn, and were not home until after three o'clock."

She didn't question his statement or ask how he had found out. She burst out crying.

"There, there," he said. "There's nothing to cry about. Just tell me why you told the police and me the wrong story. Were you trying to shield John?" he asked shrewdly.

"Yes," she said tearfully. "He's so impulsive-like. I thought at first he really might have killed my father. But then I was sure he couldn't have, but I thought if they knew he was about the College at half-past three, they might suspect him."

"I see," said Sir Richard approvingly.

"Partly that, sir—and——" She hesitated. "The shame of it."

"The shame of it?" queried Sir Richard.

"Yes, sir. You see, sir, I'd never—well, I'd never stayed out so late like in the Yellow Barn before."

The light broke on Sir Richard. He had forgotten these were children after all, he was dealing with. Parrott and this girl were only adolescents. It was all clearing itself very nicely.

"You see," she hurried on. "It was John's last night, and I mightn't see him for a long time. The Dean had sent him down, you know."

"Had he?" asked Sir Richard. This was new.

"Yes, sir. He sent for him at ten o'clock and told him he must not come back next term or ever again."

"Why?" asked Sir Richard.

"He'd failed his examinations, for one thing. And then he'd been climbing into College a lot after seeing me. And then I think I was partly to blame. That's why I—I mean that's why I stayed late in the Yellow Barn last night."

"Yes, yes. Very interesting," he said. "Well, thank you for your help. I will try to see that your young man gets into no trouble over all this, although telling lies to the police is a bad policy." He looked at her firmly. "By the way," he said, as he turned to go, "he sends you good wishes and asks you not to worry."

"Oh, thank you, sir," she said.

He got into the car and drove back to College slowly. "One minor thing," he said to himself. "I must get this sending down of Parrott altered if I can. It's essential he should stay up here long enough to get over his infatuation for this Gostlin girl: if he went down he would idealise her with his idealisation of the good parts of Cambridge. Eventually he might marry her, and that would be fatal. Damn it all!" he said as he swung the car into Fiddler and Queen's garage, "what can the Dean and Tutor be thinking of? We exist, this University exists, to educate the young men, make them take an interest in passing their examinations, make them not want to climb into College, make them less interested in shop-girls with nothing but a pair of legs and pretty face and fair hair and no conversation or brains. Damn it," he said again as he walked back to College, "I must have a word with the Dean—a very sharp word. This is all wrong."

As he went through the Porter's Lodge he stopped and spoke to Baynes, the Head Porter.

"Inquest is fixed for to-morrow, sir," he said. "Twelve o'clock. Police asked could you be there?"

"Right, I will, Baynes. Are the police still here?"

"Yes, sir, they are. The Chief Constable has just arrived, and is with the Inspector in Dr. Sanderson's room."

"Good," said Sir Richard. He looked at his watch. "Tell them I shall come and see them in half an hour, and meanwhile ask Mr. Parrott to come over to my rooms."

He climbed his staircase and entered his main room. It was five o'clock, and Kilmartin was drawing the curtains. "Some tea, Kilmartin. Tea for two."

"Very well, sir."

Sir Richard went to the telephone and dialled the Dean's number. He waited awhile. There was no reply. He put the telephone down.

"Isn't the Dean in to-day, Kilmartin?"

"No, sir. He slept in last night, but left early this morning, before I arrived."

"Ah, ha." It must have been the spiced beer, or perhaps his preoccupation with Parrott and the crime, but Sir Richard did not give that statement the attention it deserved. In any case, at that moment there was a knock at the door, and John Parrott came in.

"Good afternoon, sir," he said. "You sent for me?"

"I did," he replied. "Draw a chair up to the fire and have some tea."

"Thank you, sir."

"That will be all, Kilmartin," said Sir Richard. He poured out tea for the boy. "Sugar? Milk?" he queried. "Help yourself, and help yourself to some toast."

"Thank you," said the boy nervously.

Sir Richard looked at him quizzically and then said, "Did you think the band at the Yellow Barn good last night?"

Parrott spun round. His defences were down. "So you know, sir?"

"Yes, I know," said Sir Richard, pleased with himself. "But the police do not know yet. Why you bothered to stuff them and me up with such a nonsense story I do not know."

"I was afraid, sir," said the boy simply.

"Afraid?" asked Cherrington. "Afraid of telling the truth?"

"Yes, sir. It's this way." His words were coming quickly now that he hadn't to make his lies fit. "The Dean sent for me at ten o'clock and told me it was the end of my Cambridge career. I felt rather reckless at that, and took Miss Gostlin out to the Yellow Barn, where we had been often before together. We stayed late," he said simply. "We'd never stayed late before. They drove us back from the Yellow Barn, and we left her in the Milton Road just after three o'clock. The driver dropped me at the lights, and I climbed in. I went down St. John's Lane and over the Library—that's the easiest climb—and had to go through the Screens to get to my rooms. When I got there Gostlin was lying across the far end of the Screens. I bent down over him, but he was quite dead. I was horrified."

"I suppose it was then you lost your button—when you bent over him? You must have torn it loose as you came climbing in."

"That'll be it, sir," the boy said, relieved. "Yes, that'll be it. Then I went back to my room and tried to sleep, but I couldn't. I didn't sleep at all all night."

"I believe you," said Sir Richard. "But what I do not understand was why you didn't go straight to the Lodge and summon the police."

"Well, sir, I was frightened. I thought they might try to accuse me. I had two good reasons for disliking Gostlin."

"Yes?" said Sir Richard encouragingly.

"The first was his treatment of his daughter. He hated me and wouldn't let her go out with me. Secondly, he had been watching me climb into College, and had given the Dean an account of my movements which apparently clinched his decision to send me down."

"Two good reasons for hating Gostlin," agreed Sir Richard. "But come, boy, surely not two good reasons for murdering him."

"Well, sir, it seemed different somehow in the middle of the night."

"Tell me, Parrott," said Sir Richard kindly and shrewdly. "Wasn't one of your reasons that you didn't want to implicate the girl? It still will not look too well, you know, when it comes out: the girl is making merry with you in a roadhouse miles away while her father is being murdered."

"Yes, I think that must have influenced me a lot. I got panicky and came up to my room to think things out, and then nothing would induce me to go down again."

Sir Richard paused a moment. "I've been to see your girl," he said.

"You have?" said the boy. "How is she?"

"A bit frightened, and very worried. I gave her your message."

"Oh, thank you, sir."

Sir Richard took out his snuff-box and applied himself to the taking of snuff. He pecked at his nose with an elegant silk handkerchief.

"Listen, Parrott," he said. "I am not merely interested in your story in its relation to the murder of Sam Gostlin. I am interested in you as a member of this College, of which I am Vice-President. Will you tell me your whole story from beginning to end?"

"Why, yes, sir. If you can bear to hear it." He paused. "I've been through hell during the last year, sir. I suppose a stronger man might have taken it better than I did, but I'm not made that way. This is how it happened, sir. Do you know June Westmacott, the Tutor's niece?"

"I do indeed."

"Well, I was engaged to her for two months, and was very much in love with her. Then last May term she chucked me for that—for Dr. Fothergill."

"Ah, ha," said Sir Richard non-commitally. He remembered June Westmacott, who lived not far from the Farnabys in Berkshire. At one time there had been talk of an affair between her and Giles Farnaby, but that was before they went up to Cambridge. June was one of the few really lovely girls that graced Newnham and Girton at that time and had been much sought after, was at all the best parties and dances, and Sir Richard had heard through undergraduate gossip everyone's surprise when she got engaged to John Parrott. He looked at his nervous guest with renewed interest. So this was the young man concerned. Then he remembered how June had after a few months become engaged to Evan Fothergill.

"I remember," said Sir Richard. "That was a rotten break you had."

"I got over it," said Parrott. "I didn't think I would, but I did. Of course it ruined my work, and I failed my tripos examinations last June. During last summer vacation I really got over it and began to do some work again, and when I came back in October all seemed to be fine, except that whenever I saw June with Fothergill I nearly went sick inside and wanted to bang their rotten heads together."

He paused.

"Yes," said Sir Richard encouragingly.

"Then it was I met Diana Gostlin," said Parrot. "I know she is not my 'social grade', as the Tutor kept telling me. I know that her family have been gyps and porters at Fisher College for years, and that she's only an assistant in Fleury and Driberg's, the tobacconist's. But believe me, sir, she's a very remarkable type. She's straight and honest, and that's new to me among these women I meet in Cambridge," he said bitterly.

Sir Richard made no comment, but helped himself to more tea.

"You must believe me, sir," Parrott went on, "that I was sure Diana was the answer to all my troubles. Since I got to know her I had been working extremely hard." He paused. "Then the second blow came. My mother died. I'd always been devoted to her—hellishly devoted. She was let down by my father when I was a little boy. He went off with another woman, and my mother and I have always been together. She got pneumonia in January and died. That knocked me right back again: I couldn't work and I couldn't sleep. I think that if it hadn't been for Diana I'd never have made the grade the last few months. She's been wonderful, and I've seen a great deal of her. Once or twice I've been out with her too late and had to climb back into College. A fortnight ago the Dean himself caught me climbing into College and gated me for the rest of term. Well, that was impossible. I had to see Diana, and I still climbed in and out of College to see her."

"Wasn't that very, very rash?" said Sir Richard.

"I couldn't be without her," said the other simply. "The other night I was seen climbing in by her father, who most strongly disapproved of me seeing her. He thought it the old story of young undergrad flirts with shopgirl. Believe me, it's not, sir," he said earnestly. "I mean to marry Diana—I really do."

"I see," was all Sir Richard's comment.

"Leastways, I meant to," said the other. "But now I don't know where I am. The Tutor sent for me at tea-time yesterday and told me that I had failed my examinations this year again, and although he had put in a strong plea to the Dean, the Dean, when he sent for me at ten last night, told me not to come up again."

"You told him your story?" queried Cherrington.

"I did, but he said that a man should master his sexual passions and not let them interfere with his career."

Sir Richard took off his spectacles and dangled them on their black ribbon in front of him. He was thinking of the scene he had had with Landon before Hall.

"He said that?"

"He did, sir," said Parrott. "After that it didn't seem to matter what I did, so I climbed out of College and—well, you know the rest."

There was a pause of a moment. "You have been very rash and impetuous, my boy, haven't you?" said Sir Richard. "But you have had much to go through."

John Parrott hung his head. These were the first real words of sympathy he had had from the College in the last year. Roger Westmacott had repelled his confidences and the Dean had been scornful.

Sir Richard stood up with his back to the fireplace. He put on his pince-nez and stared down kindly at Parrott. "You will do two things for me, my boy," he said. "In the first place, you will go and tell the police everything you have told me, from beginning to end."

"Including about Diana, sir?"

"If you don't I shall."

"Very well, sir."

"And secondly, you will come and see me once a week next term, and tell me how everything is going."

"Next term, sir?" said Parrott. "But I've been sent down."

Sir Richard smiled at the boy. "I said next term. And now run along to Inspector Wyndham in Dr. Sanderson's rooms."

Sir Richard remained in thought for a few moments after Parrott had gone. "That's finished my first little bit of detection," he said to himself. "Now I must get down to my real job of running this College. Really the Dean and Tutor should have told me about the case of Parrott." He went into his study and began dialling at his telephone. The Tutor's secretary said Mr. Westmacott had gone to a University meeting. There was no answer from Dr. Landon's rooms. He dialled another number and heard the telephone ring in Dr. Landon's house on the Madingley Road. But there was no answer. It is a very funny thing, he thought to himself, but no one seems to have seen the Dean to-day. And he remembered the scene before dinner last night and the way Bill Landon had dramatically produced the revolver. A vague feeling of disaster began to come over him. "I expect he will be in Hall," he said, "and now I must go and make my confession to the police. How humiliating!"

CHAPTER FIVE

SIR RICHARD CONFESSES

COLONEL CUNNINGHAM HARDY and Detective-Inspector Wyndham were discussing the case in Dr. Sanderson's rooms on A Staircase.

Wyndham had given the Chief Constable a picture of exactly what he knew so far. First, the time of the crime. It seemed moderately clear that the murder had been committed at about 2.15. Secondly, the weapon. They had now had time to study the bullet which had been found lodged in the roof of the Screens. It was an unusual calibre—a ·38—and the Inspector thought it would not be so very difficult to trace the ownership of the weapon, if known and registered. Thirdly, he had explained their only clue so far: the button off Parrott's coat. He had told the Colonel of his interviews with Parrott and Diana Gostlin and how they gave a very different picture of old Gostlin and his opinion of their association than had Rodgers and several others with whom he had spoken in the afternoon.

"We're working on two lines now, sir," said the Inspector. "The first is tracking down Parrott's movements last night, since by his own avowal he climbed out of College at about half-past ten. We've got all we can on to checking that. They certainly did not stay long in the Cam Tea Shoppe, as they say. I've got Cobb on to checking the Milton Road end, and we may find the time the girl got home."

"Yes, yes. Routine stuff," said the Colonel. "Very necessary, I suppose, but immensely dull."

The Inspector looked surprised. "Very necessary, sir," he said firmly. "And the second line is the revolver. We're going through all the registers, and trying to trace any one in this College who had a revolver."

"What's your theory, then, Wyndham?" asked the Colonel.

"I'm sure Parrott is the man, sir," he said. "He had a double motive for the crime. He had been sent down, ruined by the Dean on evidence given by Gostlin. And then Gostlin wouldn't let him see his daughter."

"No, no," said the Colonel. "Rubbish. Absolutely rubbish. Don't believe a word of it. You give him two motives for murder. Well, the father didn't stop him seeing the girl. He used to see her, didn't he? What? Can't see, myself, that murdering the father helps you to see her any more? Doesn't make sense. Then you say he's been sent down. Well, how does murdering this porter help that? He's still sent down, isn't he? What?"

"I agree, sir; but don't you think that in the middle of the night he might have murdered in sudden vindictive passion?"

"Oh, no," said the other. "Very unlikely. Somewhere behind every murder must be somebody's obvious gain. Who stands to gain by this murder of Gostlin?"

"So far, I must admit nobody, sir."

"There you are," went on the other. "There you are. We'll peer into his life. I think you'll find he was blackmailing someone. Blackmailing one of the Fellows. That's most likely. Then he was murdered; cleverly, you know—these blokes are paid to be clever—so that the murder gave two impressions. First, that it was done by a wild undergraduate—that is our friend Parrott or Parratt, whatever his name is—and second, that it was done by an outsider who had no business to be here, but was recognised by Gostlin as he was leaving the College. Those are the two traps one is supposed to fall into by the clever man who planned the murder of Gostlin. You fell into the first."

"Yes, sir," said the other, taken aback by the cogency of the Colonel's argument.

"Yes," went on the Colonel. "I haven't paid much attention to my shooting to-day, I am afraid. Been thinking over this crime. And that's the answer. It's a carefully constructed crime made to appear like a sudden act. And my line is: find out about the Fellows. Well, you leave that to me. I'll get every little bit of scandal that's known about them until I find one for which murder was preferable to disclosure. There's a dear familiar of mine in this town—Lady Gough Clarke. Used to know her in India. Her husband was a finance wallah: used to travel a lot. Saw a lot of his wife in the hill stations, what! The old boy came back and was Bursar at Fisher College for many years. What old Joan Gough Clarke can't tell me about these Fellows will not be worth hearing."

It was at this juncture that John Parrott had knocked timorously at the door, and been bidden to enter. He told his story much as he had told it to Sir Richard. He was dismissed with a very severe caution from the Inspector about misleading the police, and packed off to repeat his fresh statement to Sergeant Mossop.

Inspector Wyndham was very shaken at the new aspect the case had taken.

"Well, I'm damned, sir," he said. "I thought the boy was lying, but not in the direction of destroying his own alibi."

"Bah," said the Colonel, blowing out his moustaches. "Knew he had nothing to do with it the moment I saw him. Weak and shilly-shallying type. The sooner you concentrate on the detailed movements of all the Fellows, the better for you."

"Yes, sir. I'm getting all their statements to-morrow morning. Fortunately, there are only eight of them." He consulted the list Sir Richard had prepared for him. "There's the President and Sir Richard Cherrington, the Vice-President. Then Dr. Landon, the Dean; Westmacott, the Tutor; Wedgwood, the Organist; and Traherne, who lectures in anthropology."

"H'm," interrupted the Colonel. "Must meet him. Wonder if he'd be interested in the things I brought back from the Nagas."

"Then there's Fothergill, a Mathematics Lecturer, and finally a Mr. Gough Clarke."

"Ah, yes," said the Colonel. "Quite so. Peter—that's their only surviving son. Other two killed in the last war. Probably Peter will be killed in the next. Bad business—very bad business. But Joan Gough Clarke's a very brave woman. Yes, a very brave woman."

The Inspector coughed. There seemed nothing to say.

"Now, this is the plan of campaign," went on the Colonel. "Don't stop your routine enquiries, but get all the Fellows interviewed. Preferably to-night. And I'll get going on their private scandals through Lady Gough Clarke." He rose. "I'll be off now. Keep me in touch."

The Colonel was barely out of the room when Sir Richard arrived.

"Excellent," said the Inspector. "I was going to ask you to come round. I want to get in detail the movements of all Fellows last night. Purely routine, of course."

"Quite, quite," said Sir Richard. "But first I have a confession to make."

"A confession, Sir Richard?" said the other, surprised.

"Yes. I'm afraid I have been guilty of misleading the police, in the person of yourself. You asked me this morning if I had seen the button and piece of cloth. I said no, but I had, and, what is more, I had recognised it as of the same cloth which Parrott was wearing last night. It was wrong of me to mislead you, but I apologise."

"Thank you, Sir Richard," said the other. "You will permit me to say that I thought you were lying. Why did you do so?"

"I thought I had seen it before, but when I later realised where, I could not see how such a thing could come to be there without implicating Parrott, which I deemed unlikely. I had a talk with Parrott, and this afternoon I thought of a way in which it could have got there. A stray remark of Parrott's sent me out to the Yellow Barn, and my odd hypothesis was confirmed. More evidence was, of course, necessary," he went on, warming to his theme as though he were lecturing, "and this was provided by Parrott's confession."

"You've been busy, Sir Richard."

"Yes, I have. The problem rather fascinates me. I hope you won't mind, but I'm going to probe about a little on my own."

"Sort of private detective, sir?"

"No, not really. I'm just going to test out any theories which I get or you tell me of. I fancy myself in the role of scientific tester of theories, but not as a detective."

"What about testing your own theory?"

"My theory? Why, I'd almost forgotten I had a theory."

"What did you call it?" the Inspector said. "A cover murder, wasn't it? Have you found what it was covering?"

Sir Richard smiled. "No, Inspector," he said. "I leave you and your police mechanism to find the other corpses."

"Does your theory take into account that this may be forward cover, if I may use that phrase?" asked the Inspector, warming to the theorising.

"Forward cover?" queried Sir Richard. "What do you mean?"

"Well, sir, it is just an idea. You say the murder was done to cover a crime already committed. May it not equally have been done to confuse us when we discover the real crime, perhaps to-night or in a few days? We shall then think they are connected, and yet the murder of Gostlin is merely a gigantic red herring drawn across to confuse us."

"It's an idea, certainly," agreed the Professor. "But I think you've been reading detective stories yourself."

"Well, sir, if you will pardon me saying so, it is just as likely as yours. You say look for more corpses. I say lock your doors at night, lest you become corpses."

"It's not only an idea," said Sir Richard. "It's a very alarming idea. What others have you got?"

"A monomaniac who murders for amusement."

"I must say I don't like your ideas to-night, Inspector. Let's proceed to my examination."

"Right, sir." The Inspector pulled a pad of paper towards him. "Tell me in your own words what you did last night."

"My doings were very simple and very unconfirmable," began the Professor. "I dined in Hall, and then went up to the Combination Room for some port. I left the room at about nine-thirty I should think."

"Who was in the room at the time?"

"Now, let me see. There was the President, Dr. Wedgwood, and Dr. Traherne. The Tutor didn't come up to wine, as he had to rush off somewhere, and the Dean departed after about ten minutes. Said he had various appointments. There were really just the four of us in the Combination Room."

The Inspector consulted his list. "Mr. Fothergill and Mr. Gough Clarke were not having dinner with you last night, then?"

"Mr. Fothergill was, but Mr. Gough Clarke was dining at home. Mr. Fothergill was taken ill in the middle of dinner and had to leave."

"Really?" The Inspector made a note. "Then after the Combination Room?" he asked.

"I went back to my rooms. Read and wrote. You know, usual sort of bachelor donnish evening. Can't confirm it, anyway, except that I was awake at about eleven. Professor Shacksfield—you know the Professor of Celtic Studies here. He rang me up. Wonderful man. Likes working and discussing things well into the night. 'Fraid I went to sleep soon after, and saw and heard nothing until Mrs. Kilmartin woke me up in great excitement this morning."

"Thank you, Sir Richard. I think I have most of that down." He paused, and handed Sir Richard the note Sergeant Mossop had given him that morning. "What do you make of that?"

"Goodness me!" said Sir Richard, fitting his spectacles more firmly on his nose. "What's this? 'Sir, The Dean has sacked him, and is reporting the matter to the Police to-morrow. Please to do what you can to-night. A. Kilmartin.' " He looked up, alarmed. "Why, it's from my gyp," he said. "Where was it found? and what does it mean?"

"It was found, Sir Richard," said the Inspector, "in the rooms of an undergraduate called Farnaby."

"My dear sir," the Professor interrupted. "Giles Farnaby is on the same staircase as myself."

"That's right, sir."

"Goodness me! but that's my nephew and my gyp. What explanation do they offer of this extraordinary state of affairs? I suppose it refers to Parrott?"

"That's what I thought, sir, but they both say No. They say that the Dean had sacked a Frederick Kilmartin, your gyp's nephew, for petty larceny from the Buttery here. Two silver candlesticks. The Dean also threatened to inform the police next day and have Kilmartin brought to justice. The elder Kilmartin wrote this note, he alleges, to ask Mr. Farnaby, who apparently knew the Dean well, to intercede on behalf of the younger Kilmartin."

"What an extraordinary state of affairs! I must say you have unearthed a lot of strange things in this College."

"I'm afraid we shall unearth a lot more, sir, as we go along."

"Dear me," said Sir Richard. "Dr. Quibell will not be pleased."

"I'm afraid not, sir."

"But tell me, Inspector Wyndham," went on Cherrington. "I am interested about this Kilmartin business. Did my nephew make this intercession, and was Fred Kilmartin pardoned?"

"Apparently not, sir. Mr. Farnaby says he came home at twelve o'clock, and the Dean's rooms were locked, his—er—oak—er—sported—is that the phrase?—and so Mr. Farnaby went to bed. I think, if you don't mind me saying so, he was rather drunk. He did not actually see the note until we showed it to him this morning."

"Really," said Sir Richard. "Very interesting, but it doesn't help us materially."

"We've been unable to confirm the story from Dr. Landon. We can't get hold of him."

Sir Richard stared hard at Wyndham. His premonition of disaster was returning. "You've tried several times to-day to get hold of him?"

"Why, yes," said the Inspector. "We've called at his rooms, but he is not there, and his wife says he has not been home all day."

Sir Richard got up. "Let's go round to his rooms at once," he said.

As they crossed the Court and went up the stairs, the little scene of last night began to re-enact itself before his eyes. Bill Landon must have been more distraught than he thought. After all, he did wave a revolver about. I suppose I was a fool to think he had snapped out of his mood so quickly. What if——? Sir Richard could hardly formulate the idea. What if he had had a nervous breakdown?

They climbed past Sir Richard's own rooms and knocked at the Dean's door. Footsteps were heard coming towards them, and Sir Richard's fears were for the moment allayed. "I must be overwrought myself," he thought. But his fears were back again when the door was opened by a rather shaken Kilmartin.

"Isn't the Dean in?" asked Cherrington.

"No, sir," said the gyp. "He hasn't been in all day. When I got here this morning he had dressed and gone out."

"He had dressed and left his rooms before you got here—let me see—soon after six this morning?" asked Sir Richard. "That's most peculiar."

Sir Richard picked up the telephone and dialled a number. "Hello. . . . Yes, hello? . . . Oh Anne, it is Dick Cherrington here. . . . I am speaking from your husband's rooms. I tried to get on to you about ten minutes ago, but couldn't. . . . He doesn't seem to have been here all day. . . . What? . . . Not at all? . . . Not all day? . . . The last you saw of him was when you delivered his spectacles just before ten o'clock? . . . I see. . . . No. No cause for alarm. . . . I'll let you know." He put down the receiver.

"What can have happened?" he said. "Mrs. Landon has not seen her husband since she left these rooms at just before ten last night. Parrott was interviewed by him at ten o'clock. But he does not seem to have been here at six when Kilmartin arrived."

"The odd thing, sir," said Kilmartin, "is that though the Dean went to bed, he apparently dressed again in the same clothes as yesterday, except that he didn't put on a clerical collar nor any boots or shoes."

"No boots or shoes?" asked Inspector Wyndham.

"That's right, sir," said Kilmartin. "I know exactly what pairs of footwear he had here yesterday, and they are all still here, including his dirty shoes of yesterday."

"Oh, my God!" said Sir Richard. The presentiment of evil he had had was more than justified. "Why didn't I do more than I did last night?" he said to himself. "I clearly under-estimated the extent to which Bill Landon was unbalanced." He put his hand over his eyes, for he had a sudden vision of Bill Landon, the balance of his mind toppling in the long watches of the cold March night, stumbling out in his stockinged feet, revolver in hand. Sam Gostlin had seen him and tried to stop him, and been shot where he stood across the steps of the Screens. The Dean had stumbled on, out through the river gate and shot himself or thrown himself into the Cam, round which had been centred the years of that life which now was crashing around him. Could this be the right explanation of last night's happenings?

Sir Richard walked quickly to the Dean's desk and pulled open the top drawer. He paused. For where last night there had been a revolver and a box of bullets, there was now an empty drawer. So his foreboding was justified, his guess correct.

He turned wearily to Inspector Wyndham.

"I am afraid this sordid mystery is over," he said. "Drag the river as soon as you can."

BOOK II

MURDER AT HIGH TABLE

CHAPTER SIX

THE UNPLEASANTNESS AT FARNABY GRANGE

GILES FARNABY got out of the train at Twyford Junction and looked about to see whether by any chance a car had been sent to meet him. There was nothing on the north approach of the station. He crossed over to the south side of the line, but there was no car from Farnaby Grange waiting for him there either. He had not expected one. It was Wednesday morning, and he counted himself rather lucky to have got away from Cambridge that day, especially after the discovery of that quite harmless note from Kilmartin to himself. John Parrott had not been allowed to go down to-day, as had almost all the other undergraduates: he was being detained apparently for "further questioning", whatever that might mean.

Giles looked at his watch: it was just twelve o'clock. He had caught the early train up from Cambridge that morning and gone straight from Liverpool Street to Paddington, and caught the first train down to Twyford. Somehow, after the murder at Fisher College he had no desire to linger in London.

There was nothing for it but to walk. His heavy luggage had gone off in his trunk. All he had was a small suit-case, which he left with the porter for collecting later. It was about three miles to Farnaby Grange. If he walked briskly—and it was a bright cold morning that invited sharp walking—he would get in just in time for lunch. He started walking.

The papers had got the story of the murder in their morning editions. Poor Dr. Quibell must be shuddering at the publicity Fisher College was being given. Fortunately they had not yet got hold of the extraordinary news of the Dean's disappearance. Somehow the story to the Press had been well arranged, and it suggested tactfully that someone had broken into Fisher College during the night, committed some major crime like burglary (only it did not specify the crime), and murdered the faithful porter as he tried to apprehend him. It was a fairly good line, and reflected little discredit on the College. It was all made to appear as though a faithful butler had been killed defending the silver in a large country house.

That was a good line for the moment, but he was sure it could not be held for long. In any case, as far as he knew no major crime had been committed in the College previous to the murder of Gostlin. Of course an examination might show invaluable College deeds or records missing, or even some of their silver, or the First Folio Shakespeares. Perhaps the much-treasured fragment of the *Anglo-Saxon Chronicle*, or the manuscript of the *De Excidio* had been stolen. But were these things, if they had happened, for which the criminal would commit murder? Perhaps in a panic he may have done so. He may only have wanted to frighten Gostlin off, and pulled the trigger in his excitement. It was, he supposed, just possible.

Giles was sure that somehow the extraordinary disappearance of the Dean had something to do with it. He had learnt from Kilmartin last night that the Dean had apparently disappeared before six o'clock on the Tuesday morning, and according to Kilmartin had gone without his clerical collar and in his stockinged feet. It was very strange. Perhaps his uncle's explanation was the right one. Giles had called on Sir Richard on Tuesday night and heard from him his theory. Apparently the Dean was on the verge of a nervous breakdown, and had practically threatened to commit suicide when Sir Richard had seen him on Monday night, just before Hall. He had all sorts of troubles, including complicated domestic ones, Sir Richard had hinted darkly. There was no doubt in Sir Richard's mind that Dr. Landon had, in the middle of the night, taken leave of his senses and tottered out of his rooms half dressed and brandishing the revolver which he—surprisingly—kept in his desk. He had then met Gostlin, who, not unnaturally astonished at this strange sight, had tried to remonstrate with the Dean, and been shot for his pains. The Dean had then, according to Sir Richard, swept out of the College in a frenzy, and either thrown himself into the Cam, or shot himself on its banks and toppled in. The police were apparently so impressed by this theory that they were dragging the Cam at first light this morning. "Perhaps even now," thought Giles, as he walked along, "even now poor Bill Landon's body is being lifted out of the cold, weedy depths of the Cam."

"Well," he thought to himself, "it's a good theory, and it explains everything to the satisfaction of everyone, but I do not believe it. No, it just doesn't seem to me right. I knew the Dean quite well. I don't suppose I knew any of his inner life: naturally he wouldn't have told me all his personal and private troubles. He certainly is more likely to have told Sir Richard all this, and therefore I suppose Sir Richard is a better judge of his state of mind. But my opinion, for what it's worth, is that Dean Landon would never commit suicide. Yes, he may have suggested it as an academic possibility, but no more."

Farnaby had come to where the road bifurcated. The main road went on, while a minor road led off to the right down to Whistley Bridge and Farnaby Grange. In the angle between the two roads was a small country inn—the Cow and Snuffers. It was a favourite haunt of Giles', and he liked the old innkeeper, Thomas Eames, very well. Farnaby

Grange was now less than a mile away, and as it was still only half-past twelve, Giles went in for a drink.

There was no one in the little bar when he entered. A fire was burning brightly in the grate. The strong smell of good beer and the cheeriness of the room took his mind off Fisher College. But he was not to be left in peace for long.

A tall, bald-headed man with a large, sandy moustache came up some steps behind the bar, closed down the trap over the steps, and turned round. It was Eames, the landlord.

"Why, Mr. Giles," he said. "Good morning to you." He wiped his fingers carefully on his leather apron, and they shook hands.

"Morning, Eames," said Giles. "How's trade?"

"Not so bad, sir, not so bad. What'll you have?"

"Pint of bitter, Eames," said Giles, "and I hope it's in the best condition."

"That it is," said Eames, taking down a tankard from the shelf and wiping it carefully. "It certainly is a nice drop of beer. Your father he looked in last night on the way from the train and says it was very good."

"Did he now?" said Giles. "Now you'll have a drop with me, I hope."

"Thank you, sir; thank you, sir. I don't mind if I do."

Another pint was drawn, and they lifted up their tankards.

"Here's health," said Giles.

"Good luck to you, Mr. Farnaby," said the other. He paused, "Just bin reading the papers, I have," he said.

"Ah," thought Giles. "Here goes. Everyone I meet for the next few days will want to discuss the Fisher College murder with me. What an appalling thought! Anyhow, Sir Richard will be whisking me away to France in a week's time, and there we shall presumably have some peace."

"Yes. Very curious business indeed," went on Eames—"from all I can make out. They don't tell one much in the papers, they don't; but perhaps there isn't much more to tell?" He looked at Giles hopefully.

"I'm afraid I don't know any more than is in the papers," he said firmly.

"We thought this morning perhaps you did," continued old Eames. "Old Bond he was down here for a drink last night, and he said as how you was expected home yesterday, but then unexpectedly delayed, and when I read the paper this morning I thought as how you'd been delayed because you'd witnessed something."

"No, no. Nothing like that, Eames," said Giles. "We were all delayed a day while the police were making their enquiries."

"Quite so, sir," went on Eames. "Well, sir, the whole thing is quite plain to me. I don't attach any importance to the account in the paper. It's a poor theory. To my mind it was suicide."

"Suicide?" asked Giles. "But there was no weapon found near the body."

"Ah, now, wasn't there?" said Eames wisely. "Now, that's very interesting. Very interesting indeed. It didn't give that information in the paper. No, it made no mention of that."

Giles could have kicked himself. "I am gossiping about this lousy business," he thought. "I must finish my beer and go home. But there again everyone will want to know all I know and what my theory is and so forth. I'm sick of the whole thing already." He put down his empty tankard.

"Mind you," went on Eames, unperturbed, "the revolver might have been removed subsequently. I mean the owner of the revolver might have found it near the body and decided he did not wish to be involved in the affair."

"That's possible, Eames," said Giles. "Well, I must be off now, or I shall be late for my lunch. We must discuss the case again. Cheerio."

He began to walk quickly along the road that led down to the river and across Whistley Bridge and up to the Grange. "Must we hell!" he sighed. "I suppose we must—discuss the thing again and again until every little scandal, every little doing is thoroughly exposed to the public eye. Well, I've nothing to worry about. The hell I have! The note from Kilmartin is certainly peculiar at first sight, but it has an easy explanation. Then, of course, they will ask why I didn't do anything about it. Yes, that isn't too good. I was too drunk to do anything about it. In any case, the Dean's oak was sported when I came up at midnight," he said to himself. Then he stopped in his tracks. He began to remember waking up in the middle of the night, finding himself fully clad and tottering out to the landing with his shoes. He could have sworn the Dean's oak was open then. Had the Dean some mysterious visitor at midnight, or had he himself crept away by then, on this mysterious mission from which he had not returned? "Oh, hell!" said Giles. "What the hell! It's nothing to do with me."

He opened the front door and walked into his home. Bond, the family butler-cum-valet, was in the hall.

"Good morning, sir," he said. "We didn't know when to expect you."

"Hello, Bond," said the other. "Well, I didn't expect to get away this morning myself. Mother in?"

"Yes, sir; Mrs. Farnaby is in the drawing-room." Bond hesitated. "There's company for lunch, sir."

"Oh, bother!" said Giles. "Who?"

"Mrs. Westmacott, sir, and Miss Westmacott. They arrived a few minutes ago, and are with your mother in the drawing-room."

Giles made a face. "Well, I suppose I'd better join them."

"A moment, sir," said Bond. "Could I have your keys, if you please?"

"My keys?" asked Giles. "I've lost them. I lost them in the changing rooms of the University Squash Courts about ten days ago. Why? What do you want them for?"

"Unpacking, sir. Your trunk."

"It's arrived? That's very quick."

"Yes, it came this morning, sir. I thought it was locked, sir, and haven't started unpacking."

"There's no hurry, anyhow," said Giles, and went into the drawing-room.

His mother was pouring out sherry for June Westmacott and her mother. She turned as he came in.

"Giles, dear, how very nice!" she said.

He kissed her. "Mother dear; well, here I am," he said. He turned to the others. "'Morning, Mrs. Westmacott. 'Morning, June."

"You all right?" asked his mother. "I mean the papers?"

"Yes, of course I'm all right. So's Uncle Richard. He's coming down here in about a week, and then taking me off to Brittany for about ten days' motoring."

"How lovely!" said his mother. "You know," she went on, addressing Mrs. Westmacott, "Richard is still at heart an undergraduate or a young don. He's never grown up, really, and that's why he's never taken over the mature responsibilities of wife and children. Mind you, he's not young in years. He's my eldest brother, and must be nearly sixty now: and he looks old and distinguished with his steel-grey hair, his spectacles and his black ribbon, and his silver snuff-box. These are just the properties he uses to disguise himself as an old man. He's still the young, enquiring mind of the late twenties—running off half across Europe to see a pot someone has found or to photograph a rock-painting that has just been discovered. I'm sure that he is at the moment nosing about this murder in Fisher College, infuriating the police, but enjoying himself immensely, and unearthing some curious little fact that they will have missed."

Giles had poured himself out some sherry, and was standing in the window talking to June. They were looking out over the flooded water meadows that stretched down to the river.

"Haven't seen much of you last term, June," he said. "But then we do see rather more of each other in vacations, don't we?" There had been, indeed, a time when they had seen a great deal of each other in vacations. That was immediately before they had gone up to Cambridge, she to Newnham and he to Fisher College. Mrs. Westmacott, with an eye on the Farnaby wealth, had encouraged this promising attachment, but it seemed to have faded away once they had got to Cambridge: June had passed into a very different set from Giles. Yet Mrs. Westmacott still hoped.

"Yes," answered June, rather listlessly.

"You don't sound very cheerful," said Giles.

"I'm not very cheerful," said June, rounding on him. "I've just been chucked."

"What did you say?" asked Giles. "I mean, I didn't quite catch what you said."

"Yes, you did," she said firmly. "I've been chucked. Mind, I've been expecting it for a while. Evan's been swept away by that Landon woman. I've seen it happening."

"Evan Fothergill and the Dean's wife?" queried Giles. "But that's impossible."

"Far from impossible," said the other curtly. "If you had kept your eyes open, you'd have seen it all happening."

"I'm astonished."

"I'm infuriated," went on June. "Evan Fothergill's a rotten type. He's a Welshman, of course. Passionate, emotional, headstrong, inconstant. Bah! No use for them."

"Oh, I don't know," said Giles. "When did this happen?"

"This morning."

"This morning?"

"Yes; had a long letter from him this morning breaking off the engagement. Sentimental rubbish. Probably written when he was drunk, the tyke!" She stubbed out a cigarette end. "Didn't have the courage to face me and tell me."

Giles felt a momentary sympathy with Evan Fothergill, but all he said was, "Your mother know?"

"No; haven't told her yet."

"Ah, yes," said Giles. That would at least make the lunch-party easier. "Have a glass of sherry. Bond seems rather a long time in announcing lunch."

It was at that moment the drawing-room door opened and Bond came in. Mrs. Farnaby noticed him first. He was ashen-white, and his hand was shaking.

"What's the matter, Bond?" asked Mrs. Farnaby. "Are you ill?"

"No, ma'am"—the words seemed to come to him with great difficulty—"No, ma'am. It's nothing. It's——" He hesitated. "There's a gentleman to see Mr. Giles, please. Could he come now?"

"Why, certainly," said Giles, and he hurried out of the room into the hall. He closed the door of the drawing-room and took hold of Bond firmly by the arm. "Now, what is the matter, Bond?" he said kindly. "You look as if you'd seen a ghost."

"It's your trunk, sir," said Bond.

"My trunk, Bond? What the hell do you mean?"

"Sir, there's a man in it." He hesitated. "A dead man."

"A dead man!" exclaimed Giles, frozen for a moment into immobility. Then he ran through the hall, raced up the stairs, and threw open the door of his bedroom. The trunk was open in the middle of the room, and a few of the clothes that had been on top were thrown about. As he looked into the trunk, Giles reeled slightly and held on to a chair to support himself. For crouched in the trunk was the dead body of the Dean of Fisher College. He was fully dressed, but he had on no clerical collar, and there were no shoes or slippers on his stockinged feet.

CHAPTER SEVEN

INSPECTOR WYNDHAM LOOKS FOR A PATTERN

IT WAS ten o'clock on Wednesday evening when Detective-Inspector Wyndham came out from the Castle Hotel, where he had just finished an excellent steak and chips and two pints of beer, fixed the lamp on his bicycle, and rode home along the darkness of the Hills Road to his little flat in Queen Edith's Way. Wyndham was a bachelor, and was very proud of his small flat, although he frequently saw little of it for days on end. He made his own breakfast, and always had lunch in the town: often enough it was just a snack of sandwiches and beer in the Wine Bar behind the police station where busy students, research workers and professors from the Laboratories nearby were to be found in plenty hurriedly snatching some lunch. At night he sometimes came home and made himself some supper, at other times he had a light meal in town, and once or twice a week he did himself proud with a good steak or mixed grill in the Castle. A woman came in twice a week to clean out his flat and fix his washing. It was an arrangement that suited Wyndham very well. It was cheap, and he spent his spare money on gramophone records, for he was inordinately fond of good music.

He had done hardly more than sleep in his flat for a few hours since he was summoned away at 6.15 on the Tuesday morning. He had had two hectic days, and to-day had been the worst. He had spent the morning taking detailed statements from all the Fellows—Dr. Wedgwood and Mr. Westmacott, and Dr. Traherne and Dr. Fothergill and Mr. Gough Clarke. They had all insisted on giving him a great deal of irrelevant information, and the interviews had been long and tiring. He still had the President to do, and that he had fixed for twelve o'clock to-morrow. The sum total of these interviews had told him very little indeed, and he was disappointed.

The dragging of the river had gone on since dawn, and had been rewarded after about three-quarters of an hour with the discovery of the revolver underneath the bridge. Sir Richard Cherrington had identified the revolver as the one which he saw in the Dean's desk, and it certainly tallied with the bullet found embedded in the Screens, and with the revolver held by the Dean according to the Cambridge police registers.

It seemed that the case was at an end: two shots had been fired from the revolver, and it seemed only a question of time before the Dean's body was found and the whole matter resolved. He had let all the undergraduates go down with the exception of John Parrott, whom he felt justified in keeping another day. The inquest was held at twelve o'clock, and passed off excellently: the jury, after very clear direction, brought in a verdict of "Wilful murder by some person or persons unknown". The Inspector was preparing to go out to lunch at about one-thirty when the bombshell burst. The telephone rang, and he had heard the astonishing news from Farnaby Grange.

As a result, he had had no lunch, but had motored furiously down to Twyford, followed by Sir Richard, who brought down Mrs. Landon in his car. Then, after fixing arrangements with the Berkshire police, he had driven back to Cambridge, had a long and rather unsatisfactory interview with Mrs. Landon, who failed to come up to his expectations of the grief-stricken widow, and then an evening of conferences with the Chief Constable, the doctors, the firearms man, and with Sir Richard and Sergeant Mossop.

He was so tired and fussed that by half-past eight he announced he could do no more work that night, went out to the Castle and then home. But, once home, his mind began to revive. He was away from his files and reports and papers. He turned on the electric fire in the flat, drew up a chair, lit a cigarette and began to think over the affairs of the last two days. Could any pattern of sense be got out of them, and out of the slight pieces of information he had already gleaned? He took a pad of paper off his writing-table and began to set down his thoughts in an orderly manner.

First there was the manner of death. He wrote at the head of his paper: "1. The weapon". The firearms man had examined the bullet found in Dr. Landon's body, that found in the Screens, and the revolver dredged up from the Cam. He was of the opinion that the two shots had been fired from the same revolver, although he could not say which was fired first. In any case, a very detailed microscopic examination of the revolver was now taking place. It seemed a most reasonable belief at the moment that Dean Landon and the porter Gostlin had been shot by the same revolver, which had subsequently been dropped in the Cam. If that was so, it was reasonable to argue that the revolver had on both occasions been fired by the same hand.

He drew a line across his paper and wrote: "2. Time of murders." It seemed fair to infer that the murder of Sam Gostlin took place about 2.15. Now, did the murder of the Dean occur before or after? If Sir Richard's oft-repeated theory was true—namely, that Gostlin was murdered because the murderer didn't want himself recognised as he came away from murdering Landon; and it seemed a most likely theory —then Landon would have to have been murdered at some time before

2.15 and after 11.30, when Dr. Wedgwood, the last man to see him alive, had left his rooms.

The trunk had apparently been packed about 7. It was then put out on the landing by Farnaby and Kilmartin, and apparently left there until 7 or so in the morning, when it was collected by porters, put on the railway lorry, and sent off from the College. It was not locked, but there could be no reasonable doubt that the murdered body of the Dean had been put into the trunk before the latter left the landing of G Staircase. Indeed, the pile of Giles Farnaby's clothes and books thrust in the cupboard of the Dean's bedroom, which had been taken out of the trunk to make room for the body, surely proved this. The doctors could not fix the time of death at such a long interval, but they were sure that Landon must have been put in the trunk before rigor mortis set in.

Anybody who was going to try the risky business of sticking a man's body into a trunk would surely wait until the middle of the night. The only occupants of the staircase top landing were the Dean and Giles Farnaby. Farnaby had tottered drunk to his bed soon after midnight. It really would be quite simple to do what you liked on the top landing at, say, one to half-past one. "And remember, too," Wyndham argued, "that our murderer is a ruthless, determined man who would have shot anyone catching him at his primary crime, as he shot poor Gostlin later."

Wyndham lit another cigarette and said to himself, "Well, now, where have we got to in this exhaustive analysis? The murders were done by a ruthless, determined man at about one o'clock to two-fifteen. That's not really far." He drew another line and wrote down his third heading: "3. The evidence of the trunk".

Then he stopped. What was the evidence of the trunk? Did its use imply that the murderer knew it was going to be there and going to be unlocked? Whom did that involve? Farnaby? Kilmartin? Perhaps Parrott, and Sir Richard, who called on Farnaby while he was putting out his trunk. Then Kilmartin might have mentioned it to the porters when he asked them to carry it away, and possibly young Fred Kilmartin knew. Ah, but there was the rub. Kilmartin had asked for the trunk to be taken down at once—that is to say, as soon after seven o'clock as possible. The porters had forgotten to do this. So if the murder was planned, it cannot have been planned with the trunk as an integral part. Perhaps the murderer saw the trunk and used it to give him time to put as much distance as possible between Fisher College and himself. So he evidence of the trunk was not helpful if the murder was planned, and there he came to the snag. Was it planned?

He drew another line and wrote: "4. The evidence of the Dean's oak". It amused him to give headings to his musings. If Farnaby's evidence was to be trusted—and it must be remembered he was drunk—the Dean's oak was sported when he came up at midnight—that was apparently why he had not gone and discussed the case of the younger Kilmartin with him—but open, he thought, when he put out his shoes at any time in the night. It was certainly shut when Kilmartin senior came to call the Dean the next morning and found him not there.

All this argued only one thing. The man who did the murder had a key to the Dean's room. Now, ordinarily, Baynes, the Head Porter, had told him, the only other key of a Fellow's set would be on the gyp's staircase key-ring, and this was kept in the Porter's Lodge when not in the possession of the gyp. This meant that Kilmartin and Mrs. Kilmartin had access to the keys anyway, and it did not seem too secure an arrangement, for if they said they had left their own keys behind, any other person on the staircase could borrow the staircase set of keys, and so have temporary possession of the Dean's key. Then again, when the Dean was at home his wife would have access to his key. Here was a line to pursue. Had the Dean lost his keys recently and found them again after a few days? Why not get all the duplicate key-makers in Cambridge circularised or visited?

There was no doubt, then, that the murder was planned, and that the murderer had a key to the Dean's room and also a key to the College gates. "I wonder how easy it is to get hold of a Fellow's Pass key," thought Wyndham. "That, too, must be checked up. Surely the timing of the murder also is evidence of plan. It was carefully timed for the last night of term so that as many undergraduates as possible would have dispersed before a proper examination had taken place. It was only the necessity of having to shoot Gostlin perhaps that ruined that part of his plan. On the other hand, Gostlin's murder and the placing of Parrott's button there may only be a tremendous red herring to confuse us and make us draw the conclusion that it was someone from outside trying to get away without being recognised."

Wyndham got up and busied himself making some black coffee. He was finding this self-analysis of the murders very helpful. "Now," he mused, "we can't go any farther on these lines. We must now consider the suspects." He made a list of them.

1. John Parrott.
2. Giles Farnaby.
3. Either of the Kilmartins.
4. Dr. Quibell.
5. Sir Richard Cherrington.
6. Westmacott or Wedgwood or Traherne.
7. Rodgers, the porter.
8. Mrs. Landon, the Dean's wife.
9. Dr. Fothergill.
10. Any of the undergraduates other than the two already mentioned.
11. Mr. X from outside.

"Damn it all," he said to himself, as he contemplated the list, "I must be working on the wrong lines if a list of this length is possible at this stage of the case. Yet it will be helpful if I can rule out some of them.

"First, John Parrott. I have always suspected him of being mixed up somehow in the case. He seems to touch it everywhere: the Dean, Gostlin, and the button. Let's suppose the boy was desperate: his career depends on staying up, and his emotional life depends on this girl, or so he thinks. He goes to the Dean at ten o'clock and finds there is no reprieve for him. He therefore comes back late at night. Wait a minute. Wait a minute. I am a muggins," thought Wyndham. "Of course, when you look at it, the evidence of the Dean's oak means absolutely nothing at all. A man like Parrott could have climbed in through the Dean's window (check to-morrow if that is possible), shot the Dean, let himself out, closing the door behind him, shot Gostlin, thrown the revolver into the river and gone to his bed. After all," he thought, "we are only going on Willerby's evidence for the time of the murder. It could all have happened as Parrott climbed in (and we know he did climb in somewhere) at 3.30. All we shall have to prove is that Parrott knew the Dean had a gun, but we have to prove that guilty knowledge in any suspect. What's in favour of this thesis? Why, the button, of course. What's against? The way Parrott tried to fake his times of entry? But was that double bluff? No, it was just silly, and anyway he freely told people that he had been sent down. Anyway, I can't remove him from the list of suspects.

"Next Farnaby. There's no real case against him, because as far as we know there is no motive. But he had the opportunity—in fact, no one better—and, as a frequent visitor of the Dean's, he might know he had a gun. Then it was his trunk, wasn't it?" He paused. "H'm. It would take a very hard man to send a corpse to his own home in his own trunk; and yet what better way of throwing off suspicion? But then it was he who asked for the trunk to be sent down to the Porter's Lodge that evening. On the other hand, we have only Farnaby's evidence for the opening and shutting of the Dean's oak. What if it was always open? Then he had no problem of getting in. We only have his evidence that he himself was very drunk that night. Still, without an adequate motive, and a motive that would make a man murder, I am afraid we must delete him from our list of suspects.

"Next the Kilmartins. The younger Kilmartin, Fred by name, says he went to see the Dean at a quarter past ten and saw Parrott coming down the stairs as he arrived. That is confirmed by Parrott. He next says he told the bad news that the Dean was sacking him to his uncle, and then went straight home. He's got a motive, I suppose, and yet, like Parrott, he keeps telling people of his motive. The elder Kilmartin had less of a motive, but he had the opportunity, if our timings are right. He says that after talking to his nephew he wrote the note to Farnaby, and then went home. His wife confirms that this was so and that they were both in bed by half-past eleven. Looks as if I shall have to strike out the Kilmartins.

"H'm," he thought, looking at his list. "Not so bad. Only Parrott has survived so far." He took some more black coffee and lit another cigarette. "Dr. Quibell, now. Well, I must leave him until I see him to-morrow, but with him it would be the same case as Sir Richard. Sir Richard could have murdered both these men. He himself admits that he knew the Dean had a revolver. He's an old bachelor. Say he planned it all as a tremendous jest with the police. Perhaps that's why he is fussing around and enjoying himself so much. Now, that is an idea. He selects a man whom nobody likes: the Dean fills that bill very well, as far as I can make out. Good! He arranges to kill him in circumstances which point to anyone (look at my list of suspects). Then he adds two master touches: the murder of the porter, and the placing of the button from Parrott's jacket near the porter's corpse. It draws attention to Parrott; and he then goes to considerable pains to prove Parrott's alibi. Now, how did he know Parrott was at the Yellow Barn? Suppose he found an undergraduate with a cast-iron alibi and then put the button there. H'm. Not so good. How did he get the button? No, it's not so easy when you work it out in detail, but Sir Richard must definitely be kept on our lists. He has a passionate interest in crime: his bookshelves are full of detective stories and the Famous Trials Series and books on criminology and forensic medicine. I wonder if in the end it is a try-out at a perfect murder? Or is it possible that Sir Richard or Dr. Quibell are dying of cancers and this getting rid of a much-disliked Dean is their one good act before they die? Who knows? Stranger things have happened.

"Come, come, Wyndham," he said to himself. "You've been reading too many detective stories yourself. Nevertheless," he said, "I shall leave Sir Richard on and put Dr. Quibell on to-morrow unless he provides me with a very strong alibi. The trouble about all these dons living in college is that they have no alibis, and cannot reasonably be expected to have alibis. That goes for Dr. Quibell, Sir Richard, Westmacott and Fothergill. They all say they were in their beds before midnight and did not come out of their rooms again until the news of the murder reached them next morning. Of course, they can't prove this; but, then, I can't disprove it, or reasonably suspect it to be untrue.

"What about the two dons—Wedgwood and Traherne—who lived out of College? What of their alibis? Both alleged they got home before midnight. Traherne said he had worked in his rooms after Hall, finishing off a review of Landon's recent book. Then about half-past ten, or just after, he had gone across to see Landon and read out bits of the review to him. That had started a furious argument, and about eleven o'clock Traherne had stamped out of the Dean's room and cycled home." Inspector Wyndham looked through the notebook he had brought home with him. "Traherne's wife corroborated the fact that he had got home about twenty-past eleven. They lived on the Hills Road, and Traherne could just have cycled it in the time. But, wait a minute": Wyndham looked at his notes again. "Traherne said his wife went to bed soon after he got home, but that he stayed downstairs in his study until two o'clock. It was just possible he could have cycled back to College, let himself in the back way, committed the murders, and cycled back again. We have only his word for it that he went to bed at two o'clock.

"Then Dr. Wedgwood. He lived in Grange Road, very close to the College—indeed, not more than a five-minutes' walk. He was apparently the last person to see the Dean alive. He had gone to his rooms after Hall and been working there until about eleven o'clock. As he crossed the Court he saw the Dean's lights, and had gone up to have a word with him. He gave him the service list for next term, and immediately they had started a dispute about the position of music in the College services. Like Traherne's dispute, this seems to have been a violent one, and Robin Wedgwood was apparently extremely cross when he left the Dean's rooms. He could not swear when he left them, but it was about half-past eleven, he thought. He walked across the Backs to his house, and let himself in with his own key and went to bed. His wife was already asleep. There really was no alibi here again. Wedgwood could have murdered the Dean at 11.30, popped him in the trunk, and walked home. Then he comes back at two o'clock, knowing a porter will be on his rounds then, and murders Gostlin so that suspicion shall fall on someone from outside, and also someone who was not known to leave the Dean's room at 11.30. I wonder," thought Wyndham, "did Wedgwood take any steps to be seen by anyone as he went away at 11.30? That will be interesting to find out. What if Wedgwood murdered the Dean in a great fit of passion and thought out the ingenious business of a second murder as a perfect alibi. It is just possible.

"The whole thing boils down to the plain fact that none of the dons have alibis, whether they live in College or not. That gives me six straightforward suspects. This man Gough Clarke I know nothing about as yet." Wyndham looked despairingly at his notes. "An awful lot of people seem to have called on the Dean the night before he was murdered. Let's see if we can get the whole sequence of things straight." He wrote in his notebook:

9.45. Mrs. Landon calls with the Dean's long sighted spectacles.
10.00. The Dean interviews John Parrott and tells him he will not be allowed to come up next term.
10.15. The Dean interviews Fred Kilmartin and refuses to reconsider his decision about the College thefts, and informs Kilmartin he will get in touch with the police in the morning.
10.30. Dr. Traherne brings round his review to Dr. Landon, and they have a furious dispute about it.

11.00. Wedgwood calls in on his way home with the Chapel service lists for next term and they have a furious dispute.

"Wedgwood leaves at about 11.30, either leaving the Dean dead, or, as is really most likely, some fresh visitor arrived later in the night and left about two o'clock. Farnaby's evidence, if it is to be believed, would suggest a fresh visitor in the middle of the night."

Wyndham sighed. It really was very difficult. Not only all the dons, but all the undergraduates, had perfect alibis and had opportunity to commit the murders. So did Rodgers, the under-porter. But for what reason? Means and opportunity seemed to lead nowhere in this case. He must concentrate, then, on motive. That's why he determined to concentrate on Fothergill. Here was a strong, real understandable motive. The Chief Constable had been true to his promise, and had spent the morning golfing with Lady Gough Clarke. As they went round the St. Ives golf course—they had chosen that for privacy, and had dispensed with caddies, for, after all, their main concern was scandal, not golf, Colonel Cunningham Hardy had heard the inside scandal of the Fisher College high table. Most of it was the scandal of any small community—likes and dislikes, disputes and intrigues. But nothing touched the murder standard until Lady Gough Clarke came, in her exhaustive way, to Evan Fothergill and Mrs. Landon.

"Ah, ha," the Colonel had cried out when he heard of the growing attachment of these two as noted by Lady Gough Clarke, who lived next door to the Landons. "This is more like it, what? Reminds one of the jolly old Hill Station in India again. What? Bad business. Bad business. Go on. Go on, my dear; tell me more."

There really wasn't very much more to tell, except that it appeared the attachment was a very serious one.

"Serious enough for murder?" the old Colonel had queried sharply.

"Och, tut, tut, tut," exclaimed Lady Gough Clarke, striking the ground with her club. "The very idea," and she did not explain whether it was a likely or an unlikely idea.

The gist of this conversation had been retailed to Inspector Wyndham by the Chief Constable. It did, after all, provide some kind of tangible motive. He could not see Mrs. Landon engaged in the difficult task of putting her dead husband in the trunk, and in any case, according to her, she had been in all night since she returned from College about eleven o'clock. Fothergill's evidence was far less satisfactory, or so the Inspector thought. He deposed to having left Hall not feeling very well, and then gone to his rooms, where he had stayed until he went to bed about eleven o'clock. "I must have another talk with that young man," thought the Inspector; "his behaviour is a little odd, and he certainly seemed to be concealing something."

He stubbed out a cigarette and looked through his notes. "Now, who have we got left in our list of real suspects? Just four: Parrott and Sir Richard and Fothergill and Mr. X from outside."

He got up. "To hell with this case; it's too complicated. I think the trouble is I'm trying to solve it before we have all the information that is really available. We must get more evidence. Anyway, there's lots to do to-morrow." He made a final note.

(1) Interview Dr. Quibell.
(2) Question Fothergill again.
(3) Test the alibis of Traherne and Wedgwood.
(4) See if it is possible or easy to climb into the Dean's room.
(5) Get someone to go round the Cambridge locksmiths and check up on the whole problem of keys.

"Yes, that is quite a lot to go on with. I'll deal with them in the morning." He bundled his notes into a file. "Now for some music, and to hell with the other occupants of these flats."

It would have surprised Sir Richard, and certainly Dr. Wedgwood and Colonel Cunningham Hardy, if they could have seen the Inspector's collection of gramophone records. He had the keenest appreciation of music, and was passionately fond of the early classics up to and including Bach, who was his great favourite. Like so many of his twentieth-century contemporaries, he had passed from a delight in the primitive rhythms of hot jazz and swing, direct to the cultivated contrapuntal delights of the early polyphonists. He dismissed very unfairly everyone after Bach as noisy or saccharine, and only thought well of Mendelssohn because he had rediscovered Bach.

To-night he put on some Pachelbel, then a Chaconne of Buxtehude's, and lastly Scarlatti's "Cat's Fugue". But he was not swept away, as he expected to be: his mind was stuck on the two men, Dean and Porter, who had been violently done to death so recently. That was why he liked the early German composers and clung to the fugue as the perfection of artistic expression—all the music had a pattern, a perfect pattern. "That is what is the matter with the Fisher College murders. No pattern. Someone appears out of the blue—perhaps through the window of the Dean's room, perhaps stealthily unlocking the oak, perhaps boldly knocking at the door and being readily admitted—commits the murder, creeps away, kills a man who has seen him creeping away, and then vanishes.

"It's just as though I have the central phrase of a fugal subject," he thought to himself—it was late at night and he was tired—"the opening phrase escapes me, and I don't know how it finishes. If I get the opening phrase and add it to the middle one, perhaps I can find the end. The trouble is, the beginning is so shadowy: I don't even know whether it starts quietly with the window-curtains parting and someone coming in through the window, having climbed up from outside; or stealthily, as they fit the key they have stolen or copied into the Dean's lock; or with a flourish, as they boldly knock on the Dean's door.

"Ah," he said, "that's another thing that is missing. Of course. There should be two short, sharp notes in the middle phrase—the shots. How is it no one heard the shots? I suppose at two o'clock in the morning anyone who did would have mistaken them for a car backfiring. After all, one doesn't normally expect to hear revolver shots in a respectable College in the middle of the night. Or perhaps a silencer was used? But, then, no silencer was found."

He stopped suddenly in his pacings up and down the room. "Good God!" he said. "Now, that's the oddest thing in the whole case, and one which, I am afraid, hadn't occurred to me until this moment. It certainly affects the beginning of my pattern. The Dean's clothes. He was fully dressed but had on no clerical collar and no slippers or shoes. It looks as if he had taken his collar off and taken his shoes off, and was perhaps reading or preparing for bed when his murderous visitor arrived. But, then, the bed appeared to have been slept in. What would make a man get up in the middle of the night, nearly dress himself completely, and all just to be shot? He was certainly dressed when he was shot. Wait a minute, wait a minute," he thought. "What if it is a trick to make us think the Dean was murdered after he had gone to bed and in such circumstances so that he would readily get up and dress again? Suppose it was Wedgwood who did it. He was the last person to see the Dean alive, or to say he did. Well, now suppose he murders the Dean while visiting him normally at 11.30, puts him in the trunk, and ruffles the bed to give it the appearance of having been slept in. He goes home, and then in the darkness of the night creeps back, murders the porter at 2.15, and again creeps back to his bed. Two things point to the murder having been committed after midnight—the Dean having gone to bed, and the murder of the porter. I suppose I must add Wedgwood to my list of real suspects.

"Oh, hell," said Inspector Wyndham. "What's the use? The thing's too complicated." And he put out the light and went to bed.

CHAPTER EIGHT

ANNE LANDON

SIR RICHARD CHERRINGTON woke next morning blissfully unaware that he was on Detective-Inspector Wyndham's list of suspects, and that his large library of detective fiction and trial literature was now counting against him in the world of real crime and detection. Nevertheless, despite his ignorance of this, he was unhappy: perhaps one might almost say he was worried. First of all, he was surprised at the President's refusal to see the police until to-day. Two whole days and nights had gone by since the discovery of the crime, and still he had been unable to effect a meeting between Inspector Wyndham and the President. It was true he had at last fixed a meeting for twelve o'clock to-day, and that Dr. Quibell had pleaded that he had been indisposed for two days; but it was, nevertheless, a trifle odd.

His second worry was Anne Landon. He had been so involved in the details of the two murders, and the problems of College administration involved by them, that he had had no time to give much thought to the remarkable revelations made to him by the Dean before Hall on the night when he was murdered. Although he would not as yet admit it openly, he could not help sensing that these revelations, and the liaison effected between Anne Landon and Evan Fothergill, had something to do with the murder. He was not prepared to consider that Evan Fothergill had actually murdered the Dean; that itself, of course, was a possibility, but somehow it did not recommend itself to him. In the first place, there was his natural prejudice against supposing a Fellow of Fisher College had committed murder, and then there was his conviction that the two murders had been done by someone from outside the College, and that the second one—that of the porter Gostlin—was unnecessary to the success of the first murder as planned, but necessary because Gostlin had recognised the murderer, or was just about to do so. Surely, if Fothergill was the murderer, he could have crept back through the Courts to his rooms without being seen, and if necessary he could have climbed over the roofs back from the Dean's room to his own.

No, it was not the performance of murder by Evan Fothergill that worried him as he ate his breakfast on this Thursday morning in March. He did not suspect Fothergill and Anne Landon even of complicity in the crime, but he was loth to suppose that the fact of their proposed elopement had nothing to do with the circumstances of the crime. Did Bill Landon tell him all when they had talked together on Monday night? Was there more to it all? Some blackmail or threats of some kind? Is that why he had made the dramatic gesture with the revolver and hinted at possible suicide?

"There is, of course, another possibility," he thought. "What if the Dean's depression got worse after Hall, and in a fit of mad fury he arranged a diabolical scheme to end his own malaise and to bring unhappiness on the wife who, in an unchristian way, as he no doubt thought, was preparing to leave him and commit adultery with a young Fellow; he would at the same time involve the wretched Fellow in suspicion. That was possible if the balance of his mind was disturbed. He might have asked Fothergill to come over and have a talk with him late at night, and when he got there Fothergill would have found him dead. Yes, that was possible. The Dean might well have taken off his clerical collar with some sort of mistaken respect for not committing suicide dressed as a priest. Yes, that would be it, no doubt. Fothergill would arrive and, finding the Dean dead, might fly into a panic. After all, the boy did look miserable in Hall on Monday night. In his panic he might try to hide the Dean's body for a while by putting it in Farnaby's trunk, and he might have taken the revolver away to throw it into the river. As he went to the river in his panic he would have met Gostlin, and, in a reflex of panic, killed him. Dear me," he thought, "what an unpleasant series of possibilities! Perhaps the crimes are by separate hands. Who knows?" And then he remembered that the Dean's bed had been slept in, and felt vaguely reassured.

Nevertheless, it was his first duty to-day to see both Anne Landon and Evan Fothergill and tell them he knew of their proposals, and warn them of the suspicion that must attach to their continued association in the immediate future. Ugh! Not really a pleasant job. He would tackle Anne Landon first. He reached for the telephone to find whether she was in and would see him, and then changed his mind. He would walk out to St. John's Close: the walk would do him good, he reasoned. He did not admit to himself that if Anne were not in he would not be upset.

He picked up his silver snuff-box, his silver-mounted malacca cane and put on a smart black hat with bound brim. Gone were his rough tweeds. To-day he was dressed in a trim black suit with thin hairline stripe, a white shirt and neatly tied spotted bow tie. To-day he was the University and College administrator: it was his London disguise, as he called it, in which he appeared at the British Academy and the Society of Antiquaries. The rought tweeds and the field archæological ways had been put aside for a time. Next week he would resume them in Brittany: for a while he was the responsible officer of his College, meeting with one of the strangest episodes in its history.

He stepped briskly across the College lawns, let himself out by the River Gate and crossed the Backs to Queen's Road. He glanced from side to side admiringly at the flower-decked lawns of Trinity and St. John's. The crocuses were in their early glory, and the Backs were triumphant in their stretches of blue and yellow. There were few crocuses on the Fisher lawns, but there were daffodils under the trees in the Fellows' garden. The glory of the Fisher College Backs was earlier, when, in late January and February, they were a mass of aconites and snowdrops, harbingers of the spring, when the Trinity and John's Backs were still winter-barren.

He let himself out through the wicket on to Queen's Road and walked past the back gate of St. John's and round the corner into the Madingley Road. Past the St. John's cricket-ground with its immemorially lovely elms, he came first to Lady Gough Clarke's house, and then to St. John's Close, where the Landons lived.

He walked up to the front door and knocked diffidently. It was answered by a little wisp of a girl with mouse-coloured hair.

"Is Mrs. Landon in?" he asked.

"Well, sir, she is in," said the girl. "Leastways, in a manner of speaking she is. That is, she is in the garden at the moment. I'll fetch her for you." And she disappeared, leaving him on the doorstep.

In a very few minutes Anne Landon arrived. She certainly did not look the conventional grief-stricken widow. There were lines of anxiety in her expression, but she appeared as if years of trouble had left her. She seemed wrapped in a new peace and happiness. Sir Richard, looking at her, thought she had never been so beautiful. Certainly not when he first met her six or seven years ago—wasn't it at a lunch-party with Dr. Quibell?—or the May Ball, when her engagement to the Dean had been announced. His heart sank. "I'm afraid the Dean was right," he thought; "she is in love with this man Fothergill. God! I hope it is going to turn out all right."

"Oh, it's you, Sir Richard," she said.

"Yes. Good morning, Anne. How are you?"

"I'm fine," she said. "I'm so sorry you were kept waiting at the door. The maid's new, and I'm afraid she's not trained."

"Increasing your establishment, Anne?" he queried, for want of something better to say.

"No, not really. I've had to get rid of the old one. Gossips too much. Packed her off this morning, and this is all I've been able to get instead so far. But come in, do," she went on, "if you want to talk to me." She led the way into the hall. "H'm," she said. "Let me see. There's no fire in the drawing-room. Come up to my little boudoir upstairs. I've got a gas-fire there."

He followed her up the stairs and into a little room on the first floor. As she busied herself lighting the fire, he glanced round the room with a slight pang of sudden sympathetic understanding for her. This room had obviously been meant as a dressing-room, but she had turned it into a little study-cum-sitting-room for herself. There were bright curtains, an easy-chair and a settee covered in warm colours, and some cheerful prints on the walls. It was a woman's room: surely this woman's private room into which she had escaped from the boredom of her married life with Bill Landon. It was really a tragic thought: the good Dean sitting in his room in College of an evening, working away, and she sitting in this little escape room, reading and perhaps wondering what the future could hold for her. Into this barren prospect had come Evan Fothergill, with his youth and good looks and ardour. It really was little wonder that she had been swept away. He looked up to the mantel-shelf. It had on it two photographs, both of handsome young men, and both taken by Wellbeck and Summers, the Cambridge photographers, who contrived to make their subjects appear even more handsome and youthfully abandoned than they were. One was of Evan Fothergill in an open shirt. The other was of somebody in a black roll-top sweater, somebody he did not recognise, but who seemed vaguely familiar. In a way he was not unlike Evan Fothergill. Perhaps Fothergill's predecessor, he suggested to himself, cynically.

She intercepted his gaze at the photographs. "Do you think it indecent?" she asked.

"What do you mean, my dear?"

"You know what I mean, Richard. I was wondering if you thought it indecent of me to flaunt the photograph of my lover so soon after my husband's death."

"Er——" he began.

"But I'm not flaunting it, you know," she said. "It's been there for a long while."

"Has it?" he said. "What did Bill say?"

Her face seemed to shut up at the mention of her husband by his Christian name. "He never came in here. That was part of the bargain. This was my room—my sanctum; my world in a way. This is really the only place I've lived for two years until I met Evan."

"You don't have to tell me, you know," he began.

"Ah, but I want to," she said quickly. "I want to very much. There's been gossip in the past few weeks about me, I expect."

Sir Richard waved his hand deprecatingly. "Oh no."

"I know there has. And there'll be a lot more, I expect, now. I'd like one of the few honest, sane, respectable men—bachelor though you be—in this rotten University to know the truth."

Sir Richard flushed. "My dear, you're overwrought," he said. "You don't know what you are saying."

"Now, Richard. Believe me, yes, I do; and I've wanted to say it to someone for a long while. You and I used to know each other quite well in the first years of my marriage, but somehow we haven't seen very much of each other in the last year or two."

"You forget, my dear," went on Sir Richard apologetically. "I was away in America for a year."

"Yes, of course. Well, I think it was then I lost contact with you. And it was then my marriage with Bill Landon became the hollow mockery I should have seen it was bound to be when I married him."

"Anne——" he started.

"No, don't interrupt," she said. "You will have to explain the Landon-Fothergill scandal, as it is bound to be called"—her tone was contemptuous—"to so many people. You may as well get the facts straight. Anyhow, I want you to know them. Richard," she said, after a pause. "I'm only twenty-eight. I married Bill when I was twenty-two and he thirty-five. It was the great mistake. My brother Oliver was so dead against it that he wouldn't see me for over a year. He was right, and I was wrong. The marriage was a complete failure. The moment I got over my fleeting infatuation for Bill Landon I saw then he did not love me—not really. Not with an overwhelming sensual passion that could not be denied. No, I'm afraid he came even to his marriage bed a husband, not a lover. He had married me so that he could have someone to go with him to the President's dinner-parties, someone who dressed well to be with him at the Vice-Chancellor's garden-party, someone to help him with the Choir School boys' sports, someone who would hand the tea round and make pleasant conversation to the undergraduates on Sunday."

She paused.

"Well, I wasn't prepared to do that—not when I realised what I was supposed to be: the nice donnish wife; that and a convenient vehicle for the occasional and restrained relief of his passions."

She stood up and stamped her foot.

"So you see how it was. I was not prepared to lose a whole part of my life and pass from being a young girl straight to being a middle-aged married woman. It wasn't a natural thing to ask me to do—to forgo my life as a young woman—was it?"

There was a long pause. Sir Richard was a little uncomfortable. It is difficult to make conversation with someone who has just bared her soul to you.

"I wonder if he knew what he was asking," he said softly.

"No," she said. "That was the trouble. That was why I stuck it so long, made this escape up here and tried to create a life of my own with books. He didn't understand me. He had no idea of the barren cruelty of his unwitting neglect. I was a wife, and there was an end to it. There really was no problem. Oh, I tried to explain it all to him, but he didn't understand."

"Yes," said Sir Richard. "He asked me to come and see him on Monday night—the night before he was murdered. He told me you had determined to go away and live with Evan Fothergill. He could not understand it. I tried to persuade him to take six months sabbatical leave and travel. He seemed to have agreed to this coruse when I last saw him. But now, of course," he ended rather lamely, "that can't happen."

She was silent.

"What do you propose to do," he asked, "now you are free?"

"Evan is resigning his Fellowship at once," she said. "We shall get married and go and live in America. He's bound to get a job fairly quickly, with his qualifications, in a school or a University. My brother has just gone to the States, you know."

"That's really what I came to talk to you about," said Sir Richard, rather diffidently. "I mean, do you think it wise to get married again so soon after the tragedy?"

"Wise? Why? But we're in love, and for me Bill Landon didn't die yesterday or the day before. He died three years ago."

"I know, I know. But don't you think a sudden marriage will attract undue publicity to you both?"

"But we shall be out of England. Don't you mean to the College? You won't like the headlines, will you? 'Murdered Dean's Wife Marries Junior Fellow'. No, it won't do you all much good, I'm afraid, and it might even kill old Quibell."

Sir Richard was stung into reply. "That's true, of course," he said. "But I'm thinking of the police. Your behaviour will surely attract their attention."

"But why? It surely won't do so much more than what they have already heard. I mean, Evan and I are so obviously suspected from the start that nothing we do will make us less or more suspected. You see," she added, with a frank smile, "neither of us had anything to do with it."

"You can prove that to the police?" queried Sir Richard quietly.

"Yes," she replied easily. "I went to see Bill in his rooms after Hall and took him his spectacles, which he had left behind. He tried to detain me and start a long talk on our married life. He even suggested I go away with him on a long holiday. I told him it was three years too late, and that if he wouldn't divorce me I should just go away and live with Evan. I left him and came straight home. I read and was in bed early, and slept until wakened by the maid in the morning."

"I see," said Sir Richard. "And Evan Fothergill?"

"He has already told the police of his full movements. He was not well in Hall, and retired early to his rooms. He slept until next morning, when his bedmaker woke him with the news of the finding of the Porter's body."

"I see," said Sir Richard quietly. "But unfortunately none of these statements are susceptible of proof."

"Nor of disproof," she quickly replied.

"I hope you are right," he said. "I hope you are right. But remember that suspicion is bound to centre on Fothergill. I wish he had a really strong alibi."

She flushed. "But that would be so odd," she went on. "Evan's story rings true because it is just what happened. I know he couldn't have committed the crime, so that's the end of the matter."

Sir Richard got to his feet. "I wish it were," he said. "I wish it were."

She accompanied him down to the front door and out into the garden and down to the gate.

"Thank you for your confidences," he said. "I'll respect them."

"Thank you for listening," she replied.

"But do let me warn you again," he went on, "that the next few days and weeks will not be pleasant for you or for Fothergill. There's the inquest, to begin with, and the memorial service I am afraid we are bound to hold for Bill. And the funeral."

"Why can't we miss all that?" she asked. "He's dead, and there's the end of it."

"Then there's all the police investigations," he went on. "It's our duty to help them in every way to bring the criminal to justice."

"I've told them all I know," she said. "And I can't help them any more."

Sir Richard turned at the gate. "But surely you want the murderer to be found out?" he asked.

"No," she said. "No. Let's leave the whole sordid business. There's been enough suffering and unhappiness already," and she turned and walked quickly back into the house.

Sir Richard glanced at his watch as he walked sadly away down the Madingley Road. It was ten o'clock, and he would not have time to see Fothergill this morning. He had a meeting of the Syndics of the Press at 10.30, and then he had to take Inspector Wyndham to the President at twelve. He would see Fothergill in the afternoon, and meanwhile walk along the Backs to the Press. This would make him just in time for the meeting.

He paused at the corner of the Madingley Road. A large red bus came round and swung towards Bedford. The groundsmen were rolling the St. John's cricket-field. An errand-boy with bicycle basket filled with bread and cakes went by whistling. A late and earnest female undergraduate cycled off in the direction of the University Library. The sun broke through the clouds and for a moment lit up the tall trees in Queen's Road.

Sir Richard sighed as he started off along the Backs. "There was something," he said—"something she told me that I know was not true. Now I wonder what on earth it was?"

He walked on under the tall trees to his meeting.

CHAPTER NINE

THE PRESIDENT IDENTIFIES THE MURDERER

THE MEETING of the Syndics finished soon after half-past eleven, and Sir Richard walked back to Fisher College along King's Parade and Trinity Street, pausing here and there to gaze into a book-shop or a clothes-shop, or to pass the time of day with some acquaintance. Inspector Wyndham was waiting for him when he got back to College, and together they went across to the President's Lodging. They were shown into the President's gallery, a sort of large drawing-room used by the President for parties and meetings. A fire was burning in the grate, and on a table near by were decanters of madeira and sherry and a plate of hot saffron biscuits. They were obviously expected, and, judging by the preparations, Dr. Quibell was obviously looking forward to the meeting as an occasion.

After a few minutes the President came in from his study. "Good morning, Richard," he said. "Sorry to keep you gentlemen waiting."

"Good morning, sir," said Sir Richard. "May I introduce Detective-Inspector Wyndham of the Cambridge C.I.D.? Mr. Wyndham, the President."

"How do you do?" said the President affably. "I am sorry I was unable to see you sooner, but have been indisposed. This tragic affair," he added, and a shade of anxiety passed across his face. "A glass of wine, gentlemen?" he continued. "Sherry? Madeira? Or, if you prefer, my man can bring you some draught beer up from the cellar?"

When they were served with drink and seated round the fire, Dr. Quibell began.

"I need hardly say," he said, "how deeply I deplore what happened in this College on Monday night. It is the first time, gentlemen—the first time in the history of this College—that violent murders have been done within its walls, and it is a great shame to me that I should hold the high office of President at the time when this violence should break out." He paused. "I have thought of resigning," he said. "But it might do no good at all."

"My dear Mr. President," protested Sir Richard: really the old man was going off his head.

"Ah, but you see," went on the President quickly, waving aside Sir Richard's remark, "I am in part responsible for this murder."

"Sir?" said Sir Richard.

Inspector Wyndham sat up.

"And so, in a way, are you, my dear Sir Richard," Dr. Quibell went on. "It has been our job to educate the young men who pass through this College so that they should not resort to violence, murder, rape, adultery, disregard for the traditions of the College and the University"—he gave the crimes in ascending order of importance as he thought them, and his voice rose as he did so—"and we seem to have failed. We have left a few—I hope it is only a few—uncultured and uncultivated, and therefore, I am sure, unhappy persons to pass through this College."

The interview was not going exactly as Inspector Wyndham had planned it, but he waited patiently and relaxed in his chair.

"Then you think these murders were committed by a member of this College?" queried Sir Richard.

"That is the trouble, Sir Richard; that, Inspector, has been my anxiety in the past few days. You see, it is not a matter of thinking. I know who committed the murders."

If he had been seeking for an effect—and in his day he was one of the most accomplished lecturers in the University—he certainly was rewarded.

"What, sir?" asked Wyndham, sitting up again.

"Mr. President, are you sure?" said Sir Richard.

Dr. Quibell shook his head sadly. He took another sip of his glass of Madeira. "As sure as I can be. That is what has worried me in the last two days. In the end I came to the regretful conclusion that I must pass this information on to the police. I have asked Sir Richard here to be present. I hope he will agree with my decision."

"But, sir," said Wyndham, getting rather hot, "it is your duty to pass on to the police any information likely to bring the criminal to justice."

"Justice—duty," said the President lightly. "I am an old man, Inspector Wyndham, and you will forgive me if I say they are empty words. Duty to the State—what is that? The State is a machine, and I do not know it. I think of my duty to this College—that I know and can understand, and after two days of earnest thought I have decided that it is better the sad scandal of the College should be finished with, than drag on, an unsolved mystery, for many years. It is, I think, better we should get rid of this man now than keep a double murderer at our High Table."

"At our High Table?" said Sir Richard.

"Yes, I fear so," went on the President. "Let me tell you my story, and let me tell it to you in my own way.

"On Monday night I returned from the Combination Room to my lodgings and wrote some letters. I remember one in particular: I wrote to my young sister in Westmorland saying that I hoped to come and stay with her for a week or so in the Easter Vacation, but did not as yet know the dates. I suppose now, with this terrible tragedy associated with Fisher College, I shall be unable to show myself anywhere."

The old man paused.

"At ten o'clock," he went on, "my man Partridge brought me some hot milk, as is the invariable custom in these lodgings throughout the winter months. I poured into the milk a generous helping of rum, added some honey and took this nightcap with me to bed. I was soon asleep."

"Yes," said Inspector Wyndham, impatient at the old man's slow method of unfolding his story.

"I did not sleep very well, and was presently visited by a nightmare," Dr. Quibell went on firmly. "I dreamt that the whole College was upside down, and that the Dean had established some sort of dictatorship over the College and was sending down some of the Fellows. In fact, he had just dismissed Wedgwood and Fothergill and Westmacott and Traherne. It was very sad and worrying. I remonstrated with him. I remember this horrid scene vividly, for he turned on me and said, 'Careful, Mr. President. I shall dismiss you next.' From this horrid scene I took refuge in consciousness with a start. The clocks were striking all over the place. I looked at the clock rather blearily. It was two o'clock."

He paused.

"I tell you these details, gentlemen," he said, "so that you may see I most clearly recollect all that happened to me that night, and so that you may judge the truth of what I am about to tell you.

"I got out of bed and went into my dressing-room to find some sleeping tablets. I could not find the light-switch, and for a while fumbled idly about. Then I found what I wanted by the light which came through the open bedroom door. I was then by my dressing-room window."

He paused very dramatically.

"Gentlemen," he said, "I have to tell you that as I looked out through the window a shaft of moonlight was clearly illuminating the opposite bank of the river."

"You saw—somebody?" asked Wyndham eagerly.

"Yes," said Quibell. "I saw a man dressed in a loose-fitting dark overcoat standing on the lawns. It was as though he had been looking into the river. Suddenly he turned, crammed a soft hat on his head and walked away towards the back gate and Queen's Road. Whether he saw my bedroom light go on or not I do not know."

"And you recognised him?" asked Wyndham. The atmosphere was very tense.

"Yes," said the President, sighing. "I recognised him without any doubt. I gather that the murders were committed round about two o'clock. Perhaps it was the sound of a shot that woke me up. I gather also that the murderer left the College by the river gate and threw the revolver into the river as he went by. Gentlemen, the figure I saw standing by the river was exactly opposite where yesterday you dredged up the Dean's revolver. I have no doubt, therefore, that I practically saw the murderer discarding the revolver."

"But, sir——" began Sir Richard.

"I have spoken to the man concerned," went on the President imperturbably. "Naturally I did not tell him that I had seen him or when; but of his own accord he tells me that he was in bed before midnight and slept through until his bedmaker woke him next morning."

"His bedmaker?" said Sir Richard. "Then it was someone who kept in College?"

"My God!" thought Wyndham. "Where are we getting to? That only leaves Sir Richard and Westmacott and Fothergill. Could it be Sir Richard all the time, and is that why we have been summoned here together?"

"It was," said the President; "I am afraid it was. I pay little attention to College scandals as a rule, but it would appear that this young man had some reason for wanting William Landon out of his way."

"Then it was Evan Fothergill you saw, sir?" asked Cherrington, quietly.

"It was," said the President. His early jaunty manner had left him. "I have written down all I have told you, Inspector. Here is a statement." He paused. "I think it has to be signed in your presence and witnessed." He took out a two-page document from his pocket, removed his spectacles and put on his reading glasses. "There," he said, blotting his signature. "Now perhaps you and Sir Richard will sign it."

Inspector Wyndham picked up the document and put it in his pocket. "Thank you, sir," he said. "And thank you for your invaluable help. I hope I may come and see you again some time."

"Do, do," said the President vaguely. "Any time you wish. And now, gentlemen, I must wish you good morning."

He was clearly anxious to terminate the interview, so the Inspector and Sir Richard, mumbling thanks and good-mornings, took themselves off down the stairs and into the Court.

The President stood looking out through the window on to the Backs. "I suppose he will be hanged," he said to himself. "Praise God, they will find a great deal of other evidence against the man, and I suppose he may be made to confess. It would be intolerable if I had to go into a court of law and give this evidence." He shuddered. "And yet, even if I do not do that," he went on, "I suppose I have given the first piece of evidence that starts his journey to the Gallows-tree." He gazed out into the Backs; someone was coming along the main pathway on a bicycle. 'Who, I wonder, is this?" said the President idly. He peered at the cycling figure, but could only make out a blur. Suddenly an awful thought struck him—but only for a moment. "Oh, how stupid of me!" he said. "I've still got my reading glasses on."

II

Once out in the Court, Inspector Wyndham and Sir Richard Cherrington stopped and gazed at each other.

"That was a bit of a shock, wasn't it?" said Cherrington.

"It certainly was," agreed the other.

"Now what do you do?" asked Sir Richard.

"First thing is to see Fothergill and confront him with the President's evidence. It'll be awkward if he sticks to his former story. You know, I don't think we have enough to make an arrest on—not yet. But now we have a line to work on we shall be able to get to work seriously at last."

Sir Richard shuddered. The awful machinery of justice. Grinding on. Statement after statement. Questioning and cross-questioning. Checking and cross-checking. Times and distances and identifications. And the end of it. A long drop early one morning. And he had thought crime interesting, and detection a fascinating study. Now he met it personally and saw that it did not end with the apprehension of the criminal; he saw all the awful personal human problems afterwards. For a moment he thought of Mrs. Fothergill, Evan's mother, whom he had once met when she was on a visit to Cambridge—a trim, neat, quiet, Welsh farmer's wife, immensely proud of her son, but rather terrified of the University, and anxious to get back to her dairy and the Carmarthen market on

Saturdays and making tea and currant buns to take out to the workers at hay-making time. Would she be proud now, he thought? Would her Chapel find solace for her wounded soul? And in a flash, too, he thought of Anne Landon. He could not bear to think what fresh anguish that passionate creature must suffer.

Inspector Wyndham interrupted his reverie. "It's only half-past twelve," he said. "I'll try to see Fothergill at once. Will you come with me?"

Cherrington almost said no. He did not want to be involved further in these purely police and legal proceedings. Once the intellectual interest of detection had gone he was no longer interested in it. And then, he thought of Anne and her passionate desire for life and happiness. Surely she could not be involved in this charge? An accomplice? An accessory after the fact? It was not possible, but he must watch her interests. He went up the stairs with Inspector Wyndham.

Evan Fothergill was standing with his back to the fireplace, smoking a cigarette. He seemed surprised and displeased to see them.

"Come in, come in," he said. "Come in, Inspector. Hello, Sir Richard. What can I do for you?" went on Fothergill, rather nervously. "Cigarette? Drink?"

Sir Richard gazed round Fothergill's rooms. They were typical of a young, hard-working Fellow with few interests but his work. Yes, this man certainly needed a woman to humanise him and turn him into a sensible human being who earned his living by scholarship and teaching, rather than a scholar and academic teacher who in the intervals of work lived in a brief and fitful way. That was the trouble with the University, and that was the justification, in part, of the world's condemnation of dons as eccentric and unworldly. It was all so unnecessary. If only people would realise that the don was really no different from the business man, but instead of seven hours a day in an office, he spent slightly more time in lecturing and research and, as he grew older, in University Committees. Fothergill might have made a really good, reputable citizen and don if he had met Anne earlier and in happier circumstances. And now it was all shattered. He looked round the room again. On the mantelpiece was an excellent photograph of Anne Landon. Really, people were strange nowadays. "When I was a young Fellow," thought Sir Richard, "it would have been considered strange to have a photograph of another Fellow's wife on my mantel-piece." But there, perhaps it had only been put up since the Dean's death. And there, over on the bookcase, was the photograph of another woman. His sister, perhaps. No, no, wait a moment. Yes, of course, June Westmacott. For a moment he had forgotten Fothergill's engagement to the Tutor's niece. And in a flash as he looked at that photograph a vague uneasiness began to settle on him. And he turned to Fothergill with renewed interest.

"We've come up to put a few more questions to you, Mr. Fothergill," began the Inspector. "I'm sorry to trouble you, but there are one or two points to be cleared up."

"Oh, yes; anything I can do to help," said Fothergill, but Sir Richard thought his eyes closed slightly and his manner became more watchful and wary.

"When I examined you the other day," went on the Inspector, "you made a statement of your movements on the night of Monday of this week."

"Yes," said Fothergill. "I did."

"Well, sir, in that statement, if I remember correctly, you said that you felt unwell during Hall, and went to your rooms straight afterwards, and did not stir out of them until awakened next morning."

"That is so."

"Now, I must ask you a serious question, Mr. Fothergill. Are you prepared to swear to that statement in a court of law and on oath?"

Evan Fothergill smiled a trifle uneasily. "Are you suggesting I am a liar, Inspector?" he said.

"No, Mr. Fothergill, certainly not. That would not be my province," said the Inspector promptly. "I merely suggest that you have not told us all your movements during the night."

Fothergill looked up sharply. "What do you mean?" he said.

"Come now, Mr. Fothergill. I'll be frank with you," said the Inspector. "We have received testimony—very reliable testimony—that you were seen about in the College after midnight. Now, in view of this, we wonder if you would care to amplify your earlier statement."

Sir Richard, while full of admiration for the way the Inspector was carrying out his examination, could not help noticing that something in his last question seemed to have relieved Fothergill.

"Well, Inspector," Fothergill said. "You are right to be cross with me. I have misled you, and I am sorry for it. But I'm afraid the real facts implicate me in the murders somewhat. That's why I tried to hide them hitherto."

"Yes," said the Inspector cautiously.

"It was a lie I told you about going to bed soon after Hall. A silly lie. I expect by now you will have unearthed all the scandals in this College." He lifted his hand as the Inspector was about to speak. "Please," he said. "I am not criticising you. It is your job. But you will have found out that I have been engaged to the Tutor's daughter, June Westmacott, for some months. You will know, too, that when she became engaged to me June was already engaged to John Parrott, and that since then Parrott has regarded me with very open loathing."

He paused.

"Recently," he said, "I have realised that my attraction for June Westmacott was a childish, schoolboy affair, and that our engagement should never have happened. I wrote her on Monday night a letter breaking off the engagement. It was a difficult letter to write, but when it was finished I took it down and posted it at the Porter's Lodge. This was about a quarter to twelve. No one was about, and no one saw me post this, as far as I know."

"Yes," said the Inspector encouragingly. All this was interesting, but he could not see where it was leading.

"The real reason for breaking off my engagement with June Westmacott," went on Fothergill, "was that I had fallen hopelessly in love with the Dean's wife. I realised this was the most important thing in my life. She returned this affection," he said simply, "and we wanted to get married. I went to see the Dean on Monday afternoon, but he would have nothing to do with me. He refused to discuss a divorce, and said we were both mad. I made another attempt to see him late on Monday night."

"You did?"

"Yes, I did. After I had posted the letter I went up to his rooms, but he would not discuss the situation with me."

"This was presumably between a quarter to twelve and twelve."

"It was. The Dean said he was going away for a long holiday and would probably take his wife with him. He packed me out of his rooms and sported his oak with a vicious bang."

"Ah, he did sport his oak," thought the Inspector. "That bears out Farnaby's evidence that it was sported when he came up at twelve."

"And then?" queried the Inspector.

"And then I was mad," said Fothergill. "I let myself out on the Backs and walked about thinking over and over again what I should do." He paused. "It must have been well after one o'clock when I got back to my rooms and went to bed." He stopped.

"That's all you have to say?" asked the Inspector.

"Yes, that's all," replied Fothergill carefully. "I repeat I am sorry I did not tell all this to you before. It was most foolish of me."

The Inspector looked up suddenly at Fothergill. "What if I tell you," he said, "that you were seen climbing along the roofs to the Dean's rooms just before two o'clock?" It was a good line.

Fothergill's eyes flashed an old hidden Welsh fire.

"That's just untrue," he said.

"What if I tell you that about a quarter past two you were seen on the Backs standing near the spot where the revolver was found yesterday?"

"I'd say the same. It's just untrue."

There was a pause. "Evan," began Sir Richard, intervening for the first time. "I wonder if you could give us more than these blank denials? You see, the evidence about you standing on the bank of the Cam at two-fifteen comes to us from an impartial and very reliable source. It was Dr. Quibell who saw you."

"Dr. Quibell?" said the other, taken aback. "But he must be mistaken. He saw somebody else. I mean it is very easy in the dark night to do that."

"He is very sure of his identification," went on Sir Richard. "And you can be sure he would be certain of it before he was prepared to incriminate another Fellow of the College."

"Wait a moment. Of course that's it," said Fothergill. "He was mistaken about the time. It was just after one, not after two, he saw me. I was still walking about at that time. As a matter of fact," he said, "I remember his light going on, and I wondered why." He said it rather lamely, and it sounded lame.

"H'm," said the Inspector. "And that's all you have to say?"

"Yes, it is."

"You went to see the Dean about a quarter to twelve," recapitulated the Inspector. "You left him before midnight, and went walking on the Backs. You walked on the Backs until after one o'clock, when you saw Dr. Quibell's light go on. Then some time later you went to bed, and did not get up until your bedmaker woke you up."

"That's right," agreed Fothergill.

"No," thought Sir Richard to himself. "No; there's something here that doesn't fit; something here that is wrong. I noticed it in the story Anne Landon told me. Now what the hell is it?"

"You walked about the Backs for over an hour in the middle of the night, did you, Mr. Fothergill?" queried the Inspector.

"I did. You must remember I was overwrought."

"Were you cold?"

"I beg your pardon?"

"I am asking if you were cold," went on the Inspector. "It was a very cold night."

"I don't remember."

"Did you have a coat on?"

"I don't know."

"A hat?"

"I really don't remember," said Fothergill. "Is it important?"

"The President says you were dressed in a dark overcoat and a felt hat."

"Then I must have been," said Fothergill lamely. "I have a dark overcoat and I have a felt hat, you know."

"Now, that strikes a chord somewhere," thought Sir Richard. "Always we seem to come to clothes in this case—the Dean's clothes, and now Fothergill's clothes."

"It's a pity you can't remember more accurately," said the Inspector, getting up. "Well, if that is all you have to tell me, we will take our leave. I must ask you to give this information in writing to Sergeant Mossop after lunch, if you will."

"I certainly will."

"And I do urge you again, Mr. Fothergill," he said firmly, "that your statement must contain the full truth and everything that may possibly assist the police in the prosecution of this case."

As they went down the stairs, Inspector Wyndham said to Sir Richard, "I don't believe him, sir. No, I'm afraid I don't believe him. He was keeping something back from us."

"Yes," said Sir Richard reluctantly. "I had that feeling too."

"I must see the Chief Constable as soon as his written statement is taken. I wonder if we have enough evidence for an arrest."

"An arrest?" said Sir Richard, stopping as they got out into the Court, warmly lit by the March sun. Then suddenly he realised the significance of June Westmacott's photograph still on Evan Fothergill's bookcase. Of course, that was it. Surely no man who was so madly in love with one woman that he would murder her husband could possibly tolerate in his rooms the photograph of a former love to whom he was still engaged?

"An arrest?" he repeated. "I should go very carefully if I were you, Inspector," said Sir Richard. "After all, while Fothergill may have kept back something from us, his facts may be right, and the President may have got the times wrong. In any case, Fothergill's psychology is all against him being the murderer."

"Ah," said the Inspector. "I'm after the facts." He added rather rudely, "We can easily make the psychology fit the facts when we've got them. Good morning, Sir Richard."

"And there, my friend, you are wrong," thought Sir Richard as he crossed the Court and went up to his rooms for lunch.

CHAPTER TEN

A CAMBRIDGE AFTERNOON

IT WAS the memory of the photograph of June Westmacott that remained most keenly with Sir Richard through his solitary lunch in his rooms. He had no desire to lunch in the Combination Room and have to discuss the whole case from beginning to end with the other Fellows, especially since Westmacott was so sure Fothergill had done it, Wedgwood that Parrott had done it, and Traherne that whoever had done it, it was a good thing for the College.

So he lunched in his own rooms. It was a cultivatedly frugal lunch. When he came into his room he had uncorked a half bottle of a delightful Mouton d'Armailhacq which he kept for drinking during solitary luncheons in the winter, and he kept turning the claret round and round as it stood in front of his fire, the while he drank some sherry and looked through the late morning mail. Here was a letter from his nephew Giles wondering whether he would still be able to get away on the motor tour of Brittany. "That'll be all right," thought Sir Richard. "We are not scheduled to leave for six days, and by that time the inquest on the Dean, and the funeral, will all be over. The memorial service had better be left until next term, of course, when all the undergraduates will be up." He chuckled at the thought of Dr. Wedgwood having to prepare a memorial service for the Dean. How they had hated each other and argued over the Chapel Services with himself and Roger Westmacott to hold the balance between their two extreme views. "H'm," thought Sir Richard, "then there is the funeral of Gostlin. Must find out when that is and attend it on behalf of the College. How tiresome all this is!"

He went to the table and ate a chicken and mushroom omelette which Kilmartin had just brought up from the kitchen. It was very good, and so were the Petit Pois á la Française which he had with the omelette. He finished the frugal meal with some Camembert and Bath Olivers. The Camembert was just as it suited him; he had prodded the cheeses in Mark's the grocers until he found one just ripe as he liked it. The claret went perfectly with the Camembert.

As he brewed himself some coffee he wondered what he should do with his afternoon. Have a knock up at squash with the marker in the University squash courts? Despite his years, he still played a vigorous game, and it was his hope he might die of heart failure on the squash courts one day. The cinema? Work? There was a long paper of his that had still to be finished and the footnotes of his last paper still needed checking. Then the Syndics that morning had asked him to read two books for them and see whether they were fit for publication. "No," he thought. "I'll just spend a nice normal Cambridge afternoon. I'll go for a walk, and then finish up with some tea in Miss Palliser's. Fortunately, the undergraduates are all down, and I shall be able to have a quiet tea chez Palliser."

He changed his clothes, put on a pair of corduroy trousers, some suede shoes, an open shirt, a neck sweater and a large shabby tweed cap. He filled his pipe and took a stick and set out. "Where shall it be?" he said to himself as he crossed the Backs. "I think the Coton footpath, and then back around Grantchester, if I feel energetic enough. That will give me all the justification I want for crumpets and jam with Miss Palliser."

As he walked across Queen's Road and up the path past the University Library, his thoughts reverted to the two murders—the Cambridge Murders, as the papers were now calling them. Indeed, it was difficult to keep one's mind off them. Somehow he could not bring himself to countenance the suggestion that Evan Fothergill was the murderer. "There is a case, of course," he said: "let us not blink at the fact that the police probably have a case. But I cannot see how Fothergill can fit the part. If he was still in the process of breaking off his engagement with the Westmacott girl, and still had her photograph in his room, the completely overriding passion necessary for a murder of this kind is just not there.

"There is, of course, the possibility," he said to himself, as he crossed the O.T.C. grounds and made for Coton—"always the possibility I envisaged this morning—namely, that the Dean committed suicide, that Fothergill had been attempting to cover up this suicide, which he found when he visited the Dean, perhaps by appointment at a quarter to twelve. He had been trying to cover it up by the murder of Gostlin, which was his first attempt at cover, and by different stories to the police.

"Of what real value is the President's testimony?" he asked himself. "It was very impressive this morning, and I must hand it to the old man that he brought it out very nicely and convincingly. He hasn't been lecturing all these years, of course, unless he can do that. But he must have convinced himself it was true before he would make a statement so damaging to the prestige and good name of his own College.

"What does it actually boil down to? That he saw Fothergill at about 2.15 or just after, standing near the spot where the revolver was found, and then that he walked quickly away into the night. Let's treat this again as if it were a statement in a scientific report," said the disciplined mind of Sir Richard. "What does it actually say? Just that the President saw a person whom he identified as Fothergill, at a spot where he thought the revolver was found next day, at a time thought by him to be 2.15. Now that's a little better," said Sir Richard. "There are therefore three propositions: (1) That the person seen was Fothergill. (2) That the place was where the revolver was found. (3) That the time was 2.15. Now I am prepared to agree to the second proposition without any objection at the moment. Do the other two hold? The President could have been mistaken about either of them. It might have been 2.15, and the person he saw might not have been Fothergill, but the mysterious Mr. X, who came into College from outside, performed these murders and disappeared into the night. It might have been Fothergill that he saw, but just after one o'clock, as Fothergill suggested: after all, Fothergill said, although with a little prompting, that he had seen the President's light go on. Or of course," Sir Richard said to himself, "in all fairness it could have been Fothergill at 2.15 or somebody different at any other time. Once you admit the possibilities of an error on the President's part you can get almost anywhere. Then, we mustn't forget the President is very short-sighted. Did he remember to change his spectacles during his nocturnal prowl? If he didn't we have two possibilities again: that he had his reading glasses on, in which case he certainly couldn't identify Fothergill, or that he put on his long-range spectacles, and so would not see the clock properly. That must be it, of course," said Sir Richard. "He woke up suddenly, heard the clocks strike, thought it two o'clock, put on his long-distance spectacles, looked in a blurred way at the clock, padded away to the dressing-room—that's right," he said, "he couldn't find the switch, which was near at hand, and then as he looked out, through the window, he focused properly and could see Fothergill."

Sir Richard paused and negotiated a small wicket gate. "It is all a little far-fetched, but I can see defending counsel making merry with the President if he ever takes his evidence to court in its present state. I must warn him of all these possibilities. Yes, I must warn him as soon as possible."

It all seemed to depend to a certain degree on the clothes. "Anybody could be wearing a loose coat and a felt hat: it doesn't help us at all. What a pity Fothergill couldn't make up his mind what he was wearing. The trouble about this case is that it seems to revolve around odd problems of clothes. Why was Bill Landon dressed at all and in such a surprising way when he was murdered (or committed suicide)? Were there two men or one on the Backs that night between one and two-thirty, both dressed in coats and felt hats? If only we could establish what Evan Fothergill was wearing that night, it would be something."

And then came one of those flashes of inward clarity that sometimes occur to all of us when dealing with a difficult problem. "Well, I'm damned!" thought Sir Richard. He had known there was something that struck him as odd with the stories of Anne Landon and Evan Fothergill. Back to clothes again. He tried afresh to get clear the events of the Tuesday morning. The bedmakers were clamouring at the main gate a few seconds or minutes after six o'clock; they were let in by Rodgers; the discovery of Gostlin's body in the Screens would be at about six-ten or a little earlier. He, himself, had been called by Mrs. Kilmartin a few minutes after this, he supposed: it had not taken him more than two or three minutes to get to the Screens—he had just put on any old clothes, with a dressing-gown over flannel trousers and his pyjama top. Yes, that's right—his arrival there must have been near enough to six-fifteen. He remembered checking Gostlin's watch just before the police came, and it recorded the time correctly as six twenty-five.

"Well then," said Sir Richard to himself, "I got there at six-fifteen, and there was Fothergill fully clad, with collar and tie and a loose overcoat on and gloves, but no hat. Now, why ever didn't I notice that before. Here's a little piece of evidence only given to me to notice, and I nearly missed it altogether. And damn it all, he's on H Staircase, isn't he? Why, that's Mrs. Harris' staircase—saw her this morning when I visited Fothergill with the Inspector, and it was Mrs. Harris who fainted at the sight of Gostlin's body and was moaning and shouting, 'Horrible! horrible!' when I got there."

He struck the tops off two withered stalks of thistle with his walking-stick. "Now, where does that get us to? It's simple. Fothergill wasn't called by his bedmaker. She never reached him, and if she had he wouldn't have time to dress so completely, and he would never have put on an overcoat and gloves at that time of the morning. Ergo, Fothergill is lying. Now why, and why should he appear on the spot at six-fifteen properly dressed?"

"I know, I know," said Sir Richard, smiting the ground with his walking-stick with such glee that two urchins from Coton cycling into Cambridge to the cinema thought he was mad. "It sticks out a mile. When Fothergill arrived on the scene at six-fifteen he was coming into College. He must have spent the night out, and I'm very much afraid probably in St. John's Close with Anne Landon. Yes, that explains so much: why Anne was looking so radiant this morning, why the maid was sacked, perhaps, why Anne was so sure it couldn't be Evan Fothergill, and why he keeps telling stories to the police which, while implicating himself a little, do keep out of the news that fact that he spent the night with the Dean's wife. Yes, that must be the explanation. I see it all now. Evan Fothergill has made up his mind, so he writes to June Westmacott, has a last interview with the Dean, and as the Dean refuses to countenance divorce, he goes and spends the night with his beloved, returning in the morning to College before many people are about. He leaves it a little late, and instead of being able to slip into his room before Mrs. Harris gets to him, he finds Mrs. Harris and several other people as well, all careering around a dead body in the middle of the College. That must have surprised him. Fothergill had no hat on," thought Sir Richard, "when I saw him, so it is very likely that he had no hat when he left College the night before, in which case the President probably didn't see him, but the actual Mr. X. Now that gives us a line on Mr. X: he was vaguely like Evan Fothergill.

"This is all supposition, though, isn't it?" he thought. "But an interesting hypothesis. How can I test it? Lady Gough Clarke, of course. The very one." He turned round on his course and walked back as fast as he could towards Cambridge. He turned off the footpath down Grange Road, and so into the Madingley Road. It was only about ten minutes to a quarter of an hour after the idea had come into his head that he was knocking at the front door of Lady Gough Clarke's house. He felt a minor pang of reproach as he passed St. John's Close, but he could not very well go straight in and ask Anne Landon if his theory was true. That would come later when he had more evidence.

Lady Gough Clarke was out. A pity! He was about to give up the chase, at least for the time being, when he turned back and began to question the maid. It was a rather difficult task, but he tried hard.

"Excuse me," he said. "You probably know who I am. Professor Cherrington of Fisher College."

"Oh yes, sir," replied the maid.

"Well, at the moment I have to make some enquiries in a hurry relating to the sad death of our Dean. Mrs. Landon is not in next door, I am afraid," he went on, glancing nervously towards St. John's Close for fear Anne Landon might at any moment come out. "The only other person who can tell me what I want is the maid there, but it appears to be a new maid. Did you know the old one, and where I could get hold of her?"

"Doris Finch, sir?"

"I don't know her name, but the maid who was there until very recently."

"That's right, sir," she said. "She had the sack this morning."

"Can you tell me where I can get hold of her? You see, the matter is rather urgent," he added.

"Don't rightly know where she is," said the girl. "But expect she'll have gone to her mother's place. Her mother's a landlady in Portugal Place."

Portugal Place was a small road full of lodging-houses not far from Fisher College. It should be easy to trace her. He thanked the maid, and looking guiltily towards St. John's Close, made his way back into College. First he put on a coat and discarded his walking-stick. Then as he was going out through the front gate he met Mrs. Harris. She had been putting her keys away in the Porter's Lodge, and was just leaving College.

He would put one part of his theory to the test straight away.

"Afternoon, Mrs. Harris," he said agreeably.

"Good afternoon, sir," she said.

He stopped and chatted to her. "Feeling better now?" he asked.

"That I am, thank you," she said. "Gave me a real turn it did. Seeing poor Sam Gostlin there lying on the paving-stones, all murdered. First thing in the morning, too; that was so horrible."

"Yes, it was a shock, wasn't it?" He wondered how to turn the conversation in the direction he wanted it without a direct question.

"I was fair put out all the morning," she said—"couldn't give my proper attention to anything. Rodgers and Kilmartin, they said, 'Now don't you go telling your gentlemen nothing about this murder here'. But I couldn't help myself: I was that upset. I went into their rooms one after the other and told them. I says, 'The most awful thing has happened in the night, and I'm that upset I can't look after you properly this morning. And as it's the last morning of term, you'd all better get up quickly. It's murder,' I said—'horrible murder. And I practically seed it happening.' "

"Yes, yes," said Sir Richard. "I don't think anyone could blame you. It was such a shock. So you went and told all the gentlemen on your staircase, did you?"

"Well, not all. Mr. Fothergill—or Dr. Fothergill, I suppose I should call him now—he had already got up when I came to his room."

"Quite so," said Sir Richard hurriedly. "Well, let's hope there'll be no more such shocks in the future."

"My heart couldn't stand it, sir," she said. "I said to Harris that day, I said, 'I mustn't be shown no more murders. Horrible!' "

Sir Richard walked off. "Right first time," he said. "Right first time, by God. Now for the maid."

He would try in Fleury and Driberg's, the tobacconists that stood at the head of Portugal Place, and see if old Mr. Driberg knew the whereabouts of Mrs. Finch. It was Thursday afternoon, and the shops were shut, but a knock at the side door produced Mr. Driberg in his flowered waistcoat, high white collar and stock. He was about to go for his Thursday afternoon walk, but was delighted to see Sir Richard.

"Ah, my dear Professor, how do you do? How do you do? What a pleasure! what a pleasure!" Old Driberg had the habit of saying all his sentences twice and of making them seem most emphatic statements when they were merely the commonplaces of everyday conversation. That is why talking to him on the most trivial matters seemed always most exhausting.

"Good afternoon, Mr. Driberg."

"What can I do for you?" went on the old man. "Alas, what can I do for you on a Thursday afternoon, with the shop shut? But I might arrange something. Yes, I might arrange something. From my private supply, of course. Yes, my private supply. Not a business transaction. No, just a gift among friends—just among friends. And you pay next time. Yes, next time. You think that a good arrangement? Surely it is. Now what can we do for you? Snuff? Some tobacco? Some cheroots?" The old man ran on.

"As a matter of fact, Mr. Driberg," Sir Richard cut through his meanderings. "I haven't really come for some supplies: I've come to consult you for some information."

"Ah, quite so, quite so," said the old man, nodding his head wisely. "These tragic happenings. So violent, so violent. Of course, of course. The young girl Gostlin is employed here. Find her very good—yes, very good. No complaints. No, no complaints."

"I'm glad to hear that, but I was only enquiring on a very minor matter. I am trying to find a landlady in Portugal Place, a Mrs. Finch. Do you happen to know where she is?"

"I'm afraid I don't. No, I'm afraid that I don't. But I can find out for you. Mrs. Baxter will know. She knows everything. Practically everything. No trouble at all." And he disappeared into his house, to reappear in a few minutes with the information, supplied by his housekeeper, that Mrs. Finch was at number twelve.

Sir Richard thanked him and went off down the road, the while the old man kept repeating, "Not at all. No trouble at all, my dear Professor."

Number twelve was like all the lodging-houses in Portugal Place, a dingy and depressing-looking building with the tenants living in the basement. Reflectors hung outside the basement windows to catch a little of the winter sunshine that penetrated into the narrow street. This time he was lucky, and the door was opened by a girl whom he rightly guessed to be Doris Finch.

"Good afternoon," he said. "My name is Sir Richard Cherrington, and I am the Vice-President of Fisher College."

"Oh yes, sir," said the girl, suitably impressed.

"I am looking for a Miss Doris Finch. Is that you, by any chance?"

"It is, sir," she said, her eyes narrowing warily.

"Good!" Sir Richard went on. "Good! I am right in believing you were, until very recently, a maid with Mrs. Landon in St. John's Close, in the Madingley Road?"

"That's right, sir," she said. "Got the sack this morning, and for nothing at all. Very unjust, I call it."

"Ah, yes." Sir Richard leaned towards her and said in a confidential whisper, "Miss Finch, I am engaged in a few special enquiries on behalf of the College. Most private, of course. Nothing to do with the police. I should be very glad if you would help me. Could you?"

Her reply surprised him. "I would indeed, sir," she said. "I've been wondering whether I oughtn't to go to the police with my story, but my mother says it was no business of mine."

"H'm," said the Professor. "Could we go and have a dish of tea together? Perhaps Miss Palliser's Café"—he thought of the crumpets and jam. "We could be private there."

"Thank you, sir. I'll just go and tell my mother and get me hat."

She ran off, feeling very important. It was not often she got the opportunity of walking down Trinity Street into Miss Palliser's with one of the College bigwigs. She hoped Mrs. Landon would see her—that would give her a shock. She powdered her face till it was nearly as white as flour, adding some cheap red lipstick to her lips, stuck a hat jauntily on her head and ran out to join Sir Richard.

But as they walked up Portugal Place and down Trinity Street, Sir Richard was unaware of her coy looks. He missed, too, the surprised stare of Baynes, the Head Porter, as they went past the front gate of Fisher College, and the astonished but interested gaze of old Mr. Bell out of the bookshop. As they went into the café he seized hold of Miss Palliser, a very old friend of his, and said, "My dear, a little table, please, tucked away in the corner and behind some curtains. Can you fix it?"

Miss Palliser gladly did, but as they crossed through the rooms of the café to get to their quiet corner they were carefully observed by Mrs. Wedgwood and Mrs. Traherne, who were drinking tea, eating sugar cakes, and discussing the Fisher College scandals at a little table near the window.

"Really," said Mrs. Wedgwood, "Dick Cherrington is to be found with the most surprising people, don't you think, my dear? Did you see him go by then with a little shop-girl, or something?"

"My dear," said Mrs. Traherne, who had just averted her gaze from the window in time to see Sir Richard and Doris Finch come into the café. "How odd!" Then—"archæologists—and bachelor archæologists at that—are a trifle odd, don't you think?"

Sir Richard and Doris Finch were safely esconced in the remotest corner of Miss Palliser's café, and had in front of them hot crumpets dripping with butter, a pot of jam, and some of Miss Palliser's famous cakes. After he had poured her out some tea, Sir Richard said casually, "And now perhaps you will be so good as to tell me your story."

"Well, it's not much of a story," she said, wiping the butter off her fingers—these hot crumpets were difficult to be ladylike about. "It's just that on Monday evening me and me boy were going for a walk. I didn't sleep in at the Landons', it being such a small house. I came every morning about seven o'clock and left every evening about six. I stayed later if they gave a party, but that wasn't often, you know. Not much entertaining there."

"Yes," said Sir Richard encouragingly, "you were going for a walk on Monday night."

"We was coming down the Madingley Road, me and Bert, and as we passed the Landon house where I worked I saw a man go through the gate quickly and disappear round the side of the house—round the back like, behind the garage."

Sir Richard pricked up his ears. "What time was this?" he said.

"It was just on eleven o'clock," she said. "I know because just after the clocks started striking, and my Bert, who is under-porter at Peterhouse, and had to go on duty at half-past eleven, he says 'Why, that's eleven; we must be getting a move on, me girl.' "

This was a surprising bit of information. Sir Richard did not see where it fitted in. "What was he like?" he asked.

"It was too dark for me to see, sir," she said. "I just saw him walk through the gate, up the drive and round the corner of the house."

"It wasn't the Dean?" he asked, and as he asked he realised that could not be—as the Dean was at that moment in his rooms in College talking with Wedgwood or Traherne.

"Oh no, sir," she said. "It couldn't have been the Dean. It was a different sort of person; more slight like, with an overcoat on and a sort of soft hat pulled down over his eyes."

. The coat and hat again. Now, was this the Mr. X we are looking for, or Evan Fothergill come hours before he said he did—if so, his latest statement was nonsense—or someone who has nothing to do with the case? It is strange that Anne Landon made no mention of her visitor, if of course he did visit her, and it was not Fothergill.

"I know about his hat," she went on, "because it was there in the morning."

Sir Richard put down his tea and elegantly polished his spectacles.

Here was something at last. He put his spectacles back on his nose, took out his snuff-case and took a pinch of snuff.

"It was there in the morning," he said slowly. "Are you sure?"

"Quite sure," she said, "because I said to Mrs. Landon, I said, 'Here, who's hat is this?' and she said, 'Oh, that's an old one of Dr. Landon's he doesn't often wear,' but I noticed she took the hat away and hid it."

"She did?"

"Yes, the hat had gone later that morning, and as poor Dr. Landon was murdered, he couldn't have come and taken it. And to my way of thinking it wasn't his hat, either."

"I see. And what then?"

"I said nothing until the news of Dr. Landon's murder was out yesterday, and then I thought, 'There's funny things going on in this house.' This morning I asked Mrs. Landon if I ought to tell the police about the strange man I saw around at eleven, and she says, 'Nonsense, Doris, you're dreaming—there were no strange men around.' Then I mentioned the hat, and she flies into a rage and says I'm an interfering busybody, and clears me out of the house at once. Do you think, sir, I ought to go and see the police? I don't want to get Mrs. Landon into trouble," she added untruthfully.

"Yes," said Sir Richard, "I think you should tell your story to the police, but leave it for a day or two. It's Thursday afternoon now—if they haven't come to see you by Saturday morning, go and see them."—"Surely by Saturday," he thought, "I can find out what did go on in that house on Monday night." He saw in front of him a rather difficult interview with Anne Landon, but in which, this time, he would play the dominant role and there would not be so much talk about the freedom of the young woman and so forth.

"Well, my dear, if you've finished, shall we go?" he said.

And they went. As he was paying his bill Miss Palliser leered at him in an affectionate way and said, "Doin' some backstairs detection, Sir Richard?"

"Really, Miss Palliser," he said, staring at her over his spectacles—"really, sometimes you shock me."

CHAPTER ELEVEN

SIR RICHARD IS EMBARRASSING

Sir Richard woke up next morning knowing that he had a very difficult day in front of him. There were two official duties: he had to go down to Twyford and attend the Dean's inquest in the afternoon, and before that he had to attend Gostlin's funeral in the morning. How very tiresome all this was! He certainly looked forward to getting away from Cambridge on Monday or Tuesday and away to Brittany on the Wednesday.

But before his official duties he had two or three unpleasant unofficial duties. First he must see the President and point out how inconclusive his evidence really was—that would not be enjoyable. Second, he must see Anne Landon and get from her the story of the visits on Monday night. Perhaps this hat was still there. Thirdly, he must speak very firmly to Evan Fothergill and tell him he must give the police a complete statement of all his doings on the Monday night. These stories he kept telling them were very wrong.

Sir Richard sat up in bed and sipped the tea Kilmartin had brought him. He took a ginger biscuit out of the silver biscuit-barrel on the bedside table and munched it reflectively. "I still don't see the whole thing clearly," he said to himself. "Yesterday when I was out walking I thought I had got it clear. The only explanation of Fothergill's presence fully dressed at six-fifteen in the morning is that he had just come from St. John's Close. Well, it isn't the only explanation, but the only one that really concerns us at the moment. The statement of his and of Anne Landon that he was asleep until his bedmaker woke him was just not true. Then the hat. He had no hat when he came into College; there was a hat left behind in St. John's Close. It was obviously his hat.

"So far, so good. Anne Landon is concealing the guilty fact of his presence there that night. That explains her behaviour to the maid, the hiding of the hat and the sacking of the maid. It is not the murderer's hat she is concealing, as Doris Finch thinks. But now we come to the difficulty. Doris Finch saw a man go into or round St. John's Close at about eleven o'clock. Let's call this man A. Evan Fothergill says he left College, was wandering about the Backs and saw the President's light go on, and he guesses this was about one o'clock. The President says he saw a man at two o'clock; let's call this man B. Now where are we?" asked Sir Richard, pouring himself out another cup of tea. "Evan Fothergill could be man B; that is the police theory. Then who is man A? Some quite different person who visited Anne Landon, stayed the night, and left his hat in the morning. Now really," he mused, "we can't have two men staying in the house, and I feel sure it was Fothergill's hat. Fothergill could be man A and have stayed in St. John's Close until the next morning; yes, that seems very reasonable, but, then, who is B—the murderer? And why does Fothergill say all this nonsense of his about posting letters and visiting the Dean and seeing the President's light go on? Is it because he knows, or Anne Landon knows, who did the murder, and they are trying to conceal the fact by making us confused over the times?

"Goodness! it is complicated," said Sir Richard as he got up and began shaving. "Then of course Evan Fothergill could be man A and man B. He arrives in St. John's Close at eleven o'clock, creeps away at half-past one, does the murders and goes back to St. John's Close, eventually returning here at six the next morning. This means the complicity of Anne Landon, and I can hardly believe it. But stranger things have happened. They would try out all sorts of defences first; damn it, they have done. The first line will be that they were both peacefully in their beds and knew nothing about it. The second line is forced on Fothergill by the fact the President saw him. If that doesn't work he will, with Anne, resort to the joint line that they spent the night together. That was perhaps why he had to murder Gostlin, who would spoil this last line of defence. The leaving of the hat and the sacking of the maid may have been deliberate. Hell!" thought Sir Richard, "what possible depths of evil have I touched on here? Should I go on rootling into this problem, or leave it to the police, who will get to it eventually? After all, the girl Finch will go to them to-morrow; this kind of evidence cannot be suppressed.

"No," he said as he began to dress, "I'm damned if I'll leave the problem as it stands. I'll see both Anne Landon and Fothergill again this morning and get their proper stories, if I can. But first the President." He went in to his breakfast with misgivings.

II

The President was breakfasting when Sir Richard called on him. He had in front of him a large dish of Fish Kedgeree, over which he was pouring some hot butter-sauce.

"My dear Cherrington, come in, come in," he said. "Have some breakfast?"

"Good morning, sir. No, thank you," said Sir Richard. "I have already breakfasted."

"Ah! to be so early in vacation is to be late in term, I feel," said the President cheerfully, with an attempt at an aphorism. "Now, my good sir, what brings you here so early?"

"Well, sir, you will remember your surprising testimony to the Inspector yesterday," he began.

"Surprising?" queried the President, a shadow passing over his face.

"Yes, sir, I am bound to use the word surprising," went on Sir Richard firmly. "In that you virtually brought a charge of murder against one of the junior members of the Senior Combination Room."

"My dear Cherrington, please, please," said the President, his uncertainty growing. "Do not imagine it did not pain me quite as much as it does you. I thought over the matter for a very long time, but I could come to no other conclusion than that it was my duty to report what I had seen to the police."

"But, sir, exactly what did you see?" persisted Sir Richard.

"But I told you yesterday," went on the President crossly. "I am afraid that I saw young Fothergill at two-fifteen or so in the morning walking rapidly away from a spot near the bank of the Cam where next day the revolver was found."

"I know that, sir," said Sir Richard, "and at the time your statement seemed completely convincing."

"At the time?" said the President sharply. "Really, Richard, I don't know quite what you are driving at."

"It's just this," said Sir Richard. "You can have made no mistake about the place at which you say you saw the person, but it is very easy to make a mistake about the time one wakes up at night and what one sees out through the window in the dark."

"But the moon was bright," protested the President.

"I suggest, Mr. President, that you woke in the night, and heard the clocks strike, and thought it was two o'clock."

"But I would have checked that by my little bedside clock," said the President.

"Would have?" went on Sir Richard. "Would have, yes. But did you?"

"I suppose I did." The President was now thoroughly alarmed.

"If that was the case," said Sir Richard slowly, "you had your near-sight spectacles on, I suppose."

"I suppose I did," said the President and paused. He got up from the table. "You mean," he went on, "that if that was the case I couldn't have recognised Fothergill when I looked out through the window. Unless, of course, I changed my spectacles, and I certainly do not remember doing such a thing in the middle of the night."

"Yes," said Sir Richard. "Or it means you did recognise Fothergill, and so had your long-sight spectacles on, and so perhaps did not check the time on the clock, and it might not have been two o'clock."

"This is all very awkward," said the President—"very awkward indeed. I thought I had gone into the whole matter most carefully."

"Please do not imagine," went on Cherrington affably, "that I am trying to shake your testimony. I am just thinking of your testimony as it would appear in a Court of Law, and I am thinking, too, that good defending Counsel for Fothergill would have no difficulty in picking holes in it."

"My dear Cherrington, a Court of Law? Surely you exaggerate."

"No, sir. As far as I can see at the moment, yours is the only direct evidence that connects Fothergill with the crime."

"The only evidence?"

"Yes. That is why I felt it incumbent on me to discuss it with you and make sure you realised all the implications. I only did so after leaving you yesterday."

"And your advice?"

"Well, sir, since you ask for it, I would get hold of the College solicitor.

Mr. Mackworth will surely advise, and will probably come with you to the police station so that your statement can be—er—amplified"—he had nearly said "corrected." "You must tell them, I think, about the spectacles."

"Yes, yes. Quite so, quite so. I will do that," said the President. "Thank you. I will ring Mackworth and go this morning."

Sir Richard took his leave, glad for the sake of the College that he had taken that line with the President, but sorry for the old man's confusion.

The President was standing looking out through his window when Sir Richard crossed the Backs. "I wonder who that is," he thought, peering myopically out the while. He turned into the room and picked up the telephone directory. "Let me see, Mackworth and Charteris; here we are." He sighed. "All this is so distasteful," he said—"so distasteful."

III

Anne Landon was in her little sitting-room when Sir Richard arrived. He was shown up there, and despite her cordial greeting he sensed a difference. There was first a difference in her manner; it seemed a little more distant. "Maybe she resents her outpourings of yesterday," he thought. "Or maybe she thinks I have discovered something." He looked round the room. Something seemed to have changed there also, but he could not be quite sure what it was.

"Well, Richard," she greeted him. "Nice to see you again, and so soon."

"Glad you are still feeling so fit and well," he said. "Remember I am calling for you in my car at one-forty-five this afternoon to take you down to the inquest."

She shuddered. "That hateful business. I wish it was all over."

"Then I understand the arrangements for the funeral are fixed for to-morrow," he said, pursuing the matter relentlessly.

"Yes, yes," she said impatiently. "It's all so sordid. The sooner we realise he is dead and the whole business finished, the better. We have all our lives to lead, and the College must return to normal," she added lamely.

"I am afraid the police will not take that view," he said.

"The police," she said contemptuously; "I've told the police all I know."

"All you know?" Sir Richard queried gently.

"Certainly," she said.

"You see," began Sir Richard—it was going to be rather difficult to explain—"the President thinks he saw Evan Fothergill leaving the College about two-fifteen."

"I know. Evan has told me," she replied; "but of course it is all rubbish. The Dean must have mistaken Evan for the murderer."

"That's not all, you see," said Sir Richard. "I arrived on the scene of the crime at six-fifteen on Tuesday morning, and Fothergill was there then and, what is more, fully dressed."

She seemed a little taken aback at this, but said quickly, "Does that make him a murderer?"

"No, of course not. But he says he was awakened by his bedmaker, and dressed and came down at once. He would naturally be in a hurry, yet he put on an overcoat and gloves, and shoes and socks and a tie."

"Well, that's possible. I don't see what you are driving at, Richard."

"Well, you see, my dear Anne, he wasn't called by his bedmaker—his bedmaker had fainted, and when she went to call him he was already up."

"Perhaps the commotion in the Court woke him up," she suggested. "In any case, it's not our business to rake up all his doings," she added tartly.

"But it is mine," went on Cherrington seriously. "I am interested both in Fothergill and yourself. Believe me, I am. And I was interested in your husband, who had many good qualities despite your—and the general public's—dislike of him. And I'm interested in getting this crime and its attendant mystery cleared from the College."

"Come, Richard, you're not making a speech now," she began.

"You must treat this seriously, Anne," he went on. "You see, I haven't told you all I know." He smiled. "I've been listening to servant's gossip, I am afraid."

She spun round. "Servant's gossip? You mean Doris Finch? That detestable girl!"

"She told me her story," he replied. "And will be telling it to the police."

"Story?" she said. "There isn't a story. It's all imagination. I'm surprised at you, with your critical mind, being taken in by such a tale."

"And the hat?" asked Cherrington.

"Some old hat of Bill's," replied Mrs. Landon quickly. "She just hadn't noticed it before."

"The police will ask you to produce it, you know," he said.

She was silent.

"And the strange man at eleven o'clock?" he went on.

"Listen, Richard," proceeded Mrs. Landon. "You must listen to me. This girl has a grudge against me and is inventing this story. There was no strange man at eleven o'clock. A great mystery is being made out of nothing."

"Aren't you forgetting that her young man also saw this mysterious stranger?"

She paused. "Oh, let's leave the whole thing," she replied. "Why should you and I bother? It's for the police to do that."

He was quiet a moment, and then he said, "I am trying to help you—to help both you and Evan Fothergill. These things must be looked at from the point of view of the police, and if necessary from that of twelve jurymen. In a court of justice the testimony of Doris Finch and her young man Bert will count as much as yours and that of Evan Fothergill."

"A court of justice?" She was shaken.

"I'm afraid all these matters will one day get there. Think of yourself before good counsel. What will be your answers to his questions? When did that hat get here? Who was around the house at eleven o'clock? Why did you sack Doris Finch? How are you so sure of Evan Fothergill's innocence?"

He paused and took off his spectacles, cleaning them with a large silk handkerchief.

"Won't you and Evan Fothergill tell the truth now?" he said. "It would be so much simpler."

"The truth?" she said, looking at him warily.

"My dear Anne," said Sir Richard, " the President thinks he saw Evan Fothergill leave College soon after the time of the murder. He was probably mistaken, but instead of telling us the truth, Fothergill invents a great story about writing letters and posting them and seeing your husband and then walking about the Backs in anguish. Why doesn't he tell the truth?" He paused. "It's because he wants to shield you."

"Shield me?"

"Surely the facts can have only one interpretation. Evan left College about a quarter to eleven, and was seen at your house by the girl Finch and her Bert at eleven o'clock. I saw him fully dressed in College, but without his hat, at six-fifteen the next morning. He had obviously just come back from this house, and left his hat behind. He had obviously been here the whole night. Now, I'm not condemning either of you," he went on hurriedly. "You are obviously both very much in love. And it won't sound very good if it gets into the papers. I mean, 'Dean's Wife Misconducts Herself with Junior Fellow as Husband is Murdered' is how the popular papers will get it, I'm afraid."

Anne winced.

"If you love Evan all that much," said Sir Richard softly, "do one thing more for him. Stop him going on in this foolish way, manufacturing stories for the police. They already suspect him, and these tales will add to their suspicions. Tell the police the truth."

She looked hard at him. "That we spent the night together from eleven o'clock and that he left at six o'clock?"

"My dear Anne, be reasonable," said Cherringfon. "It is the truth, isn't it?"

"If you say so, Richard, of course it is." Her reaction surprised him. She burst out laughing, almost hysterical laughter. "All right. Let's go and tell the police the truth. Let's go at once."

Sir Richard was startled. "It is the truth, of course, isn't it?" he said. "The time for misleading the police is surely over, if it ever existed."

"Yes, it's the truth," she said almost gaily. "It is all just as you said. You've been very clever, Richard—very clever indeed."

And, laughing, she led the way out of the house and to his car. Sir Richard followed her with some misgivings.

IV

Cherrington's misgivings increased as he drove the car round to the front gate of Fisher College. Mrs. Landon had not said a word all through the journey.

"Stay here, Anne, please," he said, not unkindly, "while I go and see Evan Fothergill. Then we can all go to the police station together."

Fothergill was not in his rooms, but according to Mrs. Harris, his bed-maker, who was tidying his fireplace when Sir Richard called, he had gone across to the Combination Room to read the morning papers. Sir Richard found him there, and in seemingly very good spirits.

"Morning, Sir Richard," he said. "By the way, last night I remembered a thing I forgot to tell the police yesterday."

"Yes," said Sir Richard hopefully. "What was that?"

"As I was pacing up and down the Backs on Monday night I noticed a car drawn up outside the back gate."

"Well?" asked Cherrington. This was not what he had expected.

"Oh, I thought it might have something to do with the murders, you know. Might be able to trace it. I told the Inspector, and he seemed interested."

Sir Richard brushed the incident of the car away as another ludicrous invention. Why couldn't these people tell the truth? They went plunging farther and farther into a morass of lies. He was more brusque than he had been with Mrs. Landon.

"Fothergill," he said, " you told me, and you told the police, that you slept on Tuesday morning until Mrs. Harris woke you. Is that true?"

"It is," he said, his eyes narrowing slightly. "I'm rather hazy about these details, you know."

"Mrs. Harris says she did not wake you. I noticed you were fully dressed in the Screens at six-fifteen. How was this?"

"Really, Sir Richard, is this an interrogation? I don't really remember. I expect the noise in the Court woke me up and I dressed and came down. I dress very quickly, you know," he added.

" You must do," said Sir Richard. "You did not forget your tie or collar or gloves, did you? Why did you forget your hat?"

"My hat?" The shaft had struck home. Sir Richard could see that, and he pursued his advantage.

"Yes," he said. "Why did you leave your hat in St. John's Close when you came away in the morning?"

Fothergill's defences were down, but he fought bravely.

" What do you mean?" he asked.

"Don't let us waste any more time, Fothergill," said Sir Richard. "You were seen near St. John's Close at eleven o'clock on Monday night, and it is fairly obvious you left there at six o'clock on Tuesday morning, leaving your hat behind. Mrs. Landon admits you were with her all the time in between."

These remarks had an electric effect on Fothergill. "She admits all that," he gasped.

"She does," went on Cherrington. "I think you should be very proud that she loves you so much she is prepared to come forward, although as a result there will be a lot of unpleasant scandal. I'm not censuring either of you. You were both very much in love, but I wish you hadn't been so foolish as to invent these stories to the police in the false hope of shielding Mrs. Landon."

"My God!" said Fothergill. "That's funny, you know. That's bloody funny. So you don't censure us?" He gave a short laugh.

Some of Sir Richard's misgivings began to return to him. "I know you are overwrought, Fothergill," he said. "But there is no time for more nonsense. Mrs. Landon is waiting at the front gate in my car, and I want you to come down and both go to the police and tell them the truth at last."

"Tell them that Anne and I were together from eleven until six?" asked Fothergill.

"Yes," went on Cherrington. "It might quite well be kept out of the papers."

"I'm ready," said Fothergill. "Let's go. I suppose you know what's best."

They went down to the car. Fothergill and Mrs. Landon greeted each other in a strained, distant way and did not speak a word to each other while Cherrington drove to the police station. Sir Richard's heart began to sink. "This is somehow not the triumphant breaking of the police case against Fothergill that I had hoped it would be," he said to himself. "And yet I can't be wrong. The facts are quite plain."

V

Sir Richard drove his car into the yard of the Cambridge Police Headquarters. Inspector Wyndham had transferred his office from Fisher College. As he went up the stairs, leaving Evan Fothergill and Anne Landon in the car, he met Sergeant Mossop.

"Sergeant," he said, " Dr. Fothergill and Mrs. Landon are in my car—the blue Bentley—in the yard. They have some rather important evidence to give Inspector Wyndham. See they don't run away."

"Certainly, sir," said Mossop.

Inspector Wyndham was poring over some papers when Sir Richard came in.

"Good morning, Sir Richard," he said.

"Hello," said Cherrington. "Don't get up, please." He drew up a chair alongside Wyndham. "How's the case going?" he asked.

"Oh, just so-so," said the Inspector, non-committally. "The Chief Constable was much impressed by the evidence of Dr. Quibell. We are working on it now."

"I spent all day yesterday working on it," said Sir Richard rather wearily.

"You, sir?" queried the Inspector. "Are you turning into an amateur detective?"

"Suppose I am. I spent a while trying to blow your case against Parrott to smithereens."

"Fairly successfully too, if I may say so, sir."

"Huh. Well, I've blown the case against Fothergill sky-high."

" Yes?"—the Inspector was still non-committal.

"To start with, the President is not sure of his testimony now. He can't swear to the times, or exactly to identifying Fothergill. He's coming along this morning with his solicitor to see you and change his statement. Amplify was the word I used myself," added Sir Richard, with the ghost of a smile.

"Oh, that's serious," said the Inspector, taken aback.

"It is, and that's not all," went on Sir Richard. "Dr. Fothergill didn't spend the night in College, as he said. There were no nocturnal perambulations on the Backs, as he declared. No, I'm afraid he spent the night in St. John's Close with Mrs. Landon. Won't make a good headline, will it, if the case comes to court?"

The Inspector registered the frankest astonishment.

"You've got evidence for all this?" he said.

"I have indeed," went on Sir Richard. "Evan Fothergill admits it. Anne Landon admits it. The maid, since sacked, but to be found at 12 Portugal Place—her name is Doris Finch—saw him arrive when walking with her young man, Bert—haven't got his name, left some work for the police—in the Madingley Road at eleven o'clock on Monday night. Same maid noticed when she went next morning to work that there was a strange hat in the house. That's probably Fothergill's hat, but I leave you to work out all that. I noticed myself that Fothergill was on the scene of the crime fully clad at six-fifteen—but without a hat—his bedmaker affirms that she didn't call him as he previously declared."

"Well, my goodness," said the Inspector. "That is a bombshell. 12 Portugal Place—Doris Finch, you say?" he said, writing on a pad.

"That's right, but I've got the two main witnesses outside. I brought Fothergill and Mrs. Landon in my car. Mossop is looking after them, and they want to make fresh statements."

"You'll have to make one too, I'm afraid," said the Inspector. "I mean about noticing Fothergill fully dressed at six-fifteen and all that. You didn't, I think, mention it in your first statement," he added, reproachfully.

"No, I didn't. 'Fraid I didn't think of it until yesterday."

The Inspector got up. "May I congratulate you, sir, on a very good bit of detection?"

"Huh," said Sir Richard. "It's my last bit. I'll make that statement for you and attend the inquest this afternoon and all that, but I do want to get away. All this is getting on my nerves. Do you think I could get away on Monday or Tuesday? I had planned to go on a motoring tour in Brittany for ten days, beginning next Wednesday."

"Oh, I think so. Yes, sir, surely. We've had all we want from you," said the Inspector, "and we shall always be able to get into touch with you."

"I don't know. I shall be touring about on no fixed plan. But I'll be back in a week or so, and Dr. Quibell and Mr. Westmacott will deal with all collegiate business in the meanwhile."

"Quite so, sir. Well, I hope you have a pleasant holiday. We shall be seeing each other again at the inquest, but I may not have a chance to talk with you then."

"Thank you."

"And thank you again for your co-operation."

"Not at all."

As he went away down the stairs the Inspector said to himself: "That really is a puzzle. Now why should Sir Richard interest himself so much in this case to the extent of questioning bedmakers and servant girls and so forth? Anyway, I shall give Fothergill and Mrs. Landon a pretty severe time. I'll see them separately, of course." He rang a bell for an orderly.

Sir Richard drove away down Regent Street. He looked at his watch. Just eleven o'clock. What a morning! And now he must change and get to Gostlin's funeral. It was all so dreary and morbid. Somewhere there must be a person in this case with a power of hate and loathing, and a violent nature such that he could commit this murder. Who was it? Who was the mysterious stranger seen by the President at two-fifteen? "It's not my job, anyway," said Sir Richard as he garaged his car and arranged for a taxi to collect him at a quarter to twelve. "I must get back to my scientific papers and my pottery sequences and my relative chronology and all the rest of it. I've finished with this case."

But, in this, he was wrong.

VI

That evening the Chief Constable and Inspector Wyndham were having a grill in the Castle Hotel before going home. It had been very late when they came back from the inquest at Twyford, and over a pair of good steaks and several pints of beer they had discussed the case in a private corner of the room.

"You've been at it now for only five days, I know," said the Chief Constable. "But I'd like your considered views and also some indication on the ways we are proposing to work."

"It's not easy, sir," said Wyndham, rather uncomfortably. "I made out a list of suspects a few days ago and have been testing out each one against the light of any new evidence we get."

"Good, yes. Now, who are on your list?"

"First, there's Parrott. We still have a possible case against him. Granted he came in at three-thirty, the murders could have been done then. It is the latest time allowed by the medical authorities."

"And the evidence of that undergraduate, Wintringham or Willowbottom. What was it?"

"You mean Willerby, sir," said the Inspector. "Well, his evidence wasn't exactly conclusive proof of the time of the murder."

"No, agreed. But Dr. Quibell? What do you think that old dodderer saw out of his window, peering perhaps through the wrong spectacles in the wrong direction. What? Do you think he saw anything?"

"I'm afraid we can't put too much weight on his evidence."

"We certainly can't. The distressing thing in this case is that every time you get hold of a fact, it turns out to be something else. Not a fact at all. Rather like the rope trick. What?"

"Of course any other undergraduate is a possibility—particularly Farnaby, who was next door—but with them the problem of motive comes in. Parrott had a kind of motive. Pretty well any of the Fellows can be included, too," went on the Inspector despondently, "from Dr. Quibell downwards. Their alibis are not perfect ones, especially this latest one of Fothergill's. Then, apart from Fothergill, it's the question of motive with the others; they had plenty of academic tiffs—disputes about the running of the chapel and about various articles and views, but it would surprise me if they were really justification for murder."

"Never know, of course," interrupted the Colonel. "Strange folk, these academics. Live together all the time. Exaggerate little things. Might murder one of themselves. Rather like two old women in a parish bazaar committee-meeting tearing out handsful of each other's hair. What?"

"Yes, sir," agreed the Inspector. "But I don't see it explains the murder of the porter Gostlin." He paused. "At one stage I'd rather favoured Sir Richard Cherrington as the murderer."

The Colonel looked surprised. "Really," he said. "I should be sorry if that were the case. Nice person. I liked him despite the fact he eats too largely at breakfast. Lady Gough Clarke says he's an entertaining body. Must get him to see my things from India sometime."

"I know I haven't got much of a case against him, sir, but I was interested in his tremendous library of detective fiction and of trials and books on criminology. I was wondering if he mightn't have planned all this as an ingenious experiment in crime. It gets rid of an unpleasant Dean at the same time."

"Don't think that will hold water," said the Colonel. "No, sir. Can't see him murdering the porter Gostlin."

"But that would be part of his plan to throw suspicion on someone from outside."

"Hm, hrmmph," barked the Colonel. "No. Somehow I don't think this old party Cherrington would commit two crimes which reflected so adversely on his College. Damn it, sir, it's like suggesting that a commanding officer would murder two of his officers in the Mess. Human nature's very odd, I grant you. Seen some mighty odd things in India. But there's always some pattern behind the oddness."

"That's the trouble I've had so far, sir," went on Wyndham. "This is a case in which means and opportunity help one not at all. I've tried to concentrate on motive, and that left me only with Fothergill. Traherne and Wedgwood disliked Landon, and Wedgwood was the last person to see him alive, but they don't seem to me motives for murder, as I've already said. And while Parrott had a motive for disliking the Dean, murdering him didn't improve Parrott's lot very much. I'm left, then, with Fothergill, and now Sir Richard's bit of detection has removed him from me."

"Cherrington seems to have been a little embarrassing to us in this case, doesn't he?" said the Chief Constable.

"Yes, sir, but we should have found out in the end all the facts he discovered." He paused. "I'm afraid I'm left with only my mysterious Mr. X who came in from outside and committed his murders and departed again unseen, except perhaps by Dr. Quibell. We know nothing about him except that he had a car and might have been dressed in a loose-fitting overcoat and felt hat."

"I didn't get the point about the car?" asked the Chief Constable sharply.

"Yes, sir. Fothergill talks about a car at the back gate of the College."

"But that was in his bogus statement that has now been recanted, wasn't it?" asked Cunningham Hardy. "If he was at St. John's Close with Mrs. Landon from eleven o'clock, he couldn't have identified cars at the back gate in the middle of the night." He paused. "And yet it is a curious thing to have invented."

"I suppose that disposes of the car," said Wyndham gloomily. "I'm left with Mr. X, about whom we know nothing except that he might have been seen by the President."

There was a pause.

"We've got no more lines to work on?" asked the Chief Constable.

"Afraid not, sir. I'm doing all the routine stuff, but it doesn't seem to get us anywhere."

"Need some help?"

Inspector Wyndham knew this was coming sooner or later.

"You mean Scotland Yard, sir?"

"Yes."

"I think so, sir. We're stuck." He sighed.

"Good man! I hoped you would take it like that. Mind you, I'm quite prepared to leave you to go on for a few days still if you have something to work on, but it all seems a blank at the moment. This is a big case. All sorts of interests involved. We can't afford to bungle it."

They walked out into the night. The Colonel had his car. Inspector Wyndham was cycling home.

"See you in the morning," the Colonel said. "Don't take this too much to heart." He leaned out of the car and said in a whisper, "As a matter of fact I shall be most interested to see how Scotland Yard tackle this case. It won't be easy for them." And he drove off.

Inspector Wyndham cycled slowly down the Hills Road to his flat. A cold wind blew across the road, and brought with it noises of engines shunting from the station near by. A great lumbering two-decker bus rode by, its tyres making a loud swishing noise. He was past the Catholic church, with its spire and illuminated clock. "Five minutes to eleven", he registered mechanically. "Five nights ago at this time Fothergill was walking towards the Landon house." Cyclists passed Wyndham in both directions. He felt chill and miserable. "I suppose," he said to himself, "I've failed—failed rather badly." He cycled despondently on into the night.

BOOK III

SUPERINTENDENT ROBERTSON-MACDONALD INVESTIGATES

CHAPTER TWELVE

SCOTLAND YARD TAKES A HAND

It was tea-time on Saturday when a large car drew up outside the main police station at Cambridge and Detective-Superintendent Robertson-Macdonald got out. He had been pleased, and not a little flattered, when the Commissioner had sent for him early that morning and said that the Cambridge Murders were now to become a Scotland Yard responsibility.

"You are not a Cambridge man yourself, I know," said the Commissioner, who in his youth had been a rowing Light Blue, " but we need someone who understands the academic world and the mentality of dons and undergraduates to deal with this case, and during your three years in Oxford," he had added scornfully, "it is possible you may have absorbed something of value which may help in the unravelling of this tiresome mystery of the two murders. Never thought much of Fisher College myself," he had continued inconsequentially, "but a chap Farnaby, now in business in town—he was up the same time as myself, and rowed in the boat with me. Good chap! Apart from this man, I'm afraid I know nothing about the place."

Robertson-Macdonald had been given a free hand to select his assistants, and had come down with Detective-Inspector Fleming and Sergeant Waddell, both of whom had worked with him on several big cases. He had spent the whole of Saturday morning working through the Scotland Yard dossiers of the Cambridge murders, reading with particular care Inspector Wyndham's report. His first call at Cambridge had been on the Chief Constable, who had been out playing golf. However, Inspector Wyndham had welcomed him warmly.

"It's a difficult case, Superintendent," Wyndham had said—"an extremely difficult case. Of course it may not appear so to you, with your wide experience of these complicated criminal cases, but to the Chief Constable and myself it appears most complex."

"It's rather early in the history of the case as yet, isn't it?" the Superintendent had said gently. "I mean the murders were only committed on Monday night, and the body of the Dean only discovered on Wednesday morning. It's Saturday now, isn't it? We can't expect complete results in five days, you know. Sometimes these cases take weeks and months to unravel."

"Yes, I know," said Wyndham. "I've been impatient, and as it's our first big case here in Cambridge during my time, we have naturally been anxious to solve it ourselves without the assistance of Scotland Yard."

The Superintendent smiled. "That's quite natural, isn't it?" he said.

"I suppose so," agreed Wyndham. "But what has depressed me so much in these few days is the apparent ease of the case. From the beginning there have been clues, possible motives leading to different members of the College, both senior and junior, but in the end, when we track them down or examine them, they lead nowhere."

"Of course, that is the trouble," said Robertson-Macdonald. "Set a crime in a large household, and you will uncover plenty of motive and plenty of opportunity. Set it in a College, which is just a very large household, and you multiply your possibilities of motive and opportunity. It is only in the hotel and other artificially created situations of the detective novel that a murder happens without trace of motive. Normally our job is not to get hold of a criminal who has left behind no traces—although that often happens—but to find out which of many people could be the criminal."

"Yes," agreed Wyndham. "You've read through my notes on the case?" he asked.

"I have. They have been most helpful," said the Superintendent graciously. "But I haven't yet had time to study all the evidence in detail."

"Quite so, sir," said the Inspector. "All we have on the case is in these dossiers, and naturally I shall be at your disposal throughout the time you are in Cambridge."

"I am sure we shall value your assistance immensely," said the Superintendent.

"I've gone over the case carefully with the Chief Constable," went on Wyndham. "And one might say, in academic jargon"—he smiled—"that there are two schools of thought at the moment. The Internal School—that the murder was done by an undergraduate or servant or don; Giles Farnaby or John Parrott or Sir Richard Cherrington or Evan Fothergill, or practically anyone else you care to name."

"Yes?" said the Superintendent encouragingly.

"Most of these people can be connected in some way with the deaths, but the motives are weak and the connecting evidence by no means conclusive." He paused. "The other school is the External one—murder by some person or persons unknown from outside. That's the trouble: our murderer, if he came from outside, was unseen, unheard, unknown—unless of course he was seen by the President. It looks as if the murderer, if he came from outside, got away without being seen or without leaving a clue."

"In fact, you mean the perfect murder?" queried the Superintendent, smiling.

"Something like that, sir."
"No," said Robertson-Macdonald slowly. "The perfect murder doesn't occur."
"Really sir?"
"No. Well, not in my experience of these things," qualified the Superintendent. "I mean it is often impossible to bring a man to court and produce evidence on which an English jury are prepared to convict, and in that sense, of carrying out a murder the legal consequences of which you can reasonably hope to avoid, I am afraid there are perfect murders. But in the sense of carrying out a murder of which the police are not eventually satisfied that they know the author—no, in that sense there are no perfect murders."
"I'm very glad to hear it," said Wyndham. "I hope this case will not turn out to be a perfect murder in either sense."
"It's too early to say yet."
"Yes, quite. May I ask how you propose to get to work?"
"You may," said Robertson-Macdonald. "I've brought with me Inspector Fleming and Sergeant Waddell. They are down in our car at the moment. With them and with your assistance and that of your staff I hope to get a lot of work done in the next fortnight. First I want to go to Fisher College to-night and see very briefly the scene of the crime. Then I should pay my respects to the College authorities—let me see, it's a President they have in Fisher, isn't it?"
"It is, but he isn't really very much use in the administrative concerns of the College. He's an old man, and rather a recluse, I should say. The real power in the College is the Vice-President, Sir Richard Cherrington."
"Ah, yes," said Robertson-Macdonald. "The archæologist?"
"You know him?"
"Know of him. Read one or two of his books allegedly written for the public in a popular style. Damned dry, but quite interesting if you plough through them. Let's go and meet him."
"And all these papers and dossiers that we have prepared?" the Inspector asked.
"Put them in my despatch-case. I'll take them with me and go through them carefully."
They walked to the Scotland Yard car and drove down Regent Street and Sidney Street and drew up outside the Front Lodge of Fisher College in Trinity Street. Robertson-Macdonald looked attentively at everything he saw.
"Excellent," he said, looking up at the Gate Tower and the front façade of the College, lit by the late March afternoon sun. "Whatever it's criminal interior, this College has an æsthetically satisfactory exterior."
They went into the Porter's Lodge, and were met by Mr. Baynes.

"Good afternoon, Mr. Baynes," said Wyndham. "I've brought Detective-Superintendent Robertson-Macdonald to see you. Scotland Yard," he added. "He's in charge of the case now."

"How do you do?" said Baynes, eyeing the Superintendent with suspicion. "Pleased to meet you, I'm sure. Wish you all luck."

"I shall need it," said the Superintendent agreeably. "At the moment I shall be glad if you can find out if the President can see me."

"President is out," said Baynes. "He left College in cap and gown about a half-hour ago, to go to a meeting of the Council of the Senate. Won't be back until nearly Hall time."

"I see. And the—er—Vice-President, Professor Cherrington. Is he in?"

"I'll find out, sir." Mr. Baynes went to the internal telephone exchange in the Porter's Lodge, and while he was busying himself ringing up Sir Richard, Robertson-Macdonald looked round carefully.

"Quite like my undergraduate days," he said to Wyndham. "I mean, being back in a College and dealing with porters. The salt of the earth, you know," he added. "The salt of the earth. No," he said, ruminating, "he shouldn't have killed Gostlin. That was bad—very bad. It gives me an added reason in tracking him down."

Inspector Wyndham looked puzzled.

"Ah, well," said the Superintendent, enlightening him, " it's possible there were very special reasons why the Dean had to be killed, and if they were tremendous enough, I can see a man nerving himself up to the ordeal of doing it. In a way, that is courageous—anti-social, of course, but one can appreciate it. But the murder of the porter in cold blood—no, that shows a brutal, callous, hard nature. Probably all the more difficult to catch, but we must do so. After all," he said, smiling at the still rather puzzled Wyndham, "we can expect to be murdered for our misdeeds, but in a reasonable society we should not run the risk of being murdered because we happened to be present when someone else's misdeeds were being expiated. No; we must get this man and see he is hanged."

Mr. Baynes came back. Sir Richard would be delighted to see the Superintendent.

Roberston-Macdonald told his assistants to take a look round, and went into the College with Wyndham. They walked first through First Court, then through the Screens, crossed Second Court, went out through the river gate on the bridge and back again to Sir Richard's staircase. Wyndham pointed out the main places in the case—the Screens the President's Lodging and the Backs, and finally G staircase.

Sir Richard welcomed them both cheerfully.

"My dear Superintendent," he said. "How charming to see you! Do sit down. Now, something to drink, gentlemen? Sherry? Beer? Whisky?"

"That's very kind of you, Sir Richard," said the Superintendent. "Some beer would be delightful."

"Yes, some beer. Very kind of you," echoed Wyndham.

"I see you are a man of taste, Superintendent," said Sir Richard. "It is, as you rightly appreciated, a time only for beer. It is a little too early for sherry, and one's palate should never be spoiled before dinner with the rougher and more violent drinks made with whisky and gin and other spirits."

He went into his gyp-room and drew them pints from the barrel he always kept there. He brought them back and handed them round.

"Here's health," he said. "And I drink to your good luck in this case, Superintendent."

"Cheerio; thank you, sir," said the Superintendent. "A very good drop of beer, if I may say so."

"I'm glad you like it. It's our ordinary College beer."

"It's very fine. Almost as good, if I may say so, as the B.N.C. draught when I was up at Oxford."

The Vice-President looked at the Superintendent with renewed interest. "You are a 'Varsity man, are you?" he said. "What attracted you into the police?"

"Various things," answered the Superintendent. He had answered this question many times before. "The war broke out after I had finished my course in Oxford. When it was over I was unsettled, tried my hand at a number of jobs, and eventually joined the Metropolitan Police, hoping to get into the C.I.D. eventually."

"And you achieved your desire?"

"I did, sir, and have never regretted it."

"I can only hope," said the Vice-President, "that your experience and ability will solve our mystery here. I have been interested in crime myself for many years—not as a participant, I should hasten to add—but merely as an observer. I have a large library of detective fiction and of books on crime and criminal science."

"Sir Richard has helped us on one or two points," interrupted Inspector Wyndham. "You will see all his evidence in the dossiers. We were interested in the movements of John Parrott and Dr. Fothergill, and he helped us to get the truth on them."

"It was nothing," said Sir Richard, brushing the matter aside. "As a matter of fact, the little adventures in detection interested me, but the major problem is one for the professional."

"I am sure we are very grateful to you," said the Superintendent.

"I shall watch your work with great interest," went on Sir Richard—"great interest indeed—and perhaps when it is done, as I am sure it will be done, successfully, you will let me know how you went to work over it. At the moment it seems to me you have to start with no clue whatsoever. Will you promise to tell me just how you went to work, and the whole process? It will be of fascinating interest as an intellectual problem."

"I will indeed," said the Superintendent. "But most of these things resolve themselves into very simple and dull routine. There are not many startling deductions and discoveries. I cannot agree with you, for instance, that there are no clues. There are a great number."

"Really," said Sir Richard, and Inspector Wyndham looked up.

"But certainly," said the Superintendent. "We are particularly fortunate in this case in having a number of statements—particularly a number of statements from the same people." He looked up. "Even, Sir Richard, from you."

"Quite so," said Cherrington hurriedly. "I was foolish to conceal the evidence of the button. Most stupid of me."

"You see, sir," Robertson-Macdonald went on. "If people are lying, or even if they are merely making statements in which the major facts are hidden, particularly if they are hidden from them themselves, a succession of different statements is of fascinating interest. One must work out all the discrepancies between everybody's statements, and also the differences in successive statements of the same witness." He paused. "It is my belief there must always be a good reason for every discrepancy. I haven't yet had time to study the statements in this case in full, but I know that they hold tremendous clues."

"So that is how you will begin?" said Sir Richard.

"Yes. First I shall go through all the papers and statements that exist in the case and note down every difference. These I shall check on. It will probably mean re-examining several of the witnesses."

"I see," said Sir Richard. "I was hoping to go away myself on Tuesday of next week. I am planning a short motoring holiday in Brittany. I have some archæological sites to see, and I am taking my nephew, Giles Farnaby, of this College, who needs a change. Will that be all right?"

"Surely, surely," replied the Superintendent. "I shall know in a day or two the extra questions I will want to ask you, sir—that is, if there are any."

"Yes," said Sir Richard. "I shall be glad to help if I can. Where will your headquarters be?"

"Oh, at the police station. I have two assistants, Inspector Fleming and Sergeant Waddell. I myself want to go away alone for a day or two and go through these statements. Then I shall come back and begin to re-examine everyone."

"You mean you are going straight back to London?" queried Inspector Wyndham, astonished.

"No, not back to London. I want somewhere just outside Cambridge where I can be reached telephonically, but where I shall not be disturbed until Monday morning at least. I want to go through all these papers. Is there a suitable place?"

"Why not go to the Yellow Barn?" suggested Sir Richard. "It has good food, and there are usually a few rooms free looking down over the Fen. The place itself is a gay one over the week-end, but you can get quiet in one of the farmhouse outbuildings that have been converted into rooms."

"That's an idea," said the Superintendent. "Isn't that the place where Parrott and the girl were on the night of the murders? The name is familiar."

"Yes, that's right, sir," said Wyndham. "But it's about eight miles from Cambridge."

"Just suit me for the week-end," said Robertson-Macdonald. "Just what I want."

"I know the proprietress well," said Sir Richard. "Would you like me to telephone and fix you a room, if that is possible?"

"That's most kind of you."

"Not at all," said Sir Richard. "And your—er—lieutenants or assistants, or whatever you call them?"

"No, they will remain here in Cambridge."

"I see. If you will excuse me, I'll go into my study and telephone the Yellow Barn, and see if you can be accommodated there."

Sir Richard appreciated the Superintendent's desire for an undisturbed day or two to think out the large problem he was tackling.

Not so Inspector Wyndham, who thought the Superintendent's approach to the problem was a very strange one.

"You won't be in to-morrow, then?" he asked.

"No," said the Superintendent. "I shall go through all the papers to-morrow, and probably on Monday, perhaps not until after lunch, I will come in and discuss the whole matter with the Chief Constable and yourself, and we will plan our future campaign."

"You'll see the Chief Constable before you go to-night?"

"Oh yes. We will go back and see him straight away," said the Superintendent. "And, of course, I shall leave Inspector Fleming and Sergeant Waddell here in Cambridge. Waddell I shall leave with you, to be on the spot and to deal with all routine matters and get into conversation with everybody concerned in the case. I have the greatest faith in both the men I've brought down with me from the Yard. They are both excellent types, and have really been responsible for the solution of all the cases in which we have worked together. Fleming will get drinking with the porters and College servants and so forth who figure in this case, and he will get me the picture from that angle."

"I see, sir. And Sergeant Waddell?"

"Well, Waddell is my sort of historical expert."

"Historical expert?"

"Yes," went on the Superintendent, smiling. "You see, one is first presented with the characters in this murder without a background. It is just as if the curtain goes up on the first act of a play. We see them all in the sudden glare of the footlights. I always want to know, when I tackle a case, what the characters were doing before. Waddell does that for me. In a very short while he will have the family histories of everyone in this case: what the shady parts of their pasts have been, whether any of them have ever been in gaol or been under suspicion for anything. You have no idea what Waddell unearths when dealing with a murder case. Of course, lots of it is irrelevant, but when we have it we feel that we begin to know the people. The glare of the footlights is toning down."

Inspector Wyndham looked a little dubious. He was certainly put off by the Superintendent's easy and, as he thought, slightly extravagant conversation. At this moment Sir Richard came in, saying that he had fixed a room for the Superintendent at the Yellow Barn, and with a further exchange of compliments, the Superintendent and Inspector Wyndham took their leave. "Huh," thought Wyndham, "these College types are all the same. Lots of talk. I wonder will the Superindendent make anything of this job, and I wonder, too, what the Chief Constable will think of him."

As he sat in his rooms, Sir Richard thought much the same thought. "A trifle confident, this Robertson-Mac-what's-his-name," he said to himself. "His talk about discrepancies and statements and plenty of clues was a little facile. Perhaps it was put on to impress Wyndham—the Scotland Yard man doing his stuff in the provinces. And yet, is there anything in it?" Sir Richard drew himself another pint of beer and set it down on the table beside his desk. He took out his snuff-box and inhaled some tobacco. "Didn't like his reference to the discrepancies in my statements, for instance. Now, let me see, I only made two statements, didn't I? First, that I was asleep all night and knew nothing about it all until woken up in the morning. Then, of course, I lied about the button and then admitted it. Damn it!" said Sir Richard, "then, of course, I remembered the bit about Fothergill being dressed. The man's quite right: I did really make three separate statements. I wonder if it was the same with everyone else? I suppose he will work on what we told last and why we suppressed it before. Well, I wish him luck. This mystery has nothing to do with me. As an intellectual problem it is no longer of interest: I have no lines to work on. It is now just a routine police matter of checking statements and so forth. As a human matter it is finished: I am fed up with the Landon–Fothergill intrigue. Bill Landon is dead and I do not know anyone who hated him really hard enough to do the murder." And yet, something said inside him, it's bloody intriguing.

He turned to his desk, a very untidy collection of papers and books and notes. Sir Richard was always engaged on several pieces of work, and never had the strength of mind to put some away in a drawer while he was working on others. He picked up the draft of an article he had written for *Antiquity* and began to go through it, altering a word and occasionally getting up to check a reference in a book.

After a while he came to a footnote reference that wanted checking in *Archæologia.* It was always one of Sir Richard's regrets that he did not possess a complete set of the early volumes of *Archæologia.* It meant him having to trudge down to the College Library to check it. Should he do it to-night, or leave it until the morning? No: this article must be finished before he went away, and there were several other pieces of work to be done as well. He looked at his watch. A quarter to seven. The Library would still be open. He picked up his typescript and walked down across the Court, through the Screens and over to the Library. It was a typical evening out of term: no one about, the Courts dark and cheerless, a few lights burning from behind heavily curtained windows. As he passed through the Screens a slight shudder went through his body. "This violence," he thought, "all the violence involved in these murders is revolting. The idea of murder as an intellectual exercise I can enjoy: and the intricacies of detective fiction I enjoy, but the thought of the violence involved and the dark passions that must have been engendered—the plotting and planning, and then—now, what was the murderer thinking? Was he happy, his purpose achieved? Or was he waiting, watchful, afraid, lest the police get on his track?"

He shrugged his shoulders, opened the heavy oak door of the Library and passed into its scholarly calm. The smell of the early bound books and of the polish on the bookcases met him, and he was reassured. The Library was empty save for Peter Gough Clarke, the Librarian. Peter Gough Clarke was the Junior Fellow of the College, a young historian of promise, and, in addition to undertaking the teaching of history in the College, he was also Steward and Librarian, which were official jobs, and Editor of the College magazine, which was an unofficial job. He was the son of Lady Gough Clarke, of whose gossipings on the St. Ives golf course with Colonel Cunningham Hardy we have already heard.

Sir Richard checked his reference in the early and very musty volumes of *Archæologia,* and was about to leave the Library when Peter Gough Clarke stopped him.

"Good evening Sir Richard," he said. "Did you find what you wanted?"

"Yes, Peter, I did," said Sir Richard. Gough Clarke's query had obviously only been a polite one to open conversation, as Sir Richard knew his way about the Library much better than did the young Librarian. "What's worrying you?"

"Oh, there's nothing worrying me, Sir Richard," he said. "I wondered if you knew how the case was going?"

The case. Sir Richard groaned inwardly. Everywhere, everyone, would be talking about the Cambridge murders—"the case". It really was insupportable.

"'Fraid I don't," he lied. "The police don't take me into their confidence, you know, but I do know they have summoned Scotland Yard into it at last."

"Scotland Yard. Really?" The other was impressed. "And what are your opinions, sir?"

"Haven't got any," said Sir Richard shortly. "The whole thing is a great mystery to me, and a very unpleasant one. I liked Dr. Landon," he said rather firmly.

"Oh, yes, Sir Richard?" went on Gough Clarke hurriedly. "Yes, of course. So did I. But I think the real key to the murder is with Gostlin."

"With Gostlin?" Sir Richard's interest revived.

"Why, yes, sir," said Gough Clarke. "You see, we know someone murdered the Dean, and we could make a list of people who wanted to do so. My mother is quite prepared to make such a list," he said slyly.

Sir Richard smiled. "Yes," he said encouragingly.

"But no one is prepared to make a list of the people who wanted to kill Gostlin," went on the other quickly. "That's the point. There was only one man who wanted to kill Gostlin."

"Yes?" queried Sir Richard.

"Yes. The man who had murdered the Dean."

"But that gets us nowhere," said Sir Richard.

"Pardon me, sir, but it does," continued Peter Gough Clarke. "He murdered Gostlin because he couldn't have it reported that he had been seen in College that night. Don't you see, that must follow? If it had been an undergraduate or a Fellow who had met Gostlin, he could have bluffed it out. When the murder of the Dean was discovered some days later, Gostlin would remember that he had seen one of the Fellows at two o'clock walking through the Courts. It would be easy for a Fellow or an undergraduate to explain away his presence."

"Yes, I've always appreciated that," agreed Sir Richard. "But only if that Fellow or undergraduate lived in College."

"The undergraduate could say he was climbing out from a party."

"Yes, that's so," said Sir Richard. "So you think it must be a Fellow who resides outside. Wedgwood or Traherne or, of course, there's yourself." He smiled.

"No, sir," said Gough Clarke. "Not a non-resident Fellow. Somebody who would be easily recognised and who should not be near the College that night."

"Yes, but who?"

"I'll show you a photograph of him, Sir Richard," said the other triumphantly.

"You'll show me a photograph of him?" asked Cherrington, astonished.

"Yes, sir. Come this way," and Peter Gough Clarke took out from a drawer of his desk five large group photographs.

"But these are College groups," said Sir Richard.

"Yes, sir," said Gough Clarke. "I know they are. This is how it all seems to me. Gostlin was porter here from 1932 to 1937. In each Michaelmas term the undergraduates would be photographed, and Gostlin would pose with them and the other porters."

"Yes?" said Sir Richard, a trifle impatiently.

"As a porter," went on Gough Clarke, "he would know all these undergraduates very well by sight, and might even remember their names."

"Ah, yes," said Sir Richard, beginning to see what the young man was getting at. "You mean it might be one of the people who came up in these years. He would come back to murder the Dean, having some special relations with him after he went down, and would be recognised by Gostlin."

"Yes, sir," said the other excitedly. "That's the idea. It would be perfectly planned murder. Gostlin was the only person who could spoil it. Any of the newer porters might not have known him. Even if Gostlin didn't know his name, he would, perhaps, remember his face, and might in a week or so remember where he had seen it before."

"It's possible, of course," said Sir Richard—"possible, but far-fetched. In any case there are so many photographs, and so many young men in each photograph." In spite of his statement, he picked up the photographs Gough Clarke had got out.

"There are really only six of them, Sir Richard," said Gough Clarke encouragingly, "and there are only about fifty undergraduates on each."

Sir Richard went through the photographs idly. He did not expect to see anyone whom he could associate with the crime. All he did see was a succession of young men vaguely familiar to him. He put away the 1932 photograph, but the moment he looked at the 1933 one he was suddenly electrified, for in the middle of the photograph was a face that had somehow become familiar to him in the last week, a face he had seen for a moment and then almost forgotten. It was no one he knew, and yet it was someone he had seen, perhaps when the boy was an undergraduate. He could have sworn that he had seen this undergraduate under unusual circumstances in the last six days. "I never forget a face," he repeated to himself, "but, by hell, as I grow older I do seem to lose the contexts in which I see these faces. I wonder where the hell I've seen this man before?"

He looked up, but Peter Gough Clarke was looking through the other photographs. Should he mention his discovery or not? "Damn it all!"

thought Sir Richard, "I don't want to start some great wild-goose chase. Leave it to the police. Robertson-Macdonald looks efficient, has lots of experience and a large staff. If he can't succeed, I certainly won't—and in any case," he reassured himself, "I've no proof that this face I dimly remember is one that has anything to do with the matter." He looked through the other photographs perfunctorily, and wishing Peter Gough Clarke good night, returned to his rooms with their warm fire and sherry and books.

Detective-Superintendent Robertson-Macdonald had seen the Chief Constable and had given Fleming and Waddell their jobs to do—Fleming to mix with everyone he could connected with the College and hear what was going on; Waddell to concentrate on all the mentioned personalities and get their histories. He would meet them at lunch-time on Monday, and until then he was to be left undisturbed with his thoughts and the dossiers. Despite his assurances to Wyndham and the Chief Constable, he could not help feeling this was going to be an extremely difficult case. There were no real clues at the moment. Nevertheless he would work through everything he had. There must be some strange points. "After all," he thought to himself, as he shrugged his shoulders and drove up the Newmarket Road and past the aerodrome, heading his car towards the Yellow Barn, "a murder should not really be more difficult to solve than a crossword puzzle. And I can solve them fairly quickly." He bit on his pipe and drove on.

CHAPTER THIRTEEN

SUPERINTENDENT ROBERTSON-MACDONALD

Superintendent Robertson-Macdonald had spent a quiet and very enjoyable week-end at the Yellow Barn, and he was grateful to Sir Richard Cherrington for directing him to such a pleasant spot. There had been plenty of noise and merriment in the main part of this well-run and agreeable roadhouse-cum-hotel, but the Superintendent had stayed for the most part in his room, which was in a converted cottage on the edge of the Yellow Barn grounds. Here, with a fire burning and the room filling with the smoke from his pipe, he had gone in peace through the papers collected from Inspector Wyndham, only venturing across to the main part of the Yellow Barn for his meals and for drinks.

He had rung up Inspector Wyndham on Sunday morning to say that all was well with him and that he hoped to see the Inspector and the Chief Constable on Monday afternoon for a conference, and to ask Wyndham to fix accommodation for him in Cambridge itself from Monday evening onwards. Then Sergeant Waddell had rung him up and said he was going up to London on Monday morning because he wanted to check up some facts in the Scotland Yard dossiers.

Apart from these telephone calls he had been left undisturbed with his dossiers. He had seen no one connected with the case except Miss Chilcott, the proprietress of the Yellow Barn, and the driver Piggott, both of whom in conversation had confirmed their earlier statements about the time when John Parrott and Diana Gostlin had left the Barn late on the night of March 10th—or perhaps one should say early in the morning of March 11th.

Superintendent Robertson-Macdonald was treating the Cambridge Murders in the same way as he had dealt with so many of his famous cases between 1925 and 1939. Whenever he took over a case which had already been dealt with for a week or longer by other police organisations his technique was always the same. First, he set one of his staff to wander about the scene of the crime and get to know by sight, by conversation, and by gossip the principal actors in the case. Here in Cambridge this was the job he had given to Inspector Fleming, his right-hand man. Secondly, he set one or two members of his staff to rootle out the past histories of all the people whose names had been mentioned in the case. He worked on the saddening but very true assumption that no one is in the eye of the law the blameless citizen he pretends to be. "After all," he had once said to the Assistant Commissioner, who had protested against his employing two men in one case solely on building up the past histories of the people in the case, "the fact of evil is one of the most important in the world, and as the world is made up of individuals, evil must play a very large part in everyone's lives. Quite a lot of evil—like spite, hatred, gossip, meanness, uncharity—is unfortunately outside the penalty of the law, but quite a lot is not, and there must be few people aged thirty who have not several interesting and evil things in their lives which they wish to keep hidden. Until I know what these things are in the lives of all the people figuring in a case, I am trying to solve a mystery of chess, whereas any case is a mystery of human beings."

In the Cambridge Murders he had brought down Sergeant Waddell from the dossier and records section of Scotland Yard to develop this historical approach. It was one at which Waddell was particularly good, and the news that he was going to London on Monday made the Superintendent hope he had hit on something interesting.

Thirdly, the Superintendent himself retired to study all that was known of the case up to the moment of his taking it over. Only when he had arranged all this information in the order in which he liked it, and was sure that he knew all the facts of the case, was he prepared to start on the next stage of his investigation, which was re-examining all the persons concerned and investigating special points which had appeared curious to him or which his assistants had unearthed.

It was dinner-time on Sunday before he felt he knew perfectly all the statements which Wyndham had collected. On Monday morning he was sitting in his room thinking over all the information he had up to the present. The amount of fact, as distinct from statement, was surprisingly small. When you came to think of it, there were perhaps only two real facts in the whole case: the first was that two bodies existed—one of the Dean, Dr. Landon, and one of the porter, Sam Gostlin—and that they both had been killed by bullets fired from the same revolver, which had subsequently been thrown in the river Cam, presumably at the spot where it was found—namely, outside Dr. Quibell's windows. That was the first fact, and the specialist's report on the revolver did not enable one to say which of the two bullets—that found in the Dean's body or that embedded in the Screens—was fired first. There was no doubt, then, that there were two bodies and that they were killed by the same gun, although of course the same hand may not have fired the gun. There were no finger-prints on the revolver save those of the dead man, Dr. Landon.

The second fact was that both men met their deaths on the night of March 10th/11th: Sam Gostlin certainly between midnight and six o'clock, probably between 1.30 and 3.30, as the doctors said, and perhaps just after 2 o'clock, as the undergraduate Willerby suggested. The Dean certainly met his death before six in the morning, when Kilmartin went to call him and found that he was not there, and certainly after eleven the night before. Medical evidence could not fix the time of death more closely than that, and it was difficult to know who really was the last person to see the Dean alive. Although Dr. Wedgwood left at 11.30 or so, and the man Fothergill called to see the Dean at a few minutes to twelve and alleged that he found the Dean alive then, there was nothing to prove any of these statements.

The Superintendent sighed. There really were very few facts, absolute unshakable facts, in this case. Everything else he classified as unverified statements. That was the trouble with Inspector Wyndham's reports. He assumed that, when a man made a fresh statement, the most recent statement was fact and the others lies. The Superintendent had arranged all the statements in a chronological table, and he had not excluded several statements from the same person, even where they were clearly contradictory. This is his table, and he sat studying it over a mid-morning pint of beer in his room in the Yellow Barn. It was entirely derived from the statements and reports in his dossiers.

First the events of March 10th, the Monday, as far as they concerned the case and were known to him through Wyndham's dossier:—

1 p.m. to 2.30. The Dean and his wife have lunch together in their house in Madingley Road. Dean asks his wife to come for a walk with him. She refuses, and goes up to her room with a headache. Dean goes into College.

4 to 4.30. Dean has tea in his rooms in College and is visited by Fothergill.

5 to 5.45. Fothergill supervising in his rooms. Sees one pupil at 5 and another at 5.45.

6.30. Fothergill goes round to the Bishop's Arms for some drinks. Seen there by Rodgers, the assistant porter. About this time Farnaby is finishing the packing of his trunk and having a conversation with Kilmartin senior.

6.50 The trunk is carried out on to the landing and John Parrott arrives. Farnaby is talking to Parrott and Sir Richard until about 7.15 or 7.20.

7.20. Sir Richard visits the Dean and drinks some sherry with him. They talk on for about twenty to twenty-five minutes.

7.45 to 7.50. Sir Richard Cherrington and the Dean go from G Staircase to the Combination Room.

8.0. Dinner is served in Hall. Among the undergraduates present are Parrott and Farnaby. High table consists of the President, Vice President, the Dean, the Tutor (Westmacott), the Organist (Wedgwood) and Fothergill and Traherne.

8.30 or thereabouts. Fothergill gets up from the table saying he feels ill and leaves the Hall.

8.45. The Fellows move up to the Combination Room for dessert and wine. The Tutor excuses himself and does not go up.

9.0. The Dean excuses himself and goes back to his room, saying he has a lot of work to do and a lot of people to see.

9.30. The Combination party breaks up. The President and Sir Richard Cherrintgon go to their rooms and stay there all night. Wedgwood and Traherne go to their rooms, and later walk or cycle back to their houses.

9.45. The Dean's wife arrives in College. She is seen arriving by Mr. Baynes. She calls on her husband, is with him only a few minutes, delivers the spectacles and leaves by the front gate.

10.00. Parrott calls on the Dean and is given a sound rating by him and sent down. About this time the President is making his drink of milk and rum and honey.

10.15. Parrott leaves, and meets Fred Kilmartin on the stairs. Kilmartin learns from the Dean that there is no pardon for him and that all the facts will be with the police on the following morning.

10.30. About this time Kilmartin senior is leaving the note with Giles Farnaby, and Parrott and the girl Gostlin have met at the Cam Tea Shoppe. Dr. Traherne calls on the Dean to read him his review, and they have a bitter argument.

11.00. Parrott and the girl Gostlin arrive in a car at the Yellow Barn. A strange man—possibly Fothergill—is seen round St. John's Close, where the Dean lived. Sir Richard Cherrington is telephoned by Professor Shacksfield, the Professor of Celtic Studies, and they have a long talk. Fothergill, according to the last story of his and of Mrs. Landon, leaves College and spends the night with Mrs. Landon.

11.00. By this time Traherne has left the Dean, both of them being in a furious temper. Shortly afterwards Dr. Wedgwood arrives to dispute over the College services with the Dean.

11.30. Wedgwood leaves the Dean. Rodger's, the under-porter, goes to sleep in the Porter's Lodge, leaving Baynes and Gostlin there.

11.45. Fothergill, according to his second story, posts a letter to June Westmacott, and then goes up to see the Dean, who refuses to see him and practically sports the oak in his face.

Between 11.45 and 12 midnight. Parrott comes into College, according to his first story.

12 midnight. Farnaby gets into College just as the gate is being closed. Goes to his rooms and notices the Dean's oak is sported. The Head Porter, Mr. Baynes, leaves, and the front gate is locked for the night.

So much for the events of that period of the murders known to the calendar as March 10th. The events of next day, March 11th, as far as the Superintendent could work them out from the dossiers, were as follows:

1.45 or thereabouts. Fothergill, according to his second story, is pacing about on the Backs, unable to sleep. He sees the President's light go on, and he later makes a curious statement about seeing a car on the Backs parked outside the back gate.

1.30 to 2.0. The undergraduate, Poynter, walks about the College, admittedly rather drunk, but declares that there were no bodies visible anywhere. Perhaps it was at this time, or slightly later, that Farnaby woke up and found himself lying in his clothes on his bed, and got up, put his shoes outside his door and then noticed the Dean's oak was unsported. (We have no real knowledge, added the Superintendent, in pencil, that this event took place during this half hour. It might have been much later or earlier.)

2 o'clock. The undergraduate Willerby sees Gostlin making his two o'clock rounds of the College, and thinks he hears a suspicious noise.

2.15. The President looks out through his window and sees a man whom he believes to be Fothergill walking away from the place where the revolver was found.

3 o'clock. John Parrott and Diana Gostlin leave the Yellow Barn.

3.20 to 3.30. Parrott climbs into College and sees the porter's body, according to his second story, and presumably drops his button there.

Then a break until six o'clock.

6.0. The bedmakers at the front gate, and Rodgers opens it to them after some delay.

6.5 or so. The discovery of the body by the bedmakers.

6.10. Sir Richard Cherrington is sent for.

6.15 or thereabouts. When Sir Richard arrives he finds Fothergill already there and fully clad, although he was not called by his bedmaker. In his first story he says he was called by her, but Mrs. Harris denies this.

6.30. Police arrive, and find Sir Richard bent over the porter's body.

8.0. Inspector Wyndham goes and breakfasts with Sir Richard, who lies about recognising the button and the piece of Parrott's coat.

Then no more relevant facts or statements until at 6 that Tuesday evening it was established the Dean was missing, and at 7 o'clock the following morning the revolver was found in the Cam, and at lunch-time the Dean himself was found dead in Farnaby's trunk in Berkshire.

The Superintendent went through the chronological table of events again and took another drink of his beer. It was a formidable array of alleged facts. He repeated firmly to himself, "Alleged facts," because he refused to treat more than two or three of the statements as established facts. Certain things he marked down for checking at once. This business of Cherrington's 'phone call with Professor Shacksfield, for instance. Why was that mentioned at all? A possible alibi for Cherrington? If he was the man lurking around the Dean's house at eleven o'clock, he might be producing this 'phone conversation as his alibi, and if Shacksfield was an absent-minded man he might not be able to say exactly at what time it happened. But, then, Cherrington said it was Shacksfield who had rung him up. What a lot there was to check. Still a tremendous amount of routine work to be done. He thought he would hand over a copy of this chronological statement to Inspector Fleming and get him to check and countercheck everything that was susceptible of checking, so that they might reduce the apparent number of alleged facts.

There was, of course, one great external discrepancy in the statements, apart from the discrepancies between the various statements of the same individuals. This was the discrepancy between Fothergill's movements in the night and the evidence of the President. It could, of course, all be explained away as Cherrington had done, and as Wyndham had noted in the dossier, by supposing the President had got his times or his identification wrong. Certainly Cherrington's point about the spectacles was a most ingenious one.

Anyway, no more could be done by pure meditation in isolation. It was time to move into Cambridge and, armed with the facts, start on the big enquiry. The Superintendent paid his bill, had his bags put in his car and drove into Cambridge. Inspector Wyndham was out when he called at the police station, but had left a message to say that a room was booked for the Superintendent in the Blue Boar, the large hotel conveniently across the road from Trinity and Fisher Colleges, and that Inspector Wyndham would meet the Superintendent in the private smoke-room bar of the Blue Boar at 12.30. The Superintendent drove round to the Blue Boar, unloaded his bags, and had them taken up to his room, and put his car in the yard at the back. There was still some time before 12.30, so he sauntered down Trinity Street, which, it being the vacation, was delightfully free of undergraduates. Dons' wives were coming out of Miss Pallisser's café after their morning coffee, dons were coming in and out of Deighton and Bell's bookshop, while the managers of the many gentlemen's wear shops in the street were wondering how best to do up their windows for next term so that the young men might be tempted to buy more clothes they did not need and could not pay for.

It was outside the bookshop that the Superintendent walked into Sir Richard Cherrington.

"Good morning, Superintendent," said Sir Richard affably. "Had a nice week-end out at the Barn?"

"Good morning, sir," said the other. "Yes, I have indeed. I enjoyed myself immensely. Thank you for recommending me to go there."

"Solved the mystery yet?"

"No, not yet," the Superintendent smiled. "These things take time, you know. But, I believe I've got the hang of the case by now."

"Any theories? Or shouldn't I ask?"

"None at all, I'm afraid," said the Superintendent. "I'm still fact-collecting and verifying."

"Well, I'm off on Tuesday afternoon."

"Yes?" queried the Superintendent politely.

"Down to stay with my sister—Mrs. Farnaby, you know—at Twyford, for a night. She was pretty upset by the unpleasant happenings in her house."

"Quite so," agreed the Superintendent.

"Yes," went on the Professor. "Not a nice thing to find corpses in your house." He paused. "Then I'm going off to Brittany with Giles Farnaby. I think I told you all this on Saturday, when you came to see me."

"You did, sir."

"Still no objection to me going away?" asked Sir Richard.

"Oh no, sir, none," said the other. "You were only going for ten days or so, I think you said. We shall see you when you come back."

"I hope so," said Sir Richard. "And I hope by then you will have solved the whole business. All luck to you." And away he went down the street.

The Superintendent retraced his steps to the Blue Boar, and found Inspector Fleming waiting for him in the bar.

"Hello, sir. Had a nice time? What'll you have? Beer?" was Fleming's greeting.

"Hello, Fleming. How's life?" said the Superintendent. "Yes, a pint of beer will do me very nicely."

They sat down in a corner and lit their pipes.

"Everything solved, my Flamingo?" asked the Superintendent playfully. "Or is this case too much for you?"

"No, no, not at all," said the Inspector. "I find it quite fascinating. There are lots of interesting people to be met, and the whole series of events is really most puzzling. Waddell got most interested in something he got his teeth into—some little scandal or other—and he shot up to London this morning to look at his records."

"Yes, he telephoned me he was doing that," said the Superintendent. "Tell me what lines you've been working on."

"Oh, I've just been talking to people generally," said the other. "Wyndham is a good chap. Had two talks with him. He's very puzzled over the whole thing. I agree with him that the most puzzling thing is the clothes in which Dr. Landon was dressed when he was murdered."

"What's puzzling about that?" asked Robertson-Macdonald.

"Well, it seems such an odd collection of clothes to be wearing. Everything all right except for his clerical collar, and just socks on his feet," said Fleming.

"My dear old Flamingo," replied the Superintendent, "I don't find the Dean's clothes in the least bit puzzling. There are all sorts of explanations."

"Really, sir?"

"Why, yes," said the Superintendent. "In the first place, the Dean could have changed his shoes and taken off his collar to sit comfortably in his room before going to bed."

"Yes, I suppose that's true," reluctantly agreed Inspector Fleming.

"Or he might have part undressed to go to bed when his murderous visitor called on him," went on the Superintendent. "Or again, his visitor might have called when he was in bed, and he may have part dressed to come out and talk with him. Remember, his pyjamas were flung about as though they were used that night, and Kilmartin thought the bed had been slept in."

"I see you've been working hard over the week-end," said the Inspector.

"Not very hard," said Robertson-Macdonald. "But the problem is not where you put it. There are enough snags without turning the Dean's clothes into one." He paused. "Here, let's have some more beer. It's a cold day."

They paused while the beer was being brought. "What do you consider the key problem then, sir?" asked the Inspector.

"Here it is, my Flamingo," said the Superintendent, and took out from his despatch-case the table of times he had prepared. He passed it over to the Inspector. "Make several copies of this," he said. "And we can all study it. Somewhere in those statements is not the answer to the mystery, but a clue to start working on."

The Inspector studied the document. "And have you found a clue, sir?" he asked.

"I have!" said the Superintendent. "Why, it could hardly be missed. It sticks out a mile."

"Does it, sir?" said Fleming. "I'm afraid I'm rather stupid this morning."

"My dear Flamingo," went on the Superintendent. "As you know, as well as I do, there is nothing so helpful to a detective as the man who makes several statements, especially when they are detailed ones. Now, here in this case we have three different statements from this man Fothergill."

"Yes, sir. I noticed that," agreed Fleming.

"Good! But what conclusion did you draw?"

"That in his first two statements he was lying to shield the lady," answered Fleming.

"Agreed," snapped the Superintendent. "But does that make his third statement, or any of his statements, necessarily true or untrue?"

"I suppose it doesn't," said the other. "I'm afraid I had assumed, with Wyndham, that the third statement was fact, supported as it was by Mrs. Landon."

"You were both meant to think that," said the Superintendent. "And we are all supposed to be chasing a mysterious stranger seen by the President at two-fifteen in the morning."

"And what do you think, sir?" asked Fleming.

The Superintendent took out his pipe and made his points with it. "Let us examine Fothergill's statements," he began. "He has made three. The first one says he felt ill during dinner in Hall, went out and retired to his rooms, went to bed, and was still fast asleep when called by Mrs. Harris."

"Well, sir, we know that to be untrue," broke in the Inspector.

"We know nothing to be true in this case yet," said the Superintendent tartly. "Then the second statement," he went on, "declares that he went to his room and wrote a long letter to his fiancée, Miss Westmacott, breaking off the engagement, and that he went down to post this at about eleven-forty-five and then up to see the Dean at eleven-fifty-five and got thrown out, following which he paced up and down the Backs, noticing the President's lights go on at one-fifteen and observing a car outside the back gate."

"Yes, sir," said the other.

"The third statement," went on Robertson-Macdonald, "said he went to St. John's Close at eleven, where he was seen by the servant girl Finch, or whatever her name is, and that he left at six next morning, leaving his hat behind and arriving fully clad, to be noticed by Sir Richard at six-fifteen."

"Yes," said the Inspector encouragingly.

"Now what strikes me so forcibly," went on the Superintendent, "is that the third statement gets rid of the circumstantial points of the second statement. The second statement has the ring of truth. Posting letters and going for walks on the Backs at night and seeing the Dean's light and noticing things like cars—all these are circumstantial points that incline me to believe the second statement."

"And the third, sir?" queried the Inspector.

"I believe the third was made because they could no longer hide the fact of Fothergill and Mrs. Landon having spent the night together. Old Cherrington nosed that out. So they produced a third statement which, while gracefully admitting they spent the night in sin, gives Fothergill a complete alibi from eleven o'clock to six the next morning."

"I see, sir," said Fleming. "And you believe that alibi to be correct?"

"I believe nothing as yet," said Robertson-Macdonald cautiously. "But I want to check the whole thing. I suspect the alibi may be correct in part—after all, there's the hat left behind and the facts that Cherrington saw Fothergill dressed at six-fifteen, and that Fothergill lied over the calling business. All the end part may be correct, but he still may have arrived in St. John's Close after two-fifteen, having committed two murders and been seen by the President as he went away."

"I see, sir," said Fleming, intrigued.

"But this is all speculation," went on the Superintendent. "You and I have got to get down at once to the problem of testing out the Fothergill statements. I want you to take the end part."

"The end part?" queried Fleming.

"Yes," said Robertson-Macdonald. "I'm intrigued by what Fothergill said about seeing a car while he was walking on the Backs at one-fifteen. This car is one of the reasons why I think he is still lying when he says he was with Mrs. Landon from eleven o'clock until six the following morning. There is no reason to invent this car, you know. It's a piece of circumstantial evidence likely to be correct. Find out if police patrols saw a car there, and when? Was it there in the morning? Concentrate on cars, my Flamingo, and get every movement of cars connected with Fisher College during the night of the murders." He suddenly thumped the table with his fist. "How stupid of both of us not to notice it before!" he said.

"Notice what, sir?" asked the dutiful Fleming.

"Why, Wedgwood's statement," said the Superintendent. "Wedgwood deposes to have left the College by the back gate after eleven-thirty. Question him, and find if he saw a car there. If he didn't, it must have gone away, since Fothergill went out before eleven, or, as seems to me very possible, it arrived much later, and friend Fothergill, in mentioning the car, has tied himself to an event later in the night when, according to his final statement, he was in bed with Mrs. Landon."

"Good, sir. I'll get down to this immediately after lunch."

"Stout stuff!" said the Superintendent. "I've got to see Wyndham and the Chief Constable after lunch, or else they will think I am most peculiar. When that is over I shall attack the first part of Fothergill's statements. I shall concentrate on this letter. Was it ever sent? How long did it take to write? When was it sent? The letter, like the car, is so circumstantial that it must be true. Did anyone see Fothergill post this letter? How does one post letters late at night in Fisher College? I shall probably have to go and see the Westmacott girl. The letter may have some interesting indications of Fothergill's state of mind that evening."

"It is good to be on the trail of something concrete, isn't it?" said Fleming.

"Yes," said Robertson-Macdonald, "it is a good feeling. I am quite sure there is plenty of work to be done on this case. I can't for the life of me see why the Cambridge folk called us in at all. Still, that's their look-out. Let's go and have lunch."

CHAPTER FOURTEEN

THE LETTER

IT WAS just after four o'clock when Detective-Superintendent Robertson-Macdonald left the Cambridge police station and walked to Fisher College. He had had a rather fruitless conference with the Chief Constable and with Inspector Wyndham, and had refused their invitation to stay and have some tea. He was anxious to get his teeth into the problem of the Fisher College murders. He had had his period of inaction over the week-end, and now wanted to test out some of the ideas he had mentioned to Fleming at lunch-time in the Blue Boar.

A thick fog was rolling in from the Fens and making the March afternoon more cheerless than it normally was. The lights were already burning in the shops as he walked down Regent Street, and the porters' lodges of Christ's and Sidney Sussex were lit up. Crowds of women with laden shopping baskets were waiting outside Holy Trinity Church for the big, red, lumbering buses that would take them away to the suburbs of Cambridge and out into the fenland villages and to Ely and St. Ives. He turned down Green Street, and paused for a moment outside Miss Pallisser's tea-shop. The cosy, curtained warmth within attracted him, and the side tables in the passage, piled high with chocolate and cream and sugar cakes. But he went on past the Blue Boar and turned in to Fisher College.

Here his luck was in. Rodgers was on duty, and Mr. Baynes, the Head Porter, was in his inner office drinking some tea. Baynes was delighted to see the Superintendent, and quickly got him another cup and poured him out some tea. In the Head Porter's inner sanctum munching toast and drinking the good, hot tea which Baynes had poured out for him, Robertson-Macdonald sat close to the little fire.

"How's the case going, Superintendent?" asked Baynes.

"Oh, it's just beginning still," said Robertson-Macdonald. "Mustn't expect results too soon, you know. Only in detective novels is the mystery solved in no time. Our police cases usually take a long time, filled with routine work."

"Is this some of the routine work, if I may ask?" queried Baynes.

"My questioning you, you mean?" said the Superintendent, smiling.

"Yes."

"Well, I suppose it is," agreed the other. "I think you can help me on a particular point."

"Only too delighted if I can," said the Head Porter. "You must realise how terrible it is to have a thing like this hanging over Fisher College. I've been here now for thirty-five years, barring when I was away in the war, and this is fortunately the first time anything of this kind has happened."

"I've been going through the statements made to Inspector Wyndham," said the Superintendent. "And I am just wanting to get straight the movements in the Porter's Lodge here just before midnight on Monday."

"Ah, ha," agreed Baynes.

"If I remember rightly," went on the Superintendent, "there were three of you here at about eleven o'clock: Rodgers and Gostlin and yourself."

"That's correct," said Baynes. "I'm not normally here as late, except on special nights, such as the last night of term or Bump Supper Nights and so forth, when the young gentlemen need special watching. I had put Rodgers and Gostlin on last night. Gostlin came on duty about ten-thirty, and the day porters went off about then. I know because I was in my office here checking up some forms that the Tutor wanted next day."

"Mr. Westmacott?" queried Robertson-Macdonald.

"Yes, Mr. Westmacott, the Tutor," went on Baynes. "He telephoned me round about eleven o'clock about these forms, and I told him they would be ready first thing in the morning. Rodgers and Gostlin were in the outer office then. Rodgers, he went to bed sometime after eleven o'clock—say about eleven-thirty—and I went away at midnight. Gave some special instructions to Gostlin. Not that he needed them, being an old hand at the job, but I thought he just might have forgotten the sort of things that go on the last night of term. Told him not to be too hard on late-comers and odd climbers into College, like. We want to know the facts about the gentlemen." He smiled. "But it isn't always necessary to communicate them to the authorities. We exercises our discretion. It's only right."

"And did you see anybody during this time?"

"Only once, when I was looking at the trunks about ten o'clock. I saw Mrs. Landon go out of College. She walked past me very quickly. And then, when I was talking to Gostlin near midnight, a lot of men came in. Young Farnaby was one. Seemed a bit tight, like. Not that he is usually. His father now, he was a one. Always the better for drink. 'Baynes,' he used to say, 'a man is always the better for drink, never the worse. Remember that.' And I have. But there," he added pensively, "he was a real gentleman."

"You didn't see Parrott come in?" queried the Superintendent.

"Parrott?" asked the other. "Why, no. I thought he was supposed to have climbed in much later?"

"I was only asking. It was an odd chance," said the Superintendent. "Now tell me one other thing, please," he went on. "If anyone wanted to post a letter in this College without going out to the public letter-boxes, what would he do?"

"That's quite simply answered," said Baynes. "We have four private letter-boxes in the College. One in the Senior Combination Room, one in the Junior Combination Room, one in the Screens, and one in the Porter's Lodge."

"Would anyone coming to post a letter in the Porter's Lodge here necessarily be seen by the porter on duty?"

"Oh, no, not at all. Certainly not at night," said Baynes. "The box is outside in the wall, and if the porter on duty was answering the telephone or writing in a book, he wouldn't notice anyone posting a letter. In any case, on a dark night the most he would see was someone popping a letter into the box. He wouldn't know who he was."

The Superintendent's hopes dropped. "Oh, that's a great pity," he said. "I was hoping you might be able to confirm that someone posted a letter on Monday evening."

"'Fraid not, sir," said Baynes. "I'll ask Rodgers if you like, but he won't know, I'm sure."

Suddenly the Superintendent sat up. "No, wait a minute," he said. "Wait a minute. You say there are four boxes in the College?"

"That's right."

"One in the Screens?"

"Yes."

"Then why in heaven should a man walk past the Screens and come all the way to the Porter's Lodge to post his letter? Or why should he say he did that?"

"Was he going out of College, perhaps?"

"No—leastways, not by the front gate."

"At what time is this supposed to have happened?"

The Superintendent thought a moment. Fothergill had said he posted the letter to June Westmacott between 11.30 and 11.45, and then went to see the Dean, but of course there was nothing to show he had not posted it earlier in the evening, say before he left College and got to St. John's Close at 11 o'clock. He could always have posted it then, as he left College before 11 o'clock. But why say he did it at 11.45? Was there the making or, alternatively, the breaking, of an alibi here? The Superintendent looked up.

"That's the trouble," he said. "I don't really know. Sometime after ten o'clock, I should think, and sometime before midnight."

"Ah, well," said Baynes. "There is a reason why he should come to the Porter's Lodge with his letter."

"There is?" asked Robertson-Macdonald sharply.

"Yes, there is," went on Baynes. "You see, the four boxes are cleared at twelve o'clock noon, and then at six o'clock, and finally at eleven o'clock at night."

"At eleven o'clock at night?" said the Superintendent, brightening up. There was going to be something in this letter business, after all.

"Yes. It is one of the last jobs of the second porter on, to collect the four boxes and take the mail out to the pillar-box at the corner of Jesus Lane. It catches the eleven-fifteen collection there."

"Yes?" said the Superintendent.

"But we have one more collection," said the Head Porter. "We collect from the Porter's Lodge box at eight in the morning, and get the letters away to the main post office. So, you see, anyone wanting to get a letter away after eleven o'clock would bring it to the Porter's Lodge so that it could catch the morning despatch."

"I see," said the Superintendent, but he did not see anything very clearly. Somehow there must be some very important clue hidden in this matter of the letter and the clearing at eleven o'clock. "Now let me get this straight," he said. "If this letter was posted before eleven o'clock on Monday night, March 10th, there was no reason why it should be posted at the Porter's Lodge."

"No," agreed Baynes. "But then the person you have in mind might just walk to the front gate to post the letter for no reason at all."

"I suppose so," agreed Robertson-Macdonald. "But if the letter was posted before eleven it would have been collected by"—he paused—"let me see, by Rodgers. Rodgers was on then, wasn't he?"

"That's right. He'd have taken the letters out and put them in the pillar-box at about eleven-ten. That would have been one of the last things he did before going to bed."

"Yes. And if the letter was posted after eleven it would be a reason for bringing it to the Porter's Lodge, and it would be collected next morning, the 11th, and posted about quarter past eight?"

"That's right, sir."

"Now, I wonder does Rodgers remember what he collected?"

"I should doubt it very much. But we'll ask him."

They walked to the outer part of the Lodge. Rodgers was busy at the telephone switchboard. When he was finished, the Superintendent said:

"I wonder if you can help us a bit more, Rodgers?"

"If I can, I will," said Rodgers.

"Tell me what you did in the way of clearing the College letter-boxes on Monday night and Tuesday morning."

"Clearing the letter-boxes?" asked Rodgers, rather surprised.

"Yes, it's rather important."

"Well, sir, I cleared the four boxes as usual at eleven o'clock, and took them out to catch the eleven-fifteen collection at Jesus Lane."

"They caught this all right?"

"Oh yes," said Rodgers. "I always switch on my torch and look at the next collection label, for fear we've been late. We very rarely are, and we were not on Monday night. Some nights we get delayed and when we get there the label is down for eight-fifteen the next morning."

"Yes, go on," said the Superintendent encouragingly.

"Well, then I came back and went to bed," said Rodgers. "Next morning there was so much coming and going, what with the discovery of the body, and the arrival of the police, that I nearly forgot the mail. But I got it to the outer Jesus Lane box just in time. I handed the letters personally to the postman who was clearing the box."

"Were there many?" asked the Superintendent.

"No, not many," said Rodgers. "There never are in the early morning collection."

"Now then, Rodgers," said the Superintendent, "I want you to be very careful in answering the next point." He paused. "Did you by any chance happen to notice among the letters you took out at eleven o'clock, or those at eight the next morning, one addressed to Miss June Westmacott?"

He looked at Rodgers hopefully, but his hopes were quickly dashed. "No, sir," said Rodgers. "'Fraid I can't help you. I didn't notice any of the names."

"Yes," said Robertson-Macdonald. "Well, I could hardly have expected you to do so." He turned to Baynes. "Well, Mr. Baynes," he said, "I think that's all I want at the moment." He turned to Rodgers. "It was just a possibility you might have seen this man post a letter or have noticed it when you collected it. I don't suppose you saw Dr. Fothergill post a letter at the Lodge on Monday night?"

"I'm afraid I didn't, sir," he said.

"Well, never mind," said the Superintendent. "Thank you for your assistance, both of you. And thank you, Mr. Baynes, for the very nice tea. Good evening."

He turned up the collar of his coat, bit firmly on his pipe and walked out into Trinity Street. "Not really very much there," he thought. "I'll have a look at the pillar-box, though; not that it will tell me anything." He walked round into Sidney Street and halted opposite the end of Jesus Lane. Yes, there was the letter-box, let into the corner wall of Sidney Sussex College. He gazed at it, and could just make out by the street lights the words "Next Collection Six-Fifteen", on the movable metal strip on the box. He shrugged his shoulders and walked away, then stopped suddenly and retraced his steps. He peered at the box again, took the pipe out of his mouth and whistled softly. "I wonder," he said to himself. "Now, I wonder."

He turned to the policeman on duty at the cross-road, and asked where the main post office was, and learnt it was two buildings away from the main police station in Regent Street. He walked quickly up Sidney Street and Regent Street, and had no difficulty in identifying the post office. Once inside, he asked for the supervisor, and was shown to a small, quiet, bespectacled, middle-aged man who gave his name as Briggs. Briggs looked up from his desk as the Superintendent was shown in. He was just preparing to leave and cycle away to his little, semi-detached house on the Milton Road.

"Mr. Briggs?" asked the Superintendent.

"Yes," said Briggs, blinking mildly.

"How do you do. I'm Superintendent Robertson-Macdonald of Scotland Yard. Here's my card."

"Gracious me! gracious me!" said Briggs, blinking again and thinking of the time when, as a boy, he had once stolen a book from the stall in the Market Place, and of the time he travelled from Cambridge to Ely in a crowded bus without paying his fare. "What can I do for you?"

"Just a little information, if you could spare me a moment," said the Superintendent.

"Anything I can tell you," said Briggs, still apprehensive. Perhaps it was about some train mail robbery. "Do sit down."

"Thank you," said Robertson-Macdonald. "It's just this. I am investigating a certain letter which could have been posted in the Jesus Lane box at eleven-fifteen on Monday night the 10th or at eight-fifteen on Tuesday morning the 11th of March. Now, what happens to the letters from the Jesus Lane box when they are collected?"

Briggs sighed with relief. So his sins had not yet been found out. "That's very easy to tell," he said. "The Jesus Lane box is one of the last collected on one of our town rounds. The postman also collects the Lloyds Bank box and the one in Christ's, and would normally get here within half an hour of leaving Jesus Lane. Probably less. Say, twenty minutes."

"Yes," said Robertson-Macdonald. "And the letters leave here—when?" he queried ungrammatically.

"Well, the late-night collections are designed to catch the one-fifteen mail for London."

"Good!" said the Inspector. "And the eight-fifteen collection?"

"That would catch the ten-thirty mail to London," said Briggs. "But there," he added, "I am assuming that the letter was going in the London direction."

"I think it was," said the Superintendent. "It was addressed to Twyford in Berkshire."

"Oh, yes," said Briggs. "I know. Well, that would go through London. I suppose you want to know the times. There may, of course, have been some extraordinary delays, but normally the letter which caught the one-fifteen mail would be delivered in Twyford on the Tuesday afternoon—that is, unless the people to whom it was addressed lived miles out in the country and had no afternoon delivery. The letter that caught the ten-thirty to town, however, would not be delivered until the following morning—that is, the Wednesday morning."

"Good!" said the Superintendent. "Good!" This was a further check. He had not expected the dates of arrival to be significant. "I was wondering," he said, "about the franking marks."

"Yes?" said Briggs.

"How would you frank the letters brought in by the postman at about half-past eleven or a quarter to twelve?"

"You mean the date?"

"Yes."

"Ah, quite so," said Briggs, "Well, all the letters coming in off the late-night collection and catching the mail at one-thirty to London would have the 10th March on them. The next morning collection would all have the 11th March. I gather you are hoping to check exactly when a letter was posted?"

"Something of the kind," said the Superintendent. "And what you have told me is of the very greatest value. I am much indebted to you. It may be necessary, too, for you to give this evidence in court later."

"Oh, really?" said Briggs.

"Yes. But until then I must ask you not to discuss this with anyone."

"Of course, of course. Never dream of such a thing," said Briggs, as he showed the Superintendent out. "Well, well," he said to himself after the Superintendent was out of his office. "Well, well," as he polished his spectacles. "The wife will be interested in all this."

II

It was just after lunch on Tuesday before Superintendent Robertson-Macdonald had been able to get away from Cambridge. Ever since his interviews with the porters at Fisher College and with the timorous Mr.

Briggs in the post office it had seemed essential to follow the clue of the letter just as far as it could be followed. He did not really expect a very great deal from it, but it seemed essential to have all the information that could be obtained. In any case, an interview with June Westmacott would acquaint him with another character in the case, and at the same time he would be able to see the Farnaby's and exactly where the Dean's body had been discovered. He had telephoned June Westmacott on Tuesday morning, and she had agreed to see him at tea-time that day. His morning had been taken up with interviewing the President, who was singularly unhelpful and seemed most distressed that his own evidence was not absolutely certain, as he had at first thought it to be.

After the President the Superintendent had visited the Tutor, Mr. Westmacott, and here he had felt the first check of his short investigation in Cambridge. He could not help feeling that Roger Westmacott had a lot to tell him, but would not do so. He had been very cold when the Superintendent had questioned him about the relations between Evan Fothergill and his niece, June Westmacott, and had expressed disapproval and surprise on hearing that the Superintendent was going down to see his niece that afternoon.

As the Superintendent drove along through Hertfordshire on his way from Cambridge to Twyford, he could not help wondering why Westmacott had been so stand-offish that morning. He was one of the dons who had not figured in Wyndham's reports very much. Was it possible that he had been wrongly neglected? The one person who was suspected at the moment was Fothergill. However much the Superintendent tried to confine himself to facts, he could not help seeing clearly that despite the third statement, and that statement's apparent support from Mrs. Landon, Fothergill was first on the list of suspects. He had a very strong motive—he was in love with the murdered man's wife; he certainly had the means—which were in any case the murdered man's own gun. He could have had the opportunity—it really all depended on which of his three statements you believed. Then there was the President's evidence of having seen a man at two-fifteen who resembled Fothergill.

It looked, therefore, as if all the indications pointed at Fothergill. "But," the Superintendent asked himself, "is this a diabolically ingenious crime? Let us suppose someone wanted to get rid of Fothergill. One way is to murder him, but another is to murder other people so that the suspicion falls heavily on Fothergill. This would be diabolically ingenious. The police would keep looking for proofs of Fothergill's guilt, whereas what they should be looking for is the man who has so carefully framed Fothergill. Who was this man? There was no doubt it could be Westmacott, who had been in College all night and who had no real proof of any alibi. Ah, ha! that's interesting," thought the Superintendent. Westmacott had telephoned the Head Porter about forms. This might be a clever move to suggest he was in his rooms when actually he was away somewhere else. Where? Perhaps he was the mystery man that visited St. John's Close at eleven o'clock. It was worth checking whether the 'phone call happened round about eleven o'clock, and where it was made from.

But the motive? What motive could there be? A secret love for the Dean's wife, and a way of getting rid of her husband and lover at the same time? A desire to revenge his niece for the bad treatment she had had at the hands of Fothergill? Just professional and domestic college hate for both Fothergill and Landon? Perhaps Westmacott was a demented person. All these things must be looked into, and perhaps Waddell at the moment was finding some extraordinary pieces of information about Westmacott in the Scotland Yard dossier and records section.

Anyway, these were unprofitable speculations. The Superintendent drove on through Beaconsfield to Marlow and out on to the Bath Road and to Twyford. Here he asked the way, and was soon driving up to Twyford Grange. June Westmacott received him with mingled curiosity and coldness, and gave him some tea. The Superintendent could not help admiring her as she capably dealt with the tea. She was an attractive, well-built girl with fairish hair and a pleasantly-snub nose.

"Well, Superintendent?" she said, when she had finished pouring out the tea. "What can I do for you? I have had a telephone call from my uncle telling me I have no need to tell you anything, but if I can be of assistance I will be. You are investigating the Fisher College murders, I understand?"

"I am," said the Superintendent. "And you can give me some valuable information, despite your uncle's assurances to the contrary." He paused. "You see," he went on, "I am really investigating a letter sent by Dr. Fothergill to you recently in which, I believe, he broke off his engagement to you."

June stiffened. "What on earth has that got to do with the case?" she asked.

"Believe me," said the Inspector, "a very great deal. I can assume, then, that you did get this letter?"

"I did."

"May I ask what time it arrived?"

"What time?"

"Yes," said Robertson-Macdonald. "Did it arrive on Tuesday evening, or Wednesday morning?"

"Wednesday morning."

"You are sure of that?"

"I am indeed," said June. "Quite sure. We get no post here on Tuesday evening."

The Superintendent's face expressed his disappointment. "So it might have been in the Twyford post office on Tuesday?" he asked.

"No, it could not have been," said June. "We often go in for letters in the afternoon, and I called in myself and asked for letters at the post office."

"Why, that's splendid!" said the Superintendent. This surely must mean the letter was posted after eleven o'clock, so that Fothergill could not possibly be the man seen at St. John's Close at eleven, and he could not have been with Mrs. Landon from eleven onwards.

"I don't suppose you noticed the date on it?" he asked.

"Yes, I did," said June. "It was dated Monday the 10th, and was written by Evan after Hall."

"He says that?"

"Yes." She went on, "If it is any help to you, I can get the letter for you to read. He says he is most anxious to marry Mrs. Landon, and that our engagement is through."

"That's most kind of you," said the Superintendent. "I would like to read it."

June Westmacott was away a few minutes, and then came back with the letter. "Here it is," she said, handing it to the Superintendent. His heart gave a sudden quick beat when he saw that the letter was in its original envelope. The franking mark was blurred over the stamp, but the last three letters "DGE" of Cambridge were visible, and also the date. The Superintendent smiled when he saw it. It was quite clearly March 11th. If Briggs' description of the Cambridge postal system was correct, then the letter was posted after eleven o'clock without any doubt, which fitted in with the time of its receipt. It was clear that Fothergill must be interviewed as remorselessly and as quickly as possible. The Superintendent read through the letter quickly and gave it back to the girl. It was a very sentimental letter, and it all fitted in with the notion of having been written, as Fothergill said in his second statement, late on the Monday night.

"Sorry I had to read this," he said rather shyly. "I mean, it is rather embarrassing for you."

"Not really," said June. "I did the same to John Parrott myself a few months ago. These things happen, you know."

"Now I have to make another request," said the Superintendent. "May I keep the letter and the envelope long enough to have a photostat copy made?"

The girl was surprised. "By all means," she said. "Keep it as long as you like. I only wish I knew how it fitted into your case." She paused and stared at him. "You were surely not thinking that Evan Fothergill is a possible murderer, were you?"

The Superintendent smiled. "Why not?" he asked.

"My dear man," said June, "that's quite impossible. I know him very well, and I can assure you here and now that if you are starting off on a line of investigation to try to pin the murders on him, you will be quite wrong. I know I dislike him and despise him at the moment," she added hastily, "but once I liked him a great deal and knew him well. You are quite wrong, you know—quite wrong."

And with this assurance the Superintendent drove away with his letter as a treasured possession. He drove to Farnaby Grange and had a few words with Bond the butler, as well as with young Giles Farnaby and his mother, but they could add nothing to what was already in the dossiers prepared by the Cambridge and Berkshire police.

As he drove away down the road from Twyford to Marlow he passed a large blue Bentley driven by Sir Richard Cherrington, who was on his way from Cambridge to Farnaby Grange. They waved to each other. "Of course," thought the Superintendent, "I remember now. Cherrington is going to collect his nephew and they are going off on a trip to Brittany." And Sir Richard thought to himself, "Now what in hell has Robertson-What's-it been doing in these parts? Visiting Farnaby Grange, I suppose." But when he was told that the Superintendent had also been to see June Westmacott and had taken away with him Fothergill's letter breaking off their engagement, and been particularly anxious to keep the envelope, he began to think to himself furiously. He went all over the case again while he was having a bath at Farnaby Grange. There came back to him vividly the face he had noticed in the College groups which Peter Gough Clarke had made him look at. "Damn it," he said to himself, "I know I have seen that face somewhere recently. Now where?" But neither the bath nor the excellent sherry he drank afterwards would refresh his memory.

The Superintendent did not drive straight back to Cambridge. He drove his car into the Compleat Angler at Marlow, and sat with a pint of beer in the warm lounge looking out over the river as it danced noisily over the weirs. "Where does all this get us to?" he asked himself. "Surely I must accept as a fact, and not an unverified statement, that the letter was posted after eleven o'clock, and in the Porters' Lodge box. This must mean that the third statement of Fothergill's supported by Mrs. Landon was not true. He did not get to her house until after twelve o'clock. Now I wonder," he said to himself. "If the letter was posted at eleven-thirty and Fothergill did walk about on the Backs for a bit, he might have been seen by the President at one-fifteen and then gone on to St. John's Close. I suppose he was there, and I suppose it was his hat. Yes, I think if Sir Richard Cherrington's evidence is correct, about seeing him dressed at six-fifteen next morning, then he very probably was out most of the night. Of course if he did not arrive until after two-fifteen he might have been seen by the President, who, after all, could have put on his long sighted spectacles, and could have correctly heard the clocks strike. Now, is that why Mrs. Landon and Fothergill are trying to produce an alibi for the whole night? The letter proves the alibi wrong.

Ergo," thought the Superintendent, "either Fothergill did the murders and there was a different man at St. John's Close at eleven (or Fothergill was there and returned to College afterwards), or Fothergill did not do them, and we are back where we were. Who was at St. John's Close at eleven? I haven't got so far, after all," he thought as he got into his car and drove to Cambridge. "I hope Fleming and Waddell have done a little better."

CHAPTER FIFTEEN
THE KEYS

INSPECTOR FLEMING was waiting for Superintendent Robertson-Macdonald when the latter got to his office in the Cambridge police station on Wednesday morning.

"Hello, sir," he greeted the Superintendent.

"Had any luck?" asked Robertson-Macdonald.

"Well, I think so, sir, in a manner of speaking," said Fleming.

"Good! That's fine! Any news of Waddell?"

"Yes, sir," answered Fleming. "He telephoned last night to say he would be down by the first train this morning and was coming straight to the police station."

"Sounds as if he's on to something, doesn't it?" said the Superintendent. "Now let me have your news."

"Well, sir, I got going on this car, just as you told me. Of course, we had no proof at the time that such a car did exist. It was only mentioned in Fothergill's statement, and then as a sort of afterthought." He paused. "Well, the car does exist all right."

"It does? That's fine!" said the Superintendent.

"Yes, sir," went on Fleming. "The constable on duty along the Grange Road and Queen's Road area noticed a car outside the back gate of Fisher College when he went by at about half-past one. There was no car there when he passed that way again about four o'clock. I questioned Dr. Wedgwood, who appears to have been the last person—bar perhaps the murderer or Fothergill—to use the back gate. He says he left the Dean in a great temper at half-past eleven and walked to the back gate, letting himself out, and so home. There was no car outside the back gate then."

"So a car arrived there between eleven-forty-five and half-past one, and had gone away again by four o'clock," said the Superintendent.

"That appears to be so," said Fleming. "It struck me, sir, that Fothergill would notice a car much more if it was in his way as he made to leave the College, than if he was just pacing up and down the lawns, as he said he was."

"You mean, Fleming," said the Superintendent, "that Fothergill must have left the College grounds between eleven forty-five and four o'clock?"

"Yes, sir," said Fleming.

"And his third statement, supported by Mrs. Landon, could not be true," went on the Superintendent.

"That's so," said Fleming. "I've established it was his hat that was left behind in Mrs. Landon's house. After a great show of reluctance, the hat was produced. I impounded it, and the maid who was sacked—Doris Finch—alleges it was the hat she found. Anyway, Mrs. Landon now admits it was Fothergill's hat, and that he left it behind."

"So what with the hat and the evidence of Sir Richard Cherrington, there seems no doubt that Fothergill left St. John's Close after spending part of the night there, and got back into College just in time to be in at the finding of Gostlin's corpse?"

"Yes, sir."

"And that he went out of College by the back gate sometime between eleven-forty-five and four o'clock?" said the Superintendent. "My evidence, slight as it is, can confirm the eleven-forty-five time, derived from Wedgwood not seeing a car."

"That's a good thing," said Fleming.

"Yes," went on the Superintendent. "I have been tracking down the letter which Fothergill wrote, and, while all the evidence is not quite water-tight, it looks as if it was posted much when he said, and certainly after eleven o'clock."

"That's a very nice confirmation," said Fleming. "But I haven't told you all my news, sir," he went on. "Not only have we established the existence of this car, but I think I know whose car it is."

"What?" said the Superintendent. "Come, come, Flamingo, you've been holding out on me."

"Well, sir, I'm not quite sure," said Fleming. "But when I was interviewing Mrs. Landon I had a look round the grounds—just as a matter of routine, of course—and noticed there was no car in the Dean's garage. So I asked Mrs. Landon, casually like, did they keep a car, and she says yes, but the Dean very kindly lent it to two undergraduates who were going on a fortnight's motoring tour in France. She didn't know their names."

"Goodness me, Flamingo!" exclaimed the Superintendent. "This is most important stuff you've been unearthing."

"Thank you, sir," said Fleming. "I questioned the girl Finch, who hadn't been quite so noticing as she pretended to be. She couldn't say whether the car was there on the Tuesday morning, but it was certainly there on Monday when she left."

"Ah-ha," said the Superintendent. "And when does Mrs. Landon claim that these two undergraduates drove the car away?"

"Oh, Tuesday morning," said Fleming. "She did not see them, because she was out at the time they called."

"You got the number and description of the car, of course?"

"I did. It is a small twelve horse-power Humber with number AP 1936. A black saloon."

"What does the police constable say to this description?" queried Robertson-Macdonald.

"Glad to see you are thinking on my lines, sir," said Inspector Fleming. "The constable can't describe the car he saw outside the back gate, but the description of the Dean's car would fit approximately. He didn't note the number, unfortunately."

The Superintendent filled his pipe. "That's a very fine piece of work, Fleming," he said. "Now let's see where all this gets us." He numbered the points with his fingers. "Point one: a stranger is seen hanging about St. John's Close at eleven o'clock on Monday night. It may be Fothergill, it may not. He disappears behind the garage."

"Yes, sir," interrupted Fleming. "I've checked all that with Doris Finch and her boy-friend. They can't add any more, but they stick to their story."

"Point number two," went on the Superintendent: "Fothergill leaves College after eleven-forty-five and before four o'clock. Point number three: possibly Fothergill, possibly someone else, is seen by the President of Fisher College at a time which may be anywhere in the night, but is more likely to be a quarter-past two or a quarter-past one than any other time. Point number four: a car, perhaps the Dean's, is driven to the back gate before two o'clock and driven away again before four." He paused. "Those are all the points we have, I'm afraid," he went on, "and they don't tell us definitely whether it's Mr. X or Fothergill."

"Quite so, sir," said Fleming, "and it might even be Fothergill with a few red herrings—such as lurking round the garage at eleven—to suggest the presence of a Mr. X."

"Yes, even that's possible," agreed the Superintendent.

"What's our next step, then?" asked Fleming.

"Why, the car, of course," said Robertson-Macdonald. "We must find the Landons' car. That's where you come in. More good staff work. Send a telegram, reply paid, to every undergraduate and graduate of the College who was up on Tuesday the 11th, and ask them or their relatives to say whether they were given the loan of the Dean's car. Put out a nation-wide search for the car, and thirdly get all the ports on the Channel crossing to check whether such a car went out of the country on Tuesday morning, or at any subsequent date."

"Good, sir! I'll get cracking on that."

"Meanwhile," said the Superintendent, "I shall probably get further statements from Fothergill and Mrs. Landon after I have demonstrated to them how very untrue their present statements are. First I'll go and tell Wyndham what we are working on."

"By the way, sir," said Fleming, "there's one little piece of evidence I learnt that I can't quite fit into the picture."

"Let's have it," said Robertson-Macdonald.

"You know the only new building in Fisher College is on the other side of the river, and comprises the baths and also a garage. The man who looks after this block is called Lupton. He sees the water is hot for the baths and supervises this block generally. Now, on the morning the murders were discovered he came to work in the normal way at six-thirty. He was delayed by hearing the surprising news, so that he didn't get to the bath block until a quarter to seven. One thing he noticed as it got light was that there were fresh car tracks on the cement outside the garage."

"Go on. This is interesting."

"I've checked with the police on duty in the town on the night of Monday–Tuesday when the murders took place, and it seems it was a dry, cold night, with clouds and the moon occasionally breaking through. You will remember, sir, that the President said the moon had broken through for a moment and shown him the man on the Backs."

"I do indeed," said Robertson-Macdonald.

"Then about five-thirty in the morning there was a short, sharp shower of rain. Lasted only about ten minutes. I checked up with some of the bedmakers and College servants, and they confirm the shower of rain, saying it caught some of them as they were starting to work in the morning."

"And your deduction from all this?" asked the Superintendent.

"That someone drove a car into the garage at the back of Fisher College between five-thirty and seven o'clock."

"That seems justified, but I'm damned if I see where it fits in. Who normally keeps cars there?"

"There are four cars there," said Fleming, "belonging to the four resident dons—Dr. Quibell, Sir Richard Cherrington, Westmacott and Fothergill."

"H'm," said the Superintendent. "You certainly have given me something to think about. Now I must off to Wyndham and tell him exactly what we are working on."

It was while he was with Inspector Wyndham that a constable came in with the news that Sergeant Waddell had arrived.

Waddell was very cheerful, and full of news.

"Well," said the Superintendent, "what sort of luck did you have in stirring up the dirt?"

"Got some good stuff, sir—really good stuff for you," said Waddell. "Didn't start off too well. Only got silly lines on the President and Vice-President."

"What have they done?" asked Robertson-Macdonald.

"Nothing serious," said Waddell. "Apparently the girl who runs the Yellow Barn used to be Cherrington's mistress."

"Ah-ha."

"Yes, and many years ago the President used to be a great frequenter of the same place."

"The devil he was!"

"But I don't think those snippets of gossip are really of very much value. I tried to concentrate on the woman."

"The woman! You would, of course. But what woman?"

"Mrs. Landon, of course," said Waddell. "The key person in the case."

The Superintendent liked the way Waddell always laid the law down about any case he worked on.

"I figured out," continued Waddell, "that her past would provide me with all I needed."

"And it has?"

"You bet it has! Just listen, sir," went on Waddell. "I find that she appeared in Cambridge six years ago. That is to say, in 1933. She came up in the summer term of that year as the sister of an undergraduate of Fisher College called Oliver Hartley. Hartley came up in 1932, and he brought his sister to the dances and the May Ball of 1933."

"This all seems fairly straightforward so far."

"I know, sir," said Waddell. "She was very beautiful, and the talk of that year's May Balls. Scandal number one. The tutor of Fisher College, Roger Westmacott by name, made a dead set at her, and everyone thought they would become engaged, and then, surprisingly enough, her engagement was announced to Dr. Landon. She was aged twenty-two at the time. Dr. Landon was thirty-five."

"H'm," said the Superintendent. So there was some connection, as he had guessed, between Westmacott and Mrs. Landon.

"What's scandal number two?" he asked.

"This man Oliver Hartley comes up an undergraduate in 1932 and, with his sister, is in the limelight in May 1933. The wedding to the Dean takes place in August 1933."

"Yes?"

"Young Mr. Hartley is not among those present in Fisher College in October 1933, nor does he appear in the College records again."

"Why not?" asked the Superintendent.

"It was found that he had put up some most tremendous blacks. He was heavily in debt and had, to all intents and purposes, stolen ten pounds from another undergraduate. It was all hushed up and explained away, but the Dean and President had no alternative but to send him down."

"May I ask your source for all this?" said the Superintendent.

"Rodgers the under-porter and Kilmartin, sir," said Waddell.

"The private room in the Bishop's Arms, and as much beer as I could hold and just a little bit more than either of them could."

"Good work! Any more?"

"They couldn't tell me any more about this young Hartley except that he had been up to Cambridge once or twice staying with his sister since he was sent down."

"Must have been an awkward ménage," commented the Superintendent. "Hartley, and the Dean who sent him down, and the Dean's wife who is his sister."

"Yes," went on Waddell. "As I couldn't get any more from this end, I went elsewhere to track Hartley. My first thought was the original home of the Hartleys at Rockbourne in Dorset. But purely as routine I looked at our records as I went through town."

"And you found him?" asked the other eagerly.

"I did, sir," said Waddell. "He seems to have carried on his tricks as soon as he was sent down in 1933. In early 1934 he is involved with a number of other young fools in a large confidence-trick swindle. He got let off under the First Offenders Act. Then in 1935 he is up for forging cheques. Went in for two years, and came out in February 1937. Went abroad, and not known of much since, except for one or two visits made to his sister between then and the present."

The Superintendent nodded his head. "Bloody good show, Waddell," he said. "You've turned up a most tremendous amount of valuable material. Trust our old Waddell to stir up the dirt in any case," he added, turning to Inspector Wyndham.

Inspector Wyndham smiled wanly. He did not see where all this was leading. It seemed to him the Scotland Yard folk were making a tremendous mystery of what had at first been a very straightforward case.

"Mind you," went on the Superintendent, turning to Waddell, "it's good, I admit, but it's only a beginning."

"Yes, sir," agreed the other, a trifle crestfallen.

"But a good beginning," conceded the Superintendent. "There's a lot of work to be done now. First I want you to get on to Fothergill. Get me all his past. Rake the whole thing up and give it me on a neat little plate."

"Right, sir, I will," said Waddell.

"Then get to work on Westmacott," said the Superintendent. "Let me have the whole lay-out there."

"Surely you don't suspect Westmacott," broke in Inspector Wyndham.

"I don't suspect anyone," said the Superintendent. "But I want to know about everyone. Now, Westmacott has lain pretty doggo in this case. He is the fourth resident Fellow, but we have heard precious little of his activities. Sir Richard Cherrington, Fothergill, the President—these three have figured time and time again, but we hear nothing of Westmacott. Isn't that suspicious?"

"Maybe he was asleep," said Wyndham practically.

"Quite so," agreed Robertson-Macdonald. "Quite so. But it's odd; and Waddell brings up a point. What if Westmacott has nursed a grievance against Landon since Landon took the girl away from him?" He paused. "Well, that's possible, isn't it?"

"Oh yes, it's possible," said Wyndham grudgingly.

"Of course it's possible," said the Superintendent, warming to the subject. "He nurses this grievance, and then two things finally decide him on getting rid of the Dean."

"Two things?" queried Waddell.

"Yes, two things," went on the Superintendent. "All those years he had nursed his grievances. Landon stole the woman he wanted to marry. Landon crosses him everywhere in the College life. Landon makes the girl's life a hell. He contemplates getting rid of Landon, and then—two things decide him." He paused. "The first is the sending down of Parrott, whom he apparently liked. He reasons with the Dean on the Monday night; the Dean refuses to be reasonable. Westmacott's temper cracks. All his pent-up hatred storms out. He makes a plan that will get rid of the Dean but apparently involve a number of likely people. It is he who arranges for Parrott's button to be by Gostlin's body, and so fixes the first red herring. The second thing that moves him is that Fothergill, who has been trifling with June Westmacott, his niece, now throws her over and proceeds to make passes at Anne Landon. So Westmacott decides to revenge June Westmacott and involve Fothergill at the same time." He stopped.

The others look at him.

"Gosh!" said Waddell. "That's a very plausible story."

"You really mean," said Wyndham, "that you think Westmacott did it?"

"Oh no," said the Superintendent. "Nothing of the kind. I merely mean it is possible to build up a case against him, as against so many other folk in this mystery. That's why I insist on Westmacott being watched carefully and his whole history examined."

"Are you having everyone watched in this way?" asked Wyndham.

"Why, certainly," said the Superintendent. "That's only routine work. It may lead us to something."

Wyndham was astonished. "Do you mean the President and Sir Richard Cherrington are being watched?" he asked incredulously.

"Of course," said the Superintendent. "Who's on Sir Richard?" he asked of Sergeant Waddell.

"It's De Rougemont, sir," replied Waddell.

"Oh yes," said Robertson-Macdonald. "We put him on because he's half French. Speaks French so well."

"French?" queried Inspector Wyndham.

"Yes," said the Superintendent. "This tour of Sir Richard's with his nephew to France. Suspicious, don't you think? Must have it watched carefully."

"Good gracious me!" said Wyndham. He was astonished at the careful planning that had been going on. "And while all these followings and investigations and so forth are going on, what do you propose to do yourself, sir?" he asked.

"That's easy," said the Superintendent. "Yes, that's quite easy. What Waddell has told me this morning makes my own course very clear." He paused. "The woman in the case," he said. "I must see the woman in the case."

"The woman?" queried Wyndham.

"Yes," said Robertson-Macdonald. "I think the time has come when I must interview Mrs. Landon."

II

Anne Landon was in her boudoir upstairs when the Superintendent's card was sent up. As she read it a faint shiver of apprehension went down her back. She could not really explain why: perhaps it was the neatly printed "New Scotland Yard" in the corner of the card. She had dealt with Richard Cherrington and the Cambridge police easily. Something told her this was not going to be so easy.

At first, however, Detective-Superintendent Robertson-Macdonald did everything possible to allay her fears. He was charming, suave, polite. Quite unlike the policeman she had expected. But gradually he turned the conversation to the crimes.

"I know this cannot but be distressing to you," he said. "But I must question you again about the events of last Monday and Tuesday."

"Really," she said, bridling. "Is it necessary? I told all I knew to Inspector Wyndham."

The Superintendent smiled. "I am afraid you did not tell him the truth, you know," he said blandly.

"I beg your pardon," said Mrs. Landon.

"Granted," said the Superintendent, bland as ever. "But you told him three different stories, you know. I mean first you said that you went home alone and did not see Fothergill until next day."

"I didn't say that," she protested. "I wasn't asked anything about whether I had seen Fothergill."

"No, but you implied you had been alone, and you certainly denied any knowledge of his hat," said the Superintendent.

She was silent.

"You will appreciate my difficulties, I am sure, Mrs. Landon," the Superintendent went on. "They are sufficient already, without having to battle with conflicting statements given at various times by the same person." He paused. "I am suggesting to you that you have still not told me or the police the truth."

"If you have come here this morning just to call me a liar, Superintendent," said Anne Landon, flaring up, "I cannot see any point in prolonging this interview."

"One moment," said Robertson-Macdonald suavely. "You see, I am not merely guessing or trying to be rude. I know you have not yet told us the truth."

"You know?" asked Anne, her eyes narrowing.

"Yes," went on the Superintendent. "You and Dr. Fothergill now assert that he came to this house about eleven o'clock and was here until nearly six o'clock next morning, when he dressed hurriedly and went to Fisher College, leaving his hat behind. It is therefore obvious that your statements give Dr. Fothergill a complete alibi for the period of the murders. With the doubts about the President's eyesight and his spectacles, and the confusion about whether it was two-fifteen or one-fifteen, it will be difficult to shake your statement in a court of law unless we have other evidence that it is a suspect statement." He paused. "And we have that evidence," he went on.

"You have?" she asked. "What do you mean?"

"Well, Mrs. Landon," he said, "I have proof that Dr. Fothergill did not leave College until well after eleven o'clock, that he was certainly in College after half-past eleven."

"We may have been mistaken about the details of the time, you know," she said hurriedly. "It may have been half-past eleven when he arrived here."

"And the man seen here at eleven o'clock?" asked the Superintendent.

"Just imaginings on the part of my maid," said Anne quickly. "She was always an unreliable type."

The Superintendent smiled. "It won't do, you know, Mrs. Landon, I'm afraid," he said. "You see, this man at eleven was seen by not only the maid Doris Finch, but by her young man, and there is no doubt about the time, as her young man is an under-porter at Peterhouse and was on time for duty at eleven-thirty. I have proof that Dr. Fothergill was in College after eleven-thirty, and I think he was right in his second statement, that he visited your late husband just before midnight."

Anne looked at the Superintendent warily. She did not quite know where he was taking her in this firm but unrelenting examination. "Well?" she said.

"Do, please, let me have the truth," said the Superintendent. "There are, after all, only two explanations of what I have told you. Either there were two men about your house that night——"

"Two men?" she interrupted sharply.

"Yes; one who was seen by Finch and her young man at eleven o'clock, and the other—Fothergill—who arrived later, certainly after twelve o'clock."

"And the other solution?"

"Fothergill is here at eleven o'clock and returns to College in time to post his letter and see your husband after eleven-thirty."

She laughed nervously. "You have at last got to the truth, Superintendent," she said. "Both Evan and I were fools to accept the theory which Sir Richard Cherrington planted on us out of the kindness of his heart."

"Then Fothergill was not with you from eleven o'clock?"

"I'm afraid not, and I'm afraid we didn't spend the night in sin. A pity. Sir Richard will be disappointed when he hears."

"Tell me what really happened," said Robertson-Macdonald.

"I went into College at about a quarter to ten to deliver my husband's spectacles. Mr. Baynes, the Head Porter, can confirm this, as I saw him just as I went through the front gate. I was with my husband only for a few minutes."

"Yes?"

"He was very upset," she went on. "And yet curiously triumphant at the same time. I couldn't understand him. He told me that happy marriages were made in heaven and needed no tending in a good Christian home. You know, of course, that I was planning to go and marry Evan—Evan Fothergill—and that my husband was refusing to divorce me. He then told me he was going on a six months' holiday, and would I come with him? The whole thing was so silly I left him quickly and went out of College."

"By the back gate?"

"No, I haven't a Fellow's key. I went out through the main entrance. At the corner of Bridge Street and Northampton Street I met Evan. He had apparently been to St. John's Close to look for me. He, too, was very distraught, and wanted me to go away with him that night. We walked about on the Backs for a while, and then he took me back to the house. That would have been about eleven o'clock, and I suppose he was the man Doris Finch saw."

"This really is most interesting," said Robertson-Macdonald. "Do go on."

"Evan went back to College and I went to bed." She paused. "Then at about one-thirty I was awakened by pebbles being thrown at my window. It was Evan. He was still in a terrible state, muttering that he would kill my husband, and that he couldn't go to sleep. I gave him a very strong nightcap, although he seemed to have had a lot to drink already, and I put the alarm clock with him, set for a quarter to six. I put him to sleep on the sofa in the drawing-room. When I awoke at seven and went down to let the maid in, he had gone."

The Superintendent paused. "Now, Mrs. Landon," he said, "I want you to be quite sure about the time Dr. Fothergill arrived."

"I am quite sure," she said. "I swear he was in my house by one-thirty. You may disbelieve me. I lied at first to shield Evan. His appearance here at all was open to misconstruction. Then Sir Richard seemed to have worked out that he had been here all night, and that seemed an even safer alibi, although it romantically involved us in apparent misconduct. Believe me, I am telling you the truth. I have nothing to conceal. My previous statements were only made in an attempt to shield Evan. You may think it despicable of me to do that, and it has probably involved you in a lot of work, but it was very important to me and to Evan."

"I see," said the Superintendent. It did all hang together when you looked at it. This story explained without remainder all the odd things that had been worrying him—the letter and the strange man at eleven o'clock. And of course it would have been Fothergill whom the President saw, and at one-fifteen—a Fothergill going to St. John's Close, and not a Fothergill fresh from the murders of Dean and Porter. But where, he asked himself, did this leave the case?

"I must ask you to come with me to the police station, Mrs. Landon," said Robertson-Macdonald, "and let us have your full story in writing. I have a car outside. Would you be so good as to come with me now?"

"Why, certainly," she said. "I'll do that for you."

The Superintendent got up to go. "There are just two other little matters I should like to ask you about," he said.

"Yes?"

"The first is your brother."

"My brother?" Anne Landon looked at the policeman sharply. "What the hell has he got to do with this business?" she asked.

"My dear Mrs. Landon," said Robertson-Macdonald soothingly, "nothing at all. Purely a routine query, I assure you."

"Well, I don't like it," she said. "Just because Oliver was unlucky enough to get involved with some others when young in a rotten swindle, and because he was made to take the rap when others who were responsible got off easily, you have him on your police records, and I suppose have a permanent down on him. He has forfeited for ever his presumption of innocence in whatever criminal circumstances he may be remotely involved."

"Please, Mrs. Landon," began the Superintendent.

"No, let me have my say," she went on quickly. "I may have been wrong myself in this business of misleading the police. I was afraid for Evan, and Sir Richard seemed so plausible. I'm sorry I've given you a lot of trouble, but, for God's sake, I ask you, keep Oliver out of this. Don't start up the old family scandal. In any case, he was in Canada at the time of the murder—been there a good while."

"He has?" asked the Superintendent. "I thought he lived in France."

"He used to do so, since he came out of prison in 1937. Then this year he decided to go to America and make a completely new start. Just as Evan and I will do." She paused. "He came over from France and wished me good-bye in the middle of February. He sailed on the *Ile de France* from Cherbourg in the last week of February, and landed in Montreal. I had a cable dated March 11th from Calgary."

There was a moment's silence. The Superintendent's suspicious mind noted the date: it was the morning the murder was discovered. Was there anything peculiar here? He thought furiously a moment, but all he said was, "Really? Thank you for all this information. You must believe me, however, when I say that I was merely making a routine enquiry. I am sorry it should have upset you."

"It's all right," said Mrs. Landon. "I'm a bit distraught at all this questioning."

"Quite so. I think we should be moving off, if you don't mind," said Robertson-Macdonald. "Just this one last question, if I may. When did you miss the car?"

"The car? Oh yes. Now, let me see. My husband had promised to lend it to two undergraduates who were going on a motoring holiday in France for a week or two. I expect they drove it away on the Tuesday morning. I was out at the time, I suppose. They certainly had my husband's permission, I know that."

"And their names?"

"Don't remember their names. Don't think I ever knew them."

"And the keys?"

"The keys?"

"Yes, the car keys."

"Well?"

"How many sets of keys did your car have?" asked the Superintendent.

"Ah, I see," said Mrs. Landon. "Two, I think. I had one set and my husband had the other."

"And these undergraduates. How did they drive the car away?"

"I suppose they had my husband's set. He presumably gave his set to them. I still have mine."

"You have? Do you think I could borrow them for a short while?"

"By all means," said Mrs. Landon. "I always keep them in this little bag." She gave the Superintendent three keys on a keyring with a keytag attached. "Here they are," she said. "Three of them. One for the garage door. The second is the ignition and the third the door key."

"Thank you," said the Superintendent. "I think, if you don't mind, we should be going along now."

III

Superintendent Robertson-Macdonald drove straight round to Fisher College. Mrs. Landon said nothing as they drew up outside the front gate.

Fothergill was in his rooms, writing at his desk, when the Superintendent called on him.

"Good-morning," said Robertson-Macdonald. "I'm Superintendent Robertson-Macdonald of Scotland Yard. Just another ruddy policeman come to question you."

"Scotland Yard, eh?" said Fothergill. "Well, what can I do for you?"

"Quite a lot," said the Superintendent. "And first of all, give up making any more conflicting statements."

"What do you mean?"

"Well, first you tell us you were in your rooms on Monday night from after Hall until next morning. Next you say you went out to post a letter and saw the Dean after half-past eleven and then went pacing about on the Backs in a distraught state. Then you say you were with Mrs. Landon in St. John's Close from eleven until next morning."

"I'm sorry," said Fothergill. "The first two statements were merely an attempt to protect Mrs. Landon from publicity."

"Wasn't it to protect yourself?"

"I beg your pardon," said Fothergill.

"You see, I know you did post that letter in College after half-past eleven."

"You do?"

"And Mrs. Landon has told me that you did not arrive at her house until about half-past one."

Evan Fothergill looked disconcerted. "She has?" he said. "You're not trying to trick me?"

"No."

Fothergill sighed. "We've been very foolish indeed," he said. "Especially after all the books tell you to tell the truth, no matter what the black appearances at the time."

"Will you tell me just what happened?" asked the Superintendent gently.

"I will gladly," said Fothergill. "I came out from dinner in Hall that night not knowing what to do. I had heard the Dean say he was going away on a six months' holiday, and I wondered if in some odd way he had persuaded his wife to go away with him. I could not get her on the telephone, so I walked round to St. John's Close. I went out by the back gate, but at the same time she was coming into College the front way with Landon's spectacles. I met her as she was coming back, at the corner of Bridge Street and Northampton Street—you know, by the lights. I walked to her house with her and we walked about a bit. Then I went back to College."

"You went into the house?" asked the Superintendent.

"No. I didn't go into the house then," said Fothergill readily. "I left Mrs. Landon at the gate."

The Superintendent sat up. "You are quite sure of this?" he said.

"Yes, absolutely," replied the other. "I came back into College. Must have been about a quarter to eleven when I got in."

"Nearly a quarter to eleven? You're sure of this?"

"Yes. I can't fix the time better than that. But I know it took me a long time to write the letter to June Westmacott. It was a difficult letter. I posted it, and then went up to see Landon. He threw me out, and I came back to my rooms. I had taken a lot of drink already that night, and now I took more. In my drink I did a very frightful thing."

The Superintendent looked at him sharply. "Yes?" he said.

"I planned to kill Landon," said Fothergill.

"You what?" said the Superintendent. "Do you know what you are saying?" He paused. "I must caution you," he began, "that everything you say——"

"No, no," said Fothergill. "That isn't necessary. I didn't carry out the plan. It was a very good plan," he added—"a very good plan. Along the roof from these rooms. In through the Dean's window and back again. No one would have the slightest clue." He paused. "Don't look so alarmed, Superintendent," he said. "It may be unchristian and unethical to plan a murder, but it is not yet a crime. You see, I never committed the crime. I was drunk at the time, or I wouldn't have thought up this plan. I put on my coat and hat and went out on the Backs to cool my head. It was as I was walking up and down that the President's light went on."

"When was that?"

"I've no idea, but it couldn't have been much after one o'clock," said Fothergill. "It was then I made a wise decision. Rather than murder the Dean I would go and see his wife. So I went off to St. John's Close."

"And that was the first time you were in the grounds of the house that night?" said Robertson-Macdonald.

"It was," said Fothergill. "And that's all my story. And it's true," he added.

"You realise," said the Superintendent, "that it leaves you heavily under suspicion."

"I do," answered Fothergill. "I have realised that since I came into College on Tuesday morning and saw the body of Gostlin. All the Fellows and undergraduates were under suspicion. When it became clear the Dean had been murdered I was more under suspicion than ever. That is why we have told you these various tales."

"You realise, too," said the Superintendent, "that even now your story will not sound very convincing in a court of law."

"There I think you are wrong," said Fothergill. "Let's take some distinguished member of this College as defending counsel. Say, Sir Athelstan Rowley or Mr. James Caunter. I think they could paint a good picture of me. Somehow I don't think I fit into the picture of the entirely corrupt young man who throws off one woman, murders another's husband, and then murders a College porter and finally spends the night with the murdered man's wife—all in the course of a few hours. I'm not cast for that rather heroic mould, Superintendent."

"H'm," said Robertson-Macdonald. "Maybe not. I must request you to give your new statement to the police station this afternoon," he added. "In fact, it would be better if you could come along and give it straight-away. Mrs. Landon is waiting in my car at the front gate."

"By all means," agreed the other.

When they were in the police station and were having their statements taken down in shorthand, the Superintendent went into Wyndham's room.

Wyndham was working through some papers. "How is the case going, sir?" he asked.

"Don't know," said the Superintendent. "We've got some lines. Can you do some things for me?"

"Why, certainly."

"The first is get a full description of Oliver Hartley—Mrs. Landon's brother—from Scotland Yard. Waddell can help you here. Get it sent to the *Sûrété Générale* in Paris and to the Canadian police, and find out whether such a man left Cherbourg on the *Ile de France* in late February and got to Montreal in early March and to Calgary by March 11th."

"Yes," said Wyndham, taking down the particulars. "Do you suspect Hartley?"

"No, no," said the Superintendent. "Just a routine enquiry. Can't leave any ends open in this case."

"Anything else, sir?"

"Yes." The Superintendent paused. "Were there any keys on Landon's body when you examined it down at Twyford?"

"Yes, there were," said the other—"a bunch of keys. We had them tested for finger-prints. They're back now with the other exhibits in this affair. In the other room."

They went into the other room together. Wyndham unlocked a drawer and took out a bunch of keys. He handed them to the Superintendent.

"My God!" said Robertson-Macdonald. "That's most interesting. Whew!" He whistled.

"Found something?" asked Wyndham.

The Superintendent picked up two of the keys and took those that Mrs. Landon had given him out of his pocket.

"These," he said, "are the keys of the Landon car which is still missing. There were only two sets. One held by Mrs. Landon and one by Landon himself. Mrs. Landon says the car was driven away by undergraduates on the Tuesday morning, and that they must have had Landon's keys, which is impossible, as they were on the body."

"That is interesting," said Wyndham. "And it means?"

"Either that someone had a third set made, perhaps at the same time as he had a set of keys made to the Dean's room and the back gate."

"Or?"

"Or I am afraid Mrs. Landon is lying."

"You think she is still keeping something back?" asked Wyndham.

"It's possible," said the Superintendent. "I noticed this morning a discrepancy between her statement and that of Fothergill which is most significant. She said it was about eleven that Fothergill left her house on Monday night, and that he was unquestionably the man seen by the servant and her boy friend Bert."

"Yes."

"I questioned Fothergill carefully on this point," said Robertson-Macdonald. "He swears that he did not go into the house in Madingley Road that evening, and that he was back in his rooms at about a quarter to eleven. He remembers that his letter to June Westmacott took a long time to write."

"Whew!" said Wyndham. "That'll take some explaining."

"Yes. There are two immediate questions. Who was the mystery man at St. John's Close at eleven o'clock? Who drove away the Landon's car? The mystery man or the two undergraduates? And here's a third related question. Where did the third set of keys come from, or was the second set returned to Mrs. Landon? Yes, there's a great deal to work on."

IV

Anne Landon could not have been much more worried than she was as she walked away from lunch with Evan Fothergill, if she could have known of the discussions that Superintendent Robertson-Macdonald and Inspector Wyndham were having about her. It had been a difficult lunch: the strain of the last few days and the ordeals of police statements seemed for a moment to have tarnished their fine love. She had declined Evan's invitation to walk back with her, and was crossing the Backs quickly and alone.

How difficult to believe, when the Backs were bright with crocuses and the March sunshine, that such confusion and unpleasantness were involving everything, even her love for Evan Fothergill. Perhaps she ought to have left Bill Landon months ago and gone away alone and started her life afresh. Was it too late to do so now? Go away from these Colleges and their self-satisfied dons' wives? No, it was too late. She knew she could not do without Evan Fothergill.

She had got to the back gate leading on to Queen's Road when a man came from the direction of the University Library, gave her a curt bow, lifted his hat, smiled, and went on down the path towards the College. It was Roger Westmacott. Not at first recognising who he was, for her thoughts were far away, Anne Landon had stared him full in the face, and, staring, had turned away in horror. Something in that smile suddenly struck more terror and apprehension into Anne Landon than anything that had happened in the last ten days. She remembered how

Roger Westmacott had proposed marriage to her six years ago, and how, when she had refused him and told him she was going to marry Bill Landon, she had seen that same cold, bitter-sweet smile on his face.

"You will live to regret this decision bitterly," he had said—"most bitterly."

She had often thought of that remark in the years that followed, and had interpreted it as meaning that Bill Landon would prove a disappointing and heartbreaking husband. That had been true: the marriage had been a mistake and a failure. But what if Roger had not meant that? What if he had meant that she should live to regret not having accepted him. What if——? She paused. But not after all these years. And yet. Evan Fothergill had broken off his engagement to Roger's niece. Could this have brought things to a head? What if Roger Westmacott had been lurking round St. John's Close at eleven o'clock, and had stolen the car and made the whole thing look as though it was a conspiracy by Evan Fothergill and herself?

But could it be?

She shivered as she walked up Queen's Road, and in one moment the smiling crocuses on the Backs seemed to be mocking her and the March sunshine to have no comfort. For the first time in her life she knew real stark terror, and she hurried on to her house, afraid.

CHAPTER SIXTEEN

MRS. LANDON NAMES THE MURDERER

When Superintendent Robertson-Macdonald got into his office in the Cambridge Police Headquarters on the Friday following his interview with Mrs. Landon and Evan Fothergill he was greeted by Detective-Inspector Wyndham with the good news that the Dean's car had been found.

"Yes, Superintendent," said the Inspector. "There's no doubt about it. A black saloon twelve horse-power Humber, registration number A.P. 1936. My Sergeant Mossop went over last night when we heard from the Hertfordshire police. There's no doubt about it—it's the Landons' car."

"And where was it found?"

"In a small chalk-pit off a side road just outside Baldock."

"Outside Baldock?"

"Yes," said Wyndham. "Had been driven right into the chalk-pit, and was hidden from sight of the main road. Some children playing noticed it, and told their parents, one of whom was inquisitive enough to go and look yesterday. He went and told the police, who immediately recognised it from our distress call."

"Ah, ha," mused the Superintendent. "Well, I suppose we'd better go over and look at it. Though we shan't find anything of interest."

"We've got all the answers to our telegrams to the undergraduates," said Wyndham. "None of them are abroad or had planned to borrow the Dean's car. Not that that is very interesting, now that we know where the car is."

The Superintendent turned on him sharply. "That's where you're wrong," he said. "That's just where you're wrong. You see, Mrs. Landon assured us that the car had been taken by undergraduates."

The Inspector whistled. "Why, of course," he said.

"And what's more," said the Superintendent, "she had the keys of the car—the only other set."

"You don't think she did the murders?" asked Wyndham.

"I don't think anything," said Robertson-Macdonald disarmingly. "But it looks as though that young woman has been telling me even more lies than I thought. First the way she declared Fothergill was around the house at eleven o'clock, and then the story about the undergraduates. I must go and see her again."

"It looks as though we can never get the real truth out of these people," said Wyndham sadly.

"Don't you believe it," said Robertson-Macdonald. "I'll give Mrs. Landon a very unpleasant time. What with the possession of a set of keys, and the lies about the man at eleven o'clock, and the car with the undergraduates, she has a lot to explain." He paused. "How long would it take to drive a car—a Humber 12—from Cambridge to Baldock?"

"Under an hour, sir. It's about twenty-five miles."

"So the car could have got to Baldock about three-thirty in the morning."

"I see you're thinking the same way as I was," said the Inspector. "Yes, assuming the murder was committed at two-fifteen—that is, the murder of Gostlin—the murderer could have got to Baldock in the car by three-thirty." He paused. "There is a train," he went on.

"There is?" said the Superintendent. "What time?"

"Leaves Baldock at three-fifty-five in the morning," said Wyndham. "Gets into King's Cross at four-forty-five."

"I see," said the Superintendent. "Well, that's all the more reason why we should go over to Baldock straight away. We must look at the car, and then we must enquire if anyone noticed someone getting on the early train on Tuesday morning. There would have been so few people about. One would have been bound to notice anyone buying a ticket."

"Of course, she mightn't have bought a ticket."

"Why do you say 'she'?" queried the Superintendent.

"Well, it was your suggestion we were tracking Mrs. Landon," said

Wyndham. "She had the keys of the car, she lied about the man at eleven, she lied about the car being with undergraduates."

"I know," said the Superintendent. "But she was in her bed in St. John's Close when Doris Finch came at seven o'clock to call her and open up the house."

"That's true, sir," said Wyndham. "But I've thought all that out, although I admit I was thinking it with Sir Richard in my mind. The train leaves Baldock for London at three fifty-five, as I said, but another leaves Baldock for Cambridge at five-fifteen."

"What are you thinking of?" said Robertson-Macdonald.

"Well, I admit I was thinking of Sir Richard as the murderer," said Wyndham slowly. "But it fits just as well for Mrs. Landon. I figured it out this way. The murderer drives the car away at two-thirty. Parks it in the chalk-pit at Baldock about three-thirty or a little earlier. Goes to the station."

"And waits there until five-fifteen?"

"No, sir," said Wyndham. "Books a ticket to London. Gets on the train. Gets out at Hitchin—station down the line. Changes into the Cambridge train, and is in Cambridge at six o'clock. Plenty of time for Mrs. Landon to be back in bed when the maid comes."

"My God, Wyndham, that's a bright idea of yours," said Robertson-Macdonald.

"Yes, sir," said Wyndham, immodestly agreeing with this praise, "and the alibi has foxed us all. Yes, it was not an alibi for Fothergill that Mrs. Landon was trying to fix, but one for herself. It was very effectively done with Fothergill's statement, allegedly reluctantly dragged out of them, and by planting the hat."

"Planting the hat?"

"Yes, sir. Fothergill's hat was planted at St. John's Close to be noticed by the maid. When she noticed it, it was to be further emphasised by being lied about and hidden. Gradually the alibi emerges. Very, very clever indeed."

"H'm," said Robertson-Macdonald. "Plausible and well argued. But you forgot one thing."

"What's that, sir?"

"The man seen hanging round St. John's Close at eleven o'clock."

"Could it be Fothergill?"

"He says no," said Robertson-Macdonald.

"I know he does," went on the other. "But isn't that just a slip in the agreed story he and Mrs. Landon had planned?"

"You mean that Fothergill knows that Mrs. Landon did the murders, perhaps for love of him, and is concocting this alibi for her?" said the Superintendent.

"No, sir; much cleverer than that," said Wyndham. "Mrs. Landon persuades Fothergill that he is in danger and is bound to be suspected.

So they concoct the story that they spent the night together, which gives Mrs. Landon the alibi she needs."

"I don't agree," said the Superintendent. "I cannot see Mrs. Landon in the rôle of calculating murderess and all this complex business about driving to Baldock, getting out of the train in Hitchin and haring back to Cambridge. It's far-fetched."

"Yes, but it's possible," said the other. "What other explanation have you?"

"Well." The Superintendent paused. "She might really be shielding someone. Or she might be lying because she does not know who did the murder, but suspects someone."

"That someone would have to have had a set of keys to the car," said Wyndham. "We can't trace any duplicate keys having been made in Cambridge."

"Well, anyway," said the Superintendent, "this is just theorising. We'll go over in the car to Baldock, look at the car, and find out if a young man in an overcoat bought a ticket for London on the morning of Tuesday."

"A young man, you still think, sir?"

"Yes, the young man the President saw."

"But wasn't that Fothergill?"

"Was it?" said the Superintendent. "I wonder."

II

This time the Superintendent walked from the Blue Boar, where he was staying, to St. John's Close. He had rung up Mrs. Landon at breakfast time, and she had reluctantly and shortly said she could see him. It was an exceptionally warm morning for March, and the sun shone with a clear brightness as he walked up Trinity Street and turned down Bridge Street.

He went over again in his mind the happenings of yesterday. First the finding of the Landon car at Baldock, with all the implications of that find: that Mrs. Landon was lying when she said undergraduates had taken it, that either Mrs. Landon had used her own set of keys, or lent the set to someone else, or that someone had made duplicates. Then the interview with the railway staff at Baldock. They had spent a long time getting hold of the booking-clerk and porter who had been on duty at that time, but eventually they had got their stories. A young man had booked a ticket to London on the Tuesday morning. When they had both remembered the young man independently, Inspector Wyndham's face fell, because it so obviously ruled out his two main suspects—Sir Richard Cherrington and Mrs. Landon.

Robertson-Macdonald had been delighted with the news. A theory was already forming in his mind. It seemed clear that Mrs. Landon's lies could mean only one thing: that she was protecting someone whom she knew had done the crime, or whom she suspected had done it. Perhaps Evan Fothergill? Or perhaps both Fothergill and Mrs. Landon were protecting a third person? Or just possibly they had spent the night together, and Mrs. Landon was using that to confuse the issue and protect a third person, while Fothergill had now no course but to support her.

Neither the porter nor the booking-clerk could give a good description of the young man. It had been dark, they had been sleepy and the man wore a coat, according to the clerk, but a burberry according to the porter, with a scarf and a slouch hat, according to both of them. It was a description that would fit almost anyone. The Superintendent showed them photographs of all the young men in the case who seemed in the least relevant—Evan Fothergill and Oliver Hartley, and John Parrott and Giles Farnaby, as well as six other miscellaneous photographs of young people which he had taken from the Cambridge police station. The porter was doubtful, but tentatively identified the young man as one of the six whose photographs the Superintendent had taken at random from the drawer in the police station. This was not very helpful, and the booking-clerk was no better: it might be Farnaby or Fothergill or Hartley—that was all he would say.

It hadn't really got them very much farther, the Inspector ruminated as he turned into Northampton Street. Well, they knew something—that the car had probably been driven from Cambridge to Baldock between 2.30 and 3.30, and that somebody rather young had taken a ticket for London at Baldock and had got into the 3.55 for London.

But had this young man gone to London, or had he, as Inspector Wyndham suggested, got out at Hitchin and doubled back to Cambridge? If that was so it couldn't be Fothergill, who was seen by Sir Richard at six o'clock in the morning. Unless he had come back in another car. Perhaps he had gone on to London, and was in reality someone like Oliver Hartley—the Superintendent, with his long police experience, rather favoured the villain he had not met and who had been in prison for some time. But Hartley was in America. The Superintendent stopped and lit his pipe. Now, was he? That was an interesting thought. He wished the answers would come from America and France to his query about Hartley and the *Ile de France*. "I wonder is it possible to fake that evidence about the *Ile de France*," he thought—"fake passport and faked entries on the ship. No, it would be difficult, especially with the immigration authorities in Canada."

Yet two things remained which he was sure had great significance, if only they could be fitted in. One was the strange man seen around the garage of St. John's Close, and the other was the hat—Fothergill's hat—which Doris Finch had noticed. Why was the hat left there? By accident? By design to prove that Fothergill had been there? Or by design because Mrs. Landon knew that there would be evidence of some man having been there, and the hat and her testimony showed it to have been Fothergill. Say Mrs. Landon saw this Mr. X wandering round her house, even knew he had taken the car, even suspected what he was going to do. "That's possible: then she goes into College, and persuades Fothergill to come and spent the night with her, and gets his hat left behind so that Fothergill is the obvious answer to the man who was there."

"Dear me," he thought as he rang the doorbell of St. John's Close, "there are endless possibilities, are there not? And then, if I am right about Mrs. Landon—as I think I must be—who is she consciously or unconsciously shielding. A former lover? Perhaps Roger Westmacott? Or Fothergill. Or even her brother, if only he hadn't been in America."

III

Mrs. Landon saw him this time not in her boudoir-study, but in a rather cold, inhuman drawing-room on the ground floor. She was obviously distressed, but at first the Superintendent could not make out the source of her distress. He assumed it was his visit, and perhaps the fact that she had sensed that he had seen through some of her lies.

"I am so sorry to come back and question you again so soon, Mrs. Landon," he began.

"Not at all," she said coldly. "It is your job, after all."

"Yes, quite so," said the Superintendent—"quite so. Very nice of you to see me. Now, let me see," he went on. "There are three things I wanted to ask you about, if you could spare me the time."

"Glad to be of any help," she said.

"Thank you. That's good," he said. "Now, the first thing is the hat."

"The—hat?"

"Yes, a strange hat was found here on the Tuesday morning. It was noticed by the maid, Doris Finch, and later you and Dr. Fothergill declared it was his hat."

"Why, so it is. The police have seen it."

"The police have seen a hat—yes," he began. "You assure me that was the hat seen by Finch on the Tuesday morning?"

"No doubt whatsoever," she replied.

"And that hat arrived here during the night with Dr. Fothergill."

"Why, certainly. How else?"

"I thought maybe he had left it on a previous occasion."

"Certainly not," she said. "It was left behind that night. There is no mystery about this hat, Superintendent, and I am surprised at your questions."

"Merely routine, my dear Mrs. Landon," he said suavely—"merely routine. Now, the second point. Ah, yes. The keys. Now, it appears that it was not undergraduates who took your car on the Tuesday morning, as you thought, but someone in the middle of the night." He paused. "Dr. Landon either misled you about the undergraduates," he said cruelly, "or someone took it away before the undergraduates got to it."

"Really," she said. It was clear that his words were troubling her.

"Yes," he went on. "I think that the Dean must have misled you."

"Why do you think that?"

"You really gave me that information."

"I did?"

"Yes. You see, you told me there were only two sets of keys to the car. One of these you have, and the other, which you thought the Dean must have lent to the two undergraduates, was found on his dead body."

She made no comment, but puffed nervously at her cigarette. He did not draw any conclusion, but changed his questions.

"How long have you had this car?" he queried.

"Not more than two months."

"Really?" he said. "Now, that is interesting. During that time have you lent it to anyone or has anyone driven it except Dr. Landon and yourself?"

"Does an answer to that question help you?"

"It might."

"Now let me think," she said. "Well, in the first place, Evan Fothergill and I have driven in it on two or three occasions. Three in all. Once we went to Ely. Another time we drove out on to the Gogs. A third time we went to supper at St. Ives."

"Were you with him the whole time?"

"Why, certainly. I can't see what you are driving at, Superintendent," she said.

"Anyone else?"

"Why, yes. My brother drove it when he was here."

"Your brother?" The Superintendent tried not to give away his quickening interest.

"Yes, he drove it, let me see, on two separate occasions. The first time we went over to Letchworth together."

"Through Hitchin and Baldock?"

"Why, of course," she said. "That's the obvious way. But what has that got to do with it?"

"And the other occasion?"

"My husband had injured his hand and could not drive. So Oliver drove him over to Ely for a meeting of the Discussion Group to which he belonged."

"I see," said the Superintendent.

"Now here is just what I want," he thought to himself. "If only this wretched man hadn't gone to Canada."

"Who was the third person," he asked. "I hope you are forgiving this inquisition."

"Why, certainly," she said. "The third person was Sir Richard—Sir Richard Cherrington. He was having his car mended or overhauled, or something, and wanted to go over to a meeting of the Bedfordshire and Hertfordshire Archæological Society at St. Neots. We lent him the car for the day. That would have been only a fortnight ago," she added.

"That is all very helpful," he said. "Now let me see. Yes, my third and last query. Doris Finch and her young man are sure they saw a strange person hanging round your house at eleven o'clock. You say it was Fothergill, but he says he did not come inside the gate. Can you explain the discrepancy in these two statements?"

She paused and lit another cigarette. "I can indeed," she said. "You see, I know who the stranger was at eleven o'clock."

"You do?"

"Yes," she said. "I understand you found my car in a disused chalk-pit near Baldock. I know who stole it and drove it there."

"You are quite sure of this?"

"I am indeed," she went on quickly. "You must believe me when I say that I have been growing increasingly terrified since the murders took place. At first I thought they might have been done by someone who was trying to do me a good turn, such as my brother Oliver or Evan Fothergill. They are both headstrong, impulsive men. I was terrified for them, and did all I could to shield them." She paused. "But then it seemed clear that they were quite blameless. Oliver was in Canada at the time, and Evan Fothergill asleep on the sofa in this very room. I began to wonder if the murders had really been done to harm me and Evan, and not to help us, and that the evil they started is going on and on."

"Yes," said the Superintendent in a soft voice.

"There is one man who has been nursing up evil against me for a long while. I nearly married him many years ago. I believe he never forgave me for getting engaged to Bill Landon. He has tried to hurt me in every way. He it was who made certain that my brother Oliver should be sent down. He hates Evan as well. All this was brought home to me yesterday when I met him. I have never seen such concentrated loathing in any man's eyes as in the look he gave me—loathing and a kind of triumph."

"And the man's name?"

"I have no longer any doubt," said Mrs. Landon, "that my husband was killed by Roger Westmacott."

IV

It was while he was in his bath on the morning of the day when Mrs. Landon made her surprising and dramatic accusation to the Superintendent, that Sir Richard Cherrington had his great brain-wave. It was not so much a brain-wave as the coming together at last of two facts he had been unable to associate for days. Although he had tried resolutely to put the whole affair of the Cambridge Murders out of his mind, a face kept recurring to him at the oddest moments. It was a strong, rather sinister face that he had seen in the middle of the 1933 College Group which Peter Gough Clarke had shown him. At once it seemed to him familiar, and then in his bath he identified it. It was the face of Oliver Hartley—Mrs. Landon's brother.

He stood up in his bath with great glee. Nothing annoyed him so much as not remembering a face. He now recalled vividly a luncheon-party six years ago in the President's Lodging. Dr. Quibell had been there, of course, and Dr. Landon and Oliver Hartley and Anne Hartley, as she then was. Even now he remembered coming into the room with Bill Landon. Anne was standing with her back to them, looking out through the window on to the river. She had turned round, and Dr. Quibell had effected the introductions. Sir Richard remembered how pretty she had looked, the sun catching her fair hair, and he had thought what a surly, cross person her brother Oliver was by comparison.

It was in that moment that he remembered where he had seen Hartley recently, or rather his portrait. Of course, in his sister's boudoir on his first visit. He was in a dark roll-top sweater, and Sir Richard had wondered idly if he was a previous lover. Then he pulled himself up sharply: the next time he visited Anne the portrait of her brother had gone. "I wonder," said Sir Richard to himself as he dressed. "Does she suspect Oliver? Of all the people connected with this sordid affair he is the one person with a disposition that could drive him to murder. Ruthless, already done a term in prison, with several grievances against the Dean, and a most tremendous affection for his sister."

It was at breakfast he made up his mind. "I know," he told his nephew, "that we do not leave England until the night boat from Newhaven, but if you will get your things ready straight after breakfast we will drive away at once. I want to go to Newhaven via Cambridge."

Sir Richard offered no explanation of his change of plan, and was very silent during the drive to Cambridge. He drove, as always, very fast, and they drew up outside St. John's Close at about twelve o'clock. Superintendent Robertson-Macdonald had just left, and Anne was delighted to see Cherrington.

"The most frightful things have happened in your absence, dear Richard," she said. "And first we owe you a real apology. I am afraid it was not true that Evan was here from eleven to six, as you argued." And she told Sir Richard the whole story.

He seized on one vital point. "Then there was another man lurking round the house at eleven o'clock?" he asked.

"There was, and it was Roger Westmacott."

"What?" asked Sir Richard, startled. "Do you know what you are saying?"

And she told him all her suspicions just as she had told the Superintendent about half an hour ago. For a moment Cherrington was silent.

"I suppose, Anne," he said gently, "that all the time you have been shielding Evan and your brother?"

"My brother?" she asked.

"Why did you remove his picture between my first and second visits to you?"

"You're right," she said. "When I first heard the news I was terrified it might have been done by either Evan or Oliver, but when I heard Oliver was safe in Canada, my mind was at rest. You're quite right. I did take his picture away, so that no one would notice it and think about him. Apparently you did."

"When did you last hear from Oliver, Anne?"

"He came over here to wish me good-bye in the middle of February, and then sailed from Cherbourg the last week of February in the *Ile de France*. I got a cable only the day after the murders. He arrived in Montreal on March 5th, but delayed sending a cable until he was fixed up at Calgary. He went up-country."

"Did he give an address?"

"No, he didn't," she said. "That will follow. You see, he was very anxious the new life he had made since leaving prison should never get linked up with his old life. We only communicated through the Post Office in France. I never knew what name he had assumed in France, and I wrote merely to Box 150, Poste Restante, at Rouen. Now that he has left France there is presumably no harm in mentioning these facts. Before I never told a soul—not even my husband—how I kept in touch with Oliver."

Sir Richard had got what he wanted without asking for it. He wished Anne good-bye and drove away. His nephew noted with surprise that the next call was at Wellbeck and Summers. He came out with a portrait wrapped up, and seemed worried as he got into the car.

"Thorough man, Superintendent Robertson-Macdonald," he said. "He's been here before me. Now I wonder?"

"You mean you wonder if he is working on the same lines as yourself," said Giles naïvely.

"I am not working on any lines," said Sir Richard. "I have now no doubt who the murderer is. The violence. The mysterious man around the house at eleven o'clock. The man with the felt hat and the overcoat whom the President probably saw at two-fifteen. The motive behind the murder. Why, it is all very clear—painfully clear."

"Then what worries you?" asked Giles.

"I wonder if the alibi is water-tight, and I wonder if I shall beat the Superintendent to it." He paused. "Hanging," he said, "is such an unaesthetic way of dying." And he drove off down the London road.

BOOK IV

SIR RICHARD CHERRINGTON INVESTIGATES

CHAPTER SEVENTEEN

TWO VISITS TO CATHEDRAL CITIES

As Superintendent Robertson-Macdonald walked down the Madingley Road after his interview with Mrs. Landon, he was most puzzled. "I have never touched such a really complicated case," he said to himself. "Or is it that there are so many red herrings? Parrott and Farnaby and Sir Richard and now Westmacott. I wonder whether Mrs. Landon is sincere, or whether she is engaged on some very complicated game I cannot understand. Did she drag Westmacott in just to confuse the issue still further?"

He pulled himself together and thought, "I mustn't get swayed by personal impressions, or by what the principal characters tell me. After all, I deal in facts, and the purpose of my interview with Mrs. Landon must not be forgotten. It was to find out about the keys. There were three people who might have got them copied. First, Fothergill, and he was with Mrs. Landon all the time—so she says; then Sir Richard, who had the car for a whole day, and thirdly, young Oliver Hartley. All suspects, except for Hartley's alibi. And yet the two trips of Hartley's are very significant. First through Baldock to Letchworth, and then alone to Ely. If only he was not in America," the Superintendent sighed.

Suddenly the Superintendent stopped in his tracks. "Of course," he said to himself. "What a fool I have been! He might have had the keys copied, but he might not have used them himself. Conspiracy? With whom? Sir Richard? Fothergill? Westmacott? But this is going too far ahead. I know what I shall do," he thought. "Some action would be a good thing. I'll drive out to Ely this morning and see Uncle Henry, and have a look round any likely shops in the neighbourhood of the cathedral."

The police car was brought round to the Blue Boar, and in half an hour's time the Detective-Superintendent was knocking at the door of a house in the Cathedral Close at Ely. After he had announced his name, a maid showed him to Miss Skilbeck, a tall, sharp-featured but kindly woman who was his uncle's housekeeper. She was delighted to see him, and greeted him warmly: his uncle was in his study, and would be very pleased to see him at once.

Canon Henry Boyce Cooper-Leigh was a younger brother of Robertson-Macdonald's mother. He had been a Canon at Ely for many years, and lived a quiet, scholarly life in the Close, making occasional excursions over to Cambridge and even rarer ones to London. He was a tall, white-haired man with a slight stoop and a very diffident manner of speaking. He was sitting in an armchair by a bright fire when Miss Skilbeck brought in the Detective-Superintendent.

"Here's young Mr. Robin to see you," she said.

"What, young Mr. Robin? Well, bless my soul," said the Canon, looking over his spectacles. "Bless my soul; this is a pleasant surprise."

"Good morning, Uncle Henry," said the Superintendent. "Hope you're well. You must forgive me bursting in on you like this."

"Not at all, not at all," said the Canon. "Ah, Miss Skilbeck. Some madeira and seed cake, please. And you'll stay for lunch, of course?"

"Delighted to, if it doesn't inconvenience you."

"Not at all. Why, bless my soul, not at all. That will be four, won't it, Miss Skilbeck?" He turned to the Superintendent. "My friend Dr. Landon of Fisher College is coming to lunch."

"What?" said the flabbergasted Superintendent. "But Dr. Landon is dead."

"Dead? Dr. Landon dead? But I should have been told," said the Canon, in an aggrieved tone of voice. "Miss Skilbeck, I should have been told," he said firmly.

"I did tell you, dear Dr. Cooper-Leigh," said the rather embarrassed Miss Skilbeck. "I did. It was over ten days ago. He was murdered, you remember?"

"I knew you had told me something about murders," went on the Canon. "It worried me last night when I was reading the lesson. I could have sworn you told me that Dr. Landon had murdered a railway porter, and I could hardly credit it. I was meaning to ask him about it at lunch to-day, but now I suppose," said the old man, smiling—"I suppose that now I shan't be able to do so."

"Really," whispered Miss Skilbeck to the Superintendent as she went out of the room, "the dear Canon is so unworldly. I bother him as little as possible," and she swept out in search of the madeira and seed cake with which the dear Canon always regaled his mid-morning visitors.

When she had gone, the Canon said apologetically to his nephew, "I never read any papers except the *Church Times* you know. Miss Skilbeck reads the daily papers and tells me anything of interest. She should have made it clearer that Dr. Landon was dead. It is wrong of her not to have crossed out his name in my book. I have him down for lunch to-day."

"Was he a great friend of yours?" asked Robertson-Macdonald.

"No, not really," said the Canon. "I knew him well. No affection lost, though. Rather an arid scholar, you know. No broad human sympathy. I remember Dr. Bond once telling me—that's the Dr. Bond who was Dean here and went to Chichester as Bishop, you remember, between Dalrymple and Purchas. Now, where was I?" he paused. "Wait a minute," he said. "Did you say Dr. Landon was murdered?"

"I'm afraid he was."

"By whom?"

"That's what I'm trying to find out."

"You're trying to find out?" said the Canon. "Of course, I had forgotten you were mixed up with the police. Your plain clothes and all the rest of it quite took me in. Well, I wish you luck in your hunt. Murder is a very great evil, but fortunately one that one does not often have to contend with, leastways not in a Cathedral Close. Of course there was the Prendergast case. Do you remember that? It was when I was a Minor Canon at Wells. Dear me, yes. Wrote anonymous letters to the Canons' wives and murdered a maid at the Crown with whom he had had an adulterous association, and in such circumstances as implicated the Bishop—it was poor dear Staunton then—and the organist. Then there was a strange thing happened when I was in charge of a parish in Liverpool. But, then, that is a violent city, you know—so many Welsh and Irish and so forth."

"Yes, Uncle Henry," said the Superintendent, cutting through his reminiscences. "Did you often see Dr. Landon?"

"About once a month. He came over to a small theological discussion afternoon we have. We are having it this afternoon at three o'clock."

"I see," said Robertson-Macdonald. "Then you could tell me approximately when he was here last."

"I could indeed," said the Canon, getting up and going to his desk. "Let me see, now. Yes, here it is. February the 18th. Yes, that is when we discussed the philosophical foundations of humanism. It was a long discussion."

"Could you remember when Dr. Landon left?"

"Oh, no, I couldn't do that. I remember him saying he had been driven over in the car, and I suppose he went back in his car. We have tea at these discussion groups. I don't suppose he could have left before five or half-past five. But the Dean will know. We had tea with him. Is it very important to your investigations?"

At this juncture a maid came in with a tray on which was a decanter of madeira, two large glasses, a fine seed cake, some knives and some plates.

"A little mid-morning sustenance is so essential, my dear Robin, don't you think?" said the Canon, as he poured out some wine. "It is such a long time from my breakfast at nine-thirty to my lunch at one-thirty."

The Superintendent was thinking quickly. This meant that Oliver Hartley had virtually a whole day in Ely. From before lunch to five or five-thirty. During all this time he would naturally have Dean Landon's car keys, and with them all the other keys. Surely he was on to something at last.

"This is a very pleasant wine," he said, turning to his uncle after sipping the madeira.

"Yes," said the Canon, nodding wisely over his glass. "I always keep a little canary wine in the house. The cold, dank humours of the Fens need constant combating."

"Now I am going to ask you rather a strange question, Uncle Henry," said Robertson-Macdonald.

"Please do."

"If you wanted a duplicate made of a key—say you had lost a key, where would you go in Ely?"

The Canon looked at him sharply. "You have found out that I once lost the Chapter keys?" he said. "I mean, there's no knowing what the police know."

"No, no, Uncle Henry," said his nephew. "I'm just making a very ordinary enquiry."

"Well," said the Canon, "you relieve me a great deal. When I lost the Chapter keys I went to old Thoday in Littleport Road, and he had a new set made in a very short time. He's a good craftsman—very good indeed." He dropped his voice to a whisper. "But don't tell Miss Skilbeck about the keys," he said confidentially. "Oh no, that would never do. I told no one about the whole affair. How you found out I do not know."

"Ah, well," said the Superintendent, hardly knowing what to say, "that closes the matter. Wouldn't dream of mentioning it to anyone. By the way, what does Thoday do normally?"

"Thoday? He is a general ironmonger, you know. Very good old type. Stocks everything, and quite excellent at making things he doesn't stock, if you get my meaning."

"Is he the nearest ironmonger to this house and to the Cathedral?"

"Now, let me see," said the old man. He took a drop of wine. "Yes, now—there's Skinner's, of course: Skinner's at the corner of White Street and Close Lane. They are the nearest firm to the cathedral. Not a good firm, you know. Dissenters, dissenters. No tradition of craftsmanship."

And with that the subject was dropped.

II

It was three o'clock that afternoon when Superintendent Robertson-Macdonald drove back to Cambridge. There was a look of great triumph in his face. After a week of hard work, at last some real tangible evidence had appeared. It was not a perfect clue, but, for all that, it was a clue.

He had taken leave of his uncle and Miss Skilbeck after a very good lunch, and gone in search of all the ironmongers and locksmiths in the city of Ely. Brushing aside his uncle's prejudices against Dissenters, he had first visited Skinner's, but no job for copying keys had been put in on February 18th or any day near that time. Neither Skinner nor his assistants could recollect any of the persons of whom the Superintendent showed them photographs. He had then walked on down the Littleport Road, and then it was he had his great stroke of luck. "Or was it fair to call it luck?" he mused to himself as he drove through Milton on the way back to Cambridge. "Wasn't it just good detection? I have been suspicious about these keys for several days now, and it was logical to track down the movements of all the people who could have had the Landon car by themselves for any length of time. But it was luck finding it at second shot, and Mr. Thoday remembering the whole incident so clearly."

Old Thoday remembered all about the affair. His day-book told him that it was on February 18th a young man had come in and asked for duplicates of five keys. He said that he had lost his second set. When the Superintendent produced Dr. Landon's bunch of keys, old Thoday could not identify the actual keys copied, but that was not surprising. Five keys—the Superintendent had noted. Just right—one for the College back gate, one for the Dean's oak, one for the garage door, and two for the car. It was a pity Thoday could not be more definite about his description of the young man. He was between twenty-five and thirty-five, he said, and wore a cap pulled well over his eyes. He thought he had black hair. When shown the Superintendent's selection of photographs, he had pointed to Oliver Hartley and, to the Superintendent's delight, said he thought that was the man. But he couldn't be sure: it might be Evan Fothergill, and it might be Westmacott. He picked out those three photographs from the selection.

"Dear me," he had said on being shown another of the photographs. "Why, if that isn't Sir Richard Cherrington! It certainly wasn't him. Know him quite well through the local archæological society. Now, whatever made you include his photograph?"

So that was as much as the Superintendent had got. Customer probably Hartley, but might be Westmacott or Fothergill. One thing had aroused the old man's suspicions. The man with the cap had said his name was Bagshawe, and greeted Thoday warmly, declaring he had done several jobs for him before.

"It's puzzled me, it has," Thoday had said. "I didn't recollect ever having seen this man before, and the name Bagshawe's an odd one. There's a pork butcher in Mildenhall called Bagshawe, but he's never been in my shop."

As he drove down the Milton Road, the Superintendent was jubilant. "I ought to have got on to that business of the alibi before," he said to himself. "It's a good rule to suspect all alibis. That's been my only slip so far. It hasn't really been such a long case. Let me see, now. It's Saturday at the moment. It was exactly a week ago that I started the case. Not bad going. What a good thing I took a day off to get all the existing material straight!" It was the discrepancies in Fothergill's statements that had led him to the vital clues. Of course it was all quite clear now. Fothergill was shielding Mrs. Landon, and Mrs. Landon either knew or suspected the murders had been done by her brother

Oliver. "That explains it all. The mystery man at eleven o'clock, the duplicate keys, the lying about the car, the attempt to put me on to Westmacott—they all point clearly to Hartley, who has anyhow a previous record of crime, and seems a tough customer. What a good thing Fothergill and Mrs. Landon had not perfected their joint stories enough for me to fail to notice the discrepancy about the timing of the mystery man! That was a good piece of detection," mused the Superintendent complacently. "And so was the business about the keys. Mrs. Landon slipped up very badly there. She must have noticed the car gone, and suspected it was stolen by her brother. On the spur of the moment she had presumably mentioned the story about the two undergraduates: a foolish thing to do, since it was easily disproved, and incidentally led him to the problem of the keys.

"There really is nothing left to the case now," he said to himself as he swung the car out of the Milton Road into the Chesterton Road—"nothing to it. Except break this transatlantic alibi and find Hartley. Probably lurking under an assumed name in France or Canada. For there can no longer be any doubt that Hartley is the murderer. He has several motives. Sent down by Landon, and his career thereby ruined. His sister married Landon against his own wishes, and was apparently very unhappy. The years in prison and the coarsening of his moral standards through crime would probably have brought him to a pitch when he was quite prepared to murder Landon, thus paying off an old score and freeing his sister. I see it all now quite clearly," the Superintendent went on to himself. "Hartley comes back in mid-February ostensibly to see his sister and wish her good-bye before he goes to Canada. But meanwhile he is laying his plans for the murder all the time. He gets the duplicate keys made in Ely. He notes the chalk-pit at Baldock as he drives his sister to Letchworth. He works out the detail of the trains and fixes his plan for the last night of term, when he knows Landon will be in his rooms in College. Then he goes back to France, and in some remarkable way fixes his alibi. There is no doubt I ought to have got on to this alibi business before. It was obvious Mrs. Landon was trying to shield someone, but we all thought it was either herself or Fothergill. The passage to America and the cable from Canada: it should be possible somehow to fake those. Perhaps the answers have already come from Paris and Montreal."

It was with a sense of considerable satisfaction that Superintendent Robertson-Macdonald got out of the car at the police station and walked up to Wyndham's office. He wondered if he should break the news to Wyndham straight away or wait until the Chief Constable arrived. The decision was taken out of his hands.

"Hello, sir," said Wyndham. "Just finished taking down a long message for you from Scotland Yard."

"Yes?"

"About Hartley. The check-up from the *Sûrêté* and from Canada about his passage in the *Ile de France*. Seems all right."

"All right?" queried the Superintendent. "Are they sure?"

"Appear to be," said Wyndham. "I will have it typed out for you straight away. Apparently Hartley lived in a small flat in St. Germain, outside Paris, since he came out of prison. He paid a visit to England about February 12th or 13th, and was back again in the flat by February 21st. He didn't spend much time in this flat, they say, and was often away for long periods. In early March, however, he closed up the flat, let it, and with all his luggage sailed on the *Ile de France* on February 28th. He arrived in Montreal on the 5th."

"There is proof of all this?" asked Robertson-Macdonald, as his case went tumbling about his head.

"So I gather," said Wyndham. "The special branch of the *Sûrêté* sent Scotland Yard these details, and they appear satisfied."

"My God," said the Superintendent. "And where is he now?"

"He left for an up-country address in Canada, Calgary in fact, from which he sent the cable to his sister. He has also now left that address."

The Superintendent sat down heavily in a chair. "Well, I'm damned!" he said. He passed his hand wearily over his face. It must be said he was tired. He had been working hard for a week, and was keyed up by his latest discoveries in Ely. Now it looked as if they only complicated the case a little further. Of course Thoday had not positively identified Hartley. It might have been Fothergill or Westmacott. "Well, I'm damned," he said again. It was the first moment in the case that he admitted the possibility of defeat.

III

When they had landed in France, Sir Richard Cherrington had made a surprising announcement to his nephew.

"This trip was originally planned, as you know my dear Giles," he said, as they breakfasted in Dieppe, "to visit some archæological sites in Normandy and Brittany. I had intended to drive to-day to Caen and beyond and see Fontenay le Marmion, and then on via Morlaix to Finisterre and back to Carnac." He paused. "But I am now changing the whole itinerary. We go to-day to Rouen, and after that I don't yet know."

"Is it," asked Farnaby hesitantly, "something to do with the murders?"

"It is," said Sir Richard, "but I don't want at this stage to tell you any more. I am not sure yet, myself. I'm only going on two slight things—hardly clues. An idea of Peter Gough Clarke's and the memory of a face. And then one thing which Anne Landon did. Just an old photograph and the removal of a photograph. I may be quite wrong."

"Yes," said Giles encouragingly. He was very much in the dark.

"You see, there are really four things to be considered in these, as in any other murders. The police keep on talking to you about means and motive and opportunity. Of these, the most important is motive. But there is a fourth thing more important than motive, and that is psychological disposition to murder, or the real character of the people concerned. I daresay there are a large number of us who have motives for murder, and who could obtain the means and manufacture the opportunity. But our personalities are against it. We are not disposed to violence, and we could not live at peace with ourselves after the crime was committed." He paused. "Yes, Inspector Wyndham was wrong when he said 'Get the facts and we will make the psychology fit them.' I think perhaps the Superintendent will reach the same conclusion as myself. He made a great business about finding out the backgrounds of all his characters. I am fortunate in knowing the backgrounds already."

Farnaby said nothing.

"You see, my dear Giles, Parrott couldn't commit a murder, neither could Dr. Quibell or Evan Fothergill, nor yourself nor myself. Mrs. Landon possibly could, but she didn't. She is afraid, and I cannot make up my mind whether she is afraid of somebody or afraid for somebody. Both Roger Westmacott and Oliver Hartley could commit murders. Both are violent men." He paused. "One has a good alibi for the night of the murder," he said. "Let us get on to Rouen."

The task in Rouen was not quite so difficult as Sir Richard had anticipated. He told his story first at the Central Post Office. He was a Cambridge solicitor of the firm of Cherrington and Cherrington. He was engaged in investigating a most complex and unhappy domestic legal affair. The lady in England had always corresponded with the gentleman in France through a Box Office number—no. 150—at Rouen. Now there had arisen a most difficult crisis. The lady was ill, and he must get privately in touch with the gentleman concerned. Quite so, quite so; Monsieur had understood. Very sad. Yes, under the circumstances, of course, most unusual. But—— And Sir Richard was away to see a M. Jacques Verrier in the Rue du Vieux Moulin.

Here Sir Richard made a very quick summing-up of the old man in the tobacconist's who answered to this name. It was a shrewd and accurate summing-up.

"I know," he said, "that you re-address letters coming from England with the Cambridge postmark and addressed to Box 150 Poste Restante here in Rouen."

He paused.

Verrier made no comment.

"These letters," he went on, "come from a lady in England, the sister of the person to whom you address them. She is now in very great trouble, and is a principal suspect in a murder case. Yes, Monsieur Verrier," he went on firmly, "a murder case. I represent her legally, and it is of the greatest importance that I get in touch with her brother at once. Of course I know I could get this information by going to the police here at Rouen, but I prefer to do this matter myself, and quickly." And he took out a thousand-franc note from his pocket-book and laid it on the table.

"I shall get into no trouble over this?" said Verrier.

"None at all. Indeed, it may prevent you being mixed up with the police at all, and you may save a very beautiful lady from a shameful death."

M. Verrier dropped his voice. "I was instructed," he said, "to re-address all Box 150 letters with the Cambridge postmark to M. Georges Festubert at the Hôtel de la Poste at Chartres. They pay me a hundred francs a month. It is not enough, if there are risks," he grumbled.

When Sir Richard rejoined his nephew he was mopping his face with his handkerchief. "Two very successful but difficult interviews," he said. "Now lead me to a very powerful aperitif, and then, after the best lunch that the Trois Marchands can produce for us, we are away to Chartres."

"Why this sudden interest in Cathedral cities?" asked Giles, but Sir Richard gave him no answer.

CHAPTER EIGHTEEN

THE POLICE SOLVE THE MYSTERY

SINCE THE receipt on Saturday evening of the messages which Scotland Yard had collected from America and France regarding Oliver Hartley, Detective-Superintendent Robertson-Macdonald had been a rather testy and quick-tempered man. He had been abrupt to Inspector Wyndham, had urged his assistants Fleming and Waddell on to further efforts, and had, himself, spent a very unpleasant Sunday.

In the morning he had worked through his papers in the Blue Boar Hotel and had not seemed to get any further forward. All the evidence pointed to an outsider who could quite well have been Oliver Hartley. There was someone outside St. John's Close at eleven o'clock, someone drove the car away from the back gate of Fisher College and left it in a quarry at Baldock; a young man got into the London train at Baldock on the Tuesday morning; there was no doubt that it was a young man, perhaps Oliver Hartley, who arranged in Ely for the duplicate keys to be made. He could have noticed the chalk-pit at Baldock as he drove his sister to Letchworth. There was no doubt about it, here was a man with a motive, and all the evidence went most of the way to show he had means and opportunity, but there was the American evidence.

What did this mean? That Hartley had cooked the alibi in a complicated Transatlantic way? That someone was framing Hartley? That the criminal had made the evidence appear to incriminate someone else by means of a series of strange clues, one or two of which pointed to Hartley? It really was most difficult.

The Superintendent went out and had lunch with Colonel Cunningham-Hardy, the Chief Constable, at his house on the Gog Magog Hills. It was a pleasant social lunch, with a lot to drink, and no mention was made of the case throughout, but nevertheless the Detective-Superintendent could not help thinking that the Chief Constable was saying to himself, "These Scotland Yard lads haven't done so marvellously in a week, with all their talk." And if he was saying that, the Chief Constable was unfortunately quite right.

As they parted, the Chief Constable said, "Am looking forward to our conference at eleven o'clock to-morrow, Robertson-Macdonald." They had arranged a meeting in the Cambridge police station to discuss all aspects of the case. "Am particularly looking forward to hearing your statement, d'ye know. Expect a lot from Scotland Yard and all these new methods."

The Detective-Superintendent had smiled grimly, thanked him for the lunch, and driven away out down the Hills Road and back to his office in the police station. He really hadn't the slightest notion what he was going to tell them all on Monday morning. Perhaps the best thing was just the plain truth, explaining how they had got hold of new evidence, and yet were still a long way from a definite conclusion. He wondered whether he should send someone to Cherbourg and Canada to check up the Hartley alibi and possibly see Hartley himself. Ah, well, that could wait until Monday's meeting.

He worked again at his papers through the afternoon and on until six o'clock, without getting anywhere fresh. The trouble was that when all was said and done there was still a fair case to be put up against a number of people. Hartley, who got the keys duplicated, but was in America at the time of the murder. Parrott, whose button was alongside the corpse and who had reason to get rid of both Dean and porter, yet could not have been in the College at the time of the murder. Then Fothergill, who had good reason to get rid of Landon, and, if his word could be believed, had even tried to plan how to do it; Fothergill, who had been seen—well, had he?—by the President on the Backs in the middle of the night. Then young Farnaby and Sir Richard Cherrington and the tutor Westmacott and those two dons who had gone out of College—Dr. Traherne and Dr. Wedgwood—and then, of course, there was the old President himself, or Rodgers the porter. It really was incredibly difficult to get anywhere in the case.

At six o'clock he could bear it no longer, and locked away his papers, knocked out his pipe and went down to the car. Then he had a bright idea. He would drive out from Cambridge to the Yellow Barn and have a jolly evening away from the case: lots of drink, good food, perhaps some dancing. That's what he wanted, a change.

He went to the Blue Boar and put on a dinner-jacket, had a gin and French at the bar, and drove out along the Newmarket Road. He was soon beyond Quy and, arriving at the Yellow Barn, put his car away and went in. There were not many people about yet, but in the lounge he met Miss Chilcott, Sir Richard Cherrington's friend, who had fixed him with a room during the previous week-end.

She recognised him at once. "Hello, Mr. Robertson-Macdonald," she said. "Back again? How pleasant!"

"It's nice to come here," he said.

"Do you want to stay here a few days again?" she queried. "More hard thinking to do?"

"No, I've just come this time to cheer myself up with a good dinner and some drinks."

"Well, we can give you both," said Miss Chilcott. "There's an extremely good dinner been put on to-night. Just suit you. Are you alone?" she said.

"I am," he said, and then suddenly added, "I know it is rather a ridiculous question, and rather rude of me, but would you dine with me? I mean," he said hastily, "I don't know anyone, and I should enjoy it very much."

Babs Chilcott took her cigarette-holder from her mouth and blew a long column of smoke up into the air.

"That's very nice of you," she said. "I'll be with you in ten minutes. I must just go round and see everything is all right."

She was as good as her word, and was back in ten minutes. They had a drink at the bar, and then another one, and then a third. The barman made good cocktails, and Robertson-Macdonald began to cheer up. Yes, this had definitely been a good thing to do.

"You know, Miss Chilcott," he said. "It's most kind of you to spend the evening with me like this. I do appreciate it."

"Not at all."

"You see, last time I came here I wanted peace and quiet to work, but now I want distraction, jollity, a few hours away from my work."

She narrowed her eyes and looked at him keenly. "How is the case going, Detective-Superintendent?" she asked.

"Oh, you knew I was in the C.I.D.," he said, rather crestfallen.

"I did; Sir Richard Cherrington told me," she said. "And, in any case, you questioned Piggott the driver very carefully when you were here last."

"I see."

She paused. "Now tell me, Detective-Superintendent," she went on. "Have you come here to-night for a change, or are you really here to pump me for information? I just like to know."

He seemed rather taken aback. "Pump you for information?" he said rather incredulously. "Why should I want to do that?"

"Well, I know all the principal characters in the case rather well," she said.

"Who are the principal characters?" he asked.

"Oh, I mean Sir Richard and John Parrott and Fothergill and Farnaby and Westmacott, and I used to know old Dr. Quibell very well once rather long ago."

"You don't include Oliver Hartley in your list of principal characters?"

"Good for you, Superintendent," she said. "I see you've been turning up all the dirt. Yes, I know Oliver well. He's had a bad deal. I would have included him, but I understand he was away in America." She looked at him keenly. "Didn't he go?" she asked.

"Yes, he went all right," said the Superintendent, sighing. "That's one of my troubles."

"So, as I thought," she said. "The case isn't going very well, and you came here for some enjoyment. Well, the band is just starting up. Let's go and dance."

After the dance they went and sat down at a table and began their dinner. There were oysters, some clear soup and some poached eggs Argenteuil. It was at this stage that Babs Chilcott referred to the case again.

"I'm a woman of the world," she said. "I expect you realise that. Running a place like this, I could never be anything else. But I live close to Cambridge, and I know my University very well. Perhaps I see it more clearly than someone living inside. Let me therefore give you a few words of advice."

"By all means."

"You won't think me foolish?"

"Impossible."

"Then here they are. Please don't under-estimate your opponents."

"Whatever can you mean?" said Robertson-Macdonald, startled in spite of himself.

"Well, don't treat them as though you were dealing with a lot of butchers' assistants in Camberwell," she said. "Don't apply the ordinary rules of crime detection. These people are very educated and very clever. These murders were very carefully thought out."

"You think so?"

"I have no doubt about it, and I have no doubt that the murder of Gostlin, the porter, was meant to rivet your attention on certain circumstances and a certain time."

"What do you mean?"

"It was probably arranged so that you should draw the conclusion that the first murder was done by someone outside College who could be recognised by Gostlin and who should not be there."

"But——" he began.

"You see, it is so silly," she went on. "In the middle of the night you could have heard Gostlin coming on his rounds, and if you wanted to, waited in the shadows until he went by."

"You don't think, then, with Sir Richard, that it was a cover murder?"

"To conceal the identity of the murderer of the Dean, you mean?"

"Yes."

"I certainly do not. It's a great red herring, the first of a large number in this case. It interests me that Sir Richard should have drawn your attention to it."

"Why?"

"Oh, I don't know. I shouldn't be telling you all this, but the day after the murder Sir Richard came here and asked me about the movements of John Parrott and the girl Gostlin."

"There's nothing suspicious in that."

"Isn't there? How did he know they had been here?"

"He guessed?"

"That's perhaps what he says, but I was not very happy about his manner that afternoon. I wonder if it all was another red herring."

"How could it be?"

"Well, I don't know. It drew attention to these two, and fixed their times of entry into College and so forth. I can't help thinking there was something rather cleverly sinister about it all."

"But you don't suspect Sir Richard?"

"Of what?"

"Well, I mean murder."

"Why not?"

"I beg your pardon, Miss Chilcott?"

"Well, perhaps not murder. Just complicity in the crime, or maybe he is shielding someone he thinks committed it."

"But why should Sir Richard want to commit such a senseless crime?"

Babs Chilcott held her glass in her hands and looked at Robertson-Macdonald over it. "Was it senseless?" she asked. "It freed Mrs. Landon to marry Fothergill. It freed the College of a rather unpleasant official."

"But I can't imagine Sir Richard doing a thing like that."

"Well, my father, who had considerable knowledge of these academics, alleged that all the unmarried ones became unbalanced as they grew old."

"Unbalanced? Mad, you mean?"

"Yes. I mean not certifiably insane, but just peculiar. I wonder sometimes if Sir Richard has gone that way. A most brilliant scholar. A most accomplished man. He has travelled everywhere and knows all sorts of people. He keeps a good table, a good cellar and is still the hardest worker in College. And yet? He is over sixty. He will soon retire from his Professorship. The Presidency of Fisher College will go to him at Dr. Quibell's death or retirement. You might think he has everything. And yet. What has he got? Nothing. I sometimes think he might do something extraordinary just to show how clever he really was."

There was a long pause.

"When I was a girl I went to tea with Dr. Irving, the great classic in Lancaster College. He was a bachelor and an uncle of my mother's. I remember my mother saying, as she admired his rooms, 'How wonderful to live alone in these beautiful rooms in this wonderful old college,' and I remember him answering her, 'Yes, my girl, but have you ever thought that it is not so wonderful to die alone in these beautiful rooms in this wonderful old college?' "

Robertson-Macdonald looked at Babs Chilcott very keenly. "Whatever do you mean?" he said.

Miss Chilcott took her long cigarette-holder from her mouth and blew a cloud of smoke over the Superintendent's head. Her eyes followed the smoke into the middle distance. "I was just thinking," she said quietly, "that it was just possible Sir Richard may have decided not to die in College—alone." She paused. "Come on. Enough of this. Let's dance."

II

As Superintendent Robertson-Macdonald drove back to Cambridge through the cold night, and as he lay in his warm, comfortable bed in the Blue Boar, he could not help thinking over and over again of what Miss Chilcott had said during dinner.

Supposing he had under-estimated his opponents, as Miss Chilcott had said? He recalled with sudden misgiving his days as an undergraduate at Oxford, and how the art of conversation had been so cultivated among dons and undergraduates that you rarely said what you believed or believed what you heard, and all conversation was an exercise in dialectic and repartee, rather than a considered statement of opinion. In view of this, how was he now to regard the various statements he had collected and so carefully studied? Was everyone telling him just what they wanted him to believe? Fothergill's various tales? Mrs. Landon and her story against Westmacott? Dr. Quibell and his visions in the middle of the night? And Sir Richard with his talk of cover murders and his passionate interest in the affairs of Parrott, Fothergill, and Mrs. Landon?

He remembered Miss Chilcott's remark about red herrings. How many of the alleged facts he had fastened on to were perhaps red herrings skilfully drawn across the stage of Fisher College to confuse everyone? Was this going to be a horrid collection of false clues? Was there some skilful mind behind these murders that had with masterly cunning manufactured one or two incidents that, being taken at their face value, were now confusing the police?

He admitted it was possible. Take, for instance, the business of the keys. Mrs. Landon had not really made any attempt to keep his attention away from the keys. She had lied about the undergraduates who were supposed to have borrowed them. At first he had thought that was a lie to save him concentrating on her brother. But might it not have been more subtle? After all, it was a palpable untruth, and they had soon found it to be so. And the result? He had concentrated on the keys, and got down to the strong possibility of her brother having had a duplicate set made at Ely. Then, again, she had perhaps deliberately exposed the impossibility of Fothergill being the mystery man around her house at eleven o'clock. Why? To draw attention to her brother. Then, again, she had gratuitously pointed out that her brother had driven her to Letchworth, although that meant passing the chalk-pit where the car was eventually found abandoned. Was it possible he had under-estimated Mrs. Landon? Was all this skilfully done to focus attention, rather grudgingly, of course, on her brother? Why? Because she knew that her brother was safe in Canada at the time of the murder. He had a perfect alibi.

Then attention had been very skilfully drawn to Fothergill. Was the dismissal of the servant girl the reverse of what it appeared? Was it, not a foolishly guilty action, but a clever action designed to draw police attention, again albeit grudgingly, to the hat and the mystery man, and so to Fothergill? For Fothergill was safe, quite safe. Mrs. Landon would vouch for his presence in her house at the time of the murder.

"Where is this train of thought leading me?" The Superintendent switched on his bedside light and sat up in bed. "Is Mrs. Landon the murderess, after all?" Suddenly he swore under his breath. "What a fool I've been." It was not only Mrs. Landon who had been drawing their attention to Fothergill. There was one other person who had most skilfully drawn the police attention away from himself to Fothergill. He got out of bed, put on a dressing-gown, turned on the electric fire, drew out a pad of paper from his despatch case, lit his pipe and began writing.

It all pointed that way. This man had knowledge of Landon's revolver, knew the College habits inside out, and was a sentimentalist who might, on a sudden turn of mind, commit crimes. He was also a very clever man who would see that the crimes did not come back to him. Miss Chilcott was perhaps right—or half-way so. And yet—the telephone call, and the car that returned to College in the early morning. Those were the snags, but they could be checked in the morning. It was nearly two-thirty before he finished writing and climbed into bed, a tired but a very contented man.

III

Robertson-Macdonald was up early the next morning, but he breakfasted late, and the waiters at the Blue Boar looked at him in a very old-fashioned manner as he demanded more toast and coffee at ten minutes past ten. He was in very good spirits. His first interview that morning had been with Lupton, the man who looked after the baths and garages at Fisher College. It had not been very satisfactory, but, on the other hand, it had not destroyed his theory of the night before. Lupton was just unable to say whose car had come into the garage on the fateful Tuesday morning. His interview with Professor Shacksfield, on the other hand, had been most successful, and had confirmed his idea of the previous night. Professor Shacksfield was quite sure it was Sir Richard Cherrington who had rung him up at eleven o'clock on Monday night, and not he who had rung up Sir Richard. He was quite certain on this point, and Superintendent Robertson-Macdonald left the Professor in a fine state of elation.

During his breakfast he looked over his notes again. No, there could be no flaw in them. He had been writing hurriedly in the middle of the night, but the facts and deductions stood the test of the rigorous morning examination. There really was no gainsaying them. He merely upbraided himself for not having got to these deductions earlier. And yet for a while he had been completely puzzled to explain the apparently insuperable difficulty of Hartley's having had the keys made, and Hartley being in Canada at the time of the murder. Now it was simple.

He looked at his watch. Only half-past ten, and a good half-hour to his meeting. He put his papers in his brief-case and walked out of the hotel across Trinity Street and into Fisher College. Rodgers, the under-porter, greeted him as he went through the front gate. Robertson-Macdonald walked slowly through the First Court, through the Screens across Second Court, and out of the river gate on to the Backs. The crocuses were bright in the morning sunlight: there was no one about, the lawns were level and trim and the river flowed by calmly and undisturbed. It was a shock to think of the murderous plans that had been laid and successfully carried out—most successfully carried out—among these immemorial elms and quiet gardens, these scholarly courts. And yet there could be no doubt about it whatsoever. Here a man whose identity was no longer a secret to the Superintendent had thrown the revolver into the river, and walked away across the Backs to drive the stolen car to Baldock. The more the Superintendent thought of the case, there was only one answer.

But was that answer going to be one which would bring one or more persons to justice in a court of law? Was it not getting perilously near the perfect murder: that is to say, one in which the police know the identity of the murderer, and yet cannot bring him to trial. The Superintendent walked through Fisher College and up Green Street and continued his walk to the police station. Misgivings began to assail him. Certainly he thought he had a water-tight answer: the Cambridge police would not be able to say that Scotland Yard had let them down. But was the answer a satisfactory one from the police point of view and from the point of view of the administration of justice in England?

The Superintendent shrugged his shoulders and went in to the police station as the Catholic church clock began striking the hour. As he walked through the clerks' office a telegram was handed to him. He glanced at it, and his face lit up. It was from the man de Rougemont, who was engaged in following Sir Richard Cherrington. It told him that Sir Richard had abandoned the original plan to go to Brittany and Normandy and was instead engaged in some curious investigations in Rouen and Chartres. "That settles it," said Robertson-Macdonald to himself. "That removes the last shadow of doubt. I knew the Brittany trip was a blind of some kind."

He walked into Wyndham's office, where Wyndham, the Chief Constable and Inspector Fleming were waiting for him.

"Morning, Robertson-Macdonald," said the Chief Constable.

"Good morning, sir," said the Superintendent. "Sorry I'm a few minutes late, gentlemen. Good morning, Wyndham. Hello, Fleming."

"Hope you've got some good news for us," said the Chief Constable, sitting himself down at the head of the table. "I don't mind telling you I'm looking forward to this conference very much."

"I've got a lot of news," said Robertson-Macdonald. "I wouldn't say it was very good news, though."

"Know the murderer?" snapped out Cunningham-Hardy.

"I think I do without any doubt."

"Well, I think I do, too. Hope it's the same person. Fire ahead."

Robertson-Macdonald looked at his papers. "You will remember," he said, "that when I took over this case it was, as Inspector Wyndham here pointed out, full of people with means and opportunity, had quite a lot with motive, and yet there was nothing we could pin on anybody. He favoured Evan Fothergill, but at that time he seemed to have a complete alibi provided by Mrs. Landon.

"I took over the case at that stage, and limited my list of suspects to those who could have had motives. Even this produced a total of eleven individuals—the six Fellows themselves—that is to say Dr. Quibell, Sir Richard Cherrington, Westmacott, Wedgwood, Traherne and Fothergill—and then five non-Fellows—Mrs. Landon, her brother Oliver Hartley and the undergraduate Parrott and the two Kilmartins. Farnaby and a mysterious Mr. X I excluded from my list, as also people like Rodgers. Of this list of eleven primary suspects, I straight away ruled out six. John Parrott was unfortunately mixed up in the discovery of Gostlin's body, but his motives were really so weak. He stood to gain nothing, so far as I could see, by the deaths of Dr. Landon and Gostlin. Then I could not believe that the motives attributed to Wedgwood and Traherne were really strong enough. They were merely academic disputes, and moreover to implicate either of them we should have had to break two good alibis. This seemed hardly necessary in the absence of strong enough motives. I similarly ruled out Dr. Quibell. There was no evidence against him, and it is difficult to conceive of him doing anything to affect adversely the reputation of his College. The two Kilmartins seemed to have good alibis for the time of the murders.

"That, gentlemen, leaves us with our five main suspects: Mrs. Landon, Westmacott, Fothergill, Hartley and Sir Richard Cherrington. I concentrated my study on these five, always remembering that the murderer had to be able to do four things: (1) get hold of a set of keys, (2) be present at eleven o'clock outside the Landon house, (3) commit the murders at some time before three-thirty, when Parrott found the body, and after two o'clock, when Willerby saw Gostlin alive—you see, I did not accept Willerby's evidence as necessarily fixing the time of the second murder—fourthly, gentlemen, the murderer had to be able to drive the Landon car to a disused quarry at Baldock and catch the London train at three-fifty five.

"Now let's take out five suspects. A good case could be made out against Mrs. Landon. She had access to her husband's keys frequently, or she might have asked her brother to get a duplicate set made for her, knowing he would never let her down. The complicated and ever-changing alibis with Fothergill might have been not to shield him, as we thought, but to shield her. Fothergill might have spent a great part of the night in St. John's Close asleep on the sofa, while Mrs. Landon was murdering her husband and Gostlin and driving the car to Baldock. She could have masqueraded as a young man at Baldock Station and then got back to Cambridge in plenty of time to be in her house when the maid arrived at seven. You remember the train gets in at six o'clock. She could also have been the mysterious stranger seen by Doris Finch and her boy: she might already have been masquerading as a young man to attract attention, and she dismissed Finch to draw attention to this and to the discovery of the hat. Indeed, she may have planted the hat there deliberately, so that Fothergill's presence in her house that night could be known."

He paused.

"I said deliberately that a good case could have been made out against Mrs. Landon," he went on. "But I don't believe in it. I don't see her carrying her husband's dead body and hiding it in a trunk. Nor, really, do I see her careering around the countryside on a course of murder and deception while her lover slept on the sofa in her house."

"I should say here, sir," interrupted Fleming, "that I have made most exhaustive enquiries at the Cambridge station, and that no unusual person came off the six o'clock train on the Tuesday morning. They cannot be sure at this interval, but they usually notice any strange persons off the very early morning trains."

"Good!" said Robertson-Macdonald. "But while I think we are

agreed in striking Mrs. Landon off the list of potential murderers, she remains an extremely frightened woman. I think this is because she either knows, or suspects she knows the real murderer. She has shown great concern for her brother and for her lover, whenever we have been questioning her about them. She has, on the other hand, denounced Mr. Westmacott as the murderer. She has not mentioned our fourth suspect, Sir Richard, in any way in connection with the murders. Do you draw any remarkable conclusion from that?"

He looked round the room, but no one answered what was perhaps meant to be a rhetorical question.

"Let us concentrate on the four remaining suspects," he went on. "Mrs. Landon has accused Westmacott. The motives adduced are possible. They are deep psychological motives difficult to assess. Westmacott telephoned the lodge about some business at eleven o'clock. He says he was in his rooms from after Hall until he was awakened by his bedmaker next morning. Admittedly he could have committed both the murders. I must stress that while the old man Thoday thought from my pictures the keys were given him for copying by Hartley, he wavered between Hartley and the pictures of Fothergill and Westmacott. There is a possible case against Westmacott, I give you that, but not a very strong one.

"Let's turn to Wyndham's favourite—Fothergill. It is worth stressing that all the Fellows would have back gate keys, and needn't have copied all the Landon keys. But then, again, it might have been Fothergill whom Thoday had in his shop that day. His identification of Hartley is by no means certain. Fothergill could easily have committed the murders and driven the Landon car away to Baldock. He would have come back, not by train, but in his own car, which he had previously parked somewhere between Cambridge and Hitchin. You remember there was a car returned to the Fisher College garages between five-thirty and seven. I haven't been able to find out whose car it was, and three of our suspects have cars there—Fothergill, Cherrington and Westmacott. Do you think that Fothergill might have been coming from the garages when Sir Richard saw him at six-fifteen? He would have left his hat at St. John's Close, and Mrs. Landon supplied him with an alibi."

The Superintendent paused and took a drink of water.

"I must be fair," he said. "There still is a case against Fothergill, as there is against Mrs. Landon and less so against Westmacott, but I don't think it is a strong case. We come, then, to our two remaining suspects—Hartley and Sir Richard.

"Hartley fits in very well with a large number of the facts. He was almost certainly the man who had the duplicate set of keys made by Thoday. He had very strong motives. He could have been the mystery man at eleven o'clock, have committed the murders, and driven the car to Baldock and caught the London train. He fits the descriptions well, but his case breaks on one fact—he was in Canada at the time of the murders. We therefore have the apparently insoluble problem, that the man who probably had the duplicate sets of keys made, and who best fits the descriptions for the night of the murder, couldn't have been there at the time."

He paused.

"You may say that my reconstruction is just making a good case for one suspect, and that equally good ones could be made for Mrs. Landon, or Fothergill or Westmacott. But here are two facts which to my mind clinch the matter. You will remember that Sir Richard told us Professor Shacksfield telephoned him at eleven o'clock on the night of the murder. That was Sir Richard's one slip, unless he relied on Shacksfield not remembering—he is an absent-minded person. Well, it was Sir Richard who rang up Shacksfield."

He paused.

"Do you see the significance of this? It was at eleven o'clock that Sir Richard was wanting to create the mystery man around St. John's Close. He is trying to get noticed in his felt hat and loose overcoat—noticed, but not recognised. He feels that the girl Finch and her boy Bert have recognised him. He disappears into the shadows behind the Landon house: it is striking eleven o'clock. In less than two minutes he is telephoning Professor Shacksfield from the box at the corner of the Madingley Road. He perhaps draws Shacksfield's attention to the time, and certainly quotes from books and papers so as to give the impression he was in his own rooms. It is very clever, very clever indeed."

"And the second fact?" asked the Chief Constable.

"Sir Richard Cherrington has slipped through our hands to France," said Robertson-Macdonald. "But he is being watched there very carefully by my man De Rougemont. He went there allegedly to visit archæological remains in Brittany. But at the moment he is behaving in a peculiar way in Rouen and Chartres."

He paused.

"I believe that he will possibly disappear."

"But my dear Superintendent, if he disappears," said Colonel Cunningham-Hardy, "that means he thinks his murders have not been so perfect as you allege. No," he went on. "You have given us a masterly analysis of the whole affair, but I'm not sure as yet you've convinced me that Cherrington is guilty. I grant you he may be, but this telephone business—he might have forgotten whether he telephoned Shacksfield or whether Shacksfield telephoned him. Then this trip to France. He may suddenly have decided to see some French cathedrals. What do you think, Wyndham?"

"I agree with you, sir," said Wyndham. "I think the Superintendent has given us a very fine analysis, but put the suspects in the wrong order. His case against Sir Richard breaks down on two points. I can't see Sir

Richard, despite his acknowledged ability in his youth as an actor—I can't see him with an overcoat and felt hat giving the impression at Baldock that he was a young man."

"Oh, I don't know," said the Superintendent. "It was dark, you know."

"I know, but it seems to me very doubtful," went on Wyndham. "That's the first point; and the second I don't like is this half-conspiracy with Hartley. Would Sir Richard be such a fool as to do that? I mean," he went on hurriedly, "I suspected Sir Richard at first, but I now believe that both Sir Richard and Mrs. Landon are shielding Fothergill."

"You still suspect Fothergill?"

"Almost certain of his guilt," said Wyndham. "As the Superintendent recognised himself, he could have been the man who had the keys made. I think there is no doubt he was the mystery man at St. John's Close at eleven o'clock. Mrs. Landon said he was, in effect, and it was he who put his time of return to College earlier. I suggest what happened was that, having written and posted his letter to Miss Westmacott, he went to see not the Dean, but Sir Richard, and poured out his troubles to him. He meant to go and see the Dean, but Sir Richard dissuades him, telling him that the Dean has a gun and might shoot him. He leaves Sir Richard, paces about on the Backs, is seen by the President, and either before or after that commits the murders—Landon deliberately, but Gostlin in a fright. He then tries to cover up the murders by driving the Landon car to Baldock to give the impression it was someone from away, and he comes back by train. Somehow or other he must have given the slip to the people at the station. Sir Richard and Mrs. Landon suspect him, and try to shield him—Sir Richard by saying he was in College dressed at six-fifteen. Now, this is a most important point. You will remember that it was only much later that Sir Richard gave us this information. Mrs. Harris, his bedmaker, didn't wake him—he wasn't there. He hadn't yet come back from Baldock. Sir Richard was lying: he later concocted a fine alibi for both Fothergill and Mrs. Landon that apparently closed the case against them until by very clever detection the Superintendent here broke it down. Mrs. Landon has been lying throughout to save her lover. She seized on the hat accidentally left behind on a former occasion and not noticed previously by the maid."

"Bravo!" said the Chief Constable. "A very good case. What do you say to all that, Superintendent?"

"It doesn't explain why Fothergill had the duplicate keys made. It suggests that the crime is the result of an impulse. I insist that it was carefully thought out."

"Well, then, Fothergill might have carefully thought it out?" said Wyndham.

"To the extent of being in Ely to purchase duplicate keys on the same day as Hartley? Come now, that isn't reasonable. And your theory doesn't explain the car that arrived back in Fisher College in the early morning."

"I can explain that," said the Chief Constable, rather surprisingly. "Ha, yes," he said, "been doing a little detection on my own. Believe when there is any trouble on the best scheme is to keep quiet. Wondered if the murderer had decided to do the same thing. Well, the one person among our suspects who has kept pretty quiet is this tutor man, Westmacott. Wyndham told me a day or two ago his theory about Fothergill. I determined to test it. Now, Fothergill's story is that he came in through the back gate just in time to be at the Screens at six-fifteen, and was seen there fully clad by Sir Richard Cherrington. Do you remember the first thing Cherrington asked him to do? Eh? Forgotten, all of you? He asked him to go and warn the Tutor—that is to say, Westmacott. Fothergill went up to the Tutor's room, but he was out—out already at six-thirty in the morning. His bedmaker says she did not wake him up. I've been to have a talk with Westmacott. Don't like him. A most unsatisfactory, snobbish individual. Didn't offer me a drink all the time I was questioning him. Remember he said he was in College all night? Now he tells a different story. Says he went to his room after Hall, but later on in the evening—he can't remember when—he felt bored with life, took out his car and drove to the Yellow Barn. Here he says he had some drinks and danced with some women he met. In fact, he says he danced on until the band stopped at two-thirty. Then, rather than drive home through the cold night, he took a room and slept there, getting up at six-thirty and driving back to Cambridge in time for breakfast. It was his car that came in to the garages at Fisher College."

"My dear Chief Constable," said the Superintendent aghast, "this is an astonishing story to have found out."

"Only finished finding it all out this morning," said the Colonel. "Westmacott was a bit slow in giving me all the details. But I got them out of him. So you see he could have doubled back to College, committed the murders and gone back to the Yellow Barn. I mean it's always struck me, what?, this insistence on the murders having been done at two or four, when the porters were on their rounds. Isn't that the impression someone would want to create? Say you wanted to make people believe the whole business was done by someone from outside, you would get the porter out of his lodge and murder him deliberately in the Screens. After all, there seems to me no need to have murdered Gostlin. It was a dark night, and the murderer could have hidden in the shadow of the Courts. Therefore he got Gostlin out and murdered him in a set place. This could have happened at three o'clock, and it could have been done by our friend Westmacott. Then I was struck by Robertson-Macdonald's explanation of the telephone business: you know, Cherrington and Shacksfield and so forth at eleven o'clock. Well, Westmacott could equally well have been lurking around St. John's Close, and remember he telephoned the Head Porter at eleven o'clock? May be that was from the box at the corner of the Madingley Road. It was as the Superintendent said, only Westmacott was in the box, and not Cherrington."

"Very fine, sir," said the Superintendent quickly. "But your explanation does not dispose of the car, and the man on the station at Baldock."

"I've thought of that," said the Chief Constable. "It is difficult, but Westmacott could have dumped the Landon car in the Baldock quarry earlier on Monday night. He could have driven it away straight after he left the Combination Room—Mrs. Landon was walking into College at the time—and come back in his own car, which he had earlier parked in Baldock. He would be back in time to telephone and be seen at St. John's Close at eleven o'clock, and of course it was his own car—not the Landon car—that was parked outside the back gate and was bumped into by Fothergill. If by any chance we manage to break his alibi at the Yellow Barn, he can prove that there was not enough time for him to get to Baldock, and that it would be physically impossible for him to drive two cars there."

"But the young man seen at Baldock station?" said Inspector Wyndham.

"I know that is a difficulty," said Colonel Cunningham-Hardy, "but Westmacott could have been away from the Yellow Barn long enough to commit the murders and get to Baldock. His defence would then be that he was asleep in the Yellow Barn all the time, and that, anyhow, who took the Landon car to Baldock?"

"You have made out a good case," said the Superintendent. "But, if you will allow me to say so, both your explanation, sir, and that of Wyndham's here, misses the cardinal point of the duplicate keys. The clue of the duplicate keys made in Ely is the clue to all this mystery. While Thoday cannot be sure they were ordered by Hartley, he first chose Hartley's photograph, and only later thought it might be Westmacott or Fothergill. Now, this is no proof, but Hartley was in Ely that day. Your theory demands that Westmacott or Fothergill was in Ely on the same day. And even if they were, how did they get hold of the original set of keys? No, I am afraid your theories fall to the ground on this crucial point. Maybe we can find out where exactly Westmacott and Fothergill were on the day Hartley was in Ely. That would resolve the doubts."

As he was speaking a police constable brought in a telegram and handed it to Inspector Fleming.

"Excuse me, sir," said Fleming as he read the message, "I rather think this message resolves the doubts," and he handed the telegram to the Superintendent.

Robertson-Macdonald took it and read it carefully. A smile broke out on his face.

"Yes, gentlemen," he said, "this is indeed dramatic confirmation of my theory."

"It was Cherrington, then?" asked Wyndham.

"There is no doubt about it," said the Superintendent. "This message is from De Rougemont, who trailed Cherrington to Rouen, and then to Chartres, and now to Paris. Yes, I think the detection is over: now it only remains to round up the criminal before he escapes."

"Escapes?" asked Cunningham-Hardy.

"De Rougemont reports," said the Superintendent slowly, "that Sir Richard Cherrington has booked a first-class berth from Bordeaux to Rio de Janeiro in the *Massillia* sailing to-morrow." He paused. "He is apparently using the assumed name of M. Maurice Pleydell.

"I believe, gentlemen," he went on, "that this apparently insoluble problem has been deliberately set for us by the criminal, and I have no doubt in my mind that the criminal is that very clever man, Sir Richard Cherrington."

He had never lost the attention of any of his three hearers through his talk, but at this moment they were staring at him almost aghast.

"I can reconstruct the history of the crime for you," he went on. "When Hartley came back in mid-February he must have had a talk with Cherrington. I am not suggesting that there was a conspiracy between them for murder, although that might be the case. I am suggesting, however, that Hartley confessed to Cherrington that he had had a duplicate set of keys made so that he could break in one night and give Landon a thrashing and extort a promise from him to give his sister her freedom again. Or it may be from the beginning he intended to murder Landon, but Cherrington dissuaded him from this task, saying that he, Cherrington, would fix matters.

"That is my reconstruction. Meanwhile Hartley is away on the *Ile de France*. Cherrington knows that this provides Hartley with a complete alibi. He therefore carries out a clever murder scheme, and at every stage leads one to suspect someone from outside. I suggest he was the mystery man lurking around St. John's Close at eleven o'clock. He drives the Landon car to Baldock with the keys he has got from Hartley, and then drives back in his own car. It was the Cherrington Bentley, I suggest, that came back to College between five-thirty and seven o'clock, probably soon after five-thirty, so that Sir Richard was in bed when Mrs. Kilmartin 'woke' him. It must have been a difficult moment for him walking through the College in the early morning wondering if Gostlin's body had been discovered and someone had gone to tell him and discovered his absence. But no, there it still was, and he crossed up to his rooms and to bed."

CHAPTER NINETEEN

SIR RICHARD CHERRINGTON BEHAVES PECULIARLY

When Sir Richard Cherrington and Giles Farnaby arrived in Chartres they went straight to the Hôtel de la Poste, and Sir Richard interviewed the manageress.

"Madame," he began, "I believe that a friend of mine, M. Georges Festubert, lives in your hotel."

"Ah, no, monsieur," was the reply. "He does not live here. He comes and stays here from time to time when he is on his travels. Usually once a month."

"I see," said Sir Richard, rather disappointed. "And when was he here last."

"About a fortnight ago. You can look at the register."

The register was brought, and Sir Richard studied it carefully. Suddenly he came across the name he was looking for—M. Georges Festubert—and an address in Paris—44 Avenue St. Martin de Tours. So far, so good; but he was brought up with a rude shock when he saw the dates on which this M. Festubert had last stayed at the hotel. For he had arrived on March 10th and left on the 12th—that is to say, he had been in Chartres during the time of the Cambridge murders. "I wonder am I wrong, all the time?" thought Sir Richard. "And yet, I suppose hotel registers can be fixed."

He took a room for the night, and Giles was given the room next door. "The best room in the house, monsieur," he was assured.

Sir Richard felt tired when he got up to his room. The excitement of the chase was beginning to die. Was he not rather foolish to go chasing round France on a possible clue which might lead to nothing, or, on the other hand, into very considerable personal danger? Would it not be wiser to send a telegram to Superintendent Robertson-Macdonald or to go to the *Sûrété* in Paris and tell them what he knew? But what did he know? It was very little.

He thought again of the hotel register downstairs. Wasn't it too much of a coincidence that this M. Festubert had stayed there on the night of the murders? It did look as if several alibis were being built up. Or was he unduly suspicious? He began unpacking his bags. Sir Richard was a methodical man with his clothes and packing, and for however short a period he stayed anywhere, he liked to have everything unpacked and neatly set away in drawers. It was as he was preparing to put some shirts in a drawer that he noticed a dirty handkerchief tucked away in the corner.

"Bah," he said to himself. "Careless servants," and picked it up and threw it into the waste-paper basket. It was then that the dramatic thing happened. Either as he picked up the handkerchief or as he threw it away, something on it caught his eye. He picked it up out of the basket and with bated breath opened it out carefully. Yes, there was no doubt about it whatsoever: his quick archæological eye had not failed him. He looked at the monogram again. It was almost too good to be true. For in the corner of the handkerchief the letters "G. F." were neatly embroidered.

Stuffing it in his pocket, he rushed downstairs and looked at the register again. Yes, Festubert had stayed in the very room that Sir Richard was in. Here at last was tangible proof. He walked out on to the *terasse*: his nephew was sitting at a small table with a *bock* in front of him.

Sir Richard slumped down in a chair beside him. "Order me several," he said, pointing at the beer.

"Why, what's the matter?" asked Farnaby. "I thought you had gone up to your room."

"I've just made a startling discovery," said Cherrington. "Do you remember that yesterday in Cambridge I said I had no doubt as to who the murderer was? Now I have proof."

"Proof?"

"Yes, proof," went on Sir Richard. "You mustn't press me to tell you now. We leave for Paris early to-morrow morning, and I hope I shall be able to tell you the whole story before long."

Inspector de Rougemont, who was sitting inside the hotel, would have been most excited if he could have heard the conversation between Cherrington and Farnaby. He had dutifully followed them from Cambridge to Newhaven and from Dieppe to Rouen, and then on to Chartres.

"I wonder," he thought to himself, "if this is a wild goose chase, or whether the Superintendent is right and Cherrington will lead us to the solution of this case."

II

When they got to Paris, Sir Richard first drove to the little hotel near the Odéon where, since his undergraduate days, he always stayed when in Paris. He left his nephew here, and drove off westwards along the Boulevard St. Germain. He had some difficulty in finding the Avenue de St. Martin de Tours. It turned out to be one of the many wide residential boulevards near the Arc de Triomphe. He drew the Bentley up at the kerb opposite No. 44 and went in. It was a large block of flats, and the concierge was in his little cubby-hole under the stairs.

"M. Festubert?" the concierge said in reply to his question. "He has gone away."

"Gone away?"

"Yes. Gone away some time ago. But if you want to know anything about him, M. Pleydell—M. Maurice Pleydell—who shared a flat with him, is in the café across the road at the moment."

Sir Richard crossed the road, his mind in a state of turmoil. This was becoming far too complicated. Festubert and Pleydell? What was behind it all? And yet, having come so far, he could not now stop without knowing some answer. There was no one sitting outside on the terrace of the café on this cold March morning. He went inside and looked round quickly. In the far corner a man stared hard at him, and then quickly put up his newspaper. But in that instant Sir Richard had recognised him: it was the face in the college group Peter Gough Clarke had shown him, and it was the man whose portrait had been hidden by Mrs. Landon. With feelings of mixed triumph and foreboding, Sir Richard went across to the man's table.

"Do you mind if I sit down here?" he said.

"But certainly," said the other, putting down his paper and staring at Sir Richard. "All places are free."

Cherrington looked at the man carefully. Yes, there had been no mistake. He had taken a long chance and had been right. To cover his excitement, he took out his snuffbox and elegantly and deliberately—perhaps a little too deliberately—he took some snuff.

"I am tired," he said. "I have driven a long way in the last two days. From Cambridge to Newhaven, and then from Dieppe to Rouen and Chartres, and then on here."

"Yes," said the other non-committally. "Why was that?"

"To find you, Monsieur Pleydell," said Sir Richard.

"And why did you want to find me?" asked the other, a wary, watchful look coming into his eyes.

Sir Richard took off his spectacles and dangled them on the end of their black ribbon. He had made up his mind.

"To ask you to dinner, Monsieur Pleydell," he said.

"To ask me to dinner?" asked the other.

"Why, yes," said Sir Richard. "What could be better? At Le Tour d'Argent to-night at eight o'clock. I shall have a special table set aside, so that we can talk freely, but not be overheard."

The other rubbed his chin. "And suppose I do not come?" he said.

Sir Richard stared at him, and his eyes narrowed.

"I think, Mr. Hartley," he said, "that you will come."

III

Sir Richard left the café quickly and got into his car. De Rougemont, who had been waiting a little way down the road in a taxi, said, "Follow that car. Do not let it out of your sight." Sir Richard drove down the Champs Elysées and away along the main boulevards, turning off into the Rue de Quatre Septembre, and stopping outside Barclay's Bank.

Sir Richard was gone about ten minutes before he came out and drove away in the direction he had come, stopping outside the Madeleine.

Sir Richard walked into Messrs. Thomas Cook's office and went up to the desk dealing with Transatlantic passages. He studied the sailing list for a moment, and then said, "I see that the *Massillia* is sailing from Bordeaux to-morrow for Rio de Janeiro."

"That is so."

"Is it entirely booked up?"

"It is not."

"I want a first-class berth from Bordeaux to Rio. Here is the money." And he produced a number of thousand-franc notes.

"Are your passports and papers in order?"

"They are."

"Excellent, excellent. And the name?"

"The name," said Sir Richard Cherrington firmly, "the name is M. Maurice Pleydell."

IV

Sir Richard stood at the window of the Tour d'Argent restaurant looking out over the darkness of Paris below him. Situated as it is on the top floor of a large house on the south bank of the river, and with the walls of the main restaurant built of glass, the Tour d'Argent has in summer-time the unrivalled attraction of the most superb views over Paris to add to its barely rivalled cuisine and cellar. On many a previous and happier occasion Sir Richard had dined here the while the sun went down in a ball of flame behind Notre Dame. To-night he could just discern the dark shadows that were the cathedral and the river flowing silently along.

He looked at his watch. It was ten past eight. Would his guest come? Sir Richard began to have misgivings as to whether he had been so clever in his arrangements. Should he perhaps have sought out the police in Paris or sent a telegram to Robertson-Macdonald in Cambridge? Was he being particularly foolish? He sighed. "What does it really matter," he thought, "if I have not acted correctly in this matter, if I have taken the law into my own hands, so to speak? In a year or two the whole of the civilised world will be plunged into another war much worse than the last one. Then these domestic crimes and problems will be forgotten, will be put into the perspective of the greater carnage."

His reverie was cut short by a voice at his shoulder. "Good evening, Sir Richard," said the voice. "You look rather sad."

Cherrington turned round quickly and faced his guest.

"Sad, am I?" said Cherrington. "I suppose I was. I was just wondering how many times I shall eat here again and see the night fall over Paris, and how soon this place and all it stands for in the way of cultivated living, as well as all Paris and all it stands for to me as civilisation, will be swept away—razed to the ground by explosive and fire."

The other looked at him keenly. "You think there will be a war, then?" he said.

"I have no doubt of it," said Sir Richard. "But let's go to table. We have other things to do than forecast national calamities."

Sir Richard had booked a table away from the rest of the restaurant, in a corner by the glass walls. A decanter of dry sherry was on the table, and he helped his guest.

"I have ordered you what I think is a very nice dinner," he said: "some smoked salmon; œufs pockes d'Argenteuil—a favourite dish of mine, I am afraid—then the duck; they do it so well here, and their orange salad is delightful; then some Chicken Liver Brochettes to finish. I hope it will meet with your approval."

"It sounds delightful."

"I've suggested a bottle of Chablis, and then some Château Margaux to drink. Do you think that right?"

"I am entirely in your hands, Sir Richard," said the other. "You know about these things."

"No, no, I am merely an amateur," said the other, waving his hand deprecatingly. "One can get a superb meal here. The food is possibly better at Laperouse, and the cellar is not as good as at Foyots. But the combination here is unbeatable."

They drank some more sherry, and the salmon was brought.

"Your very good health," said Sir Richard, raising his glass.

"And yours," said the other.

"Do you know," said Cherrington, putting down his glass, "I thought you might not come."

"Oh," said the other. "Well in any case I am looking forward to hearing your Cambridge news."

"My news?"

"Yes. My sister, how is she?"

Sir Richard paused. "She is very well. Naturally the whole of Fisher College and everyone connected with it are violently affected by the recent murders."

"Yes, yes," said the other quickly. "But my sister. She is not under suspicion?"

"No," said Sir Richard. "I don't think so."

"Thank God for that," said the other. "You know, my sister is the only person in the whole world who means anything to me. I couldn't bear it if she was suffering as a result of the murders."

"Really, Mr. Hartley?"

The other looked round the restaurant. He turned back to Sir Richard. "I know we are away from everyone and cannot be overheard," he said. "But I wish you wouldn't call me Hartley. My name is Maurice Pleydell. Oliver Hartley died two years ago, to all intents and purposes."

"Died?" said Sir Richard.

They were silent while the waiter took away their plates and brought them the eggs and asparagus.

"Yes," said the other, when they were again alone. "When I came out of prison in 1937 I determined to start an entirely new life. I therefore ceased to be Oliver Hartley. I crossed over to France, and have lived here ever since. But the police are interested in old criminals, and while the moment I landed in France I ceased to be Hartley and became Maurice Pleydell, we took a small flat in St. Germain in the name of Hartley, and odd people would use it as a *pied-à-terre* from time to time. A friend of mine who got out before me bought the flat in the Avenue St. Martin de Tours. I went straight to it from prison: in fact, Maurice Pleydell had been created a little while before I actually appeared."

"How did you have the money for all this?"

The other smiled. "You forget," he said, "that I went to prison for some money transactions the police didn't like."

"I see. And since you came out?"

"I have lived in various ways. Some legal and some illegal. Most not offences the law can easily punish. I am now connected with a considerable printing firm—my friend Festubert and myself."

" And your sister, she knows nothing of all this?"

"Nothing," said Hartley. "I have been very careful to see that no one connected the Hartley of the old days with the Maurice Pleydell of the new. You have been the first in these two years to make this connection, and I expect you will not betray me. I am only telling you all this because you have my sister's interests at heart and I want to tell someone."

"You communicated with your sister always through the Rouen Poste Restante?" said Sir Richard.

"That is so," agreed Hartley. "No one has traced me hitherto that way, as my sister is the only one who has the address."

"She only gave it to me because she thought you were now in Canada."

"I see," said Hartley. "I wondered how you had traced me. You see, no one else writes me from England."

"And your occasional visits to England? How were those managed?" said Sir Richard.

"That was where it was useful keeping alive the flat in St. Germain. I would go there and emerge as Oliver Hartley with Hartley's passport, leaving Maurice Pleydell behind in a wardrobe. Actually, I have only been over to England twice since I came out of prison. Once was late in 1937, and the second visit was in mid-February of this year."

Sir Richard looked at him very severely. "You have not been in England since February?" he queried.

"No, sir," said Hartley, returning his look unflinchingly.
"Where were you," said Cherrington, "a fortnight to-night?"
"A fortnight to-night," said Hartley. "Oh, I don't know. Without looking up my diary, I wouldn't know. There is no reason why I should remember that date, is there?"
"There is indeed," said Sir Richard. "It was the night your brother-in-law, whom you disliked, was murdered in Cambridge. It is the sort of thing one is likely to remember."
They were interrupted at this stage by the waiter, who brought them the duck and fussed around serving the Château Margaux.
When he had gone, Hartley said, "Ah, yes, of course. Stupid of me. I remember now. I was motoring about in North France at the time. Out of touch with the news."
Sir Richard looked very severe. "My dear Hartley," he said, "you profess a great regard for your sister and so forth, and I believe it. Yet when you learnt that her husband had been murdered you seem to have made no attempt to go across to England and see her—to see her at a moment when her brother would have been a great help to her. Why is this?"
Hartley seemed off his balance for the first time. "Well, you see——" he began.
"I'll tell you why," said Sir Richard firmly. "It's because it was in theory physically impossible for you to visit her. You were supposed to be in America." He paused, took off his spectacles and looked keenly at Hartley.
"I am an old man," he said. "I may be an academic, but I am not so very stupid. I, too, am interested in the welfare of your sister as well as that of my own College. Don't you think it might be a good thing to tell me the truth?"
"The truth?" said Hartley.
"Yes," said Sir Richard. "You see, I believe you were the mysterious man seen by Doris Finch at eleven o'clock outside St. John's Close on the night of March 10th, that you were the man who shot the Dean and Gostlin and threw the revolver into the Cam, that you were the man who was seen by the President at two-fifteen walking away through the Backs, and that you were the man who drove away in the Landon car from the back gate of Fisher College."
Hartley went very pale. He looked around the restaurant carefully. No one was in hearing distance of them. "You haven't fixed a microphone to this table, have you?" he asked.
"I haven't," said Cherrington. "I wish you would believe me," he went on, "when I say that I am not interested in this case from the point of view of bringing the criminals to justice. Landon may have done a more criminal thing to your sister than you ever did to him. I am merely curious for the truth, in an abstract, academic way."

Hartley put down his knife and fork and took a gulp of the red wine. "I'll tell you the truth, then," he said, his words coming quickly. "I've wanted to do so to somebody for the last fortnight. I shall respect your promise not to let me down.

"It began like this," he said. "Landon hated me, I think, since I went up as an undergraduate in October 1932. He was always against me. When I got mixed up in some trouble in the summer of 1933 he sent me down when a more reasonable man could have dealt much more humanely with me. That was really my undoing. It started me in what the novelists and psychologists call a career of crime. It really wasn't crime—it was just being a little cleverer than the other man, and not paying too much attention to the niceties of the law."

He paused.

"But Landon did me a greater harm than sending me down from Cambridge. He married my sister, whom I loved. We were brought up together by an aunt in Rockbourne in Dorset. Both our parents died when we were young. I was devoted to my sister. When she got married to Landon against my advice and entreaties I refused to see her or have anything to do with her for several years. She wrote to me constantly, and came to see me in prison from 1935 to 1937. It was then I began to realise that she was wildly unhappy and that Landon had ruined not only my life, but hers as well." Hartley took a sip of the wine. "It was no use me saying to her 'I told you so'—I thought how best I could really help. It was in prison that I determined to get rid of Landon. It would pay off my old score, free my sister and prevent some other undergraduates from being treated as I was, although I had few really altruistic feelings in the matter.

"I laid my plans very carefully. This was really why we kept Oliver Hartley alive in the flat in St. Germain. It was to be a perfect murder. The person of Maurice Pleydell, created to protect myself, anyhow, was perfect cover for my schemes. Georges Festubert was the name my friend assumed, and I used this in my address at Chartres, so that even if I was traced through the Rouen Poste Restante it only brought someone to the joint Festubert–Pleydell flat, not necessarily to me.

"Sometimes I wavered in my purpose. I went over to Cambridge in 1938 to visit my sister, and her unhappiness was very apparent to me. Yet I was never sure that if she were free she would be happy again. All through the latter half of 1938, as I went about my business in France, I kept wondering whether my projected action would in fact achieve the desired result of making my sister happy again.

"Then in the spring of this year I learned that my sister had fallen in love with this young Fellow of Fisher College called Fothergill. In her letters it was clear she was passionately in love and wanted to marry him. That decided me, but I had to go carefully. A young man who in carrying out one of my schemes had got mixed up with the police, and had done six months in jail, needed some help to leave the country. I arranged for him to take up the flat in St. Germain and assume the person of Oliver Hartley. He was equipped with passports and papers in this name. I told you I was connected with a printing firm, and the making of false passports and documents is one of our specialities," he said quietly.

Then he went on: "I went across to England on February 12 as Oliver Hartley. The other man laid low while I was away. I saw my sister and made plans. It was then that I learnt from a stray sentence of my brother-in-law that he kept a revolver and ammunition in his desk, fearing a repetition of the Lancaster College incidents, so he said. I drove Landon to Ely one day, and while he was at a meeting I had a duplicate set of keys made for the car and College and garage. On another day I drove my sister to Letchworth, and noticed near Baldock a suitably deserted chalk-pit where I could leave the Landon car I planned to use in my scheme. I had already worked out in detail the timing of the scheme and fixed the event for the last night of term. There was a chance that the undergraduates would have been dispersed next day before the police got into the case properly. I counted on the general end of term confusion to help me.

"I went back to France on February 21st, and the other man resumed the rôle of Hartley in the flat at St. Germain. On February 28th he closed up the flat, and sailed away to Canada on the *Ile de France.* He arrived in Montreal on March 5th, and then went up country. He sent my sister a cable from Calgary on March 12th. Thereafter he disappeared into the western distances of the New World. He will never be found. He now has a new name and new papers: it will be impossible to trace him. He has disappeared completely and will start a new life. He has done me a great service, and I have done him one.

"I tried not to leave anything to chance. One night just before I left England, and when Landon was sleeping at his house, I tried the set of duplicate keys I had obtained. They worked excellently. I took the opportunity of examining Landon's revolver. It was a ·38 bore, and when I got back to France I had little difficulty in getting one of exactly the same type with a silencer.

"You will see that I had planned a most complicated double alibi. The first alibi was for Hartley, and if it worked well, as I believe it has, it was meant to put the police off my trail, if not for ever, certainly for a very long time. The second alibi was to cover the possibility that the police got through my cover as Maurice Pleydell. What happened was this. On Sunday March 9th, Georges Festubert—the real Festubert—and I motored down to Chartres. We stayed at the Hôtel de la Poste, where I had been in the habit of collecting my Poste Restante letters readdressed from Rouen. The hotel people there knew me as Festubert, and the real Festubert registered as Pleydell. We thought that after an interval of time that would confuse the staff of the hotel if subsequently questioned as to the exact movement of both of us during that period, or any previous period.

"We got adjoining rooms, both of which had telephones. After lunch on the Monday I took the car with Festubert, who drove me to Rouen. There I went by train to Calais, and was in Cambridge about ten-thirty."

"Faked passports, I suppose?" said Sir Richard.

"Oh, yes," said the other easily. "The passports of Pleydell or Festubert will not show any entries into England during that period.

"My only worry," he went on, "was whether the car was at St. John's Close. If it was lent to someone for the night, or my sister had gone away in it, my carefully prepared plan was ruined, and I wanted to leave nothing to chance. I therefore went straight to the house and made sure the car was there. I saw a man and a girl come down the Madingley Road, but I did not know they had observed me. I slipped behind the garage, and waited there until half-past one. Then I went into College, using Landon's keys. No one saw me. I got into Landon's rooms with the greatest of ease and found his revolver. I had, of course, brought the other one, in case his had been removed. I was wearing gloves, and I easily fitted the silencer on to Landon's revolver."

He paused.

"Then a most unnerving thing happened. The light went on in Landon's bedroom. I waited, my heart beating frantically. I had been very quiet, and I knew he could not have heard me. The bedroom door opened, and Landon came out almost completely dressed, but with no collar on and in his stockinged feet. He paused at the door, fumbling for the light-switch. He stood there silhouetted against the light of his bedroom. I shot him immediately," he said simply.

"Then I thought of a good way of putting the police off the scent even further so that the various alibis could take effect. I had noticed a large trunk on the landing, and guessed it contained undergraduate effects being sent down at the end of term. There was no need to force the lock. The trunk was unlocked—merely strapped. I had little difficulty in putting Landon's body into the trunk. I put the clothes from the trunk in a cupboard in Landon's room. Then I had a second great shock. The door across the landing from Landon's room opened and a young undergraduate came out and put his shoes on the landing. Fortunately he noticed nothing and went back to his rooms. But it unnerved me slightly.

"Certainly as I crept away I was more keyed up than I expected to be. That is why, I suppose, I shot Gostlin. If I had had my wits about me I could have avoided him. It was a dark night. I was so excited that when he shone his torch and I realised he had recognised me I shot him almost before I knew what I was doing." He looked curiously at Sir Richard. "I was sorry about that," he said. "It was a mistake."

Then he went on quickly, "I threw the revolver into the river, having taken the silencer off, and made away. The President could not have recognised me. It was dark when I got away at two-thirty. He must either have been dreaming or seen someone else. I got into the car, drove to Baldock, left the car in the chalk-pit and took the train to London. I was in Calais soon after lunch on the 11th.

"While I was away from the Hôtel de la Poste, telephone calls had come through for both M. Festubert and M. Pleydell, and the real Festubert had taken them both. He had ordered a dinner for two in his rooms on the Monday night, and, poor man, had to eat the two dinners. On the Tuesday morning M. Pleydell gave various instructions by telephone, and so did M. Festubert: I don't think the management will ever get straight the events of those days. Finally the real Festubert drove over to Rouen again for lunch and fixed an interview for M. Pleydell with a firm in Calais. By a wonderful stroke of luck, the firm in Calais could not see M. Pleydell before lunch, but they could at three in the afternoon. I phoned Festubert from Calais, and was able to walk into their office just before three, and they will swear, I am sure, that I telephoned them at twelve o'clock. I was in the middle of the English Channel then.

"No," he said, "I was lucky. But the thing was well planned. Festubert and I were back in Chartres by dinner-time on the 11th, and the hotel and the hotel register will, I am certain, in all faith swear I was there from the Sunday to the Wednesday."

The waiter arrived and took away the remains of the duck and salad and brought the savoury.

"Let me give you some more wine," said Sir Richard. "You need it after that astonishing account." He paused. "May I ask you two questions."

"But certainly."

"First, why did you not get away from France as soon as the murders were done? Why not lose Maurice Pleydell in South America, as you have lost Oliver Hartley in Canada? Why have you stayed on here to risk recognition by someone like myself?"

"My sister," said the other simply. "I was struck with the fear that she might be under suspicion herself. I am waiting until I know there is no chance of that, and then I shall go away. You do assure me," he said quickly, "that she is well and happy and not being troubled much by the police?"

Sir Richard left the question unanswered. "My second question is a more difficult one. I suppose there are three people who know of the murder and how you did it. The man who went to Canada, the real Festubert, and myself. What if you cannot trust them?"

"Neither the man who went to Canada nor Georges Festubert know that they have assisted in alibis for murder, but neither would let me down. As regards the first, if questioned by the police I shall say it was a way of getting rid of Hartley and getting the man out of the country. It was a strange coincidence that Hartley's brother-in-law was murdered at the same time. As to the second alibi, I can trust Georges Festubert. We know too much about each other to be able to rat on one another."

Sir Richard poured out the last of the wine and held his glass up to the light.

"And myself," he said softly. "What about me?"

"You, Sir Richard," said Hartley. "You found me by a strange coincidence, and I presume you have my sister's welfare at heart. I don't think you would add a hanged brother to a murdered husband in her list of cares. But," he said, looking keenly at Sir Richard, "you can always go the way of Gostlin. It would be easy," he smiled. "English Professor shot at night in hotel in Paris."

"So it grows on one," said Cherrington softly.

"What did you say?" asked Hartley.

"I was just thinking," said Sir Richard. "I have never had a meal with a murderer before. It is quite a novel experience."

"Well," said Hartley, flushing slightly. "I don't think I can be called a normal murderer. I mean I didn't kill for gain or fear or revenge; it was just to do my sister a good turn. I have nothing to lose in this world, and I planned the thing very carefully. I suppose I had the detachment that the normal murderer hasn't got. I pride myself it went off perfectly. You are the only person in the world who knows my story, and at this moment you do not know whether I have drugged or poisoned your wine while you were not looking." He smiled.

Cherrington looked most startled.

"It's all right, Sir Richard," said Hartley. "I am trusting you with my confidences, but I'm not staying in France any longer. Now that my sister is free from suspicion, I shall go away, who knows where?"

At last he was silent.

Sir Richard waited until the coffee was brought and then ordered some liqueur brandy for both of them.

"Young man," he said, "I pass no judgment on what you have done. But in your long account you have made three mistakes."

"I have?" said Hartley. "I don't believe it."

"In the first place you said that I had come across you entirely by coincidence. That is not true. Peter Gough Clarke put an idea into my head—just a slight idea, and your sister's concern for you I noticed. She was afraid until she got the telegram from Canada that you might have been mixed up in the affair, and she hid your photograph. It took a long time for the two things to come together in my head, and even then it was only an idea. It seemed to me that your character and history fitted you for the part of murderer—I mean no offence. The police have been questioning the Fellows, if you please, as though a set of quiet, disputatious academics could commit such murder. I am afraid I know very little about alibis, and I paid no attention to the telegram from Canada: these things are always explained in detective stories, and, it appears, rightly so. So on the odd chance I tracked you down through the Poste Restante at Rouen and the hotel at Chartres to your flat in Paris. It was surprisingly easy."

"But what have you in the end?"

"One moment, please," said Cherrington. "Then your second mistake. You said just now that you have nothing to lose in this world. But I know you have. Your sister. I was wrong when I gave the impression that she was free from suspicion. She is very much suspected by the police, who think that Fothergill and herself fixed the whole affair between them. I think she may well stand trial for murder."

The other did not hesitate a moment. "If that is so," he said, "I shall go across to England straight away and confess to the whole affair."

"Bravo!" said Cherrington. "I had hoped you would say that. But you shall not do that. I shall decide what you do."

"You?"

"Yes," said Cherrington quietly. "I am managing this affair from now on. You see, you made a third mistake. All murderers do. You should read criminology more. The more complex and perfectly planned a murder is, the more likely is there to be a real mistake."

"I don't believe that I slipped up."

"In removing Farnaby's clothes and so forth from the trunk to the cupboard in Landon's room, you must, by a curious cruel mistake, have stuffed one of his handkerchiefs into your pocket. You left it in the corner of the drawer of the room you occupied in the Hôtel de la Poste. An even more cruel fate put me in that room last night, and I found the handkerchief with its monogram. My son," said Cherrington, "I am afraid the President of the Immortals has been jesting with you in a cruel fashion." He paused. "Or don't you read Hardy?" he queried.

The other was silent. "I don't believe you," he said. But his tone was not confident.

"At this moment," said Cherrington crisply, "your beliefs do not interest me much. I will tell you what you are going to do. You will now go back to your flat and write down everything you have told me to-night. To-morrow you will go to the Brazilian Consulate and have your passport properly visa'ed. Then you will catch the two-thirty train from the Gare d'Austerlitz and board the *Massillia* at Bordeaux. Here is your first-class ticket from Bordeaux to Rio."

"But——" said the other.

"You will do as I say," interrupted Cherrington. "I shall be at the station to-morrow and you will hand me your story in full. You will also send me a cable from Rio de Janeiro when you get there. When I receive that I shall burn the incriminating handkerchief."

"And if I decide to remove you, Sir Richard?"

"The handkerchief, with the facts of its finding, and the fact that M. Maurice Pleydell is really Oliver Hartley, I have placed in a letter addressed to the *Sûrété* with instructions to get immediately in touch with Superintendent Robertson-Macdonald at Scotland Yard. This letter is with my bankers, and will be posted at six o'clock to-morrow evening if I have not retrieved it in person by then." He paused. "I am not ready to die," said Sir Richard, "and I have accordingly taken these precautions."

The other was silent a moment. Then he said, "What if they proceed against my sister?"

"If they do, I will hand your confession to her defending solicitors. By that time you will have disappeared in South America. I believe," he added, "it is a country of great possibilities."

"And what about my own future?" asked Hartley. "How do you suppose I can live knowing you know I am a murderer?"

Sir Richard knew he was now at last master of the situation. He took out his silver snuffbox and elegantly proceeded to take snuff. "In six months time, perhaps a year, perhaps less," he said "the second part of the World War will break out. This is your chance to start life afresh. Join the armed forces. By the end of the war—and it will be a very long one—everyone will have forgotten the minor domestic crimes of Cambridge in the welter of carnage that will then take place."

Hartley smiled. "I don't know why you are doing this, Sir Richard," he said. "For the sake of my sister, I suppose. But don't your moral scruples prevent you from shielding a murderer?"

Sir Richard looked fiercely at Hartley. "Is murder, then, such a terrible crime?" he said. "Is it the supreme crime? I have seen so many people ground into poverty and death by wicked people whose actions are not recognised by the law as crime, so many people's lives made an unspeakable horror of cruelty and hatred and neglect. I do not see why such people should go free, and that only those who have killed their victims quickly and cleanly should be hanged by the neck until they die."

Hartley was silent.

"You will, of course, do exactly as I say," said Cherrington. "If you are not at the station, if your statement does not contain the necessary incriminating detail, I shall go straight to the *Sûrété*."

"And if I disappear to-night?"

"Your sister will stand her trial for murder."

Hartley got up. "I will do as you say," he said. "Thank you for the meal. Good-night." And he walked away.

Sir Richard sat on. "I wonder," he said to himself. "It really is the best course I have thought out for him. And yet, he is a wild nature and has murdered two men by now. I suppose he might shoot me." It was a most disagreeable notion. A cold shiver ran down his back.

"Waiter," he called out, "some more brandy, please."

CHAPTER TWENTY

GILES FARNABY'S HANDKERCHIEF

DETECTIVE-SUPERINTENDENT ROBERTSON-MACDONALD had been unable to get on an aircraft, the train from Calais was late, and it was not until a quarter to eleven that he arrived in Paris. De Rougemont was there to meet him and with him an official of the *Sûrété*.

"Hello, sir," De Rougemont greeted him. "Glad to see you at last. May I present M. Coquilhatville of the *Sûrété*."

"Hello, De Rougemont," said the Superintendent. "Bonsoir, monsieur."

M. Coquilhatville bowed. "Enchanté de vous connaître," he said.

"Well, now, what's the latest state of this strange affair?" asked the Superintendent.

"Sir Richard Cherrington has been having dinner with M. Pleydell this evening," said De Rougemont.

"So there is a M. Pleydell?" said Robertson-Macdonald. "It is not merely a pseudonym for Cherrington?"

"By no manner of means," replied De Rougemont. "This Monsieur Pleydell has a flat in the Avenue St. Martin de Tours. He shares it with a M. Georges Festubert. The Paris police have nothing against Pleydell and Festubert except that they think they may be mixed up in a rather small forgery organisation—supplying dud passports and papers and so forth. Nothing very large."

"I see," said Robertson-Macdonald, stroking his chin. "That is rather interesting. Now I wonder why Sir Richard Cherrington should be dining with such a person and why he should book a passage for him to South America?"

"I've no idea," said De Rougement. "They've had dinner together at Le Tour d'Argent. M. Coquilhatville has kindly provided two men to tail them, and we have just had a message to say that Pleydell has left the restaurant and returned to his flat, but that Cherrington is still in the restaurant."

They were now coming out of the station and getting into the police car waiting for them.

"Where shall we go to, sir?" asked De Rougemont.

"Just one minute," said Robertson-Macdonald. He had been thinking furiously. "What does this man Pleydell look like?"

"Pleydell?" said De Rougemont. "I have only seen him on two

occasions. He is rather difficult to describe. About twenty-five or twenty-six, not very tall, black hair—quite an ordinary-looking man."

"A very obvious Frenchman?" asked the Superintendent.

"No, he's not," said De Rougemont. "And the French police know nothing about him before eighteen months ago."

The Superintendent turned suddenly on the other two. "I wonder if we could look at Pleydell first," he said. "I am extraordinarily intrigued by the description you give of him."

As the car sped through the brightly lit Paris streets, Superintendent Robertson-Macdonald was thinking very hard to himself. The description, the connection with forgery, the association with Sir Richard—it was just possible. What if the transatlantic alibis were complete fakes?

The door of the Festubert–Pleydell flat was opened by Pleydell's manservant.

"Is M. Pleydell in?" asked the Superintendent.

"No, sir, no," said the man. "He's gone away."

Without paying attention to what the man was saying, the Superintendent walked into the outer room of the flat. There was a light burning in the next room. Robertson-Macdonald opened the door and looked in. A young man was sitting at a desk writing. He turned round as the door opened, and stood looking at the three policemen.

"What the devil?" he said.

And in that moment, apart from his instinctive use of English, the Superintendent recognised him. The man made a swift gesture to a drawer in his desk, but the three policemen were too quick for him.

"Oliver Hartley," began the Superintendent, "I arrest you for the wilful murder of William Landon and Samuel Gostlin on the night of March 10th/11th, and I warn you that anything you may say may be taken down and used in evidence against you."

Hartley broke into a stream of abuse. "The dirty double-crossing tyke," he said. "He took me in completely."

"Who did?" asked Robertson-Macdonald quickly.

"Why, Sir Richard Cherrington, of course."

"Isn't he an accomplice of yours?"

"Of mine?" Hartley laughed. "Say, what is going on? I thought he was an accomplice of yours. Don't tell me we are both suckers?"

II

Sir Richard found that when he came to leave Le Tour d'Argent he seemed to have taken rather more brandy than he had intended. Maybe it was all a reflex from the strain of the past twenty-four hours and the worry of the last fortnight, but he felt distinctly intoxicated—indeed pleasantly so—as he stepped out into the cold night air. "Must be careful," he said to himself—"must be careful: this Hartley is a really dangerous type and probably won't stop at anything." He got into a taxi, and as it drove away looked cautiously out through the back window. He saw a man emerge from the shadows near the door of the restaurant, get into another taxi and wave it to follow his. As he looked he was thrilled to see the man had on a felt hat and a loose overcoat. "Ah-ha," thought Sir Richard, "so the chase begins."

Cherrington changed the taxi's route three times, but the other taxi still followed. He paid his own taxi and got it to stop near a Metro station. He ran into the station, leapt on a train, changed three times, got back up into the night air again, took a bus back to the Odéon and walked slowly to his hotel. There was no one about. He went quickly through the hall and up the stairs and to the double-room he was sharing with his nephew. Giles Farnaby was sitting in a chair, reading.

"Hello, Uncle Dick," he said. "What's the matter? You look upset."

Sir Richard slumped down in an armchair and mopped his forehead. "Whew," he said, "that was a near shave."

Meanwhile Superintendent Robertson-Macdonald and De Rougemont were driving as fast as they could to the Odéon. They had left the protesting Hartley with Coquilhatville and the *Sûrété* officials. As they got out at Sir Richard's hotel, a policeman came up and saluted them.

"Good evening, sir," he said to de Rougemont. "I regret to say that Sir Cherrington gave me the slip to-night."

"What?" said the Superintendent and De Rougemont together. "You've lost him?"

"Well, no, sir," said the other. "He is back in his hotel here now. But I lost him between the restaurant and the hotel. Have no doubt it was deliberate. He jumped off his taxi into the Metro. I could not trace him. But he came back here some ten minutes ago."

"Good!" Robertson-Macdonald hurried into the hotel, followed by De Rougemont. He showed his card at the desk, and a page took them straight up to Cherrington's room.

The Superintendent was in rather a whirl, and indeed had been since the meeting this morning with Wyndham and the Chief Constable and the arrival of the telegram from De Rougemont. They were shown into Cherrington's room. Sir Richard got up as they came in.

"Good heavens, Superintendent. What are you doing here?" asked Cherrington.

"Hello, Sir Richard," he said. "I've come to ask you what you know about M. Pleydell, and why you booked a ticket in his name to South America, and why when you knew he was Oliver Hartley you did not immediately let us know?" He paused. "By the way, this is Inspector De Rougemont who has been trailing you round France for the last two days."

"Trailing me, Superintendent?"

"Yes, Sir Richard, and I should like to know why you behaved so peculiarly on your journey home from the Tour d'Argent this evening."

"I was being followed."

"I know that. The police were following you."

"The police? Good gracious, I thought it was Hartley."

"Why Hartley?"

"By the way, where is he?"

"We have just arrested him."

"I see," said Sir Richard, sighing. "I tried to save you that unpleasant necessity. Perhaps it is just as well you have got him at last."

"I don't understand you, Sir Richard. Why did you think he followed you?"

"He had just confessed to me the full story of the murders, and I thought he might be going to put me out of the way."

"Confessed to you? But that's excellent!" said the Superintendent. "Could you tell the whole story to us?"

They were all sitting down by now. Giles Farnaby was absolutely agog with excitement.

Sir Richard gave them briefly what Hartley had told him.

"You must admit it was damned ingenious," he concluded. "It almost deserved to succeed."

"There is one thing I don't understand," said the Superintendent. "Why did Dr. Landon come out of his bedroom? Was he disturbed by Hartley?"

"I've been thinking about that," said Sir Richard. "I don't think he was disturbed by Hartley. It was, I think, his own mind that disturbed him. Remember he was in a very uncertain state of mind. He had had a great personal shock that day, and may not have slept well. I suspect he got up and was going into his room, perhaps to write a letter, or perhaps to go home to his wife with a last appeal for her to understand him. Perhaps even he was coming out of his bedroom to shoot himself or Fothergill. We shall never know to what extent his mind was disturbed."

"I see. Yes, that explains a point that was worrying me."

"And now you tell me something," said Cherrington. "When you began on this case you promised to tell me how you had worked it all out. I should be most interested to know."

"Well," began the Superintendent. He was not very much at ease. "I discovered it was probably Hartley who had had a set of keys made in Ely that were duplicates of Landon's. He fitted well the description of the man seen outside Landon's house and catching the train at Baldock. There was, however, a complete alibi for Hartley during the period of the murder, so that either the alibi was wrong or someone was working with Hartley as an accomplice. I had all the possible suspects watched: Fothergill, Mrs. Landon, Dr. Quibell, Westmacott and——" he hesitated.

"And myself," supplied Sir Richard.

"That's right," said the Superintendent uncomfortably. "At one stage I was very suspicious of you. I attributed a great deal to your telling me Professor Shacksfield had rung you up at eleven when he says it was you rung him up."

"Very likely," agreed Sir Richard. "I don't really remember what happened. I know we had a long telephone conversation."

"In the end, Sir Richard," said the Superintendent, "it was you who led us to the criminal. A very fine piece of work if I may say so. How did you work it?"

"I had very little to go on," said Cherrington. "Nothing tangible. And yet I sensed Mrs. Landon was afraid for someone. She hid her brother's photograph after I had been there once, and I guessed she was afraid for him. I realised, too, that he was the person, of all people connected with this case, most likely to have the courage to commit these crimes. I tracked him to France, and there struck on a piece of real evidence. While making his second alibi at Chartres he had left behind a handkerchief with the monogram 'G.F.' on it. He could only have got this when he was putting Landon's body in the trunk. It was a strange coincidence I should be put in his room at the Hôtel de la Poste and find the handkerchief with my nephew's monogram on it."

"But——" began Farnaby.

"Marvellous!" said the Superintendent generously. "I do congratulate you. Although it was a piece of luck your finding the handkerchief, you did realise its significance straight away."

"But, Uncle Dick," said Farnaby.

"Yes," said Cherrington complacently. "This hasn't been a case in which deductive logic has played a very great part, I'm afraid."

"But, Uncle," said Farnaby, getting his word in at last, "I haven't got, and I never have had, handkerchiefs with my initials on them."

There was a silence in the room for almost a whole minute, and then Sir Richard said, "Are you sure?"

"Absolutely sure," said Giles Farnaby. "Don't you think perhaps the initials could equally well be for Georges Festubert?"

In the silence that followed the Superintendent gave a slight nervous cough: he was looking at the ceiling.

At last Sir Richard burst out laughing. "Well, I'm damned!" he said. "That's one in the eye for the scientific method, isn't it? I thought I had been so clever. You know," he said, turning to the Superintendent, "this is one of the rare occasions in my life when champagne is the only drink, and enough champagne to make us all quite tight."

And he got up and rang the bell.